The Influence Peddlers

The Influence Peddlers

HÉDI KADDOUR

TRANSLATED FROM THE FRENCH

BY TERESA LAVENDER FAGAN

YALE UNIVERSITY PRESS ■ NEW HAVEN & LONDON

A MARGELLOS
WORLD REPUBLIC OF LETTERS BOOK

The Margellos World Republic of Letters is dedicated to making literary works from around the globe available in English through translation. It brings to the English-speaking world the work of leading poets, novelists, essayists, philosophers, and playwrights from Europe, Latin America, Africa, Asia, and the Middle East to stimulate international discourse and creative exchange.

Yale University Press books may be purchased in quantity for educational, business, or promotional use. For information, please e-mail sales.press@yale.edu (U.S. office) or sales@yaleup.co.uk (U.K. office).

Set in Electra and Nobel type by Tseng Information Systems, Inc.
Printed in the United States of America.

Library of Congress Control Number: 2017934301
ISBN 978-0-300-22288-3 (pbk. : alk. paper)

A catalogue record for this book is available from the British Library.

This paper meets the requirements of ANSI/NISO Z39.48-1992 (Permanence of Paper).

10 9 8 7 6 5 4 3 2 1

CONTENTS

The Influence Peddlers

Part I

THE SHOCK: NAHBÈS, NORTH AFRICA, THE EARLY 1920S

1

A TREE IN THE WIND

She read more books in Arabic than in French. This had reassured her father, but he came to realize that some Arabic books were just as dangerous. Her name was Rania, twenty-three years old, statuesque, almond-shaped eyes. She was the daughter of Si Mabrouk, Mabrouk Belmejdoub, an important figure in the capital, a former minister of the sovereign. She was a widow. Her husband had died when she was nineteen. He was handsome; they adored each other. He also loved to read, and since he also loved fighting in the army, he had died in a shell attack in Champagne.

She had returned to live in her father's house, and he would sometimes say, "We have both lost our other half." After a year, he began to look for another husband for her. She didn't refuse the suitors—"If you want me to marry that idiot, I will obey"—and it was the father who found himself on the verge of tears because his daughter would add, "It will be like . . . a tomb before I die." The imbecile was shown the door.

When other men came to call, she was quick to describe them: one was violent, another toothless, yet another dirty or a gold digger. She didn't elaborate. But she reassured her father, she would one day find a good husband. He was worried because in a way she was handicapped—she was taller than the average man, she could hold a man's gaze, she had the carriage of a woman who, from an early age, had been made to carry a basket on her head. No one had forced her to carry a basket; she wanted to do what the servants did.

To encourage her not to be so difficult, her old servant had one day recited a saying: "An apple that stays on the ground is soon covered with worms." She responded that she wasn't a piece of fruit. As for books, she discussed them with her father as she had done with her husband, and she didn't intend to become the wife of someone who expected her to give that up.

Rania's older brother, Taïeb, also encouraged her to remarry. He was married to a woman whose family was even more powerful than theirs and who forced him to toe the line. "His marriage is a mess," said Rania, "so of course mine has to be worse." Her father sided with her, but he didn't forget that one day Taïeb would inherit his authority.

In the middle of the winter of 1920, her uncle Abdesslam, who had a farm on the outskirts of Nahbès, a city in the south, had asked Rania to come run his household: his wife was ill, bedridden. Rania had agreed, and Si Mabrouk granted his permission, relieved to see her put some distance for a time between herself and the scene of her unhappiness, as well as the pressure from Taïeb and from certain female friends whose husbands were increasingly hostile to the protectorate that France had imposed on the country.

Rania loved the farm. She had gone there often, as soon as she was old enough to walk. She enjoyed the open countryside; she planted bushes, herded goats, dug irrigation ditches, cut barley with a sickle. For a long time she spent her days in a big fig tree that had a tree house and a swing, until the day her aunt had decided that it wasn't proper anymore. She replaced her home in the tree with journeys through the fields and knew every corner of the property's twenty-two hundred acres. Eventually she was forbidden to wander off without dressing in a decent and pious manner and had to be accompanied by two female servants.

She hadn't returned to the farm since her marriage. Her uncle came to get her at the Nahbès train station. She walked around the car: "Is it a Renault?"

"Are you interested in such things?" her uncle asked.

"A widow can be interested in decent things."

"It's decent for a man, not for a woman."

"Maybe a car will be just the thing to get me to marry again."

She was impertinent! The uncle said to himself that perhaps it was best to send her back, but he didn't want to upset his brother. He would wait.

She had kissed her aunt, asked her uncle the name of the doctor who was taking care of her.

"It's Doctor Pagnon."

"He's a butcher!"

"He says she's doing better."

"Is Berthommier still around? Send for him." It was an order.

Doctor Berthommier, looking serious, had prescribed sedatives for the pain. Rania continued to give orders. She had taken control of the household.

"You can take care of everything around the house, like my wife did," Abdesslam had said. "I'll take care of the fields, the livestock, and the sales."

She had quickly understood that his wife had also taken care of the fields, the livestock, and the sales and that she was feared much more than her husband was. Here, too, the young widow had become indispensable. No one could work with numbers the way she could.

And while she oversaw the entire operation, her uncle could continue to focus on what was essential: meetings with intellectuals, and also drinkers, meetings he held at his home twice a week, a mixed group of men who were themselves mixed cocktails: conservatives imbued with a wish for reforms, rationalists who began to seek out marabouts as soon as their diabetes started acting up. "*Risalat al-tawhid*," Rania had said one morning while putting away the books that had remained in the sitting room along with the bottles. In response to the wary look her uncle gave her, she had replied, "Well, isn't that what's written on the cover?"

The uncle wasn't duped—she knew what she was holding in her hand: "The Letter on Unicity," by Muhammad 'Abduh, who proclaimed himself an atheist . . . He felt dizzy. He had his niece open her trunks and found Egyptian novels about the liberation of women . . . the Hachette series of great writers, Rousseau, Hugo . . . and even *The Course on Positive Philosophy!* His niece wanted to know more than men, which wasn't good for her or the family. He decided to call his brother.

"It's too late," Si Mabrouk told him. "Do you want me to forbid her to read? To beat her? Lock her up? I wanted a wonderful daughter, she grew up . . . How is your wife?" The conversation went on for a long time and ended on a cold note.

The uncle had told his wife that Rania was packing her bags and returning to the capital. The aunt didn't say a thing; a woman obeys. But the look she gave him was enough to throw her husband off-balance: the veil of death. A man is helpless against the look of death through the eyes of a wife. You constantly threaten them with it, and then there it is, rustling the folds of its shroud behind their slightest act of submission.

What was most difficult was getting Rania to agree to stay.

"My father will not be happy to know that I'm being treated like a piece of luggage!"

Finally the uncle said, "I'm not forcing you . . . it's for her."

"For whom?"

"For her and . . . for all of us."

Rania had agreed, and left the sitting room, gathering up on the way the works of Jamal al-Din al-Afghani, another dangerous reformer, and *Unnecessary Necessity* by the poet al-Ma'arri.

"Tell your friends I'll return them." She never did.

Four months later, there had been a more serious incident. Her uncle had found her with a newspaper, not a French newspaper with nice photos and advertisements, but a nationalist newspaper in Arabic that attacked France, demanded a constitution for the country, and sang no praises of the sovereign or his ministers. He shouted. She didn't answer, just took off her round, tortoise-shell glasses, put away the newspaper before he could take it, and modestly started to take her leave. But her uncle asked her questions, about the newspaper, the world; she answered, her hands on her knees, responses in a hesitant voice, broken words, scattered ideas, all that he expected to find in the head of a woman. But when all of that was put into good order, her words became strong statements, dangerous ideas. She knew a lot of things, and knew how to hide them. She fell silent after speaking a few more words, and he was forced to ask question after question. He argued against what she said, and she said he was right, she hadn't seen things that way, France was stronger, no, she didn't really know what the word *nation* meant; Abdesslam was sure she was lying. She mentioned another idea, the rights of the people . . . And Abdesslam's voice rose higher and higher even as he realized that what she was saying greatly resembled the remorse that once he could have had.

On questions of religion she remained measured, but he sensed that she was aware of everything, the visit he had made to the mausoleum of Sidi Brahim, the most famous marabout in the region. He had wanted to be discreet, perform a nocturnal sacrifice, but was a bit ashamed. Except, of course, he had brought the only red rooster in the area that would start crowing in the middle of the night, an unstoppable crowing, bringing everyone to their windows, until his knife had restored silence. She knew everything he was doing, and that he was doing everything to save his wife, sacrificing a rooster and worshipping under a tree where tiny pieces of fabric were hung. She said things only indirectly: "Some scholars think that . . ." But her uncle knew that it was exactly what she was thinking, that the cult of the saints, especially for someone who read "A Treatise on the Oneness of God," was fetishism, contemptible. And she never mentioned the bottles in the sitting room.

At the end of the first year the aunt had died; then, a few weeks later, so did the uncle, who had stopped eating. Before he passed away he said to Rania, "Be careful . . ." The farm went to Si Mabrouk, who decided to sell it and have his daughter return home. She had asked to stay, since the farm was doing well. She liked her life there, with space all around and orders to give. Si Mabrouk had refused. She had used delaying tactics. He had come from the capital along with Taïeb. Her voice had shaken when she talked about what she was leaving behind. The father and son had shouted, louder and louder. And she had won.

She had continued to live on the land. Si Mabrouk had the Renault taken away when he learned that she was driving it.

"But it's just in circles around the house."

"If you continue no one will respect you anymore!"

She had a horse-drawn carriage sent from the capital to get to town and a

one-horse cart for the countryside, a lovely cart, light but solid, easily maneu-
vered over the rough ground, the stones, the roots, the mud, everything, with
good suspension, hitched to a large, dappled gray horse. She had chosen an old
servant to drive her; he was called Ali the Vulture because of his neck and his
nose. He held the reins, but in fact it was she who was in charge, seated next to
him, moving her head to indicate the direction in which the servant should go.
She went all over the property, and when she arrived at a site where peasants
were working, she stayed in the cart, at a distance, in a place from which she
had a good view of the site. She would sometimes be distracted by the flight of
starlings or kestrels while Ali the Vulture gave orders that the peasants acknowledged while turning their faces toward the cart. She sometimes also joined the
group, picking up a clot of dirt, breaking it up, or a piece of wheat that she
crushed in her palm, and everyone waited for her decision. Her hands, with
nails that were often broken, were long and slender.

She would come by early in the morning to get things started. She would
come at the break, under the clear sky at midday. She brought not bread and oil
like other owners but mutton tagine, tomatoes, fruit. And those who blessed her
did so only once because she said that bosses who had themselves blessed were
only pagans and those blessing them were hypocrites. No one dared thwart what
they sensed she wanted: work done well, on time, without quarrels or indolence.
The cart was red; she could be seen at a distance.

She would return at the end of the afternoon to take stock. That woman has
the eye of a master, the peasants would say, an eye that fattens the livestock.
When returning to the farm she liked to get out of the cart and walk alone in
front of it, listening to the living sounds around her, letting the air play on her
face, walking with the sensation of being in front of herself, saying to herself:
*They need to take the stones out of this field, they aren't careful, you leave the
land alone and it brings back its stones, imperceptibly, and because it is imperceptible no one does anything, must tell them not to delay . . .*

The last rays of the sun cast a soft light onto the large, green fruit of the cactus that bordered a field; in the sky where the blue was beginning to darken
there was a single, small cloud . . . *My thoughts can reach as far as that cloud . . .*
"Here," her husband had written to her during the war, "we have gray clouds for
rain and yellow clouds for death." . . . Rania walked along another field, breathed
the air that traveled from the sea in gusts of wind . . . the wind is the companion
of widows . . . her eyes rested on the rapeseed, her uncle had wanted rapeseed
to please the French, it was idiotic, rapeseed in a land of palm and olive trees,
not idiotic for them, the colony must produce for the homeland, they said, idiotic even so, but she kept the rapeseed, for the cows, because she liked the great
yellow burst of its flowers, and because a Frenchman who had once come to her

uncle's house had said to her, pointing to a field in flower, "It begins here, and week after week the yellow will invade Italy, then France, Germany, Poland, Russia, as far as the Urals, the great voyage of rapeseed," . . . she went across the field, looked in the distance, toward the white cupola of a marabout that marked the northern border of the property, she also walked through the wild grass . . . *Ahdath al-yaoum mithla l'hacha'ich* . . . the events of the day are like wild grass . . . *My life no longer has wild grass* . . . *I live in two prisons, the second is the walls of my heart, to make wild grass in one's heart* . . . *I wrote him a letter and everything is in his hand, with my tears* . . . *I didn't send that letter* . . . *I burned it, I was like a leaf before the flame, shrinking* . . . *I must hide it* . . . *Love that is shown is in danger.*

She scolded herself, stopped dreaming, continued walking, between dreams and thoughts. When a little rain began to fall, she stopped, looking above the reddish edges of the wadi, and saw a rainbow appear: the peasants called that *'ars addib*, the jackal's wedding feast.

She ended up contracting the illness of rich farmers, a hunger for the earth, and she chided herself for letting a parcel of two hundred acres to the north of the property escape her. A colonist, the largest landowner in the region, Ganthier, had grabbed it up; he had bought it from another colonist who had left the country to grow old on the Côte d'Azur. She had asked her father to make an offer, but Ganthier had won. The colonist had confided in Ganthier: "Mabrouk Belmejdoub, the former minister, offered me more, but I was advised to sell it to you—it seems the French need to support each other, even in business!"

Ganthier's plan was simple: he was going to offer this parcel in exchange for another that was located between his land and that of Mabrouk Belmejdoub. That would consolidate Ganthier's land and cause the property of his neighbor and daughter to move toward the north. The parcel Ganthier was offering was larger, and Si Mabrouk had not been against the consolidation. Rania had been against it. Ultimately Ganthier would succeed in the exchange, of course. But while waiting, his workers, his machines, his animals had to cross the widow's land, on a path that was three hundred yards from her veranda . . . No, she wouldn't ask for any payment, that would have been beneath her, but Ganthier would have to request permission to pass, even for just himself, he who was so self-assured and so proud of the way he rode a horse. To those who expressed surprise at his patience, the colonist responded that one could not act with a former minister the way one could with a poor member of a tribe, especially when the former minister was what they called "a great friend of France."

Rania did not, however, spare the great friend of France some distress, as on the day he had learned that his daughter's carriage had been recognized a few steps away from the courthouse of Nahbès, during the trial of the rioters of Asmira, in February 1922, peasants who had protested with stones and weapons the sale of a parcel of collective land. There was a large wagon in front of the carriage, with food that had been distributed to the families of the accused. The authorities had not intervened: to feed those in need was a sacred duty, even when it was the relatives of the rioters. In addition, journalists had attended the trial, including a woman who had come from Paris, where she had the ears of the powerful; they had to show that the arm of France was strong but not inhuman. And that daughter of Belmejdoub, she was after all the widow of someone who had died on the battlefield of honor. A report pointed out that, coincidentally, the journalist, yes, Conti, Gabrielle Conti, left in the carriage. Just in case, they put together a rather well documented file: "That Belmejdoub girl, she reads too much, she is only a Bovary," the head commissioner had said, happy to show off his education to Ganthier. "A Bovary who reads Rousseau and Sheikh 'Abduh," Ganthier had replied, giving the police report back, "not novels for idle women. I've known her since she was a child; she is becoming dangerous."

Rania also read newspapers from Paris, *L'Avenir* and *L'Illustration*. She lingered on the photos, those of Latife Hanim, the young wife of the new leader of Turkey, Kemal Atatürk: she was wearing a black coat and an Astrakhan cap and was reviewing the troops in Istanbul, next to her husband, on horseback, without a veil. In other photos Latife Hanim was receiving ambassadors. There was also mention of preparing an official trip with her husband, a long trip, to Germany.

Rania turned the pages. She had a favorite photo. She stared at it. That photo appeared in issue after issue of *L'Illustration:* a woman "seated in the back of a sedan," said the ad. The woman looked like a princess; you could see her ankles and the beginning of her throat . . . "Chauffeur, on your way!" Rania began to dream of traveling to Germany while putting on her large, traditional robe meant to hide everything, a gray caftan that darkened her figure without hiding the movement of her hips, not a movement of a flirty woman, rather that of a tree in the wind. She wore a veil over her face when she was in town but not on the farm, or she would wear a veil in the Egyptian style, one that could be pulled up over the mouth and nose. She also dreamed of a satin slip. Gabrielle Conti was going to send her one from Paris, pale pink. They had long conversations, sitting on the veranda of the farmhouse; the journalist had been to Turkey, the entire Middle East. Rania talked to her about her own country; Gabrielle had promised never to cite her name, and Rania discreetly fed the journalist's reports. She nourished her own thinking while feeding her thoughts to Gabrielle — men, their refusal of women . . . to act above all like . . . cite the Book . . . the scholars . . . shame them . . . *L'Illustration* was a colonial newspaper, but she liked to find some of her words in it.

2

THE BETRAYAL

At the end of the spring of 1922, on avenue Jules-Ferry in Nahbès, Rania witnessed the sudden arrival of a group of noisy foreigners who were driving cars that were more beautiful than those of the French colonists, white convertibles with huge wheels with steel hubcaps and headlights as big as a horse's head. They were wearing trousers and golf caps like the ones she had seen in magazines, and they called out to each other on the sidewalks as if they were at home. She found them unbearable. She was inside her carriage and was giving the driver the signal to leave when her cousin Raouf came up and spoke to her with due respect. She hadn't needed to ask questions; at eighteen he was proud to know more than she did about them. Yes, those were Americans, they were there to film a movie, *Warrior of the Sands*. She was fascinated, and hostile, watched them silently, said to herself, *These are people of the times to come . . . but they haven't come like travelers to whom one can say "welcome" . . . nor like the French*, mitl ennar 'ala lkabid, *like a liver on fire . . . Why am I watching them? Because the times that are coming have nothing else to offer me? What kind of car is that? I'm looking at it, I see it's there . . . And those women, how did they do it? Do I want to become what I'm looking at, to bare my legs and strike a man's back while I laugh? In public? Perhaps not in public.*

In the street, passersby, North Africans and Europeans, watched while pretending not to see, disturbed less by those wearing the golf caps than by the young women who were accompanying them, some of whom were driving; they were wondering who could have authorized this; the war hadn't finished destroying the world, their dresses were revealing a lot more skin than the devil might have requested, and now they were sitting at outdoor cafés without men, which the most brazen of French or Italian women would never have dared to do.

Raouf managed to give Rania some details: A film with a character who was a sheikh played by a famous star. There must be around fifty Americans. They were noisy, but it bothered the French the most. They didn't like people watching people who were taller and richer than they were, and you know, I've heard that some of the Americans are against colonialism!

After a while the young man began to tire of standing in front of the half-covered window of the carriage. Rania and he were relatives, but that was no reason. He assumed an affectionate air. Rania sensed what was behind it; the gentleman was about to take his leave. She then abruptly told him that she had to return to the farm, said good-bye, the little light-brown lace curtain fell back over the window, and the carriage left avenue Jules-Ferry, leaving the foreigners with the scandal they were provoking and the populace with novel emotions.

In the days that followed, there was plenty of commentary in the town. At the Cercle des Prépondérants, where the most influential French people could be found, someone even said: "When the women sit down you can see everything!" and the governing board members of the Cercle decided they wouldn't be inviting "those people" to any gatherings. They held to their decision until they learned that one of the American women, a public relations person who smoked in public, had said: "The most backward people in my country, those in favor of slavery, are more open-minded!" Fear then traveled through the little colonial world, the fear of being described in American newspapers as "more backward than slavery supporters." The doors to the Cercle were opened to those young "flappers," as the Commander de Saint-André, who spoke their language, called them. Someone said something that enabled them to save face and that made the committee laugh: "As long as they leave their negro servants in the kitchen with our *fatmas* . . ." One of the women of the Cercle, the wife of the lawyer Doly, a somewhat dotty, thin woman, with ears that almost touched her neck, asked the commander what the word *flapaires* meant, with the understanding that if the answer were to go beyond the limits of decency he should disregard the question. The commander reassured her: the word evoked the noise that the wings of a young bird make when it begins to fly. "Then, let's welcome the little birds!" Madame Doly concluded, her chin raised high.

In the Cercle, the little birds behaved very well. They came in a group, wearing more fabric than usual. They showed that they knew how to take tea among people of good standing, carry on a conversation in flawless French, and remain seated on the edges of their chairs while Madame Doly explained to them what the word *Prépondérants* meant: It's very simple. We are much more civilized than all these natives. We carry much more weight. Thus we have a duty to lead them for a very long time, because they are very slow, and we meet in the Cercle to determine the best way to do so. We are the most powerful association, organization in the country! The American women talked about Balzac and Ravel so well that they put their hostesses to shame, but they also fawned appropriately over the starched dresses and straw hats with red wooden cherries sewn on the edges, the height of fashion in the colonial world. All tension had dissipated. It was even hinted that the Americans should be invited to join as honorary members, a suggestion that was made at the moment of their departure as hands were shaken and cheeks were kissed.

The American women had found the encounter "marvelous" and "fantastic," but they didn't return. They did not make the Cercle des Prépondérants their gathering place of choice. Their thés dansants, and especially their evening parties, were held in the salon of the Grand Hôtel, the most lavish and newest of the three hotels in Nahbès, on avenue Jules-Ferry, a huge salon, paneled in red cedar, whose bay windows looked out over a tree-filled garden.

These American parties were soon the talk of the city. A *betrayal!* said the French ladies because, after a suitable period of waiting, many of the gentlemen in Nahbès began to frequent the Grand Hôtel. And the worst "betrayal" was that of the garrison officers, who should have been examples of reserve and aloofness. The officers defended themselves. It wasn't a betrayal to go to these parties because they had been ordered to do so by command of the colonel in charge, to assert the presence of France, the protector of the country, to "fraternize" with the Americans who, since the declaration of their President Wilson, had a tendency to say whatever they wanted about the rights of people to govern themselves. And the officers would have been happy to bring their wives along if they hadn't publicly said such bad things about those "easy gatherings," an expression in which the adjective played a very important role because, although it primarily described "gatherings," once it was spoken it could freely—in the silence of innuendo—apply itself to the young women who were the center of them.

This outrage among the ladies of Nahbès was not, however, without certain disadvantages for them, because the presence of this large film crew had caused a crisis of inadmissible romance within their ranks, a crisis caused essentially by the presence of Francis Cavarro, the "star" of the film, as they said. All the women, even those who couldn't stand the *flapaires*, dreamed of one day being able to talk to that star the way they did out loud in their dreams, the dreams one has when one's husband is at work, the children are at school, and the maids are in the kitchen . . . to be the one who can catch Cavarro's attention . . . to be singled out from everyone else in the group . . . Cavarro was the other Valentino. He was a much better actor. To get Francis Cavarro to smile while offering him a cup of tea, to brush his fingers under the cup . . . He was tall, his jet black hair slightly slicked back, with a Greek nose, blue eyes, long hands, filled with energy—he had been great in *Escape from Zenda*—and one could forget the empty years and talk to him, take him aside, be taken into his arms, or simply listen to him, because one evening he would agree to play the piano and sing while looking through a bouquet of roses at the one who would be his chosen one and whom he would take out in the mythical car that he had brought over with him to Nahbès, his Silver Ghost, a Rolls-Royce that he drove himself.

Every day around 6:00 p.m., shortly after the end of the day's filming that took place outside the city, the Silver Ghost could be seen, its top rolled down, rolling slowly along avenue Jules-Ferry. It was accompanied by a crowd of shouting children who fought in front of the hotel for the privilege of opening the doors of a Rolls, an incomparable car, so incomparable that the contrôleur civil, Claude Marfaing, who held colonial power over the entire region, when he knew that the Silver Ghost was approaching the town limits, avoided driving his own car, a Panhard & Levassor, nonetheless, but few women truly dreamed of watching a sunset sitting in the front seat of the contrôleur civil's Panhard & Levassor, whereas the Greek nose, the jet black hair, the long hands, and the Rolls of Francis Cavarro were conjured every day by hundreds of female souls deprived of any emotional heroism but whose romantic dreams remained dreams, and the most unhappy of dreams, those that are within arm's reach but that make you feel your inaptitude all the more.

It was a regrettable situation, and more than one respectable woman among those who had condemned those "easy gatherings" had later sought to join them. None had found a way to do so, because in what was going on at the Grand Hôtel there was something worse than the liberal ways of young girls who would all the same end up getting married and having children like everyone else; something had happened that prevented every French woman concerned with her dignity and the exemplarity of her race to go down avenue Jules-Ferry when those gatherings were taking place, in one of the nerve centers of the city, a dual city, resting on a plateau on the shores of the sea and cut in two by a deep valley, perpendicular to the shore; a city that for centuries occupied only the right side of the valley, the left side having then been chosen exclusively by the French colonists; two very distinct cities: walls, the mosque, and the souks on one side, the post office, train station, hospital, and avenue Jules-Ferry on the other; a "native city" and a "European city" that could be separated in an instant, in the event of disturbance, by a company of Senegalese auxiliaries who were stationed over a ravine on the single bridge connecting the two sides, a dual city proud of what was called its "harmonious duality."

And this was exactly what prevented the French ladies from entering the salon of the Grand Hôtel. The Americans had become accustomed to inviting "natives" there—that was the word the colonials used to talk about the North Africans outside official discourse; they might also say "Arabs," but that had the disadvantage of not including in their contempt the Jews native to the country.

In short, the Americans openly treated the natives as equals in the European city, the most cultured natives, of course, those who had done or were doing their studies in French, the young bourgeois, but indeed the same ones who were pushing for a catastrophic change in the current state of affairs. And if in the modern European city there were already a few places where the paths of the two societies, the Europeans and the natives, crossed — certain cafés, for example — one didn't find women there, and patrons sat in established parts of the room or the terrace separated by some half-dozen tables that as agreed would never be occupied and from which the waiters carefully avoided removing the dust that had settled on them.

Up to then, the only worlds where everyone mingled were those of the Bolsheviks, the unions, the socialists, militants of all races who gathered to prepare a life that no one would ever have. They were small in number, and the regulations of the protectorate stated that, if need be, they could be either repatriated (city dwellers) or imprisoned (natives). There were also all the official events followed by a méchoui where everyone was invited, but here, too, things were perfectly regulated: each person had his rank, each person his zone.

But the parties at the Grand Hôtel were different, a hodgepodge, as it was called, of Arabs, Jews, even Italians, who came to mingle with the French and Americans, with music, alcohol, dancing, the clicking of heels, bracelets, and mainly laughter, the too-free laughter and shouts of those women from across the Atlantic, a swarm of actresses, assistants, make-up artists, secretaries, publicity people, journalists, and daughters of producers, all young and lively, beautifully constructed with straight backs, straight foreheads, straight noses, shapely legs, who put their hands on a man's shoulders without even knowing his name, not concerned with his origins, and any man while dancing could put his hand on a woman's uncorseted hip, even her bare skin, shimmering with joyful sweat.

Only a small number of people were involved, but the damage had been done, and those people thought they were preparing the future! At meetings of the Prépondérants it was pointed out, moreover, that on the one hand the natives were careful not to bring their wives to those gatherings and that, on the other, the "true Arabs," those of tradition, the believers — you know how they can believe here — the true Arabs, disapproved of those gatherings just as much as the most respectable French people did, and they wanted them prohibited, and the filming of that *Warrior of the Sands*, as well, a satanic undertaking, putting human beings on film. Without going that far, there was talk of putting pressure on the management of the hotel so those uncontrollable parties would have to be held at a private location instead of being the shocking attraction of the city center. Doctor Pagnon, who, with Jacques Doly, the lawyer, was considered one of the most influential of the Prépondérants of Nahbès, had alerted the heads of his organization in the capital, but they responded that they could not for the moment do very much: those people from Hollywood and New York had been received by the sovereign in the presence of their consul and the resident general of France, the sovereign had even decorated the film's director, Neil Daintree, with the medal of the Ordre des Compagnons du Trône . . .

For the resident general the film had become a matter of state and Nahbès the place where a highly respectable film was being made. The United States had come there to make a film about a good Arab, a film about a sheikh, not a hypocritical pillager or a fanaticized rebel, no, a noble horseman, head of a tribe, adversary then friend of infidels and progress, and played by a world-renowned star. The word had ultimately come down from Paris: one had to move with the times. On close scrutiny, the screenplay was not subversive; it was a hymn to a well-understood fraternity uniting Europeans, natives, and Americans in the joyful celebration of a balance that had just been established for the entire century to come. Some colonials even came to defend that policy. They said that one had to feed the rats to save one's provisions. The real Prépondérants called them dangerous.

3

HONORED GUESTS

Gabrielle Conti would sometimes visit Rania early in the morning, to enjoy the countryside in the remaining coolness of the night; it was her discovery. "You know," the journalist said, "I am what they call a hypocrite, I can write 'the fields hum softly against misfortune,' but I'm incapable of putting a name to any plant." They walked slowly but with a good stride—the air wasn't yet a burden, the earth smelled good—Gabrielle saying, "Men would say our stride isn't very feminine, not hobbled enough." She stopped often, asked: "What's that? They're everywhere!" She pointed at a stem with green leaves that were just opening up, topped with white umbels.

"A witch's plant," said Rania, "hemlock."

They started off again.

"And you can eat that." Rania pointed at a hedge of cactus whose large fruit were covered with red and yellow bumps, "*Karmus ensara*, the 'Barbary fig,' which you call prickly pear . . . but our term is correct, you imported it . . . Huge cactus to make your first enclosures . . . You can eat it, but it has to be picked carefully: the thorns are dangerous. We'll do it another time."

Up in the sky, on their left, a blue-gray hawk was gently moving its wings, almost immobile some sixty feet above the ground.

"He's hunting," said Rania, "I see him whenever I walk. I like to think that it's always the same one, a friend, but I'm not sure, and if he stays close by, it's probably because we're upsetting the shrews and the field mice. We're his beaters."

Gabrielle waited until they returned to the veranda of the farmhouse to tell Rania about the parties at the Grand Hôtel. They sat down across from each other in front of a breakfast that made the journalist sigh; she pushed away a plate full of honey and almond pastries after taking one or two and then reaching for a third, to go with her second cup of coffee . . . She started to tell her story, incapable after a time of knowing how many pastries she had eaten. Rania refrained from interrupting her. Once, though, she asked if those evenings resembled the balls at the Opéra, she had seen drawings and paintings in the Paris magazines. Gabrielle laughed, replying that the women at the hotel weren't dressed the same way, and promised to bring her photos. Rania was mad at herself for asking the question; she was also a bit mad at Gabrielle: *Why did she laugh? Because I don't know anything? Because it has become a world where it is ridiculous not to know the difference between Opéra balls and parties at the Grand Hôtel? I thought that knowing the difference between Stendhal and Zola was enough, but she laughs, not to be hurtful, but that makes it worse, when I wasn't expecting it, I shouldn't feel out of touch, I'm the one who is hurting myself, throughout the day, sa'atuna ka diba'u . . . our hours are hyenas, and it's what we read in novels and magazines that makes us want to go to those parties where I'm not allowed to go . . .* Rania also tried to get Raouf to talk, but he replied tersely that he didn't know anything and had no desire to know. The tone was forced and probably expressed something other than the words, but Rania didn't insist. She refrained from telling her cousin that he was lying and that he was quite free to go whip himself into a frenzy with foreign women at a hotel.

She was mistaken. Because it wasn't at the Grand Hôtel that Raouf had seen the life he had been leading up to then turned upside down. He had just received his *baccalauréat*, and he didn't dare appear in such a place yet. It was on the request of his father, the caïd Si Ahmed, who was the sovereign's representative in the region of Nahbès, that he met the Americans the day after they arrived.

"I would like," Si Ahmed had told him, "for you to take care of the two most important people, the one they call the director and his wife, the actress . . . They should be treated . . . as our honored guests . . ."

Raouf had understood: they should not allow the French to be the only ones in charge of the Americans' stay. But he didn't want to become the instrument of paternal politics, a strange politics, in line with those of the French — "You must always swim close to the boat," repeated the caïd — but he sometimes drifted unexpectedly and then returned to the right path just as unpredictably, and now he had to be pleasant to the foreigners about whom his father nonetheless said: "Their declarations on the rights of peoples . . . democracy . . . is madness . . . communism!" The father assigned the son the task of making the newcomers' life easier; he, himself, would remain in the background, like that . . . in the event of problems . . . No, his father wouldn't do such a thing, not that hypocrisy, and yet "Hypocrisy is the weapon of the conquered" was one of Si Ahmed's favorite sayings. Raouf ultimately said that he would do what was asked of him, though the tone of his voice made it clear that he wouldn't be putting too much energy into the effort; when you had your life in front of you in a country like this you had to be just as cautious of Americans as of the French. "One group goes down, another climbs up," repeated his friend Karim, less fascinated than his other friends with everything that came out of Europe or America.

And that evening, in the gardens of the caïd's residence, at the welcome party that his father and the contrôleur civil, Claude Marfaing, were hosting for the entire film crew, Raouf had refused to be impressed by that Kathryn Bishop whom everyone was surrounding. As soon as she turned her smoldering gaze on a man, the chosen one puffed out his chest, the most talented without appearing to do so, others, on the contrary, while placing a hand above their heart and standing on tiptoe; still others played with their mustache and devoured the actress's face with their eyes, a square, soft face, a wide mouth, well-shaped ears; some even lowered their gaze to what the dress allowed them to contemplate from its low neckline; and they all began to talk louder, other women trying to get closer to the actress to take advantage of a few leftover scraps of gallantry.

Raouf was being watched. He was expected to act predictably, the high school student in front of the blond of everyone's dreams, the native before a famous Westerner. His smile was shy and friendly without being indifferent, but since he didn't want to elbow his way in, he ended up in the second row. He left the circle to go from group to group to greet the other Americans, all those people exuding the open sea, who congratulated him on his scholarly English. Raouf thought he had reached the top of his game.

A bit later, Kathryn Bishop, escorted by her court, had said to him when their paths crossed, "I hear you're going to keep us from doing anything stupid in a country we know nothing about?"

Raouf had responded that he might not be able to devote all his time to that more than pleasant task—he had to begin preparing for his entrance into university—but it would be an honor if the occasion were to arise in the coming weeks (*Good to say weeks*, Raouf said to himself, *not days, you're not their flunky, well played!*) to show Madame Bishop and her husband some of the monuments in the city.

Kathryn had smiled, *Who does this kid think he is, with that suit that has forgotten to grow with him? He has intense black eyes, lovely lips, straight shoulders, but that is no reason!*

Then she said, "That would be perfect," and she walked away.

Raouf had understood. David Chemla, his childhood friend, was right. Those Americans, as soon as you didn't do exactly whatever they wanted, they abandoned you. That was capitalism in all its arrogance. Raouf was not a hotel bellman—he had his own life to lead! He was mulling that over when he felt someone take his elbow. It was Ganthier, the colonist whom his father had forced him to see for years, Ganthier saying to him, "So, we're being haughty?" Ganthier had seen everything.

"Not at all," Raouf replied, "but I really won't have time to take care of them, and the lady didn't like that . . . My father is going to say that I did it on purpose, especially if you tell him."

Ganthier began to chuckle: "What's the matter with you? She's gorgeous, I have rarely seen a woman with such a perky behind. She smells good, she looks at you, and you send her packing? Do you think such a package bounces back to you like a handball?"

Raouf didn't answer. He simply looked at Ganthier, a man in his forties, dry, elegant, the largest landowner in the region, a former seminarian and reserve officer. "The only Frenchman whom domination has not rendered an idiot," his father had said to him one day, "Learn to challenge him, it will make you stronger."

Ganthier knew Raouf well. They had begun to talk when Raouf was twelve. Ganthier had given him books and had been astonished to see him arrive at his house the next day with *Twenty Thousand Leagues under the Sea* or *Voyage to the Center of the Earth*, eager to discuss them with him. "You are a frightening reading machine, young Raouf," said Ganthier. "Yes, master!" Raouf responded, in a mocking tone. Ganthier didn't have any children, he was a bachelor, and in Nahbès that young Arab was one of the rare people who was interested in books and literature. It was the only thing they had in common. On all other subjects their exchanges were but a long series of confrontations that became increasingly heated as Raouf grew older and Ganthier hardened into a pure and stubborn colonial.

Raouf and Ganthier had taken a few steps together on the paths of the caïd's residence; then Raouf again began circulating alone among the guests. Some French people would raise their voices when he approached: "Those people . . . the right to vote? Not for another six generations at least." Others lectured on the new arrivals: "What you'll notice is their fatalism . . . History, progress, that doesn't interest them." He also received from time to time forced compliments on passing the *bac*, the first *ex aequo* in all of North Africa along with one of his French friends from the Victor Hugo *lycée*, the son of the head of the Sûreté générale. He thanked the people who looked down on him and whom he wanted to insult. He ended up mixing with the youngest Americans of the film crew, boys and girls scarcely older than he. They were direct, laughed a lot, and were not easily impressed. They liked the future. Raouf had been enjoying himself, then, catching a look from his father, he left his new friends and walked over to the director, Neil Daintree, who was talking with a Frenchman on the terrace.

He was wondering how he was going to approach the director when he heard him say that he was reading *Eugénie Grandet*. The man he was talking to assumed a knowing air, and Raouf boldly interrupted:

"Has Charles already arrived in Saumur?"

"He's just landed," Daintree had said, "and it's magnificent!"

"The noble genre that is slumming it in the provinces," Raouf had added.

"That fellow Balzac knew how to create a contrast. I'd like to make a film about it."

Daintree and Raouf were leaning on their elbows on the railing of the terrace.

"This place," Raouf said, "is like the provinces for the French . . . but it comes with a sense of superiority."

They delved into *The Human Comedy*. Daintree's favorite book was *The Lily of the Valley*.

"I prefer *Lost Illusions*."

"Ah, so your Balzacian hero is Rubempré, the poet!"

"No . . ."

"Rastignac?"

"No . . ."

"Bianchon, the doctor?"

"Not him, either . . ."

"*I give my tongue to the cat*," Daintree said, jokingly translating the French expression.

"De Marsay!"

"The man in power?"

Daintree had glanced over the crowd of uniforms, dresses, dark suits, and djellabas that were teeming below, then: "Are you really that interested?"

They had indulged in an orgy of references. Raouf started to talk about *The Last of the Mohicans*. Daintree kept anyone who might have tried to join their conversation away with a withering look, and seeing that her husband was hiding away at a party where he was the guest of honor, Kathryn approached them:

"You're kidnapping this young man. You're preventing him from preparing his entrance exam into the university."

"Can you believe it? He has read *Eugénie Grandet*!"

Behind the actress, some men were cursing themselves for not having read Balzac recently.

"Ah, my husband's latest passion! That girl was pitiful, when you want a man you take him . . ." Then, in a burst of laughter:

"Ask Neil what happened to him four years ago!"

Raouf tried not to look at the actress's throat. He stared at her gray eyes, and she added: "Don't look at me like I'm crazy, you're going to have to get used to it. Do you know the war cry of our parties in Hollywood? *Let's drink and fuck!*"

Daintree clenched his teeth. Raouf had understood most of it, and started blushing . . . He found the strength to respond that with that war cry they were dismissing many fictional characters, who in general were more patient. Kathryn then assumed a serious tone:

"Yes, the 'delaying of love' . . . whereas at thirty you'll be finished . . . the art of French novels . . ."

"Oh, Raouf has also read *The Last of the Mohicans*," Daintree said. "He speaks English!"

"Just a little," Raouf said, happy to change the subject.

"He's having dinner with us tomorrow, and he's going to teach me Arabic!"

"That's it, my husband wants to seduce you, but be careful, we can be big bad wolves!"

"He's also read *White Fang*," Daintree had added.

In the weeks that followed, Raouf did what his father had asked. He spent hours with the Daintrees and he became enthralled with movies, finally understanding the enthusiasm of his former teacher Jules Montaubain: "It's an art, Raouf, it's going to take over all others, it's going to complete them, in the Hegelian sense of the word!" Montaubain had communist sympathies, couldn't read *Das Kapital*, and liked to make references to Hegel. He was, like Ganthier, very proud of Raouf's having passed his *bac*.

When he was with Kathryn Bishop, Raouf had to put up with her provocations. She had decided to treat him like a teenager. He treated her like a respectable lady on purpose, which made her mad, and Ganthier commented: "Two wounded vanities, young Raouf, it's a true beginning!" Once, Kathryn had said to Raouf: "Neil wanted you with me so I wouldn't go looking for company elsewhere!" Raouf had disappeared for two days. Since Neil was worried, she came to apologize:

"We'd be better off friends, don't you think?"

"Indeed," Raouf had replied, and very happy with his reply. They started to walk together, arm in arm. People greeted them. He was happy not to experience the emotions that Kathryn provoked in the men of the town. He continued to go say a few words to Rania when he noticed her carriage on avenue Jules-Ferry, but not when he was with Kathryn, even if he knew that Rania had seen them. Rania watched him; she didn't mind, but she thought it was stupid to act like that. She said to herself, *They could come over, he could introduce her to me, she could become my friend, what he's doing is petty, I'm sure he knows it, he's not stupid, so why is he doing it?* Rania couldn't come up with a satisfying answer, but it didn't upset her to discover such behavior in a boy who everyone said would have a brilliant future.

4

AND . . . ACTION!

And then there was one afternoon . . . a few miles south of Nahbès, in the middle of the first dunes, where the Americans had set up their clutter of trucks, tents, mobile dressing rooms, lights, scaffolding, and canvas folding chairs. In front of a Bedouin tent, there was a couple, a woman whose eyes were no longer her own, in the arms of a handsome man who was speaking to her urgently.

Raouf was standing some fifteen yards from the actors, at a good distance, far enough to see everything that was going on, whole bodies, the movements of the lower bodies, the chests, everything glued together, everything that is disturbing when you watch a couple and you can also see the details, the fingers, the lips. He watched, arms hanging at his sides, his mouth open. He wasn't used to what he was experiencing; boys of eighteen didn't know women. He kept thinking of something a friend had said, a friend who had read one book more than all the others: "A woman is natural, that is, abominable," and then you go to a brothel, or you dream of a goddess, or both at the same time, but you are repulsed at the idea of being glued to a real woman, of flesh, whose will is not your own. Raouf hadn't learned the words to make plans and decide "I will have her" to end his stupor. He couldn't detach himself. He suddenly wanted to call Kathryn a whore and punch the pretty boy in the face, but she was his friend. But a whole lot of things were battling in his head and in his trousers, violence, sweetness, images, echoes of conversations between friends—the one who tells you in the tramway that he went *all the way* and that he didn't find it *all that fun*, in any case, brothels are disgusting—Kathryn's dress, slit on the side, revealing her entire naked leg. He had once heard her say: "I'll never be a great star, I don't have Ziegfeld legs." Raouf didn't know what a Ziegfeld leg was, and didn't dare ask anyone, but he found Kathryn's leg magnificent. He watched her, watched her face, her leg again, without being seen. He wanted to remain cool but everything was battling in him, very ancient poems *hasartu bifawday ra'siha*, I took her by the temples . . . *fatamayalat 'aleyya*, and she leaned toward me . . . Kathryn ten yards away, short hair, a large, lovely mouth, I took her by the temples, a pre-Islam ode *hasartu* . . . But it was that pretty boy Francis Cavarro who was leaning over her, her temples . . . Enough to make you close your eyes for a moment, his hands traveling down to her waist, *hadima lkash'hi*, her slender waist . . . squeezing it, open your eyes, remain cool, Ziegfeld leg, Kathryn standing on tiptoe, slender ankles in sandals, and again Baudelaire, "and your feet fell asleep in my fraternal hands," panic, alexandrines that blended with fourteen-centuries-old odes, *tamata'tu min lahwin biha gheira mu'jali*, I took my pleasure in entertaining myself with her . . . without haste . . . And something that resists everything, a real woman, not the woman of the poem, and in the arms of another, let her stay there, I took her by the temples, leave, leave those two rubbing against each other, and we stay, we're one too many, but you never know what can happen . . . They must be looking at me . . . She leaned toward me . . . without the eyes of a dead fish, looking at that greasy idiot who is taking her in his arms for the third time, and the other one over there who shouts in his megaphone and who couldn't care less that his wife is in the arms of another, and who shouts "Action!" so she'll start rubbing again . . . They must be watching me.

Raouf looking around, his gaze lingering on a roundish shape wearing a panama hat, Laganier, a high-level functionary of the *contrôle civil*, the head cop, Laganier acknowledging Raouf, always polite with the caïd's son, but he was still thinking: That native is an example of the mistakes that we can no longer afford to make; opening the French school to them only created enemies, and now, in addition, this one is watching women with his mouth open. If he were watching a French woman that way it would cause quite an uproar, but that is an American woman. That will teach the Americans, friends of everyone, a high-ranking officer and the grocer Ben So-and-So; it is in fact insulting, and what's more, they let themselves be called by their first names without *monsieur* in front, and the natives are getting ideas . . . Those movie people, it was like in Paris, intellectuals, and a lot of them speak French. We warned them about the natives, but they don't care; they say they got rid of their colonizers and that it has done them a lot of good. Then we pointed out that they didn't have a lot of negroes at their table, but they don't care about that, either. There are even some who have started to learn Arabic, not only to give orders — French would have worked for that — no, they're learning Arabic to understand, they said, as if the French weren't capable of explaining things! And all of this, in the end, has come from the miserable "protectorate." We should have turned this country into a colony pure and simple a long time ago. There is nothing to protect: we have the military, political, economic, technical strength; we have a predominance to exercise over the colonized, that's all; remove the obstacles and move forward! Laganier also found it scandalous that Raouf had access to the set, but he was the director's friend, he took the wife out, and he was teaching the husband Arabic, the couple's friend!

Farther away, auxiliary guards, clubs in hand, barred access to the site. They moved aside when they saw Raouf arrive, his thin figure, his gray, European-style suit, bare head. The soldiers saw Raouf every day; their French captain had told them that he was the factotum of the American boss and his wife. For the soldiers the American boss was "the general" because he was always giving orders and no one gave orders to him. They pretended to understand what a *fact-outoum* was, while thinking that Raouf was too important a person to be serving a boss—he was the caïd's son—and even if they had already seen him getting water for the actress like any servant could have done, servants never sat down to chat with bosses while laughing along, the way Raouf did with the general and his wife, the one who in front of everyone rubbed against a Christian disguised as a sheikh, *factoutoum*, can you imagine! Now if an American wants to rub against a Christian woman he has to be disguised as a sheikh and the caïd's son is *factoutoum!*

A sudden shout, one word: "Sand!" The noise of a motor, the smell of gas, two huge fans starting to roar, men throwing shovelfuls of sand into the blowing fans, the sand flying toward the couple, then another metallic shout through a megaphone: "Places!"

It was Daintree who had shouted. Kathryn had placed her body very close to that of the sheikh, her head raised toward him, behind them a Bedouin tent, rugs and cushions under the tent, other tents in the background, palm trees, and dozens of Bedouins on horseback. Another shout, Daintree again, in front of the small opening of a six-foot-long funnel lying horizontally in front of him on a tripod:

"Attention! Ready, Francis, three seconds and you kiss her," Daintree pivoting his megaphone to the right: "And when they begin to kiss, send in the camels . . . Camera! . . . Action!" To his left a man began turning the crank of a camera, and two other men, farther away, each on a scaffolding and sheltered by a large umbrella, were doing the same with their cameras. More shouting into the megaphone: "Francis! Three, two, one, go!" The couple started kissing again, two mouths on top of each other. "Cut! Kathryn, you're kissing him too soon, you look like a woman in heat . . . Let him kiss you first! And get those damned camels out of here! From the top . . . ready . . . action! . . . Kiss . . . camels . . . cut!" Daintree was holding his arms out to the camels: "Get the camels closer together! Make them go straight to Steve's camera!"

Daintree wasn't upset. A kiss and getting fifty camels to go by didn't happen by snapping your fingers. In Hollywood, he would have had well-trained circus camels, but too tame to play true, energetic beasts of the desert, with the look of wanting at any moment to escape into the infinitude of the sands—that's what creates dynamism! Circus camels were made to take orders and to eat, and their camel drivers to wait to be paid. That would be seen on screen. The director had said to the producers: "I don't want a circus ring. I want real dunes, real Arabs, real camels, a real space. I want people to sense that the background could at any moment escape the control of the leads. That's what will make the tension of *Warrior of the Sands*. I want a real, harsh world that will disturb the audience. They'll love it." And Daintree had gotten everything, or almost, because he had wanted to go to Arabia, but the producers had found that North Africa was just fine, closer, had better infrastructure, dear Neil, and just as much sand and Arabs: "You're not going to quibble, and what's more, they speak French like you, like Kathryn, like Francis." Neil had agreed to the compromise, even if North Africa was a bit too policed for his taste. He had obtained his strip of desert and the possibility of filming almost his entire film while escaping the horror that everyone was going through back in Hollywood at that time, a horror, a true horror.

He was also allowed for the first time to shoot with two extra cameras, so he wasn't going to get upset because his real camels led by real Arabs were making a real mess. Anyway, they weren't any more difficult to direct than the actors, than that couple who couldn't even act out a kiss. "Kathryn, now you're waiting too long, we won't see anything decisive on screen, do it on two counts!" Neil knew what was going on. Kathryn and he had had a fight the night before, and she was getting back at him. He wanted to tell her, *Try for once to express love without looking like you're lying*, but decided not to, and said: "He kisses you, you count one . . . two . . . while getting up on tiptoes, three . . . four . . . Then come back down on your heels, he will have to hold you tighter, whether he wants to or not, right, Francis? Be virile, damn it, give me sex!" The last word had resounded a hundred yards around. Raouf wondered why Neil dared to say such things to a pomaded actor; it was dangerous, if Cavarro took him at his word . . . Neil's voice again: "The camels behind the flags . . . Francis, this isn't the moment to comb your hair! Attention, ready? Action! Kiss, one, two! Camels! One, two! Good . . . Cut!" Daintree pointed at the fans with his fist, not the ones that were making the sand fly, but the other two, the ones that should have been sending wind into the palm trees. They hadn't started up; there was sand carried by the wind with palm trees that weren't moving. They could have filmed with real wind, but they would have had to wait, and in this country, with real wind, you can't do anything at all.

They started again, all fans at full power, Kathryn pressed, Cavarro leaned over, Kathryn pressed harder, Raouf suffered, *muhafhafatun bayda'u gheiru mufadatine*, soft, white, the stomach firm and flat . . . The camels were advancing in mass in the background, a beautiful undulation. "Good . . . like a wave arriving from the Orient . . . not too quick with the camels," shouted Daintree into his megaphone, ". . . a large wave . . . powerful . . . Control them! Shit! One of them is getting away!" One of the camels was hesitating, suddenly ran toward a tent, fell on it, got back up, was beaten with a stick, panicked, ran toward the musicians . . . "I want musicians," Daintree had said, "I'm not crazy, I know the film is silent, but I want everyone on set to hear oriental music. It gives rhythm, tone. You don't interact with someone the same way if you hear oriental music during the shoot, and Cavarro is much more expressive when he hears that music. I want musicians within the camera's range. The prince receives a young Christian woman. He's a man of the desert, but he's civilized. He has musicians prepared, violins and tambourines—it's the sign of a great soul! For sex there's the kiss, and for the soul there's music, and throughout the world, when the film is being shown, the pianist in the theater will start playing oriental music."

The camel had finished running around the musicians, who had scattered, and a little girl started to approach the camera with a basket of eggs that she was holding like a trophy, thinking it was her turn to act, starting to run toward the couple, stumbling, staggering toward Francis Cavarro, Francis having just enough time to avoid the eggs that crashed to the ground. A great professional, Francis, he saved his white burnoose—not completely, some yolk got on the bottom . . . "Cut! We'll do it again, set that tent up quickly, the camels in place, and put some sand on the egg yolk! Keith, stop that shrew from hitting the kid! It wasn't her fault, it was yours . . . Attention . . . Everyone ready? Send the sand!"

"If you want the audience to feel the sand, you have to have eaten pounds of it while we're shooting," the director had told his crew. But suddenly they couldn't hear the fans. "We're out of gas for the fans? Holy shit! Are you kidding? Too many takes? Who said that? Does someone want to direct instead of me? Too many assistants, you mean! Too much dead weight that isn't doing shit!" Daintree walked up to the little girl with the basket. He wanted to pat her on the head. The girl trembled when she saw Daintree's hand reaching out to her. He stopped. "Okay! Fill up the tanks, we'll take a break! Twenty minutes! Francis, don't wander off!" Then Daintree turned toward Raouf, his voice softer, friendly: "Raouf, my fellow, can you keep an eye on Kathryn? I don't want her to disappear! Assistants and cameramen, to the truck with me!"

Kathryn had left Cavarro's arms. He had gone to sit in front of another woman who was putting powder on his nose. It reassured Raouf that the man took pleasure in having his nose powdered. Kathryn had asked Raouf to get her some cold water. She could have asked her black maid, Tess, or one of the women who had been assigned to her, but with Raouf she was sure that the water would be uncontaminated — he was obsessed with cleanliness, even more than an American. Once she had said to him:

"It's amazing, your obsession with cleanliness, a puritan in this country . . ."

"So if you're an Arab you must be dirty?" Raouf had asked. Kathryn didn't like when he talked like that; she didn't want Raouf to think she was prejudiced. Raouf was a puritan, and that was rare here. Raouf didn't need to act like a bitter old man. What she wanted was someone who was always nice, someone attentive; that's what certain men in France were like, in the old days. Raouf could make a very presentable gallant, someone who admires you and whom you don't care that much about. Kathryn thought she was being harsh to think that. She liked Raouf, but he was ungraspable. He spent the day trying to sort out his thoughts: "I belong to a defeated country. They say I'm the future, but I belong to a defeated country."

They were sitting under an umbrella, Raouf had brought something better than water, lemonade. She told him that he was the perfect gallant. The first time she said that word, she had asked him if he knew what it meant. Raouf's eyes had shone. He was proud to be able to say, "preciousness, seventeenth century." He interrupted himself: *I'm going to sound like I'm reciting my lines*, he thought. He had also been afraid that he would blush while talking about Mademoiselle de Scudéry's *La Carte de Tendre*. Every time Kathryn called him "gallant" it made him both happy and unhappy. She pretended not to see; she never went too far, just enough to know he was suffering a little.

She drank half the glass, set it down saying, "Now that is pleasure itself . . ." The word made Raouf blush. She had said it on purpose, because he was pouting. She knew why, but continued to talk, provoking Raouf, "That's what's most difficult, you know, to pretend to feel what you don't feel, a false feeling, but which is supposed to provoke real emotion." Raouf didn't say anything, stared off into the dunes. She continued: "It's like when you played war in the olive grove with your friends, you played a warrior without being one!" She was getting annoyed at Raouf's silent pouting:

"I'm doing the same thing, I'm playing, and what's more, they pay me!"

"It's been quite some time since I played in the olive grove," Raouf had responded, "and maybe what you're doing is false, but it's a real man's mouth!" She laughed loudly when he said that. She was seven years older than Raouf.

Silence between them, they noticed the poodle, the trotting shape of the poodle that followed Daintree all day long, never more than six feet away. The "poodle" was the nickname they had given Wayne, twenty-two, red-headed, who still sounded like a boy, a recent graduate from a film school in New York.

His work on the set consisted mainly of running around with Daintree's canvas chair so that it would be available whenever the director wanted to sit down. Wayne could have been an assistant, not on this project, of course—this was the highest level of film-making—but elsewhere, supervising a camera with a lesser-known director, he would have learned things like everyone else. But no, Wayne, with a great deal of professional awareness, folded, unfolded, refolded, lugged around all day long a canvas chair on which the name of Neil Daintree was printed in bold letters, the task of a grunt. All the assistants laughed when they saw Wayne trotting behind the director: Can you imagine a student of the film academy, reduced to that! Even the local workers looked down their noses at him, an American who does that job? It can only be because he likes doing it.

Raouf watched Wayne, then, turning to Kathryn: "Now that's a gallant, a real gallant." Kathryn's voice turned hard: "Do you want to learn something today, Raouf? What person here knows better than Wayne, at any moment, everything that Neil is doing? Framing, directing the actors, tricks, regrets, strokes of genius . . . Wayne is learning the profession alongside one of the greats, just by soaking him up . . . I know a lot of people who would pay to carry around that chair . . ." Kathryn sighing, adding that Wayne had only one fault, he was shy, didn't have a girlfriend, but good for him, if he wanted beautiful women he would have to become someone very strong . . . not like the sons of notables who wait around for someone to bring them a docile virgin on a platter, in exchange for a nice dowry . . . because here the man provides the dowry, right? Unless a rich widow . . . Kathryn was talking the way she had when she had met Raouf for the first time. He was worried. By putting some distance between them, he had wanted to show he wasn't happy, and now she was widening the gap, with contempt. He had to make peace.

Ganthier's arrival diffused the tension. He was accompanied by Gabrielle Conti wearing a Saharan jacket and a long skirt, a pen on a chain. As soon as she was in the shadow of an umbrella she took off her khaki-colored cotton hat to air her abundant brown hair, shining with red highlights. Ganthier had fallen in love with her at first sight. He had discovered what he had never encountered before, a powerful woman. He had said to Raouf: "She frightens President Poincaré! Each of her articles has more than two million readers!"

Gabrielle Conti's boss in Paris, the owner of *L'Avenir*, was crazy about her: "She writes like Maupassant, can you imagine, a woman who writes like Maupassant!" He paid her very well, agreed that she could also publish articles in *L'Illustration*, and it was through her that he had his instructions and threats sent to the ministers. "She's playing an interesting game," Marfaing, the contrôleur civil, had said to Ganthier, "What she can't publish in her newspaper she sends to her Bolshevik or socialist friends, and in exchange they tell her a bit about what is going on in Russia or in their parties. She feeds her articles with that and discusses it with the ministers." She and Ganthier didn't agree on anything, and she liked to provoke him: "One day history will tumble ass backwards, and you'll find yourself on the other side of the sea." But she had discovered that the colonist spoke and read Arabic fluently, and she used him shamelessly. And she didn't hide from him the fact that men were of little interest to her. That had not discouraged Ganthier.

Neil's voice called everyone back to work.

5

A QUINTAL AND A HALF

There was something a bit bizarre about the parties at the Grand Hôtel. Ever since the Yankees had landed, the inhabitants of Nahbès were on the alert: Yankees are really wild when they drink, twenty of them, thirty—then, after midnight it is a complete free-for-all! After a week they'd seen everything, Neil, Kathryn, Wayne, Francis, Samuel, the entire crew. They were holding up amazingly well. They drank, laughed, danced. They touched each other when they danced, but it wasn't a bacchanal, which everyone expected, and there was someone called McGhill who kept saying: "We should present a redemptive image," a big, jolly, red-faced man, with cauliflower ears, ready to laugh at anything. Well, when he entered the room at the Grand Hôtel, around close to midnight, everyone was laughing as much as usual, but without missing a beat, they began to gather their things, still laughing and joking. "Present a redemptive image . . ." That didn't make sense. They were the most beautiful, the richest, the most famous people in the world. What did they need to redeem?

Eventually, some of the Yankees began to talk, when McGhill wasn't there. They told a strange story to the people who had become their friends, a show of confidence in Ganthier, Raouf, Gabrielle Conti, and even Montaubain, the teacher who was enthralled with film. Ganthier knew Americans well. He had seen them live and die during the war, and he had been to the United States twice. "They are the only descendants of Shakespeare," he told Raouf and Gabrielle. "The English are no longer Shakespearean ever since Dickens and his novels. Dickens reconciled them with decency and humanity. They are still somewhat assholes on principle, but it is only in America that you can still run into Richard III, Lady Macbeth, or Falstaff, people who have the strength to throw themselves headfirst into whatever they do, risking those heads, and that's what they call freedom, Falstaff's throwers of steel, always ready to throw it over a river, under trains, in the cement of skyscrapers, over the seas, and after six in the evening they bathe in alcohol, adulterated or not, and that's when the women take power because they are less drunk than the men, and the next day they divorce Falstaff to marry Shylock, or vice versa! Shakespeareans who also spend their time driving Othello crazy: they say they killed themselves to free him, and then they forbid him from sitting next to them."

Gabrielle Conti often joined the discussion at the hotel bar. She had also been to the States. The Americans continued to talk in front of a journalist then, but the reason they did was only understood later, and they hadn't always been so prudent—there had been another era in their country, real good times.

In the mornings after they met, Gabrielle would go to the farm to tell Rania the Americans' story, skipping the least palatable parts: It had begun the year before, in California, a scandal. That's why people in the movie business were being careful, Gabrielle adding that new conditions had been added to their contracts: "They are forbidden from getting drunk in public, two people must not be in the same hotel room if they're not married, and it is sometimes written in that they can lose their job *if negative statements about them are circulated in the media*, even if those statements are lies, they just have to be negative, Kathryn showed me her contract" . . . Rania was very interested in what Kathryn did. She asked Gabrielle if it were true that American women had as many lovers as their husbands had mistresses. Gabrielle knew only that Kathryn loved Neil. Neil had a reputation as a ladies' man, but he had fought in Europe for four years during the war . . . *"ayuha' al'ahyia*, happy are the survivors," Rania had murmured. She wondered what her husband's life over there could have been like. He had died a hero; the rest didn't interest anyone. Ganthier could have given her a glimpse of that life, but she hadn't had a conversation with him for years. He had come to her uncle's when she was a child. He was almost a member of the family. She had called him *'ammi*, Uncle Ganthier. He had given her books, *Les Petites Filles modèles*, which she had loved, and later another book by the Countess of Ségur, *Diloy le cheminau*, which portrayed Arabs as evil and cowardly. Rania had asked Ganthier why.

"Probably because the author didn't know any Arabs."

"So she's talking about something she knows nothing about?"

Rania had decided not to read that countess anymore, she had told Ganthier. She had never been ill at ease with him, except in her adolescence, and she didn't really understand why. Then she had stopped going to Nahbès, she had gotten married, she had lost her husband, and when she had come back to take care of her aunt, Ganthier hadn't come to visit them; her uncle and he had had a falling out. Her uncle said: "He is here through force, and then he wants us to call it hospitality."

Rania realized that a silence had fallen over her and Gabrielle. Gabrielle was looking at her.

"Sorry," said Rania, "I was thinking about . . ."

"I know . . . ," said Gabrielle.

She picked up the thread of her story: the Americans' story had begun with a short piece in the newspapers, a woman, a clinic in San Francisco, an actor interrogated by the police.

Gabrielle spared her friend the details, but at the bar of the Grand Hôtel, when Cavarro told it, it was much rougher: it had hit the actors like a ton of bricks on September 4, 1921. They had begun to talk about it a few days before the newspapers did, telephone calls, laughing at breakfast, a girl, not the first time she did that, they hung up, a somewhat nasty rumor; they had a pastry and then they called someone else, a blouse and a bra thrown across a room, shouts, and not at just anyone's house, a bra on a lamp, knocks at the door, people in their pajamas at three in the afternoon, at least a dozen of them. "Oh, a lot more than that!" Wayne had said, and Cavarro immediately shot him a venomous look, a look that Raouf hadn't understood even if he did understand that Cavarro wanted to maintain control of the story and couldn't stand for anyone to add anything to what he was saying: a girl in a bathtub with big pieces of ice on her stomach to ease her pain, shouts, also laughter, the day after Labor Day, the workers' holiday—in the States, it's the first Monday in September—a girl stripped while yelling, at a celebrity's place, no, not in Los Angeles . . . in San Francisco, the good city, clothes rolled up into balls, thrown across the room, they'd already seen that a hundred times, but they were talking about it because of the knocking on the door and the pieces of ice, at a million-dollar star's place . . .

In fact, said Neil, the girl hung around people in the movie industry. That evening she had been drinking like a fish and she was the star of the show. Yes, said Cavarro, a great thrower of clothing, not too bad to watch, by the way, and real coyote cries, and it wasn't at the star's home, but in a palatial hotel in the heart of San Francisco, a huge suite. They were celebrating both the star's new contract and Labor Day.

Samuel Katz, Cavarro's publicity man, had added that it was really a contract for a million per year, a gramophone, a party, contraband whiskey, and if they only whispered about it, it was because if you said bad things about a star in California, said Katz, the studios end up hearing about it, and you become shit for twenty years.

When Samuel Katz was talking Cavarro let him speak with a great deal of indulgence, then he resumed, it's not the fact that the girl took her clothes off that caused a stir—it was the type of gathering where everyone was soon naked—no, it was the shrieking, and not the sounds someone makes when they bang themselves on a table in the middle of a room, those are funny sounds.

Everyone stands around in a circle, said Cavarro, you clap your hands, the girl hangs on to the tie of the guy like in a rodeo, you sing "Oh, Susannah," and you wait for the finale, the rising shrieks, especially when the girl really knows what she's doing, because to be pleasured in front of thirty people . . . Oh, I know some who manage very well, said Kathryn before falling back into her thoughts. She hated that type of girl, Neil's specialty, they chased after him, they wanted to show him what good actresses they were, *and he pretends to believe that I did the same thing when I was their age, it suits him* . . . Cavarro continuing: that day the girl invented a new thing, the angry striptease, to create a scandal for the star! Ganthier was watching Raouf, who was looking blasé, and a voice finally pierced through, burning through Cavarro's discreet narration: the star was Roscoe Arbuckle, it was Fatty!

Cavarro had gotten up: "We said we were going to tell this to our friends like a true drama. If you want to break the suspense, you don't need me anymore!" They had gone after him, let him explain to the French and Raouf who Roscoe Arbuckle was, over six feet tall, weighed a quintal and a half, nicknamed Fatty, a comic actor, a quintal and a half of tempest, he could even do a backflip. When he arrived at a party with his retinue of already drunk girls, it made an impact! Raouf had seen the glacial look Kathryn had given Cavarro, who fell silent, Wayne taking advantage to add that Fatty was a popular comic, for millions of children, all over the country, accompanied by millions of mothers. The story, added Neil, was a lie to destroy Fatty Arbuckle. Okay, there really had been a party, in San Francisco, with around a dozen people, on Sunday, and on Monday there were indeed fifty of them. Fatty had always left his door open; he liked that, serious work, then play. But all the same, said Kathryn, a girl who was shrieking in the middle of the party, there also could have been reasons. That's what was disturbing, and on Wednesday evening, the girl was in the clinic.

Suddenly, they started to talk about the noise of the electric fans in the rooms, and the general lack of fans in Nahbès. McGhill had just appeared at the bar, greeted by a few forced smiles. He didn't stay long, and Neil resumed: Fatty hadn't done anything, people went wild at his parties, they didn't want to leave anything of the pig, everyone went wild, and no one was forced, but no one likes obese people, especially when they have money! Kathryn wasn't saying anything, and Samuel Katz added, that's exactly what was getting to people, the money, it can seem evil if people are told that the big million-dollar baby attacked women at fiestas where the tail was wagging the dog . . . Neil adding for his French friends and Raouf:

"You have the right to earn the million, but you can't dirty it, people never miss an opportunity to teach morality, back home it's a national sport!"

"That said," continued Katz, "for Fatty and the million, audiences came to see him because of what he did, not because of what he earned." And Wayne added in a slow voice, "It wasn't because of his weight that people laughed. With weight, Fatty said, you make people laugh five, six times in a half hour of film. The job is to raise that to sixty times: you have to have an idea, talent, thirty minutes, and sixty laughs."

"You might also recall that he added something else," said Kathryn, "because Fatty never managed to shut his mouth. He would say: 'If you think it's a piece of cake to make people laugh, try it for a half hour, without stopping, after that you'll want only one thing—to become a true sadist,' he said that several times, 'sadist.'" No one had contradicted Kathryn.

At the farm, Gabrielle had quickly gone on to the end of the story: they said that on Wednesday the young woman who had shrieked was in the hospital, and they also said that maybe Fatty had . . . Gabrielle didn't add anything; the details needed to stay at the Grand Hôtel bar. Rania had told her at some point that it sounded like the summary of a novel. "That's journalism," Gabrielle had said, "The narrative without the fiction . . . That said, the best fiction is what is created by real people!" Rania had given in, keeping her roaming thoughts to herself, *li habibun azuru fi lkhalawat* . . . *I have a friend I visit in solitary moments . . . His place in my heart fills all my heart . . . I die of his indifference like a bee in a flame* . . . The figure approached, she kissed his eyes . . . *I am an infidel, my heart is crazy and my tears fall one by one . . . There is the memory, but there is the desire* . . .

This is the first time we've spoken about this together, Cavarro had confided to Ganthier, when we were in California no one dared mention it—no one wanted to be summoned to testify. Wayne tried to defend Fatty in spite of the looks Kathryn was giving him: for fooling around Fatty had an embarrassment of choices, he had only to say yes. Wayne then thought that both Neil and Kathryn were angry at him, and Katz took advantage to cut him off: Anyway, that girl, she did that more often than most, she was even forbidden from getting near Mack Sennett. They said she had infected half the studio; Sennett had even brought fumigators into the building. The girl was in the hospital, her name was Rappe, Virginia Rappe. Fatty had gone back home to Los Angeles. It wasn't really a hospital, Cavarro pointed out, it was a clinic for young, single women . . . Bullshit, said Kathryn, that was invented by the men, holding her husband's gaze and translating "bull" and "shit" for Raouf.

6

THE OLD WOMAN AND THE EGGS

Raouf had a favorite ally: Tess, Kathryn's maid, had decided to become his friend. Tess's name used to be Lizzie, Lizzie Warner. She had changed her first name because she thought that Lizzie was too obvious—people automatically saw a black servant, with a white apron and a kerchief in her hair, grouchy and maternal—she had opted for Tess. Kathryn had said to her, "When you say that name you feel like you're giving an order . . ." Tess was happy with the remark, because such a first name put some clarity in relationships with bosses: they said "Tess!" and the voice didn't have time to soften on another syllable.

Tess knew how to get by. That was useful, because she said she was neither loyal nor devoted, two qualities of a slave. She made a point of having a bad character and of threatening Kathryn regularly with finding another job, which wouldn't have been difficult: she knew how to repair wigs, alter a dress, do the shopping and cook a dinner for ten people at the last minute, pack suitcases without ever forgetting anything, come to work on Sunday morning, saying she couldn't refuse because you couldn't ever give bosses a reason to be upset. She also paid very close attention to her weight. She was as thin as a reed. She said a plump maid was a slave-owner's cliché. She was very hard on men. Her skin was rather light, some white blood a few generations before her—no doubt a master or an overseer exercising his rights, she told Kathryn. From time to time a white man thought he could do the same thing, such as the time a journalist from the *Herald*, Arnold Belfrayn, had found himself doubled over, his hands over his crotch, in the vestibule of Kathryn's house. Tess always acted as if she had nothing to lose.

The friendship between Tess and Raouf had begun during the film shoot, one evening when the extras had organized a méchoui for the Americans, a real country méchoui, not some dish cooked in pieces in the oven like they do in the city. All the Americans came; they liked to show that they were a community. They were offered whole animals on platters, with sauce and hot bread. They were taught what to do, taking the food with the right hand, thumb, index, middle finger, only three fingers and very nonchalantly, while having a nice conversation with one's neighbor, and the sauce, that's what was best, the sauce with a piece of lovely, crusty bread to dip into the golden brown mixture of olive oil, animal fat, blood, pepper, salt, and saffron, and they also showed the Americans the place where they cooked the méchoui, just in time: there was still a lamb on its bed of cinders. They had made a circle around the hole, and at one point Raouf saw Tess move away, a slow walk, mistress of herself, as if she couldn't stop going toward the sunset, and suddenly she leaned against the trunk of an olive tree, a broken figure. Raouf joined her; she was vomiting. He didn't say anything. He held her, then helped her to sit down, then he went to tell Kathryn, who said, "Oh, my God!" and she rushed over with Wayne by her side. They took Tess to Kathryn's car. Raouf didn't ask any questions about what had happened. Kathryn did tell him, "No, she's not pregnant! I'll tell you one day, but not now." Since then, every time Raouf ran into Tess they spent a few moments of friendly banter on the work and the days spent filming, and Tess taught him about the moods of her boss, whose name Raouf tried to get her to say as often as possible, sometimes reciting to himself, *idha dhukirat dara l'hawa bimasami'i*, when they say her name desire wrenches me to my ears.

One evening, in a carriage, Raouf had finally kissed Kathryn's hand. She said, "When you're done, we'll talk." What came next was a very calm statement: a woman loving her husband for and in spite of everything, a fine young man whom she was happy to have as a friend, "and if you do that once more we will never see each other again."

They continued to be seen together. He sought refuge in the pride of experiencing a strong and thwarted passion, and carried the umbrella with care; sometimes Kathryn leaned on his arm to cross a hole in the road, or avoid a porter whose head was hidden under a sack of grain. She wanted to go everywhere, see how people lived, especially at the outdoor souk, which Raouf didn't like, the crowds, the dust, the shouting, the awful wares. He said: "I'm not a guide for things of the past."

Arriving at the souk they heard inhuman cries. They came from the right, from a large pen.

"The donkey pen," said Raouf.

"Donkeys for sale?"

"No, that's where the peasants leave the animals they rode in on. It avoids a mess, theft. There are hundreds of donkeys."

"Who are having a braying contest," concluded Kathryn. Raouf added: "What really makes them bray is because there are two pens, one for male donkeys, and one for females." It smelled like urine, dung, earth, cut hay. The wind blew gusts of acrid dust onto their faces. A man began to run, holding a stick in his hand. "A pen attendant," said Raouf.

"Why is he shouting?"

"It's not interesting."

"Raouf, come on!"

"He's shouting: 'Pig, you'll see!'"

"At a man?"

"No, at a donkey."

"Why call a donkey a pig?"

Both of them watched the man with the stick, and Kathryn burst out laughing: thirty yards away the head and chest of a donkey rose up above the others, a donkey that was mounting the hindquarters of his neighbor, and the neighbor was protesting. The attendant had begun to beat the delinquent, who was being stubborn in spite of the blows, Kathryn saying: "He's brave, why don't they leave him alone? After all, there won't be any consequences . . ." While the attendant was going at it, other donkeys had begun to have the same idea. Chests appeared here and there above the melee. Another attendant started in on another couple. Kathryn was laughing harder and harder. People were looking at them, Raouf saying: "Let's go," and Kathryn: "I was raised in the country, Raouf!" Among the mass of animals, a circle of peasants surrounded two men, who were shouting at each other.

"Those are the donkeys' owners," said Raouf.

"Why are they yelling at each other?"

"The donkey of Ben Zakour was mounted, so they're making fun of Ben Zakour, and Ben Zakour doesn't like that, he's yelling at the owner of the other donkey, who continues to make fun of him, so Ben Zakour says that his donkey must have been watching his owner, and the others better calm down, or the souk police will take care of them." In the background the choir of female donkeys was echoing the cries of the males. A man said something that made everyone burst out laughing and calmed everyone down.

"What did he say?"

"I didn't understand him," Raouf answered, "He must be a Berber, I can't understand very well."

"Raouf, you're teasing me!"

"It's offensive."

"Raouf!"

"He said: 'Let the one who is mounting mount the male, females only cause trouble.'"

While the owners were arguing some of the donkeys again tried to put a leg up on a neighbor's hindquarters, then gave up when the attendants started shouting.

Raouf and Kathryn went back to the souk, Kathryn noting a red cart that stood out from the others.

"That's the widow Tijani's," said Raouf, "She came to sell some animals."

"Or buy some."

"No, she doesn't buy here, and she sells very high." Kathryn was silent for a moment, then:

"Why 'the widow Tijani'? Couldn't you say 'my cousin Rania'?"

"Do you know her?"

"She's a friend of Gabrielle's."

"Did you see her at Gabrielle's?"

"No, Gabrielle goes to her house. I saw her once at the hammam. She's as muscular as an American woman, and she has true Ziegfeld legs."

This time, Raouf seized the opportunity:

"What is a Ziegfeld leg?"

"It's a long, slender leg, but not skinny, a dancer's leg. Ziegfeld has a music hall where all the beautiful girls in New York dream of going to kick their legs. You've never . . . seen your cousin's legs?"

"The last time must have been when I was six . . ."

They went into the souk. Kathryn was entranced.

"It's local color," Raouf commented coldly.

"It takes me outside of myself," said Kathryn.

"At least you're not taking photos."

She was especially interested in the artisans, in the wandering professions, basket makers, tinsmiths, outside dentists, teeth pullers unlike any she had ever seen before:

"There were some in Montana, they've been gone for a long time, seeing them here . . . My grandmother must have been treated like that."

They looked at an assortment of not very clean pliers lying on a piece of cloth, right on the ground, but when a man came up holding onto his jaw, Raouf refused to look anymore, and they left, advancing with difficulty against the flow of an increasingly dense crowd, their movement resembling a river which, arriving at its mouth, must fight against the incoming tide, and there was also the backwash, all the obstacles on the ground, crates, bundles, handicapped beggars on their haunches, and large gray stones that were used as markers. "And watch out for the nails that the kids haven't picked up yet," said Raouf, "Tetanus is no joke."

In the overall mayhem, an immobile figure drew their attention: an old, bent woman, barefoot, standing in front of a stall. They followed the direction of her gaze, and saw a piece of sun yellow fabric, and they saw nothing else but it, the old woman sticking out a hand, touching the fabric, putting it back, looking at it again without saying anything, showing a complete absence of interest. In the back of the stall the merchant didn't react. He was looking down at a notebook, a large wart in the middle of his forehead.

"That's not a wart," said Raouf, "It's a callus from the thousands upon thousands of times he's bowed down touching his forehead to the ground. This merchant is wearing the mark of his piety on his forehead."

An old woman who was saying nothing, a merchant who wasn't looking at her; she left, Kathryn commenting:

"He lost a client. An American vendor wouldn't have let her leave."

"She seemed indifferent," said Raouf, "He showed her some contempt, that's the way it works here."

Later, Raouf and Kathryn passed in front of the fabric merchant's stall again, the piece of sun yellow was still there, the old woman, too.

"That's how the souk works," said Raouf, "First you look, you visit other stalls, then you come back to buy."

This time the old woman was arguing with the merchant, two harsh voices.

"That yellow is magnificent," said Kathryn, "If she doesn't want it, I'll take it, but I'll wait for her to decide." The old woman was holding a bundle in front of her, a knotted rag.

"What do you think is in that rag?" Kathryn asked.

"I don't know."

"It looks like she wants to give him something."

The old woman placed the bundle on the counter. She pushed it toward the merchant. The merchant pushed it back at her, seeming not to want it. They argued, their voices getting louder.

"They're eggs," said Raouf, "She's talking about her eggs, there must be a dozen, no more. She says they're excellent, she wants to trade them for the piece of yellow fabric."

The merchant was shaking his head, slowly, closing his eyes. Among the words he said and repeated, Kathryn managed to understand two or three — she was very proud of her progress — the word *God* and then *no*, and also the word *douro*.

"He doesn't want her eggs," said Raouf, "He wants money, coins, he says it's the twentieth century now." The merchant gestured broadly at the passersby whom he was taking as his witnesses. On certain faces there were signs of approval, people who were trying to show they agreed, but without hurting the old woman. She raised her knotted index finger to the sky, raised her voice. She was seeking an audience. Raouf translated as she spoke: For forty years the woman had always exchanged her eggs with this merchant, him or his father, and his father, may God watch over him, had never refused any exchange. His father was watching him from above, he should be careful not to bring shame on his father! The merchant's responses became even sharper, saying that was enough—he rubbed his index finger against his thumb, *douro, douro*—he wouldn't accept anything else: the old lady just had to go sell her eggs somewhere else and come back with the money; this was the twentieth century. But the old woman didn't want to. She said this twentieth century was the Christians', not that of the Master of the two worlds and of true believers; the merchant must accept the trade. It had always been thus, under the eyes of God, in the centuries of Islam and not the Christians. It should continue as it was with the merchant's father—one didn't have the right to change God's order. Twelve eggs was a good trade for a piece of fabric: to refuse was impiety! In response the merchant's voice also rose.

"He didn't like the accusation of impiety," said Raouf, "The old woman went too far. It's as if she senses that in any case she has lost. She's telling the merchant things that he can't accept, and that his French money is money from the devil."

The merchant had taken a bolt of gray fabric, measured three feet with his forearm, cutting and serving a client who paid in bills. He gave back the change, showing the coins to the old woman: that was honest money, not eggs! The old woman looked at the merchant's hand with contempt, was silent. Yes, the merchant added, honest money and not rotten eggs, the old woman again calling him impious. People were watching them, the old woman pointing at the callus in the middle of the merchant's forehead—he couldn't have gotten that while praying—the merchant saying that he didn't need to be preached at by a pagan who spent her life cutting up frogs and burning pieces of paper instead of praying. Raouf translated faster and faster, the merchant's voice was louder and louder: a woman who adored a piece of bone instead of reciting the words of the holy book, yes, recite, and not just venerate pieces of a skeleton that were perhaps those of a dog!

He had shrieked the last word, and the old woman now appealed to the shame of the entire souk, a shame that should befall the merchant! That's it, said the merchant, the entire souk, the souk that could see that she was only a pagan who knew no more about God than she did about how people bought things, a witch, everyone saw her, God saw her, she would be seized by her hair and thrown into hell. The old woman began to scream; she was crying. "She's given up the fight," said Raouf, "She's crying that a *kafir*, an apostate, is insulting her, and the merchant is threatening to call the police, she'll have nothing."

Raouf held a bill out to the merchant without saying a word and took the piece of yellow fabric. The witnesses were looking at him with hostility; he didn't have the right to do that. They then looked at Kathryn, with even more hostility. That foreigner had the means to pay for miles of any fabric she wanted: why buy the piece the old woman wanted? They didn't have the right, even if the merchant refused her eggs. The old lady had collapsed. She had stopped shouting. She looked at the people, sought some support, didn't find any. The caïd's son had bought for the Christian who was with him. And Raouf took the eggs from the old woman, put the fabric in her hands. Without saying a word, he took Kathryn by the elbow. They left. The old lady sent blessings their way. They were already far, Raouf saying:

"I don't know why I did that, I'm making her think she is living in a world that will help her, but that world is abandoning her even before she can leave it."

"What will you do with the eggs? You could have left them with her."

"That would have been an insult. I'll give them to a beggar, it won't be hard to find one here."

Raouf was silent for a moment, then: "It should have been another poor person who did what I did, but the poor don't have the means . . . or I should have bought the eggs from her, she would have been able to enter the race without losing face, I acted too quickly, I shouldn't have . . ."

"Yes, you should have, and in any case, I really like you in the role of defender of old ladies."

"No, I'm serious. Marx is right, you shouldn't try to ease the class struggle."

"I don't like it when you talk about Marx, Marx will make you do stupid things."

"In Chemla's opinion I'm not even a Marxist, I'm only a feudal Marxist."

"That's going to make you a lot of enemies," said Kathryn.

Coming out of the souk they passed in front of the red cart again.

"Is Rania really rich?" Kathryn asked.

"Her father is very rich. She's an interesting woman. If you want, I can bring you to her house one day."

"You can go to a widow's house?"

"She's a cousin, she's family."

"Could you marry her?"

Raouf smiled. He almost responded, *she's too old.* And he knew Kathryn had understood his smile when she knocked him on the shoulder, laughing.

7

THE COW OF SATAN

In the streets of Nahbès, given the way Raouf was behaving with his American woman, people knew something was going to happen. It finally came to pass with Belkhodja. They were friends, and friends know how to hit you where it hurts.

Belkhodja was a good merchant. He borrowed money in the city, when in the countryside even the scorpions were dying of thirst, and bought rugs from the Bedouins who no longer had any goats or sheep. He made quite a good profit. Better yet, he often left them with their rugs, and loaned them money so they could buy food from a merchant whom he recommended to them, but under the condition that each household make two beautiful pieces for him each winter, with wool strips and camel hide. He came often to oversee the work, verify the density of the fibers, the stability of the colors, made threats when the women allowed little girls to work in their place. When spring came, those rugs paid for the loan. In the souk of Nahbès they could have been sold for a lot more than what Belkhodja paid for them, but a promise is a promise, and once the merchandise was delivered, the Bedouins carefully continued to place Belkhodja under the protection of the All Powerful.

Belkhodja was also a member of what people in Nahbès called the "little band," young men in Western-style dress who met in a café, La Porte du Sud, to criticize everything: they loved to say that a fistful of bees was always better than a bag of flies. In the city, it was felt that Belkhodja had a good influence over them. At their age they thought like roosters, and Belkhodja showed them the value of experience. He liked that role and to be treated as a friend by those boys who were ten to fifteen years younger than he. He refused, however, to be considered a man of the past. He defended what he called tradition, but he liked technological progress. He had had a metal bathtub installed in his house after having used one in a hotel in the capital. He also dreamed of buying a car, and as soon as he had seen that he did his best business with a French clientele, he transferred his rug trade to the European city. He joined the little band at La Porte du Sud, not far from his shop. He preached to those present and spoke ill of those who hadn't yet arrived.

Scandalmongering was Belkhodja's sweet weakness. It was never purely scandalmongering. Some claimed that Belkhodja had eaten a poisonous snake when he was a child, but he denied that: he said he was seeking above all to bring back the believers who had been perverted through pernicious innovations. He, himself, committed sins. Sometimes late in the evening he would drink a bit of alcohol, and the young men whispered that the prayer rug he sometimes carried under his arm was hiding a hashish pipe. He tried, however, never to go too far on the path of errors, which is only a downward slope, he said, for weak souls! And he added that the best way to pay for his sins in the eyes of the Merciful One was to bring back onto the right path other believers who were more lost than he.

And so Belkhodja's inveighing against Raouf—that young man full of promise but whom he considered perverted by French education—always came from good intentions, especially now that they were seeing the caïd's son parading around in the company of that actress, a "star," as they called her, a real danger to his friend. He had to, using all necessary means, bring that wandering soul back into the community. And Belkhodja quickly found a nickname for Kathryn Bishop: *bagrat eccheitan,* cow of Satan. That had spread around the city. When the stone leaves the hand, says the proverb, it belongs to the devil.

Raouf was quickly told what his friend had said. Raouf had laughed out loud, confident of himself, and had added: "Satan has good taste," and he acted even friendlier toward Belkhodja when he joined the group. Taking the fabric between his thumb and index finger, he felt the fine quality of the merchant's new tunic, and complimented him, and wondered whether he, himself, might give up Western dress, at least while he was in Nahbès. He sweet-talked Belkhodja as if he didn't know anything, and Karim, one of the members of the little band, who knew his Raouf, said to himself while observing the scene that he wouldn't want to be in the merchant's shoes in the coming months . . . *cow of Satan* . . . What a terrible thing to say . . . *ta'asat l'insan min llisan,* man's misfortune comes from his tongue.

The other members, especially those who had studied in the capital at the Victor Hugo *lycée* with Raouf, said they thought he was being very good not to throw Belkhodja into the ravine at the first opportunity: "You would only have to take that crook by the collar" . . . Raouf had laughed again, then he sang the praises of that crook, who knew how not to give in to the temptations that Satan and modernity put in his path, the proof being what Belkhodja had been trying to do since the beginning of the year, as a true believer: he wanted to bring together his actions and his words. Perhaps he would succeed, you had to respect the effort, said Raouf in a sad tone, in a world where many, to make a living, on the contrary increase the distance between their soul and reality.

It had, in fact, been several months since Belkhodja had decided to get married, and he wanted his marriage to be a lesson for his young friends. In front of their smiling faces he had stressed that he would never be the dupe in a union. He wanted a woman who was completely innocent. He didn't want to discover one day that he had in his bed one of those creatures that men talk about when they play cards. The smiles had disappeared, and he was silent a moment to allow his friends to imagine the shame that could befall a too-confident husband, then he had reassured them, because it wasn't difficult to avoid such a woman: one had only to listen to public rumor, which can be very cruel, but at least it didn't spare the guilty. Belkhodja liked to interrupt himself as he was preaching. He was holding his audience. He took the opportunity to rub his handlebar mustache. For once they didn't make fun of it. That said, he resumed, no matter the precautions a good man might take with those creatures that serve the moon, isn't there always a risk, which one cannot foresee? And throughout the final months of winter they heard his stories about catastrophic marriages, men in a hurry who became victimized husbands and disgraced victims. He wasn't what you would call an intelligent and clever raconteur, but as soon as he started telling them about women, the young men no longer cared about intelligence. They were happy to feed their apprehensions.

From anecdote to anecdote, spring had finally arrived, but they stayed inside the café, where a wood stove emitted irregular heat, a dozen of them around three tables that they had moved together. It was the afternoon. They struggled against drowsiness, regretting they hadn't gone home to take a nap. They looked at the first flies that had been caught on the strips of sticky paper hanging from the ceiling. They looked at Belkhodja again. He had recently turned down a girl who was too young. That's okay for old men, he had said. "What's more," someone added (maybe Raouf, but they didn't really remember), "girls who are too young don't know how to do housework."

Pushed by his friends, the merchant described his ideal wife, a true young woman, with already (he eagerly made a gesture) something to hold onto, and beautiful, but above all not a seductress, that always ends in catastrophe, it's much worse than finding yourself eating bad meat because you wanted to buy too quickly! Belkhodja's laugh sent to hell all those who didn't have his lucidity, and they laughed with him because, the day before, the conversation had been interrupted to let the din of a truck loaded with two donkeys pass. "It's Hammou's truck," one of the young men had said, "He is proud, he revs the motor, he's going to the animal market."

"It's pretty late for the market," Raouf had replied (that time they remembered perfectly: it was in March, before the Americans had arrived, the last

Saturday in March), "Hammou is pretending to go to the market. In reality he is going to the slaughterhouse. Tomorrow there will be people who buy veal that they'll find a bit tough!"

"Remember," Belkhodja had continued, "remember the marriage of Rahal (that name had brought silence down on the group), Rahal the proud one and his so lively bride!" The merchant's voice had turned sarcastic: an intelligent bride, who spoke well, and modern! I don't want an idiot, Rahal kept repeating, this is the twentieth century! He settled in the capital, he had taken a girl from the capital, and he had his twentieth-century marriage on the sheets the next morning. The old servant woman had done her work, not too much chicken blood, or it would have looked like a big lie. She poured just enough to make it look real. A discreet servant. But a lot of people knew: Rahal, of course, the best placed, and then the bride's sister, and an in-law who was also related to the husband's family. It remained a family secret, until it reached the one who had been informed last, Rahal's father, who then went to see the bride's father. They talked calmly for several hours. The young modern woman, intelligent and lively, had been a virgin, of course, but she wasn't really right for his son.

The rest of the story was murky. Some spoke of an annulment, others of a separation, an illness, perhaps the beginning of tuberculosis. The girl admitted that she didn't feel well. Moreover, she was pretty thin. Her family should have said something, especially a daughter to be married. She was ill, not seriously. She was going to put on weight, be cured, but she should have said so before: that could be a cause for annulment. People talked without being sure. She left to seek treatment in the mountains. In the end, no one talked about it anymore, and Rahal was free again. He had saved face, but a rumor continued: Hadn't he been contaminated? Maybe he was free, but he wouldn't find a good match soon.

Belkhodja laughed in front of the young men, whom the story had made thoughtful. He liked to provoke silence and be the only one to laugh, a laugh that enlarged the bottom of his face and revealed two rows of good teeth, intact, already dyed with old ivory, which makes men look respectable.

The merchant had continued enthusiastically to tell his anecdotes on marriage. Rahal was a successful merchant, his family was more powerful than the girl's, he ended up free, he could have been worse off . . . Belkhodja lowered his voice, and the attraction of what could have been worse made the worried faces lean toward him. They were entering into the realm of serious indiscretions. They watched the waiter's movements. They watched each other.

"Worse than Rahal's story," the merchant added, "is when the girl's family is more powerful than the husband's, because that type of modern girl comes from the best families. They make a very good match. A pretty girl. She can read, write. She's rich. Her parents are powerful. She has everything. You get her, and you triumph in front of your friends. You won out because you are the most virile!" Belkhodja's arms had left the table, his forefinger pointing. His voice, accompanied by sharp movements of his arm and his hand, pounded his words home like nails: "And then you realize too late what that girl is capable of!"

Then Belkhodja's voice became less violent, talked about a young married couple in their sitting room, the husband saying that the trip to Europe . . . They were facing some expenses . . . When you're a responsible husband and you first want a car, you say, "No," and what you get is, "I didn't know we were in trouble." The voice is reedy, but the young wife doesn't give up, returns to the subject every day. The husband tells her that to be the wife of a young entrepreneur with a brilliant future is not the same thing as being the daughter of the richest millowner in the land. His voice is hard. He will inherit one day, of course, and her father is not just anybody, but while waiting he can't give her everything, and the wife also talks about buying furniture, a European-style sitting room, and other things, and you begin to believe that she's asking you on purpose for things you must deny her, to make you feel like you can't live up to the standards of the place where you went looking for your wife!"

Here Belkhodja glanced around at the more or less threadbare jacket sleeves of his young friends. "And to the husband's latest refusals," added the merchant, "the response is coldness, or silence. He believes that this is the life of a couple. He begins to tolerate it less. He, himself, becomes intolerable. He starts going out at night again, finds his friends from before, enjoys himself, says that if he had stayed a bachelor he would go out less often—that makes everyone laugh. He treats his wife harshly, and she becomes contemptuous and cold, even in the bedroom!"

Around the table jaws were clenched and eyes were glazed. Too bad for them, Belkhodja said to himself, they think they're men because they go to the café and talk politics, when they couldn't even manage things in their homes if they had one! As soon as they have a dark blue suit they see themselves leading the country, with a *constitution*, which isn't even an Arabic word, what heresy, just like their modern women, heresy and prostitution!

"And one day" (Belkhodja's voice had become cold) "the modern wife has accumulated enough resentment, she goes in search of a single great pleasure to compensate for all those that she hasn't been given . . . I repeat, all . . . and when her husband learns, he suddenly has in front of him a wife he didn't know, who despises him, threatens him . . . He could beat her, renounce her, or even resort to the punishment of the past when a hole was dug and only the adulteress's head could be seen . . . But he doesn't do any of that, why? Because his wife's father and mother are very powerful people, even more powerful than his own father, and it is up to the son-in-law to be docile and silent." Throwing his head back, his eyes to the ceiling, Belkhodja took great delight in his conclusion: "The qualities of a good, traditional wife are now expected of the husband of a modern wife!"

He didn't cite anyone and began grooming his handlebar mustache. No name circulated among his audience. Everyone recalled hearing the same stories, but they didn't want to be the ones to publicly point a finger at a family whose head could at any moment summon from some village a few dependable, obedient, and violent men.

So don't ever look for the perfect match, Belkhodja had concluded, what they needed was a modest and respectable wife, a wife to take care of things around the house, but careful! . . . That wife also has to be a woman . . . The merchant's eyes had opened wide and the words came out: "who smiles!" Belkhodja was proud to have added that, a smiling wife. He had thought of it the day he had seen his sister-in-law, a woman beyond reproach, scold her husband for having gone into the sitting room with muddy shoes, the bitter voice of the housekeeper within her rights, the voice that became just loud enough to spoil the evening of a good man, the voice of a wife who made a point of not calling the servant and who herself mopped up the floor in front of their guest to show him what the inconsideration of a husband could reduce his wife to. "There's a real scourge of respectable women," said Belkhodja, "Good men don't think enough about what daily life can become with a respectable woman who doesn't smile."

He was happy. He had abandoned his customary role with the "little band" at La Porte du Sud, that of the man who reminded the boys of all the dull virtues. This time even Raouf had listened to him attentively, his elbows on the table, his chin in his hands, a smile on his lips, seeming to say, *good job!* Belkhodja didn't want to be Rahal, or the son-in-law of a powerful man, or his own brother. He would find a country girl, a good housekeeper, but above all, someone who smiled! The rug merchant was happy. It was with this type of presentation that one captivated an audience of insolent boys.

A SORT OF TACIT AGREEMENT

They told the Fatty Arbuckle story only at the bar of the Grand Hôtel, a sort of tacit agreement among Francis, Wayne, Kathryn, Neil, Samuel, and a few others. Each person provided a fragment, was corrected, corrected someone else in turn, or fell silent in a fit of pique that forced his friends to let him talk. Sometimes one of them was seized with a mute rage, like someone who is forcing himself not to speak, said Ganthier, so as not to alert the snitch, McGhill, and so as not to cause a bomb to explode in front of us: we are their safety net!

And so Francis Cavarro continued with the story of Fatty, a rumor of a dead woman, a secondary infection, at the Wakefield clinic, reporters on the hunt, a dead actress, Virginia Rappe, who at twenty-five years old had had to fight for the right to a few minutes on film. That in itself was enough to slander the victim, said Kathryn. And the cops talked about a suspicious death, peritonitis. They had questioned the girl who had taken Miss Rappe to the clinic on Wednesday evening. Her name was Maude Delmont. And they had questioned Roscoe "Fatty" Arbuckle: Yes, he had returned to Los Angeles with his lawyer, a tight jacket, golf pants, low shoes. In the photo he was laughing.

"Do you remember his cowboy film?" asked Wayne, "*The Round Up*, the quote on the poster: 'Nobody likes a fat man.'"

"Yes," said Samuel Katz, "but under the fat he was a dancer, and could do amazing backflips."

"Still, not the sort of man," replied Cavarro, "who attracts women!"

Kathryn hadn't reacted.

A certain Virginia Rappe had died after a party given by Fatty Arbuckle at the Saint Francis Hotel, and many people said: "Those actors do that in broad daylight, like animals!" Fatty helped the police with their investigation, the sort of help that could lead directly to the noose, or the gas chamber, the latest technology. There was a principal witness against Fatty, Maude Delmont, Virginia Rappe's friend. Virginia had supposedly confided in her while crying, "He hurt me," and Delmont swore that she had seen Fatty carry Virginia off and spend a half hour with her in a bedroom with the door closed.

Later, Ganthier had told Raouf that, according to another rumor, Daintree and Cavarro had attended the party. Daintree swore that they hadn't, but the press hounded them. That's why Cavarro shot Wayne an angry look when he recalled that there had been a lot of people at Fatty's party.

"They love big parties," Ganthier had added, "The more people, the livelier!" Ganthier also remembered a party in Chicago, after a visit to the slaughterhouse where he accompanied the old Clemenceau. Everything was white, noisy, huge, and clean. The pigs advanced one after the other on a conveyor belt, smoothly — their squeals. A man attached one of their hind legs to a chain. The animal was raised up, its head about five feet from the ground. It writhed, squealed louder. In the next room another man opened its carotid — white tile, white walls, everything hosed down, steam, a gust of air every fifteen seconds, a regular humming. That's what was frightening, peaceful machinery: I saw hell, it was white! The slaughterhouse manager had said to them in front of a collection of metal boxes: "Here we use the whole pig." Ganthier still had Clemenceau's remark in his head: "Everything but the squeal" . . . And more squealing, too, during the Franco-American party that same night, in a nightclub in Chicago, the shouting, the four-legged races, everyone naked, free beasts, each had a rider, and a band of old Gypsies in tuxedos on the mezzanine, impassive. Samuel continued: Anyway, Fatty wasn't very refined, abandoned at thirteen, set off on his own, did cheap theater, fifteen years of that, completely broke, and if they found torn clothing, it was murder in the first degree, and death, like any other pig.

Seeing that Raouf was lost, Wayne continued: Fatty had been accused by Maude Delmont of having raped Virginia Rappe, who later died because of it. Samuel Katz resumed: Fatty claimed he was innocent. A group had come to visit him on Monday morning. They had drunk, danced. A very drunk Miss Rappe arrived. She tore her clothing. Fatty had asked two women to look after her. They had placed Miss Rappe in a bathtub, with large pieces of ice on her stomach to ease her pain. Fatty had called a doctor, then he went to catch a boat for Los Angeles, and on Friday, September 9, Miss Rappe was dead.

The main accuser, Maude Delmont, was joined by two other women, Nancy Blake and Zey Prevon. They confirmed that Fatty had stayed alone in a room with Virginia Rappe for a half hour, and they heard her yelling through the door. Other people maintained that she had begun to shout and throw her clothes around the living room before that. There was also a man who said Fatty had hurt Virginia Rappe, Kathryn noted, someone named Semnacher. Neil Daintree's voice interrupted Kathryn: Semnacher, Virginia's agent, of course! And Neil added that they had found telegrams from Maude Delmont to her lawyers: "WE HAVE ROSCOE ARBUCKLE IN A HOLE HERE. CHANCE TO MAKE SOME MONEY OUT OF HIM." Delmont also had a criminal record for fraud and bigamy, and was going to have problems. The district attorney was Matthew Brady. A high-profile case — he wasn't going to miss that.

"Could Kathryn have participated in such things?" Rania asked later, and Gabrielle responded with a smile: "People are innocent until they are proven guilty!"

"Here, women are considered inherently guilty," said Rania.

"Even in the cities?"

"Especially in the cities! The most modern of men want to marry girls from the countryside, and when they don't find one, their mothers do it for them, *misfortune to those who have abandoned the virtues of the country for the darkness of the city.*"

"Is that what you think?"

"The virtues of the country are only one more example of hypocrisy, the hypocrisy of jailers." Rania thinking that to escape the jailers one had only to close one's eyes, or to be alone, among the rustling grass, on the path where she could talk to herself out loud, *nazala l'hub manzilan fi fou'adi,* love has taken a place in my heart . . . to speak to the other voice that rose up in her own, a desire . . . The figure came to meet her . . . *Everything became faster when I saw him . . . What is a flame if it remains in the flint? I left his hand on my stomach and morality to everyone else . . .* The figure disappeared under the white disc of the sun. Rania came to herself, lifted her head to Gabrielle, who had respected her silence while looking at her wide eyebrows that a razor had transformed into pure and distinct curves.

And in San Francisco all of that had ultimately turned into a maelstrom of stories and substories of a jury, a grand jury, perjury, defamation, questioning, retractions, the testimony of the coroner . . . Fatty found himself in front of the grand jury, the police chief saying that he had looked under all the rocks and that the death of Virginia Rappe was rape and murder in the first degree, adding: "There is no way an Arbuckle is going to come to San Francisco to do such things and escape scot-free."

"In San Francisco," Neil pointed out, "people don't like Hollywood. They say, 'This is the North!'"

"You have to explain," said Kathryn, "They mean the South is full of 'darkies.'"

The prosecution's strongest ammunition was the testimony of the three women: Delmont, Blake, and Prevost. With Semnacher, Virginia's agent, D.A. Brady had his four aces. And there was also Lehrman, the victim's boyfriend, Neil continued. Virginia was at that point, the years go by, the weight is gained, but no real roles. And Samuel added: Lehrman had a wide forehead, the eyes of a rat, and a droopy mustache. His sweetie had left him in New York to go party on the other side of the country. When he learned that she was in the hospital, he was happy to send a get-well-soon telegram, but after she died, he called the undertaker to ask him to whisper in the dead girl's ear, "Henry loves you." Afterward he began to play the role of avenger, and newspapers ran headlines: "Virginia's fiancé wants to kill Arbuckle." He said that in the beginning Fatty cleaned out spittoons; a cleaner of spittoons had been turned into an idol. That tub o' lard took my fiancée into a room to rape her: she tried to fight him off!

When Gabrielle told Rania about Fatty's youth, Rania commented: "At six years old my husband, to survive, had begun by sweeping out the school in his village. It was either that or become a petty thief . . . One day the teacher had surprised him writing numbers on the blackboard. He didn't understand them, but he liked numbers. That had charmed the teacher, and my husband quickly advanced . . . He was on his way to becoming the best financial lawyer in the capital. He did it all by himself, but I never understood his love of weapons and fighting: it wasn't his world. He wanted to imitate the lords who in any case are gone . . ."

"Do you think of him a lot?"

"I'm angry at him for going off and getting killed for a country that despises us."

Throughout the United States Fatty's films were removed from theaters. The grand jury deliberated very quickly.

"Back home," said Samuel Katz to Raouf, "the grand jury is the one that decides which cases will go before a judge."

Maude Delmont gave the damning testimony: Fatty holed up for a half hour in a bedroom with Virginia. Then there were doctors, peritonitis following a rupture of her bladder, and for the district attorney the proof of a violent struggle were the torn clothes, thus rape and murder. But others noted that the body didn't show any proof of violence.

And then there was high drama when Maude Delmont, the first accuser, changed her testimony. She admitted that she had drunk a dozen whiskeys and that Virginia Rappe had gone into the room alone. And that, said Neil, was a problem for the newspapers that had depicted Fatty carrying away a girl who was fighting him off!

Kathryn had made a face that seemed to say that was a detail that didn't detract from Fatty's perversions. Neil was silently having fun while observing his wife. Kathryn had a difficult role. She would have liked to have hanged Fatty, tell about what happened in his troupe, but she would have also had to tell about what she had done while she was with them. Raouf didn't understand anything about that tension between the husband and wife, but he tried to seem as if he did, which then prevented him from asking questions of Gabrielle or Ganthier. And he didn't dare ask Kathryn, either.

Cavarro continued: The Delmont girl confirmed that she had put Virginia into the bathtub with pieces of ice on her stomach to ease her pain, and Semnacher, Virginia's agent, had testified that he had heard the actress say, "He hurt me," but only on Tuesday morning . . . "On Monday I thought she was just drunk," said Semnacher, "That's why I had gone home, yes, to Los Angeles, with one or two of Virginia's torn clothes. I was planning to use them as rags . . . for my car."

Cavarro was acting as if he wasn't taking sides, while bringing up only the worst of each episode. To me, Ganthier told Gabrielle, he looks like someone who is watching a shipwreck which he is almost certain to have escaped, but since he is constantly returning to it he could be carried away on a wave, and Neil with him. Gabrielle was intrigued by the director/actress couple: "They work together," she said, "They live together, but you get the feeling that if we weren't here they would be at each other's throats."

They kept bringing up the gas chamber, but Zey Prevon, the other key witness for the prosecution, let Brady down. She refused to confirm the victim's "I'm dying, he killed me." It was on the police statement, but she hadn't signed it, in spite of threats by Brady, who said he would charge her as a conspirator in the murder! Brady had only one main witness left, Maude Delmont, who said different things depending on the jury she was talking to; there was also Semnacher, who contradicted himself. It didn't carry weight, so Zey Prevon was brought back to the stand, and she confirmed what Maude Delmont had said.

In the streets, the Women's Vigilant Committee demanded Fatty Arbuckle's head. They rarely called him by his nickname, Fatty, which they considered to be too friendly. They are called Vigilantes, Kathryn said, they defend the rights of women and the morality of the old, Neil adding that with Prohibition they had killed taverns, and now they wanted to ruin the film industry: "They can't attack us for what we show and what we say, because of freedom of expression, so they take aim at our lifestyle, in the name of virtue, and that spreads vice! For alcohol they have succeeded in turning us from a country of boozers to a country of criminals. There have never been so many bottles of milk sold in the States ever since bottles have been painted white and contain a mixture of caramel and woodgrain alcohol, and cost five times more than the real whiskey they took away, a 'milk' that paralyzes legs."

At the beginning of the trial the Vigilantes had sat in the first row of the gallery, wearing all black. They were confident: Fatty was going to end up like a snowball in Satan's hands.

9

AT A NICE SCHOOL

Kathryn knew the contents of her Baedeker and Guide Bleu by heart. She was proud to show off her knowledge to Raouf: "That's a madrassa!" she had said to him while squeezing his arm. In front of them, a dozen or so boys were chanting in a shed. Behind the teacher, hanging from the wall, was a large stick with a length of rope attached to each of its ends.

"And that's what he hits them with when they don't know their lesson!"

Raouf laughed:

"He better not! It would kill them!"

Kathryn fell silent. She was disturbed by Raouf's laugh. She didn't want to hear any more details, Raouf continuing:

"But it's still used for discipline, in a certain sense." He was waiting for a question from Kathryn, which wasn't coming. She changed the subject:

"Did you get hit at school?"

"Which one?"

When he was a boy Raouf had attended two schools at the same time, a French school during the day and what Kathryn called the madrassa in the afternoon. The madrassa wasn't too difficult. You just had to learn verses from the Koran by heart. His only problem was that he chanted rather badly. The teacher, Si Allal, scolded him for wanting to first understand the meaning of what he was supposed to chant, and Raouf didn't like bending to the established rhythm. It was a sin to do otherwise. The teacher said, "It is while chanting that one makes the suras enter into the soul, don't you have a soul?" Raouf ended up having two texts in his head, the one he was asked to chant and the one he tried to understand.

For those who didn't have a good memory, Si Allal used not a stick but a large, solid, yet supple switch. It caused the most pain and blood that could be inflicted without breaking a bone. The stick with the rope attached to the ends was only its complement, and on a first, somewhat serious mistake, at a sign from the teacher, two students quickly approached the guilty one. They put him on his back, put his feet through the rope on the stick, then slowly turned the stick to pull the rope around the well-bound feet, and then lifted the stick horizontally up to their chests. The guilty one found himself hanging by his feet, offering his bare soles up to Si Allal, who, before striking, said, *The teacher's switch comes from paradise.* The two students in charge of the victim were usually large and strong. It was a sought-after task, because one couldn't be a victim and a torturer at the same time. They rarely laughed, except when the victim, upside down, pissed on himself.

Other times, for more venial sins, on another sign from Si Allal, the guilty one brought the tips of his fingers together, turned them upward, and presented them to the teacher: quick blows, and double punishment if you pulled your hands away before the strike. You were then forced to present not just your fingers but both palms, which promised even worse blows. The times when Si Allal gave proof of great inventiveness was with students who let their hair grow when poverty, scabies, or lice didn't force them to have their heads permanently shaved. The teacher would pinch a lock of hair in a break at the end of the switch, and he slowly rolled the hair until the student began to cry. He would pause, allow the victim to find the words that he was unable to recite, then start turning again, until there was true crying, from pain, another pause, the saccharine voice of Si Allal: "Do you remember now?" and he slowly raised the switch higher, like a fishing rod. The student stood up, trying to add to his pleas the words to be recited that his friends were whispering to him, until he found himself on tiptoe. Si Allal then stopped pulling the switch higher; the guilty one became the artisan of his own pain; and as soon as he couldn't stand on tiptoe any longer, his pleas started up again. Si Allal was careful not to bend his switch too much — it rarely broke — and the guilty parties themselves were careful not to cause that catastrophe; they always stayed one step ahead of the pain; they played with it. It was not as bad as their cries indicated, but there was always the moment when it got the better of them and their ability to breathe, and those who had proven the most resilient at the beginning would start to beg.

When Raouf would say: "It's bad form to beg," his friends responded that he could say that because the teacher never tortured him. No student could ever remember seeing Si Allal raise a hand or a switch to Raouf, whereas that immunity was a blemish on the way in which Si Allal exercised his profession. No one would dare mention it, of course. A student would never have dared to say: "You hit me, but not him . . ."

He was happy that the caïd's son was a good student, and there was no one like him to recite the suras the teacher ordered him to recite without mistakes in front of officials; but that lack of common punishment was a bad sign for the community. No, it wasn't because the caïd was a powerful figure that the teacher refrained from punishing Raouf. Other students were sons of figures who were almost as powerful as the caïd and they were still taken by their hair or beaten bloody. If the teacher didn't touch Raouf, it's because the caïd hadn't said to him, as all other fathers did when they brought their sons to him: *dbah wa ana neslakh*, cut his throat, I'll skin him! The caïd had said something more complicated, about dignity, about men who only become worthy if they are treated with dignity, and dignity doesn't need to be beaten in. The teacher didn't agree — his switch had created dozens and dozens of believers — but the caïd had had a cold tone when he had spoken, and above all he hadn't repeated himself.

"So, if I understand you, you would have liked to have been beaten," Kathryn had said.

"Sort of, and to get used to being beaten. I made a point of fighting after school."

Then Raouf fell silent, ashamed at having revealed himself. Kathryn had tricked him. It was her turn to talk. It was an exchange. She started to talk about her childhood, early adolescence, very personal things: "I was chubby, I had a huge behind, large calves — my mother made a point of coming into the bathroom when I was in it. I've changed, haven't I?" Raouf blushed. She also talked about her school, her dance teacher, a friend of her parents: "He was generosity itself. He knew everything, loaned me books, gave them to me. He got my father to agree to let me go out in the evening — he told him, 'Youth must prevail.' He was the best dance instructor in the city. He was always joking. He taught me two or three very solid things that I still remember today. He had me read Mark Twain and Dickens in a school where it was best not to admit you read books . . . His wife was in a sanatorium, which cost a lot. He had the dance school; he taught half the lessons, and in the evening he wrote ads for the neighborhood store owners; I never saw him not working. On Sunday he visited his wife on the bus, seven hours round-trip. Sometimes he bought lottery tickets, but he never won; he knew how to comfort me when I had bad grades in school, and he went over my math homework with me. I would have preferred for him to help me before I turned it in, not afterward, but I never dared ask him: he was a moral person! I owed him my strength, and when he showed me his penis I didn't understand, except I didn't want to, and I was stupid enough not to turn him in; I didn't want to seem like a tattle-tale — rather, I wasn't sure that my parents would have defended me. I was thirteen. I just managed to say that I had twisted, then retwisted my ankle. I stopped dancing," Kathryn started to laugh, "and I was so disgusted at what he had done that I lagged behind my girlfriends who were already spending Sunday afternoons with boys watching the river flow with *something in their hand*, as they said . . . I didn't lag too far, but even so . . .

Then my aunt offered to let me stay with her in Hollywood, and I made a lot of progress there."

Kathryn knew that Raouf was shocked and she was having fun seeing him pretend not to be, someone trying to share the same sort of confidences with him. "He doesn't know anything about women," said Tess, who sometimes talked with her. He pretended to have a lot of mistresses back in the capital, he got tangled up in his stories, and in front of Kathryn, he quickly returned to his school memories. Kathryn interrupted him: How did Rania receive her education? A bit like I did, Raouf had responded, in a French school, and for Arabic a teacher came to her house; she told me once that he was the only pious man she respected. When she finished at the French school she didn't continue at the *lycée*; she was the only "Arab" in her class, and she couldn't stand it. She could have gone to one of the convent schools, but they only teach sewing and housekeeping, so her father brought in teachers so she could continue studying French, math, geography, natural sciences, a sort of home school, like Egyptian princesses had.

Raouf responded to Kathryn's questions about Rania, but he didn't offer more information, so Kathryn brought him back to the previous subject. At the French school there were also teachers with switches, not all, but some hit, yes, everyone, even the French kids, and the Arabs, Jews, Maltese, Italians. Monsieur Desquières told all of them sternly how privileged they were to be studying under him. He had his own method: he brought his chair out from behind his desk, put it in the center of the platform where the desk was standing, facing the class, sat down, sighed, smiled, and everyone knew what was going to happen next, especially on the days when he returned homework. He proceeded in alphabetical order, deadly silence in the room because he made a point of speaking very softly. The beatings were for grades below 3 out of 10. When a student heard his name he stood, went up the row to the platform, and there he had to kneel down in front of Monsieur Desquières, put his head between the teacher's knees, and Monsieur Desquières squeezed that head like a vise. Then he took the large iron ruler that he always kept on his desk and began to beat the victim on his buttocks, slowly and strongly, noting the shouts and the kicking by saying: "Ah! The gentleman is resisting! He is resisting!" and then beat him even harder. On some mornings, when homework was being returned, there were always one or two students who became ill on the way to school. And the punishment lasted even longer for those whose names had to be repeated because they couldn't find the strength in their legs to stand up.

Once Raouf had had the courage to say to him: "Sir . . ." It was the day when Desquières had set upon David Chemla. Chemla was the son of a tailor. No one really understood the reason for this beating. Chemla was a very good student. The first blows were understood, because Chemla had laughed when the map attached to the blackboard had fallen: Monsieur Desquières didn't like laughter in his classroom. Chemla had laughed so it was normal that he be beaten, but Monsieur Desquières had beaten him in an unusual way, not on his buttocks. He hadn't put Chemla in the usual vise: he had come directly in front of him, and he had beaten the boy's head with his hands while calling him a *dolichocephalic*, a word that the class had just learned in natural science class. He hit him harder and harder, sought the right angle to really hurt him, sometimes closed his hand into a fist while shortening his trajectory. His blows were spread apart. It was as if he tried each time to experience with his body the pleasure of inflicting punishment, to avenge something he wasn't saying. Raouf had said *Sir* . . . trying not to shout out, not to provoke the teacher, not to create an obstacle. He would have been incapable of saying what he had wanted to put into his voice, not begging, not an appeal. Raouf hadn't liked the sound of his own voice when he had said *Sir* . . . a sort of plaint, but not indignant. He couldn't seem to want to interrupt Monsieur Desquières. That would have made him furious. No, he wasn't furious yet. He wasn't furious, he was methodical.

Chemla took the blows without saying anything, without making the slightest noise. He didn't beg. The others were afraid, at least those who were sitting next to Chemla. Those who were farther away endured the spectacle while enjoying it. Some laughed each time Monsieur Desquières said, *do* . . . blow with the left hand, *licho* . . . blow with the right hand, . . . *cephalic*, and the back of the right hand hard enough to surprise even Chemla. Raouf had said, *Sir* . . . and another student, Walther, Guy Walther, the son of the police commissioner in Nahbès, had also said, even more softly, *Sir* . . . and that had calmed Monsieur Desquières. He hadn't looked at Raouf, or Walther. He continued to hit, not as hard, fewer and fewer blows, like a runner who keeps running slowly after the finish line in order not to abruptly stop the movement of his muscles. Later, many years later, while thinking about that scene, Raouf wondered why Monsieur Desquières had given in to their discreet appeal. Perhaps he had realized that blows to the head could have been more dangerous than those of a ruler to the buttocks. Raouf and Walther had enabled him to save face. He had ended by saying: "You hear, your friends are begging me to spare you, they are better than you, they know true solidarity, you dirty . . ." He had hesitated—everyone expected a final *dolichocephalic*—but he spit out, "You dirty . . . money-grubbing Commie!"

The map whose fall had made Chemla laugh was that of the colonial French empire, a map of the world with its large spots, red for colonies, yellow for pro-

tectorates, over Africa, Asia, and the oceans. And much later Raouf would learn
what had been behind all that. Chemla's family was communist, not the father,
a gentle tailor, but the uncle, the one who worked for the railroad and called
for the destruction of empires. He was a *dolichocephalic*, too. Monsieur Desquières knew all that.

During his walks, conversations, and confidences with Kathryn, Raouf felt
less and less prey to amorous suffering. He even started to worry about it, to
wonder with fear, *Are we only friends?* But he also found peace in this new state,
which to him seemed at least to be sheltered from upsets and breaks. Ganthier
had even said to him: "Bravo! The journey has been completed! From the gallant to falling in love, and from being in love to being a true friend in record
time!"

10

A WELL-PLANNED MARRIAGE

In the discussions he led with his young friends at La Porte du Sud, Belkhodja had always been very self-assured—marriage was within his realm of expertise—but the more time that went by, the more anxious he became. It was almost the end of spring, and he didn't have anything specific in the works yet. He was going to lose face. Some of the young fellows would notice, and that's also why he brought up *the cow of Satan*, a term that was meaner than strictly necessary, when Raouf had begun to strut around with his American woman: he wanted to make the first move.

They were now sitting on the terrace under umbrellas, and one day one of the young men, Karim, said to Belkhodja:

"If you were really clever, you would marry the widow Tijani."

To speak in front of Raouf about his cousin, even if she was distant, was a provocation, if not a crime. Karim had done it on purpose. He had just been discussing politics with Raouf, who had criticized his bourgeois nationalism, his contradictory tastes for alcohol and theology, and his willingness to force women to wear the veil until better times. Raouf chose not to acknowledge Karim's provocation and to take advantage of it to tease Belkhodja:

"Si Mabrouk's daughter? He's too afraid!"

"Afraid of what?" Karim had asked, "She's a true believer."

"He's afraid she'll give him theology lessons! She knows ten times more than he does."

"She wears glasses," Belkhodja said, "She knows too much, too much learning is the learning of unbelievers!"

And to change the subject, he grabbed Raouf's French newspaper and made fun of the photos of women in bathing suits:

"Even the French are starting to raise skinny cows!"

They all laughed. It was a jab without apparent ill-will, but what Belkhodja had said about Kathryn Bishop and the *cow of Satan* had already made the rounds in the city. For Raouf, to allow this latest jab to pass was to bow before Belkhodja. The merchant hadn't spoken at random. He knew that the caïd's son wasn't comfortable when he talked about the Americans. He had the awkward-

ness of a lover. The time had come to jab him harder, to push him, to find out
who was strongest. But Raouf was quick to reply: A beautiful woman, according
to their dear mentor, has large thighs, large breasts, a large behind, and can carry
three gallons on her head; otherwise she is a . . . concession to colonialism! . . .
Everyone laughed . . . Raouf continued:

"A beautiful woman can even have a mustache, as long as it doesn't look like
his . . ." More laughter.

Belkhodja was caught off-guard. He planned to continue with cows, but first
he wanted to defend himself against liking large behinds and mustaches. He
knew what the others had understood, it was infamy, but if he defended himself
Raouf would ask him why he was blushing at an innocent joke . . . They would
laugh even harder . . . It would be best to continue with the cow of Satan, but
he had to refresh it. Belkhodja tried to come up with a new phrase, maybe another animal. He was hesitating as they watched him. Around the table everyone thought he had already spent too much time thinking. Café conversation is
pitiless. They once again turned toward Raouf. It was his turn to speak because
the merchant was too slow. It was his turn to continue, and they knew how he
would.

Belkhodja told himself that he had made a mistake in provoking the caïd's
son, because what he was now going to use against the merchant was not popular ideas, the fashion of skinny women or perverted innovations, it was something else: it was the Arabic language. Everyone knew it. They were silent. That
was the problem with Raouf. He walked around with foreign women, but he
could speak the language within the language, the one that they revered all the
more since they were in the process of losing it while saying *toumoubile, cami-
oune, birou, tilifoune, ventilatour*, or putting verbs after their subjects like the
infidels; and, in contrast, Raouf for years had been going back in time. That ink-
licker wasn't content to learn the Koran by heart. He knew what they had given
up knowing through centuries of stagnation: the most beautiful texts, those of
the earliest times–Ibn al-Muqaffa', Abu Nuwas, al-Jahiz, Badi' al-Zaman, Abul
'Ala al-Ma'arri–the elegance before the reign of the devout, and Belkhodja
could not respond. One didn't interrupt in a vulgar language someone who is
resurrecting the language par excellence. Raouf was going to recite. They preferred to listen to him rather than run the risk of a serious incident by allowing
Belkhodja to return to his jabs. They were waiting for some immortal verses on
feminine beauty and desire, and the tragedy of desiring beauty.

Belkhodja stood up: "Fat or skinny, when they want a rug, I have to be there."
He added half a proverb: "Work, and you will become strong . . ." No need to
tell them the rest. They knew it: *Stay seated and you'll stink.* He really liked re-

minding them that he was the only one to earn his living without depending on anyone. The others had deigned to laugh, and said good-bye to him. He had stepped away from the joust. They were grateful that he had anticipated his defeat and, above all, Karim had said, that he had spared his friends another display of Raouf's pedantry.

Everyone assumed it was only a lull in the storm, but in the days that followed Belkhodja had practically stopped talking about women, marriage, or cows. And if he no longer talked about them, it was because one doesn't catch a hare by beating a drum: he had finally found the right path, thanks to a friend of his aunt's. No, he hadn't consulted his mother—there are things a son doesn't talk about with his mother, especially when she doesn't miss an occasion to make him feel the degree to which he still needs her—so a friend of his aunt's who was also a distant relation of Raouf's dead mother and whom Raouf avoided because she wanted him to marry a girl *of quality*. She was reputed to be an excellent matchmaker. For Belkhodja, it would have been ironic to succeed in his undertaking thanks to a relative of that young jackal who spent his time laughing at him. He had spoken with her discreetly. He had been telling her personal things since he was an adolescent, since she had told him not to go with perverted women, or at least to talk about it with Doctor Berthommier, a useful Christian, who had given Belkhodja good advice. When they had met during the winter Belkhodja had told the woman: "I want her to smile, I don't want a wife who yells, I want her honest and really smiling. I don't want one of those women who rest on their virtue and the children they give you to make your life miserable. There is worse than a perverted wife, it's the wife who gets it into her head that virtue implies rights!" Belkhodja was proud of that phrase and to see that it elicited respect in his interlocutrice.

The search had taken a long time. Money never passed between the merchant and the matchmaker. The first time he had brought her a superb tribal mat, and she had thanked him: "You are so kind, Si Hassan, but I don't have any more room for rugs. Once is good, you're generous, but be careful, a marriage costs a lot, really a lot!" He had understood. She only liked raw silk, at each visit a large bolt of the finest quality. All of that was more expensive than gold coins, but he didn't have anyone else he could talk to about this. For hours she described what she had been doing, the time she was spending, her poor legs, her poor nerves. She above all described for him the charms of his future life as a married man, the births, the first steps, the circumcisions, and the day when he would accompany his eldest son to school for the first time, and all the other children, at least three sons and a daughter, the youngest, his favorite, a true joy, but the sons would be his pride, which is more important than joy. She knew how to flavor each of their meetings, without forgetting to mention the difficulty of her task: "You understand, Si Hassan, you can find beauty, you can find virtue, you can find virtuous beauty, but someone who really smiles . . . You're asking too much, that is only found in paradise, there is something excessive in your request, that's what people tell me, you know, or they lie to me. You're going to have to be patient . . . We'll find someone, Si Hassan, with the help of God!" Then came the best part, the tale of the life that awaited Belkhodja, buying a little donkey to amuse the children, meals under the large willow tree, his wife's smiling face.

Belkhodja felt the weight of time passing more and more heavily, and sometimes doubted the matchmaker's abilities. But at the end of the month of June she finally found him a very promising match, a nice young girl, not too tall or too short, not skinny but not too fat, just what he needed, not a chatterbox, and no mustache, "pretty, appetizing, modest and calm, and smiling, as you asked" . . . Her family? Not too demanding but well regarded, a chance that shouldn't be missed. Yes, from the country, thirty miles from Nahbès, but not uneducated. The road has gone by them for ten years. "The girl's skin is very white; she blushes even when she moves. There are days when I would like to be a man . . ."

Belkhodja then became a man in a hurry. His young friends, including Raouf, found out what was happening and warned him: beware of sleeping water. Send other women to see her, to see her mother. The girl will become the mother. You're the one who told us of the faceless risk. Take your time. Raouf had said, "Women often change" . . . Belkhodja's upper lip was pulled up. He said, "Another word of wisdom from the Christian" . . . Raouf acted as if he hadn't heard. He had recited *ankartu ma qad kuntu a'rifuhu minha* . . . and I no longer recognize anything of what I knew of her. He fell silent after those words to give Belkhodja time to complete the phrase, but Belkhodja knew no more about the verses of Bashar than he did about French authors, and the ending Raouf recited in a sad voice didn't please him: *siwa almaw'udi wa lghadri* . . . apart from promises and betrayal . . . There wasn't any sarcasm in Raouf's voice, but in veiled terms Belkhodja said that he had found the opposite, the exact opposite of a cow of Satan, adding that he didn't need poetry, that he had the clarity and insight of religion! A flat response, he knew. He lacked the panache of a reader, but at least commerce had taught him not to hesitate when a true opportunity presented itself. There would always be risk, but if his interest in the girl became too well known, there could be competition, vultures. People knew of his experience. Someone else would jump on the opportunity to take advantage of Belkhodja's expertise. Belkhodja quickly concluded the marriage, to shut the vultures'—and Raouf's—mouths, since he suspected Raouf of preparing some sort of revenge.

And at the beginning of July 1922 there was a wonderful celebration. Belkhodja was overjoyed to hear a very friendly Raouf call him a "lucid guide of youth" in the speech he gave in front of all their friends a few days before the wedding, at a party where fig alcohol and whiskey had ultimately played an excessive role, in Belkhodja's opinion. Only Ganthier, whom he had invited along with some other big European clients, maintained a reserve which made him Belkhodja's favorite interlocutor. Belkhodja told him everything that he had laid out for months in front of the little band, refusing a girl from too good a family—the powerful are dangerous for a good man—innocent chastity, and a smile, especially a smile . . . a choice that won unanimous support. He pointed to Raouf: "Even he, what he said, for once, wasn't salt in my jam!"

On his way home, Ganthier was accompanied by Raouf, walking under the stars. Ganthier was amused at Belkhodja's choice:

"That man likes the money of today, but he has chosen a girl from the past. He would never have chosen a girl from the city, for fear of finding a rebel." Ganthier stopped, faced Raouf:

"Do you know why here you are so afraid of women who have a bit of strength?"

"I'm not afraid!" Raouf said.

"Alright, but that lovely blend of women and fear, doesn't that remind you of anything? Your childhood . . . servants . . . You wanted to stay in the garden when it was getting dark, so they threatened to call the creature from the outside, the ghoul, the female with the hands of an octopus, the head of a hyena, and teeth as long as fingers, furry like a spider. Did you disobey? She was going to eat your privates! That has an effect, doesn't it?" Raouf didn't answer. His father had forbidden the servants to tell his son stories of ghouls. It was paganism, said the caïd, and not long ago, for less than that, they burned people. There is divinity only in God! It happened, however, that Raouf regretted not having known such fears, and never having had dealings except with real enemies. He answered Ganthier, a few words, the ghoul . . . the universal ghoul . . . Then he was quiet, as if observing the scruples of friendship, and Ganthier understood. He, himself, wasn't doing so well right now with a free woman. He, too, had his "man-eater," who in fact didn't want to eat, and Raouf was expressing even more irony than if he had openly mentioned Gabrielle. His silence caused Ganthier real anguish . . . to each his ghoul.

The first month of marriage was a great month for Belkhodja, with a wife who was always joyful, maybe not such a good housekeeper, but Belkhodja had agreed that she could bring a female servant who picked up the slack, and the young wife got along well with her mother-in-law: Your wife is very good, she said, at least she doesn't talk too much! Belkhodja let the "at least" go by. The family relations were in order, and order, as a German client once told him, is half of life. The young wife answered "yes" to all of her husband's requests — *na'am a sidi*, a model of smiling modesty — she rubbed his back when he was in the bath. She didn't object to things during love, but didn't take any of those initiatives that could have led him to believe that she might be leading another life, either active or imaginary.

There was one thing that annoyed the merchant: his wife was very upset, almost ill, at the idea of joining him in the bathtub after bathing her husband. She obeyed, but derived no pleasure from it, which deprived Belkhodja of his. She would smile with a forced air, her gaze became increasingly vague. He didn't like that absent air. He asked her to exchange it for a happier face, which she couldn't manage to do. She was on the verge of tears while still looking like she was smiling. He liked that bathtub, but decided to no longer inflict on his wife something she didn't like. As for his water games, he kept them for his stays in a hotel in the capital, with other women. As for his wife, she went four times a week to the hammam. At La Porte du Sud, no one dared tell Belkhodja that four times was a lot.

11

THE STORY OF THE ICE

Raouf thought that the Americans were pushing it a bit at the bar of the Grand Hôtel with their story of the trial, but for Ganthier that's what they were all about, an oversized character, an oversized story, an enormous scandal, a crazy amount of money. What they love, said Ganthier, is to dream, and they fashion their dreams from blows of an ax, punches in the face, sledgehammers or hydraulic drills, with dollars. They have to have the biggest dream, and if there are several of them to fight for who has the biggest, it's even better. They love battles with the sound of bones cracking, like in their football. They have to knock heads, and in the end there aren't any winners, there are just survivors . . . When they arrived at the front in 1917, they had no experience, but they really wanted to knock heads. They kept saying, "Hit fast, hit hard." I ran into one of their colonels who was commanding a tank brigade. As soon as there was an opening, he set off. They had to hold him back. He dreamed of being the first to cross the Rhine. He wanted a redo of the Battle of Ulm. His name was Catton, or Vatton. He told me about the Battle of Ulm over an entire night, with whiskey. He knew it to the last detail, better than Napoleon! When I asked him how he remembered so many details, he hesitated, and then confided in me, "I was there" . . . He wasn't joking. He believed in reincarnation. He was crazy, and that's why he won.

And for Fatty Arbuckle, the catastrophe, Cavarro had said, was the ice. They had already talked about the ice, about when Delmont and the others had testified that they had placed large pieces on Virginia's stomach after putting her in the bathtub, but this was something else:

"What did Mr. Arbuckle say to you the next day, Tuesday, in Los Angeles, regarding the ice?" the district attorney asked Semnacher. Semnacher refused to respond directly. He wrote on a piece of paper, and the district attorney read out loud. Tuesday, in his house in Los Angeles, Fatty had said to Semnacher: "You know, I even put a piece of ice in her vagina!" The newspapers talked about *unpublishable proof.* In fact, it wasn't proof, no one who was at the bathtub and ice scene, even Maude Delmont, had claimed that Fatty had put anything anywhere—it was the joke of the next day, said Samuel Katz, Fatty and his disgusting jokes. The district attorney knew, what was important was that it got around.

"I'm almost sure that Cavarro and Daintree were at Fatty's party," Ganthier said to Gabrielle. He was facing the death penalty, but the grand jury charged Arbuckle only with involuntary manslaughter.

"And there was a lot more talk about the power of the rich," Kathryn had added. Gabrielle didn't tell Rania the story of the piece of ice.

At the end of September Fatty was released on bail, Neil Daintree saying that that was when there was some real drama, from the Vigilantes, who were watching the crowds. One of them had brandished an enormous hat pin saying she was going to kill that assassin. The others had applauded, but when Arbuckle appeared, he's the one everyone applauded, with "Way to go, Fatty!" and so on. Cavarro pointing out that everyone then talked about female fickleness: they love angels but they applaud the beast, because they need him, like in the time of the Indians, or maybe they were playing two roles at the same time, defending a dead girl and supporting a living man!

At the farm, Rania had repeated: "Two roles at the same time . . ." She found that interesting, if they hadn't been *vigilantes*, would their husbands have allowed them to watch the trial? When you want to fight you do it in the clothes you are given . . . and you have to wait, she thought, *For pleasure you also have to fight, and wait for darkness . . . He turns off the lamp, the stars slip through the window . . . He with me, my heart is breaking . . . He will break me out of prison . . . or he will forget me . . . I can't stand the idea that he might forget me . . . I tear off his clothes . . . He is every pleasure . . . and pain . . . I want him to watch me, and I'm afraid of the moment he will, I must wait . . .* aniyatu l'hawadith—*in the basket of hours events remain hidden.*

The judge wanted the trial to be over before the end of 1921. The jury was quickly selected. Fatty had a new lawyer, McNab, quite a presence, said Samuel Katz, a serious face, a man who fears God, and who makes him fearsome. He looked down on everyone from a height of over six feet. He was the one who looked like a district attorney, and Brady, across from him, with his assistants, looked like neighborhood ruffians. McNab was also the only one who looked the Vigilantes in the first row in the eye so they would think about their own sins. He didn't say that women were the root of all evil, Samuel chuckled, but it was clear that he was persuaded of that. Ganthier realized that Samuel Katz was the only one who had attended the entire trial, the only one who tried to see things clearly, but the problem was all the contradictions. Some witnesses had spoken to the police and signed their statements, then retracted them. Others had refused to sign, and said the opposite on the stand, then they had confirmed, or not, the first statement they had signed, or not. The district attorney made accusations of corruption by "the defense of a millionaire." The defense asserted that the district attorney was threatening and sequestering the witnesses . . . A true American story, Samuel continued, of sex, alcohol, principles, money, and emotion: the public came, morality was exalted, death hovered, the press made money . . .

Cavarro was proud to see his publicity man become the center of the conversation, even if he was sometimes afraid he would veer onto radical ideas.

When they took the stand, the doctors weren't in agreement about the cause of the ruptured bladder: external force, internal rupture, the shock of the cold bath, or contractions from vomiting, at least ten whiskeys, the witnesses said— McNab had the number repeated while claiming that he didn't want to sully the victim's memory—ten whiskeys, and vomiting. There was also another woman who had drunk ten whiskeys: the accusing witness, Maude Delmont, she had admitted it. And after the weekend, Zey Prevon claimed that Virginia Rappe had shouted in the bathtub, "I'm dying, I'm going to die!" Then Fischbach, one of Fatty's friends, swore that he hadn't heard that. He had seen Miss Rappe tear off her clothing in the living room, and he had carried her, himself, to the bathtub. Judge Louderback asked him how he had done that. Fischbach tried to grab the judge by the right arm and the left leg. The judge panicked, and the audience burst out laughing.

Gabrielle apologized for telling Rania these details. Everything had become grotesque.

"No more grotesque," Rania said, "than a twelve-year-old girl being married to an old man, and who swallows a bottle of bleach . . . But here there aren't judges to deal with it." She was silent . . . *The despair of the girl . . . bleach, burning, agony . . . disgust greater than any pain, and I dare call pain what I am experiencing?*

Arbuckle finally took the stand, telling about that Monday, Miss Rappe on the ground in the bathroom: I went to tell Miss Prevost. Miss Delmont joined us. Miss Rappe was pulling off her clothes. I went out. When I returned she was in the bathtub. Miss Delmont was rubbing ice on her body. I took a piece. She yelled at me. She told me to put it back where it was and get out. Soon afterward, with the hotel manager, we put Miss Rappe in another room.

A doctor testified after Fatty. He had treated Miss Rappe in 1918 for a chronic infection. We were a bit lost, only the Hearst newspapers were clear, said Samuel, a large drawing on the front page, a spider web, Fatty in the center, with two bottles of whiskey, and around him the faces of seven women, Rappe, Delmont, Blake, Prevost, and others I don't remember, Virginia Rappe, with her eyes to the heavens like Mary Magdalene, and the headline: "They Walked into His Parlor," Neil recalling Hearst's declaration: the trial has "sold more newspapers than any event since the sinking of the *Lusitania*."

The trial lasted until the beginning of December, said Cavarro, and in the end there were ten votes for acquittal and two against! A new trial was set for the beginning of January 1922. With such results it would be only a formality.

And what was really something at the second trial, Kathryn added, laughing, is that Fatty's wife had come back to live with him. If Fatty lost she wouldn't have had a cent, of course, but that was something, a bastard husband, a wife who is still there when things are going badly—a lot of American women could identify with her!

If I understand correctly, Rania later said to Gabrielle, with Americans it's money that forces a woman to stay married, not love? Gabrielle had laughed without answering, keeping something Kathryn had said to her in confidence to herself: *Love forms knots, and then it pulls them apart, I have been knotted and pulled apart more often than is fair, now I'm staying put.* Rania turned her head to look out at the countryside and thought of the one who only came alone, *wa an tamaneitu chei'an, faenta koullou attamanni,* and when I desired something, you were all my desire . . . *He and I, under my eyelid . . . To be two, again, a home . . . But choose him . . . Is it a sin? So that one is punished before having committed it?*

You never liked Fatty's wife, Neil said to Kathryn, I wonder why. Kathryn clenched her teeth. One day her friends had forced her to hide because Fatty's wife had found a gun and was looking for her all over Hollywood—that crazy woman got it in her head that I was trying to steal her husband from her . . . That made him worth more.

The district attorney Brady had again chosen not to have Maude Delmont testify. She had just received a one-year suspended prison sentence for bigamy. The two other girls at the party, Zey Prevon and Nancy Blake, were enough, but now they were accusing Brady of having sequestered them and threatened them with prosecution for conspiracy in the murder if they didn't say what he wanted! The next day, the district attorney questioned Semnacher: he wanted to talk about the ice again. Semnacher refused, and the district attorney called him a liar . . . The prosecution was now insulting its witnesses! McNab then questioned his witnesses, about the victim, gently, the glasses of whiskey, the drunk woman, the outbursts of rage, she tore off her clothes . . . The witnesses didn't voice any judgment, even the one who said he had seen Virginia Rappe "puke her guts out" during a party, but the rumor was buzzing in the opposite direction, a nasty rumor, the pack against the woman, said Kathryn. District Attorney Brady was flabbergasted, said Samuel. McNab had sworn that he would not attack the dead girl and here his witnesses were tearing her apart. He wasn't encouraging them. He even seemed to want them to stop! When it was a matter of the witnesses for the prosecution, he forced them to speak. But the defense witnesses, they knew so much that out of respect for the jury he held them back, and all of that regarding alcohol, abortions, chronic infections.

Gabrielle asked if they might pass over those details. "American justice," Neil said, "loves the facts!"

"And money," Kathryn added. Later, Gabrielle continued to fill Rania in: in America money is practically a sign of divine election, and if they fail, they give themselves a kick in the behind and start again. Gabrielle had seen how things worked at a big newspaper in New York, the notices from the management in the elevator, with the amount of money paid to such and such a journalist for such and such a story, permanent competition among those people, the ease with which they showed you the door, and the one leaving was even more fatalistic than a Nahbès peasant: he left the place with his cardboard box, "no hard feelings." I'm firing you without negative thoughts, so you shouldn't have any. They'll take you back one day, perhaps, leave them with a good impression — that was the rule of the game — so that her own newspaper, managed by a sort of blackmailer, seemed like a haven of familial stability to her.

Brady couldn't even count on his victim anymore, and to shorten things, McNab decided not to have Fatty testify. The jury's deliberation lasted several hours, with two interruptions for additional information, and the results were the same as in the first trial, ten for and two against, but this time Fatty was found guilty! McNab had blown it, said Cavarro, he should have had Fatty take the stand. The jurors hadn't pardoned him for that defection. Or perhaps they had seen the truth, said Kathryn.

12

A LOVELY SUMMER

Overall, it was a lovely summer, with demanding film shoots, then the pool, the beach, walks, parties, talking with friends, people were careful not to break any ties. Many found that Ganthier had intolerable ideas, but Neil and Francis liked him. Francis enjoyed provoking him: We let you French talk, you call us decadent materialists, and in the meantime we make more and more cars, airplanes, machines, and we're not at all sure we'll come to your aid the next time the Germans decide to beat you up. Gabrielle had asked the colonist why he didn't go more often to mingle with his own Prépondérant friends.

"They're idiots," Ganthier had replied, "They don't know what a great nation should be."

"You are our charming reactionary," Gabrielle had said.

To show that he had good taste, the colonist asked the journalist to read the poetic chronicles signed by a certain Lousteau, in a magazine published in the capital.

"No, I didn't write them, it's not a pseudonym, believe me, I wish it were . . ."

Gabrielle flipped through the pages without saying anything, then:

"Your poet is amusing, when there are colors they're 'red, blue, green,' and his landscape is 'the sea, the mountains, flowers'!" Gabrielle marked each element with her hand, "the sun, kisses, perfumes," always in threes, in each phrase, in a line, like the Father, the Son, and the Holy Spirit . . . She kept tapping the table in rhythm, "houses, temples, public squares," and with verbs it was the same thing, "abandoned to the world, returned to heaviness, beaten down by the sun" . . .

"Ganthier, do you really like that? Wait, here's another: 'I learned how to breathe, I became integrated, and I fulfilled myself,' long live the ternary! He easily uses a half dozen per page!"

Ganthier had stopped doing battle with the wasp that was interested in the jam on his toast. He looked up at Gabrielle; she was waiting for his reaction. He took advantage of that to linger on her forehead, which was covered by a lock of brown hair, her dark brown eyes, and he criticized her for not being sensitive to the rhythm. She shrugged her shoulders: It didn't have any rhythm. It was sis boom bah, the fanfare of an army. Real rhythm can't be bought ready-made. It has to be created! Ganthier held his ground:

"His prose is uplifting!"

"No, it's like a tune in triple time. Is your Lousteau an officer? Is he Commander de Saint-André?" Ganthier didn't answer, he thought Gabrielle was reading too closely. It wasn't fair, he almost said, *even your skin, seen under a microscope* . . . But he kept that to himself and said:

"No one reads like that. With a magnifying glass Flaubert would be tossed in the trash. Lousteau has wonderful images, you're jealous!"

She blew up: Flaubert on the contrary hunted down such things, and sis boom bah from beginning to end was numbing.

"Your Lousteau should try a fourth term every once in a while, it would make him much more interesting. As for his images, my hairdresser uses the same ones!"

Gabrielle continued to read other fragments out loud, shaking her head: ". . . 'delicate edges of long blue irises,' you can tell the author wants to please women! And this . . . 'drops of color that tremble on the ends of her lashes,' I would tremble . . ." She turned the pages, parodying shivers, then she sighed with satisfaction: "Ah, so Monsieur Lousteau can be more vigorous: 'the rocks sucked by the sea with the sound of kisses and the smile of its brilliant teeth.' Can you imagine, the sea that sucks and the sea that shows its teeth, it's going to bite! Ganthier, aren't you ashamed to be reading such things? Is your poet Saint-André?" Ganthier didn't want to give her a name. It was a true secret. Gabrielle responded that she was going to do some investigating. She would find it, and would tell everyone, "but if you tell me in confidence, it will stay a secret between friends . . ."

Ganthier gave in because of the warmth with which she said the word *friend*:

"Lousteau is a high-ranking bureaucrat. In fact, he is Marfaing."

"That doesn't surprise me," Gabrielle said, "The colonizer who wants to become sublime through poetry . . . And it's good to confide in me." Ganthier was furious with Gabrielle and with himself. He would have preferred to defend those chronicles better. He liked them, but something in him also agreed with Gabrielle's contempt for Marfaing's writing.

For fun, Gabrielle sometimes asked Ganthier if he didn't want her to reconcile him with the one he called the young widow. He refused. The journalist teased him:

"You're afraid your energy will dry up if you don't have any more enemies!"

"I wonder what you can find interesting in that zealot!"

"Rania's not a zealot, she's a nationalist who dreams of the West, but only partially, and that's why you don't like her, and men want to shut her up!"

Ganthier remembered a little girl who loved to laugh who sometimes called him "uncle" and told him he had ears like the devil . . . At fourteen, fifteen, she became hostile toward him, appearing only with a scarf covering her face when he visited Abdesslam.

Occasionally there was also a picnic, the specialty of the colonials. "At my farm!" Pagnon had said at the beginning of the month of August, "Don't bring a thing, I'll take care of it all . . . and my wife will supervise." More than a hundred people came, at an hour when the sun was still far from setting, but had softened a lot. They had set up trestle tables with white cloths, bottles, glasses, platters of salads, meats, Spanish rice, couscous, potatoes with harissa. Everyone filled his plate, walked around the braziers and the pits to smell the merguez, grilled sardines, sides of pork or lamb chops, then went to sit on a rattan chair or one of the Louis XV chairs that had been brought out from the house. Some men even sat on large rocks to show how hardy they were. The more agitated ate standing up going from one group to another. It made you thirsty. Pagnon's wine was easily at 55 degrees—it was a wine that didn't last and that quickly went down one's throat to the bladder—and some even put pieces of ice in their glass.

Thérèse Pagnon was the perfect hostess. In a dress of orange silk that blazed on her hips and chest, she gave every man the impression that she found him the most interesting one there. She was like the wine: she put everyone in a good mood. Even the boar—that's what they called Pagnon—was smiling. He liked seeing his wife standing out, not because it made her happy, but because he became the husband of a wife whom one noticed, a real wife of a head surgeon.

Thérèse was also smiling. She smiled at her husband, who waved at her. She also smiled at Claude Marfaing, who understood what was in that smile, because he was laughing with Gabrielle Conti. And Thérèse thinking that Gabrielle is trash, a Parisian, always wearing trousers, but today with her legs hanging out, the famous legs of Gabrielle. Thérèse is sure that one of them is larger than the other, but men don't see that sort of thing, and they like those legs, chiseled, as they say, a treat. Thérèse doesn't agree. They are too muscular, too visible. She doesn't seem feminine, plus she does a man's job. They say that's how she spent the war, instead of taking care of the wounded or watching children, and she doesn't know what that's like—she doesn't have any, over thirty and not married. And men are interested in her. They don't understand. They don't understand anything, that she couldn't care less about men. *And there's that idiot Claude, who is laughing to make her laugh, that woman is a public danger, a brunette without shame!* And Claude Marfaing knows why Thérèse is smiling at him, because she can't do anything else. Her husband is there. He's watching her. Everyone is watching Thérèse, who is watching her lover flirt with the journalist from Paris, a madwoman. You remember what she wrote two years ago, when she came the first time, at the time of the riots at the Grand Sud, her articles on that visionary, Ben Something or Other, a tramp, a sort of backward-looking preacher, with his beard and his rags. She had compared him to Christ—worse than crazy, a provocatrice!

All around, people pretending not to notice anything, but everyone sensing that something was about to happen. It had been some time since the contrôleur civil had been pulling her chain. You could easily see what he wanted to do with Gabrielle Conti. He was Ganthier's rival. It seems they joked about it between themselves, a competition that rejuvenated them, and there was Marfaing flirting right in front of Thérèse, who was becoming furious, and you could understand . . . You know . . . A wife, when a whore arrives, she can control that, but it's trickier for a mistress—there's no contract, no common goods—and when she wants to control, it's a lost battle. The paradox with Thérèse was that she held things together only by threatening to make the first move, to break things off while creating a scandal. She forced Marfaing to stay with her by threatening to make an exit that would be more terrible than all the good-byes he could have imagined, and the day had perhaps arrived. People weren't voyeurs, but they didn't want to miss anything. Pagnon's picnic was going to be a success, and no one cared about what would happen to Marfaing. When the loves of a pretentious man are falling apart in public, the only thing to do is fill your glass and wait!

At some point Thérèse decided to intervene. She needed a pretext. She grabbed a bottle, and headed at a right angle toward Marfaing, who immediately understood what was coming. Anything to avoid an incident, he bowed to Gabrielle Conti: Excuse me, dear friend, there's another question of protocol to settle with our hostess . . .

Gabrielle was not the type of woman who was left alone at a gathering. Two officers took advantage of her solitude while Marfaing went to Thérèse, his face joyful, the contrôleur civil, the man in charge in the region, his glass almost empty. He held it out in front of him. He's going for a refill from the wife of a great notable. All is for the best at the best of all possible picnics. The glass out in front of him was also meant to keep his mistress at a safe distance; she was probably quick to slap a face. Thérèse served Marfaing his wine while scolding him under her breath, all smiles and clenched teeth. He didn't respond that he was paying her back for looking at Cavarro. He said that he was obligated to talk with other women, otherwise people would think he was under a thumb, and

they would start looking for whom that thumb belonged to, and they would ultimately find out, or they would think he was queer.

"Are you joking? Everyone knows we're lovers!"

"Yes, but they're pretending they don't, and we must help them pretend."

"And so it's to help them that you make that whore think that you want to
jump on top of her . . ."

"Jump on top, that's a bit much . . . It seems she always likes to be on top."

He shouldn't have said that, not an image like that. Thérèse doesn't like that
image at all. He could see that right away, her mouth in a scornful arc, eyelids
getting narrower, and the face as white as a porcelain sink. Marfaing remembers
the remark of one of his Paris friends: There is nothing more dangerous than
being involved with a woman in a small town. He's suddenly afraid of the way
his mistress looks. He regrets everything, but is also amused to see her in such
a state. It's a professional revenge. She has caused so many baseless scenes with
Marfaing that he takes pleasure in provoking one for which for once he knows
the reason, a nice jealousy, murderous, but held in check by the presence of her
guests, her cheeks red now, her ears, too, under the pink of the hat. She looks
good, and she controls herself. She's the hostess of the event. A hostess can do
anything except create a scandal. Thérèse understands:

"And do you believe that I will hesitate to put my hand on your face? Or on
that of your fat whore?"

"She's not really fat, tall, rather . . ."

Thérèse doesn't say anything, she becomes white again—that's bad. Marfaing changes his tone: he says that he'll stop, no, he is absolutely not trying to
. . . sleep with that Parisian woman. He pronounced the verb with a pleasure that
upsets Thérèse—don't upset her:

"No, I'm not a hypocrite." Marfaing is seeking a concession, the avowal of a
venial sin:

"Okay, I was having a bit of fun, not paying attention, a bit of picnic flirting."

"You think it's funny, to make me ill?" Thérèse isn't getting any calmer. Don't
let her start with illness, don't let her climb onto her own words: take the initiative. She is also going to say that I infuriate her, so:

"I just wanted to make you jealous, just a little bit . . . It's sweet . . ."

Marfaing could add that he was jealous of how friendly Thérèse is toward
Cavarro every time she runs into him, but he doesn't. He's never mentioned
that. Maybe Thérèse doesn't even realize what she is doing with the actor—no
need to wake a sleeping dog. And anyway Marfaing knows that with Cavarro,
who isn't even there today, there is no risk. The police reports are clear. So he is
content to admit his sins. He will be pardoned, say to Thérèse that she's beauti-

ful when she's like that, almost as beautiful as when she's in his arms. He knows that when Thérèse is jealous she thinks she's ugly, and her jealousy becomes uglier and uglier. That's dangerous because a jealousy that thinks it's ugly can seek to sully everything. Luckily, with Thérèse you just need to reassure her: "You have never been so beautiful, you have the loveliest backside of all the guests at the picnic." Thérèse thinks she has a large behind. Marfaing adds that she is splendid. All the men want her — she just has to look around: "Your husband is coming over. He's not like you. He at least knows that I love you. He has no doubt, and that makes him dangerous." That's what he needs to do, put Thérèse on alert, in the face of a danger greater than that of a lover who flirts: a husband who revolts. Pagnon approaches the couple, slowly, looking even more like a boar than usual. It's not his fault. He never learned how to be pleasant with anyone. He knows that it sometimes hurts him in his profession, a surgeon with a head like the guardian of the gates of hell . . . That's why I decided not to work in the private sector, he sometimes says, but on the other hand, it makes me look serious. A doctor doesn't have to sell his wares on the street: we're not fishmongers.

13

AN EYE ON EVERYTHING

"Now there's a triangle that's becoming dynamite, if you'll allow me a mixed metaphor," Ganthier said to some other guests who were observing from a distance. He didn't like the game Gabrielle and Marfaing were playing. *She's pretending to be interested in him to get me to react, and when I react she sends me packing, she doesn't like anyone, she only likes what she does: show up, dig around, write, provoke, disappear.* Around Ganthier, people were silently delighted. Pagnon's face was more sinister than usual. The scandal was going to explode, but no, that would have been too good to be true; in two months the elections for the Grand Conseil were taking place, and no one could play around with that, neither the contrôleur civil nor a notable like Pagnon, and Thérèse knew it. This wasn't the time to blow everything up in public. Anyway, scandal for Thérèse was a gun with one bullet, and the presence of all the people would hold her back. "No," said the most impatient of onlookers, "The crowd may prevent the incident today, but when one of them decides things need to blow, we will make a wonderful echo chamber." At some point the group of observers changed the subject to compliment a child who went by wearing a golden yellow dress:

"You're not afraid?"

"No, he's really nice, I even gave him a fly."

She was walking a lizard with a string attached around its middle.

Pagnon was approaching the couple while thinking, *That idiot Marfaing is upsetting Thérèse, and I'm the one who's going to suffer for it later, he can't just be happy sleeping with my wife, he has to go and infuriate her.*

"So, dear contrôleur, what did our big Gabrielle have to say? Be careful, you know those Parisian women, they're all hysterics, real ones, and all those openings . . ." Pagnon was oozing fury, but not at what everyone thought. He was furious at his wife's dress, too low-cut. *She's showing too much breast, and what she hides she allows to be guessed at. You can see everything underneath the fabric. She's standing in front of that idiot Marfaing, and you can see everything.* Marfaing also noticed what was going on. The two men were thinking the same thing. *She must have gotten one of those American bras, an unspeakable vul-*

garity. That's why Pagnon immediately sank to a smutty level, to be even more vulgar than that bra, Marfaing tensing up, Pagnon thought he was still in the staff room. The contrôleur civil forced himself to smile at what the doctor had said, to show his manly complicity, but not too much. They didn't know how Thérèse would react. Her face had become a mask, the corners of her mouth rising even so, for the gallery. She's standing there, a bottle in her hand.

The head surgeon was enjoying himself:

"Beautiful Gabrielle, you flirt with her right in the middle of the picnic, and she'll ask you to perform the Duc d'Aumale position in the field over there . . ."

Now Thérèse's chin starts to tremble. She hesitates. She doesn't know whom to attack. Pagnon adds that with those crazy ones, one should be able to give them a poke where they need it. He can feel that his wife is about to explode. He continues:

"And what's more, my dear, that Gabrielle, she's your fault!" He's silent a moment: "You do too much with her. You talk to her, you invite her. She must think you are making advances. One of these days you know what she's going to do? She's going to leave Marfaing and throw herself on you, or even on me, although everyone knows I only like the young ones." A benevolent smile from Pagnon to his wife. He puts his hand on her shoulder. Don't push her over the edge: she must continue to preside over the picnic. Pagnon knows how to host. People feel good when they're in a group with him. They will remember that at the time of the elections. It's not easy to get elected by the colonials when you're a doctor, even when you have a farm, but it should happen, thanks to Thérèse, to his connections, and with Marfaing's support. Pagnon smiles at his wife and at the contrôleur civil.

"I must leave you, I need to keep an eye out everywhere, well . . . almost."

It was perhaps a final jab at the lovers, but Pagnon's eye really was drawn by what was going on over by the parking area, far behind it. He went into his house and came back out on the veranda with his hunting binoculars. About a half a mile away a man was climbing a mound of stones, then running, followed at a distance by three men. At one point the runner turned around. Pagnon recognized him: Mohand, one of the workers on the farm, not the worst, and Mohand recognized the large white shape on the veranda. He had started to run when he saw the three men coming toward him with a rope. He immediately understood: there were two bottles of wine missing from the hundred fifty that had been taken out for the picnic. He had heard Saïd, Pagnon's right-hand man, count the empties and the full ones, recount while swearing, order a search, without luck. No one likes stories of theft, especially where the French are concerned. In the opinion of the French, when Arabs are present a French person can't steal—it would be too shameful. It's always an Arab who is blamed, and now, seeing the three men, Mohand understood that they wanted him, *That will teach me to agree to take care of the bottles, I should have done like the others, talk about religion, they would have found a Maltese to take care of them, I wanted to please . . .* Mohand running, far from the people, far from the picnic, the smells of méchoui, merguez, sardines, far from the laughter. The three behind him weren't in a hurry. They were auxiliaries, soldiers for small tasks, not very well trained, but who knew in advance what would happen when the sky is blue, the sun is still hot, when the stones on the ground are there to cut, when one's side hurts, when nothing in the entire countryside likes escapees. Mohand could go left, go back down to the bed of the wadi, run on the soft ground, barefoot, faster. He doesn't go there. After five minutes he has slowed down, stopped. He is gasping for breath. It doesn't do any good to run. It makes them mad. It's better to be caught after a little run. The three guys will seem to have accomplished a serious mission. They'll be in a good mood. Maybe they won't beat him as hard. Mohand picks up a large stone, makes sure there isn't anything underneath, sits down, and puts his sandals back on.

They caught him and brought him back without excessive violence to the party, but at a distance from it, in the middle of the parked cars. They tied his hands to a luggage carrier on a roof, in the sun. He couldn't sit. Saïd, Pagnon's foreman, didn't ask him anything. He put a rag in his mouth and began to beat him with a knotted club. Then Pagnon arrived, looking angry:

"Did you need to do that? What good will it do? You steal and you run away, and when you're caught you don't admit it? Are you sick? Are you hot? It's going to be cold tonight, Mohand. If you don't admit it, you know Saïd, he'll give you to the soldiers, all night, and tomorrow everyone will be talking about it." Mohand finally confessed. He was untied. He could sit on the ground, with his back against a car tire. Saïd gave him back his gag so he could wipe his face.

Later, Neil Daintree said to Pagnon:

"You told me you don't beat your employees," Pagnon responding that he didn't, it was Saïd, his right-hand man, who took care of that. In the past, Saïd had also stolen, and was sentenced to a term of six years of forced labor for aggravated theft. It was Pagnon who kept him from going to prison, his suspension being on the condition that he would work for Pagnon. Saïd was efficient and devoted—it was rare—and what's more, he had an eye:

"We Europeans should never strike the natives. We must show that we are not like they are. When I beat my dog, it is always with the leash. It thinks that it's the leash that is beating him. From time to time he chews up a leash, but he continues to love me."

Saïd was Pagnon's leash, and Mohand wasn't too angry with him. He knew that those were his orders.

"And since I'm not the one doing the beating, and it stops when I arrive, he isn't too angry at me, either."

"What are you going to do with him?"

Mohand had confessed. Pagnon was wiping the slate clean. Mohand would work without pay for a month or two, probably two, but at least he could stay on the property.

"If I fire him he would die in three weeks."

Standing around the méchoui, some had followed everything, discreetly. They had seen a man chased at a distance, then brought back behind the cars. They had lost sight of him. They had imagined what had happened next. They didn't really know what had happened. They didn't ask. Maybe he had gone to watch the women in the toilets. No, no, it was a theft, probably money, from a car. Then Pagnon had talked with one of the officers. People heard some of what they were saying: Bottles of wine, that's the worst, you know, because they don't know how to control themselves. Wine is forbidden by their religion, so when they have some, they drink it all as quickly as possible, thinking it won't be noticed, neither here nor on high. Those things have to be punished right away, very hard, the club, anyway, they like justice, you know! Those who heard about Mohand's story chuckled about it while stuffing their mouths with pieces of meat and slices of bread dipped in the cooking fat and oil. The méchoui is good, I'm taking advantage. Next month I'm going on the Vichy diet.

An hour later, the youngest son of the gendarme captain, Marchal, vomited in front of everyone, and his older brother went over to a tree to do the same; it smelled like sour wine, those kids, thirteen and fifteen years old. And the rumor circulated among the more alert, not because it proved Mohand's innocence, but because it was a good boost to the festivities at the gendarmes' expense, with another good laugh for conversation, happiness for the officers of the Legion and the Spahis, who couldn't stand the gendarmes. The rumor was quickly denied, but wine, when it goes through the warm entrails of a human being, has a distinctive odor.

Pagnon knew that Daintree knew. He hadn't tried to cover it up—Daintree was worthy of the truth—and without preliminaries:

"In fact, it was those young fools . . . My innocent worker, I'm relieved, truly. I will pay him his salary, with a bonus."

"What about the thieves?"

"An escapade, two kids, two bottles! We've all done that, but we weren't the sons of gendarmes, incapable of doing something stupid without throwing up! We'll forget them."

As for Mohand, he would be forgotten, too. He would be paid. No, not exactly exonerated. Here you could never admit that you had punished the wrong man—you would lose face. You have the right to be blind, but not to be wrong. To excuse yourself is a loss of authority.

"He is innocent," Pagnon added, "but we were right to punish him."

"He's going to be known as a wine thief?" asked Daintree.

"No, everyone already knows he's innocent . . . the Arab telephone . . . He didn't steal anything, he won't lose face, nor will we. I know, it's not really fair, but for him it's destiny. He was there at the wrong time, *mektub*. You know what that means . . ."

"I know, the great book . . ."

"Exactly . . . their fatalism."

Daintree had joined Raouf and Ganthier. He reported his conversation, citing Pagnon's *mektub*. Raouf became lost in contemplating a plant with large, velvety green leaves that spread out a few inches above the ground. They were covered with white crystals that shone in the last rays of the sun. He commented without raising his head:

"*Mektub* helps them control people . . . They criticize us for it, but they know how to use it . . . and if we try to escape it, they say we're revolutionaries."

Ganthier continued: "And in your families they say that you have become atheists, dear youth caught in the trap of history!"

Daintree had dust on his shoes. He wanted to wipe them off with the green leaves. He decided not to, seeing Raouf contemplating them, and asked:

"What is that plant that can thrive on rocks?"

"It must have a scientific name," Ganthier had said, "but here they call it the 'glacial grass,' a strange name for here. The crystals are water, and you can eat it in a salad, with oil."

At a distance Pagnon was watching the three men in conversation. He said to his wife that it was bizarre, those three. They had every reason to hate each other, and they spent their time talking:

"The one I like least is the young *bicot*, with his air of a little chief. He shouldn't be here, Ganthier never should have brought him. Ganthier is playing a strange game. He's more of a colonist than all the colonists, but always hanging around with Arabs, and he talks to them in Arabic. When he's not with the son, he's talking with the father."

In Pagnon's opinion, Ganthier wasn't providing a good example, his land regrouping plan that he let linger . . . The natives saw that and they began to linger, too.

"Presumably, he respects her, that widow What's Her Name, or maybe there's something else . . . He's known her since she was a kid . . . He claims that he supports strong-arm tactics, but when one is a supporter of strong-arm tactics you don't interact like that with these people." Thérèse pointed out that her husband spent his life taking care of *those people.*

"Maybe, but it pays, and I'm getting experience for when I'm in private practice. And it shows them that they need us."

14

TWO HATREDS

Yes, Samuel Katz answered Ganthier, the third trial was in March, about a month before we took the boat to come here. That gave the Vigilantes weeks and weeks to attack movies all over the country. In the studios they were beginning to say that you couldn't let one rotten apple ruin the whole basket, and the press kept talking about the ice! As soon as the new trial began, McNab quickly announced that his client, Mr. Arbuckle, would testify on the stand. The district attorney then had Doctor Wakefield, the head of the clinic, testify. He repeated that the tear in the bladder could only have come from an external force. McNab cross-examined Wakefield:

"Did you participate in the autopsy?"

"Absolutely, it was my clinic."

"Did you have the right to do so?"

"No, but . . ."

"Isn't that a punishable offense?"

"Yes . . ."

"Three years in prison, if District Attorney Brady decides to pursue you?"

"Yes . . ."

"Thank you. No more questions."

That was where McNab showed his stuff, said Wayne, when he let the facts talk. Later it was Nancy Blake's turn, at the end of her rope, muttering that she had never been sequestered, she had stayed with the mother of Mr. Duffy, a deputy district attorney . . . Yes, Mrs. Duffy had slapped her, but it was to wake her up . . . McNab pounded her: Why had she gone from a Virginia saying "I'm dying," in the first deposition, to "He hurt me" in the next one, then "He killed me"? Blake didn't say anything. McNab asked her who had ordered her to say, "He killed me." Blake started to cry, McNab on the offensive. When he looked at Brady you could see he hated him. The district attorney thought he was the only one who had a right to hatred, hatred of corruption and crime, and now, right in front of him a man showing a hatred that was just as moral, a hatred of blackmail and manipulation, and Blake said that the district attorney had forced her, that Mrs. Duffy really had slapped her, she was drunk and she slapped me . . .

I'm afraid . . . McNab had no more questions, Blake tried to breathe, and Brady didn't question her, said Samuel, he didn't want to flog a dead horse.

Everyone was waiting for another great moment, Fatty on the stand, which occurred two days later. The assistant district attorney, U'Ren, led the questioning. He did a wonderful job. He shot out his questions while walking around the room. He watched for the moment when Fatty would let down his guard. He made him talk about his career, his profession as an actor, his talent. He put him at ease. He had taken a friendly tone: "In your opinion, Mr. Arbuckle, what is a good actor?" Fatty was delighted, but many in the room had understood, Fatty was about to hang himself, and he answered: "A good actor . . . is someone who . . . experiences the truth and expresses it . . . He is a servant of the truth!"

An angry look from District Attorney Brady to U'Ren: the accused had just screwed them. Brady had more witnesses of morality file through for Virginia, while announcing that he would begin investigations into false testimony against those of the defense. People were getting bored, and that's when McNab did something strange, something disgusting, said Kathryn, no, said Neil Daintree, it was reality. In the other trials the prosecution had also used reality, the two doors, that of the bedroom and that of the bathroom, set up right in the middle of the courtroom, with a discussion of Fatty's fingerprints and those of Virginia. They had reality before their eyes for days and days; they were the district attorney's doors, the doors of death. So McNab had the right to produce a piece of reality, too, and a court clerk entered with a large box, silence in the courtroom, the type of silence that makes you smell the heat, the sweat, the cloying perfume. He put the box on a table, took off the lid—you would have thought you were in a great hatmaker's shop—he found a spot of light on the table and took out a large jar, put it in the ray of sun, and the sun revealed a diseased bladder. McNab didn't say a thing, the prosecution didn't dare say anything: it was no longer just by way of the doors that Virginia Rappe was present. Everyone was nauseous. That's exactly what McNab wanted. It was his turn to talk. He said that he would simply read the report of the doctors, whom the prosecution had not accused of perjury: it was a great strategy. Brady had gone after so many people that an unaccused witness could only be telling the truth, and McNab read: first abortion at fifteen. Brady tried to object; the judge overruled. McNab sometimes shot a glance at the Vigilantes. Treatment for chronic alcoholism, treatment for urogenital tract infections, 1908, 1911, 1914, 1917, 1919 . . . The voice of science, McNab, then he set down his paper and stopped talking. That was all. In the summaries U'Ren attacked Fatty, Kathryn saying: He mainly described his parties, and he wasn't wrong! And Neil replying that the prosecution lacked material evidence and testimony that was true.

At the bar of the Grand Hôtel that had been the most serious incident between Neil and Kathryn, a terrible moment, unbearable, when Kathryn had asserted that people were afraid to talk, fear and money helps make the rich innocent; Neil's smile, it seemed to pierce his wife's story. She suddenly fell silent.
Cavarro seemed to enjoy that silence, but everyone sensed that there was going
to be a real catastrophe, Fatty and Kathryn . . . He had helped her at the beginning of her career, in exchange for what? Fatty wasn't much the type to ask for
permission, they knew that, Neil adding that when girls went out with Fatty they
were well aware of what might happen, Kathryn becoming very pale. It would
have taken only a few more words, and they said to themselves that Kathryn was
going to say what they already more or less knew, that Daintree and Cavarro had
participated in the party at the Saint Francis. She could also give the age of the
girls who generally accompanied her husband, and McGhill would quickly find
out: he would make them all go back home, right away. Kathryn had a fixed,
cold stare . . . And it wasn't just a lull in the conversation, Ganthier would later
comment, we might have been there as safety nets, allowing them to tell a tell-
able story. That didn't prevent the devil from lighting a fire under them.

After Gabrielle told Rania all that, Rania took Kathryn's side:

"Your men also have their ways of reducing women to silence. They make
a woman think she can live, then they remind her that she doesn't have the
right to have lived, I mean, to have made mistakes. Do you think one day we'll
have the right to make mistakes and to benefit from them?" *To be in the right,*
thought Rania, *in the right while making mistakes . . . the just feeling doesn't
trick . . . his hand on my stomach . . . the sensation of happiness . . . and we
both fight sleep . . . a look, nothing is finished . . .* wa sukrun, thumma sahwun,
thumma chawqun, *drunkenness then sobering, then desire . . . and the proximity
then the abundance then the intimacy, and when I pass him I don't dare say anything to him.* Rania didn't want to ask if Kathryn had really slept with Mr. Fatty,
and Gabrielle had no idea. Fifty or so yards from the veranda there were cypress
trees. Gabrielle was surprised by a sort of mute explosion in the trees, followed
by a small cloud. Those are pollens that are being freed, Rania said. Nature is
much freer than we are, isn't it?

Samuel broke the silence Neil had provoked. He told of the end of Brady's
summary, his words to the jury: If you don't find this man guilty, you will be
breaking your oath, you will be perjurers! For weeks, each time Brady and his
men accused someone of perjury, they then dragged him in front of a judge;
some jurors were going to see that as blackmail. When it was the defense's turn,
McNab first sent Schmulowitz in front of the jury. Schmulowitz was very calm,
very logical; he appealed to the intelligence of the jury, the foundation of law,
reasonable doubt:

"We don't claim to know absolutely the cause of Miss Rappe's injury, we simply know that there are other possibilities, just as strong, if not more so, than external violence, and that is enough to establish reasonable doubt as to the guilt of the defendant."

He had concluded by saying that he left it up to the soul and the conscience of each juror.

Then McNab got up. Schmulowitz had done the work of Fatty's innocence. McNab was going to take care of the lie. He attacked strongly, saying that the district attorneys had transformed into a hateful pack. They had manipulated, threatened, sequestered the witnesses for more than six months, Miss Blake and Miss Prevon, one of them shamefully beaten in the name of the American people! And they had constructed an untrue idealization of the victim, "a human being whom I respect, but the prosecution can't turn her into a saint, she was a victim of society, but one who didn't belong to the world of real women." McNab had thunder in his voice. He looked at the Vigilantes, then the jury, and he paraphrased Ruskin, "Wherever a true wife comes, her home is always around her . . ."

McNab had finished, and Brady let Friedman conclude in the name of the prosecution; he didn't do it himself. McNab had just stolen their thunder—no question of making any comparisons, especially since Friedman had a final card to play. Brady and all his colleagues had stayed up all night perfecting it, the irrefutable argument that McNab hadn't anticipated:

"If we had, as the defense claims, forged all these testimonies, if we had built our case on 'moonbeams,' wouldn't we have been more careful with our work? Would we have presented to the jury the hodgepodge of witnesses that we were forced to present?" Brady was clearly steaming. They had perfected the direction of Friedman's speech but hadn't chosen those words, "moonbeams," "hodgepodge." McNab and Schmulowitz looked at each other: Friedman had just admitted that the prosecution had screwed up.

The judge had instructed the jury to deliberate, and within a few minutes the jury came back into the courtroom. McNab's face turned white. Were they requesting additional information? Like in the earlier trial? The jurors entered. The district attorneys were all smiles. Some jurors had very hard faces. A piece of onion skin paper was passed from the jury foreman to a bailiff, from the bailiff to the judge, who read it in silence, a stern look at Arbuckle. Everyone was sweating. In such moments, said Samuel, everyone feels important, that's why people come. There was finally a unanimous verdict: not guilty!

Mayhem! Everyone wanted to touch Fatty. The jurors began to sign a sheet of paper that was put on the table. It was their apology. Mr. Arbuckle had been the victim of a great injustice. No bit of proof had ever been provided by the prosecution. Mr. Arbuckle was in no way responsible. They hoped that the American people would accept the unanimous verdict of twelve free men who had reflected for a month. Fatty Arbuckle was innocent of everything!

In the bar of the Grand Hôtel Kathryn concluded that it made a very modern story, the opposite of Dickens or Hugo. With them you have a good person who is found guilty—it makes you cry—whereas with Fatty you had an innocent who was still a real bastard. It wasn't easy to talk about that affair, she told Gabrielle later, we managed to sweep everything under the rug, but it might well come back to haunt us one day. McGhill would really like us to tear each other apart in front of him!

15

AT THE MARKET

They strolled through the aisles of the central market, three women, two Christians, as the shopkeepers called them, although neither of the two had been Christian since they were old enough to give up their dolls, but in Nahbès "Christian" enabled the locals to talk about all foreigners without having to get tangled up in distinctions between Europeans and Americans. So they were two Christians and a Muslim whose eyes were the only thing they could see, the two Christians dressed decently, Hamid the butcher had said to his son Aymen, as if they had given up their eccentricities so they wouldn't upset the woman who was accompanying them or whom they were accompanying, difficult to say, so equal did those three seem, some of the shopkeepers having recognized the veiled woman and greeting her discreetly in passing, caught between the general rule, which said a woman was not to be acknowledged, and the specific rule, which applied to trade, which was that a widow, and one from a powerful family, should be shown respect, especially this one, who in addition had brought food to the people of Asmira during their trial, and who also refused to let her land be taken by a colonist. Of course the central market did most of its business with Christians, but that wasn't a reason not to greet a courageous Muslim woman, even if some shopkeepers refused to do so. Some women can be the exception and move around certain places but not receive gestures that are reserved for men, and furthermore, they shouldn't have to do the shopping, which should remain a man's business, the most important men of Nahbès having even brought their buying habits from the market of the old city to that of the new city, not for all products, of course, because it wasn't worth buying things here that cost twice as much as on the other side of the wadi, but you could buy new products—jams, for example, those famous jars of Félix Potin from Paris, or even, for the more daring, some said, or those who were more influenced, said others, those famous cheeses, also imported, the glory of our table, said the French, and perhaps even those daring or influenced ones also came to buy . . . No, wine certainly wasn't sold here. They had it delivered to their homes in the evening. It was the curse of the times, when believers contravened the prescriptions of the Book on that subject and on many others, and that's why a woman shouldn't leave her house. That's what Hamid's neighbor, Abdelhaq, the most traditionalist vendor of fowl in Nahbès, whom tradition had not prevented from setting up his shop right in the middle of the European city, that place of all perdition, and who begged pardon from his interlocutors each time he was forced to utter the word *woman* in conversation, was now asserting to Hamid. Yes, Hamid had responded, this city is perdition, but do you really think that wine waited for the arrival of the French to flow into Arabs' mouths? I'm a good Muslim, I don't drink, and if I want to greet the Belmejdoub girl, a respected widow, I'll greet her, even if she doesn't have to respond to my greeting. And Abdelhaq didn't pursue it, so as not to start the day with a quarrel with his neighbor, but even so, that widow, Abdelhaq knew she was an atheist—he had been told that more than once—a false Muslim who used religion for politics, whereas the only message from On High was that politics was fully contained in religion, and that woman who was helping the relatives of rioters wanted religion to be contained in politics, like the Turks, and we know what that led to. Politics weren't good. The colonists were there. For the pious Abdelhaq it was the will of the On High, and it was no use trying to change it. It was like trying to wash a crow.

The three women were coming straight toward them, each followed by a little porter holding a new straw basket. Kathryn couldn't get over all the colors and smells.

"Colors are the most difficult to describe," said Gabrielle.

"How do you do it when you write?" Kathryn asked.

"You have to follow one that you find in others, yellow, for example. I really like following yellow. It really stands out, and it also flows into the green of the leaves, the tails of leeks, the blue of the flowers, the orange of fruit, of saffron and birds of paradise, and the brown of dates, and the beautiful matte yellow of the melons that make you think of some mustards."

Kathryn asked: "Do you know how to choose a melon?"

"No, never. In Paris I rely on the vendor."

Kathryn and Gabrielle bought without restraint, filling their baskets without much discernment, Kathryn asking Rania why she wasn't buying anything, Rania responding that it would be scandalous if she started buying the fruit of the earth, a scandal here and a scandal at the farm, and my very presence is a scandal: can you imagine me returning with tomatoes? I'll buy something on our way back, some spices. There are two vendors who sell good spices. I'll buy some from both!

"Why do you want to go to the market?" Neil had asked Kathryn, "when you always eat on the set or at a restaurant?"

"Because I want to see it," Kathryn had said, "and smell it, and touch it, and it will give me ideas."

"What sort of ideas?"

"I don't know, but the market is exciting, I haven't been to one in years!"

The women walked around, talked, took it all in, hesitated, went down the aisles. It was nine in the morning and it was already very hot.

When they first entered the large covered market, Kathryn and Gabrielle had initially wanted to refuse the services of the boys, who were undaunted and who remained planted in front of them, their hands already on the baskets the women had just bought, as if the refusal of the young American and French women had only been a formality before an agreement that would in any event be concluded. Kathryn had turned toward Rania, saying that she was against making children work. "I am, too," Rania had said, "but that's how these children live, and if you don't use one of them, they're all going to harass us . . . Do what you want . . ." Gabrielle was thinking that Rania knew how to argue well, to help the poor, escape harassment, exercise your will, just by speaking softly to Kathryn . . .

The friendship between the two young women was unique, spontaneous and cautious at the same time, as if they were both afraid of a harshness that would have needed only a slight push to be established between them. The journalist had taken some time to introduce these two friends, and she wasn't yet convinced that she had done the right thing. It had happened at Rania's. Kathryn's name kept coming up in conversation, which was odd, anyway, when the great subject in Nahbès among the women was Cavarro. Rania never talked about him, nor was she ever the first to bring up Kathryn's name—she left that to Gabrielle, and Gabrielle always found herself mentioning Kathryn, even when she had decided not to, *Why do I talk to her about her? Because I sense that she wants to? Because I'm incapable of stepping away from what could become a story? Because of Raouf? Or to annoy Ganthier?*

And Gabrielle had ended up persuading Kathryn to visit Rania. The young widow would be happy to see them, to have the world in which she would have liked to come and go freely come to her. "Sometimes," Rania would say, "I feel much freer than other women, but I become angry at myself for being satisfied with crumbs!" There was vehemence in her voice. She had liked Kathryn; she wasn't like the European women; she immediately broke the barriers, laughed, spoke loudly, said intimate things, asked her after a few minutes if she knew Raouf well, yes, ever since he was very young, a cousin, distant, on our mothers' side, and Rania found that she, too, was confiding in her, telling about how she brought him to the hammam with her when he was young. At that time he could have been taken for a girl with his long eyelashes, his lovely lips and sweet voice. He was in love with me. The other women adored him. He rubbed their backs, they tickled him, he fought back—Rania wondering then how she could say such things to an American woman whom she had known for only an hour, when she should have had her talk about Raouf, ask her what she had done to turn him into an escort, Rania continuing: I remember a day when a woman said to him, "When you were younger you were nicer"—he wasn't even six—and he replied, "I didn't know you as well." That day we understood that he loved words and that he no longer belonged to us.

Rania didn't know why she was telling those stories, but she liked the laughs she brought out of Kathryn, and Kathryn was happy to have become Rania's friend, as if that friendship gave her permission to keep her cousin as an escort in a world that was proving basically to be more welcoming than she had been told. "The women especially are horrible," Marfaing had asserted, "They are prevented from having contact with the outside world, so they would like the same, or almost the same, for the men. *Hchouma,* shame—they are constantly assaulted with that word, so they seize it and throw it in the faces of their lords and masters. You saw So-and-So at a reception of the *contrôle civil? Hchouma.* So-and-So is going to France on business? *Hchouma.* So-and-So had a European-style suit made for himself? *Hchouma.* They don't dare say anything about the presence of men in the cafés of the medina, but if it's a café in the European city, *hchouma.* They have become the guards of the guards of their prison. Marfaing didn't allow for any exceptions, but Rania was indeed one. She wasn't ashamed to be seen with two "Christians" right in the central market.

At one point the three women saw an older European woman who was walking with her back to them, a very large, overweight woman wearing a voluminous, billowing flowered dress, which was sticking to her sweaty skin, a half dozen boys behind her, who burst out laughing and shoved each other while pointing her out to the entire market. The woman was carrying her two baskets by herself:

"You see what happens when you refuse their help. They cause a ruckus," said Rania. Then she pointed at Kathryn's basket, "You're going to put all of that in your hotel room?" Kathryn trying to find a pretext for going back to the Grand Hôtel with her provisions, and suddenly a cry of triumph:

"I'm going to host a dinner!" Gabrielle asking:

"Where?"

"At your place! I'll take care of everything, okay? Neil will agree, I'll make an American dinner, there will be a dozen or so of us, right?" She hesitated for a moment when she realized Rania couldn't come . . . "No, fewer people, we'll invite only women, a dinner of women! Like in New York! Rania, you'll come!"

Rania didn't say anything. Gabrielle was a bit taken aback, but Kathryn reassured her, Tess, her maid, would be there to help:

"Tess knows how to do everything and when she doesn't she learns very quickly, that's how she has survived."

Kathryn pounced on everything, vegetables, fruits, flowers, spices, then she led her friends to the fowl vendor, Abdelhaq, who was suddenly obsequious, of course, the most beautiful of my turkeys, signaling to one of his helpers, who came back holding in his arms a beautiful live turkey that was throwing its head in every direction, Abdelhaq himself sharpening a knife that sent out reflections that the turkey was trying to catch, fifteen minutes and it would be ready, Kathryn paying, immediately setting off to a stall selling potbellied onions. Behind her it wasn't just one but now three small porters who were following her.

"May I ask you a very indiscreet question," Rania asked Kathryn. Kathryn on alert, Gabrielle plunging into an examination of a bunch of leeks. She would have given anything to have avoided this.

"Anything you want," Kathryn had said in a flat tone, caught off-guard, an aisle in the market . . . The question would seem nonchalant . . . Gabrielle would necessarily hear . . . And Rania, quite emotional at daring to ask such a thing:

"Would you tell me the story of *Warrior of the Sands?*"

Kathryn, relieved, quickly launched into a synopsis of the screenplay right in the market. The hero was called Jamil, yes, that's the role Francis plays: he's a soldier in the Turkish forces during the war between Syria and Turkey. He is a member of an Arab tribe. He deserts, and in a remote village he discovers a clinic for orphans run by American missionaries, Doctor Field, and his daughter, whom I play, Kathryn suddenly wondering if Rania had ever seen a movie in her life, not knowing if she should give more details, Rania understanding her hesitation and saying:

"We have a projector in my father's house. I've even seen *Broken Blossoms.*"

They stopped talking when they saw the older woman with the baskets passing in front of them. The woman shot a venomous look at Kathryn.

"What did I do to her?" Kathryn asked.

"Don't play the innocent," Gabrielle responded, "To other women you're public enemy number one."

Kathryn continued: "The chief of the village wants to appease the Turks and decides to hand over the children, who would be slaughtered, so the horsemen of Jamil's tribe arrive on the scene."

"That," said Gabrielle, "is like the cavalry in your Indian stories."

"Yes, and with some dramatic license, Jamil, the one who deserted from the Turks, is the son of the chief of the Bedouin tribe, and at that moment they learn of his father's death . . ."

Rania: "Isn't that another example of theatrical license?"

"In the theater they wouldn't dare do that," said Gabrielle.

"You can in the movies," said Kathryn, "if it makes a good scene."

"That's called boulevard theater," Gabrielle concluded. Kathryn said to Rania:

"Gabrielle is the only friend I have who dares voice reservations about film . . . So Jamil becomes the chief, and he risks his life to save the children, he fights the Turks . . ." Rania says:

"Do the missionaries convert the children?"

"No," said Kathryn, "It seems that would cause some problems."

"I can guess the ending: the chief of the tribe marries the doctor's daughter."

"You don't like that?"

Kathryn had laughed at Rania's awkward silence. Rania was keeping to herself a too harsh thought about marriage with foreigners, *How can I say we are against it, but without bitterness? No, we're not against it, open the borders, but in both directions, and it would be enough to decide that no one would ever be merchandise again* . . . Kathryn had added:

"Basically, I'm like Neil, I'm wary of conclusions that are too simple, but you have to make a living, right? The real movie will be *Eugénie Grandet*, but first we have to bring in money with *Warrior of the Sands*."

"I have confidence in Neil," said Gabrielle.

"Gabrielle is from Paris, Parisian women are very critical," said Kathryn.

"You mean they don't like true feelings?" asked Rania.

"We didn't learn about life in *David Copperfield*! Look at that!" Gabrielle was pointing at the older woman whose back was again turned toward them, sweating in the aisle, the fabric of her flowered dress now stuck in the large crevice between her buttocks. The kids were shouting, making fun of her, imitating the woman's walk.

"You see what happens when you refuse the porters," said Rania. The kids' shouts transformed into a clumsy chorus, in French: "Madam, madam, your ass is eating your dress! Your ass is eating your dress!" The woman didn't seem to understand. Maybe she was Italian or Maltese, or she was pretending not to understand.

"She's not French," said Rania, "Otherwise the market police would have already intervened. She's not French, but she understands."

"How do you know?" asked Gabrielle.

"She's not turning around."

"You'd make a good director," said Kathryn.

As they were leaving they ran into Raouf and Ganthier. Gabrielle was afraid

Rania would be troubled, but on the contrary, she reacted first and gestured to the two men who acknowledged them. Through the veil that covered her face she had called them "the protectorate in two volumes," then, turning to Gabrielle: "You know what is happening? They see each other so often that they are blending into each other, and one of these days each will see the other in the mirror!" Ganthier didn't say anything, his face severe, as if hardened by the impeccable part that divided the hair on his head. He was holding his hat in both hands in front of him. Raouf was acting proud, and Rania knew that it was a sign that he wasn't comfortable in his role, either.

16

A SMILING WIFE

As the weeks went by Belkhodja started to notice that his wife sometimes stopped listening to him. She smiled but she didn't hear. He had to repeat himself. Her face assumed a vague look, like someone who was off in a dream. He didn't like that. He was worried. He tried not to think about it. Then, at La Porte du Sud, he surprised the members of the little group who were smiling, smiles of connivance. His worries returned, but he stopped thinking about them because his wife had apparently stopped dreaming. But another time, one of the young men called out to him just as he was arriving, as if to warn the others, who in turn began to call to him with a gaiety that he found false. He was sleeping badly, calmed himself down, tried the next day to catch the group unawares by coming through the back room. That day they were silent. Silence is much worse. It's meant to hide something, because it's serious. He dared to ask the reason for it. The silence had settled before he arrived because of the absence of Farouk, their favorite waiter: his father had died.

That death comforted Belkhodja. He slept better, but his worries returned, more frequently, heavier, at each dreamy smile from his wife. The matchmaker had gone north, no one knew where. He chided himself for not continuing to visit her with bolts of silk. There was no one to talk to now, to help him battle the return of what he called his hyenas. Up until then he had only known the terrors that came with his trade. Now others had come. He sometimes said to himself that the matchmaker had put into his arms the opposite of what she had promised. He chased away that thought, scolded himself, chased away the hyenas, but in the shop a client said something about a fool: "He's being cuckolded and what's more he helps with his hand," and the hyenas returned. He could see his wife smiling at him. She was accompanied by a figure that he couldn't place. He ran home to find his wife busy rolling out the couscous in the company only of their servants.

He pulled himself together. He had always had anxieties . . . In his activities as a rug merchant it happened that he would wake up in a sweat at three in the morning after having the day before sent two rugs with an invoice to a compatriot living in Marseille, and he was suddenly sure that he would never receive the money, not even the deposit that should have been paid to him immediately. It was madness to work that way. He used to say that there were things worse than theft, such as showing that one is afraid of being stolen from, and that's how you get stolen from, he would say to himself without being able to fall back asleep. It would soon be dawn. He neglected to do his first prayer. He scolded God for tolerating bad payers in his creation. He got ready to go out, too early, squeezed an imaginary throat with his two hands, caught himself, finally left his house, walking briskly, to go squeeze the payment from his client's brother. And on his way he met an employee of that brother who was bringing him the deposit. And it was the same thing with his wife, it wasn't her fault. Belkhodja calmed down. He was filled with tenderness. Then he thought of the moment when he would catch her in the act: he killed the man with a knife, attacked her, and woke from a waking dream that ruined his digestion after lunch. He thought he was stupid, reconciled with the world for two or three days, went crazy because at La Porte du Sud someone had said: "The best chicken is the one your neighbor has fed." And then calmed down again.

One morning, looking at his sleeping wife's face, he cried tears of tenderness and remorse. He had chased away his suspicions. She had begun to move. He hadn't wanted to wake her. He was leaving the room when he saw her move her legs, still sleeping, a smile on her lips. His wife had strange dreams. Women who dream are the worst. He knew what was behind that smile: he knew the dreams of other women, girls in the capital, those who lived in the Sphinx and the Miramar, who greeted him gaily while telling him that for weeks, even in the daylight, they dreamed of certain parts of his body; and those words that, in the capital, enchanted him, now came back to him like blows from a whip.

He was suspicious of the servant she had brought with her, neither young nor old, an ordinary face, with smallpox scars. She could have been a madam. He ordered the little maid to watch the servant on the pretext that someone was stealing from him. The little maid quickly reported that the servant had conversations on the terrace with someone she didn't know. The images returned, the warm ground of the terrace around three in the afternoon, a couple who hides behind sheets hanging out to dry, and people think it's the wind that's making them move. He no longer dared leave Nahbès. He no longer went to the capital—he who really liked making good deals, finding some pleasure, spending and dreaming of grandeur—now he was sacrificing his dreams for those of his wife, but he continued to wax his mustache and look elegant in front of his friends. There is someone more laughable than a cuckold, Raouf had said one day, it's the man who thinks he is! Belkhodja said to himself that the caïd's son was seeking revenge for the cow of Satan. He wanted to reply, but decided not to. He was careful not to be the last to laugh when they told a dirty story.

Then the madness returned, but not to the point of blinding him, or preventing him from realizing that the little maid was telling the master who had promised her money each time she had something good to tell him what she thought he wanted to hear. Belkhodja sent her away. And two hours later he brought her back, because it was better to have a frightened child under his roof than to condemn to the street someone whom the punishment would have rid of any scruples. He asked one of his friends to watch the servant, citing the same motive: someone was stealing from him. The friend took the mission seriously, even sacrificing part of the time he spent at his hardware shop. He quickly summed up the situation and said: "No, no theft, nor anything else." He liked romantic songs and thought Belkhodja was stupid for having married without love and then becoming insanely jealous.

Jealousy had become Belkhodja's second profession. He was capable of dropping everything and running to the old city to try to catch a man who had just been brought up in conversation; a crazy pursuit, follow his nose to the suspect, decipher what he could from the face of that new suspect: fear? sarcasm? calculation? And once he was in front of the man Belkhodja was nothing but friendly, he was pleased to have met him, it was destiny: I'm having a gathering of friends, this evening, a few young people, too, who admire you, they want to talk to you, don't insult me . . . You will be the guest of honor! The man put his hand on his heart, accepted, and Belkhodja returned quickly to his shop, sent his helpers to go invite some people for an impromptu party, and to let his wife know there would be a dinner with his friends that evening.

The man came to the dinner, was friendly with everyone. Belkhodja calmed down, watched him, was mad at himself for suspecting him, hugged him while joking, offered him a kidney cooked to perfection, shining with a dark, dense sauce, and at that moment caught the look of another guest, a look directed at the door that opened onto the private rooms. Suddenly there was a huge hole in his chest. He had allowed the cat to guard the meat! That other guest was the friend he had asked to investigate and who was caressing with his eyes the most sacred place in his home.

The next day, at dawn, he went to pay that friend a visit, then decided otherwise: if he were guilty, he would be expecting his visit . . . Be patient, then, surprise him when the tension has let up, and in the middle of the afternoon Belkhodja went to verify whether the friend was indeed in his hardware shop. He wasn't there. Belkhodja, enraged, went to his own house, this time taking a closed carriage to escape the eyes of watchers, and burst out in front of his wife, who was surprised, smiling, beyond suspicion. He went back to his shop, calmer. Your friend has just left. He was looking for you. He came to thank you for the dinner. He went to La Porte du Sud. Belkhodja hurried to the café, afraid his friend would mention the surveillance missions he had undertaken, but no, the man remained discreet. Belkhodja promised himself, however, to keep him away from the gatherings of the little band, then reassured himself: they never talked about his marriage there.

Except that Raouf, one day when they were talking about the role of look-outs in the service of lovers, had seemed to give Belkhodja an ironic look, citing Ibn Hazm's old code on the art of love concerning the endless wandering of the jealous man, and Belkhodja said to himself that the caïd's son must know something, no doubt through his father. There must be a police report on certain movements around his house. Raouf knew. He was perhaps involved, out of vengeance? Belkhodja gnashed his teeth without arriving at any real conclusions.

He went to see a sorceress in Nahbès, an Italian woman. He had his Tarot read. The prudent sorceress didn't see anything, but he knew that he would again fall prey to his hyenas. His suspicions grew and shrank like the phases of the moon. He no longer talked about the Americans or the cow of Satan. He was afraid he had called the evil eye upon himself by invoking the devil. He thought he was living the worst of what an existence could endure, but when he began to no longer have the strength to run after shadows in the streets, he soon discovered that the worst was yet to come.

As the days went by he kept to himself in the back room of his shop, leaving an employee to ruin deals that he would have concluded with no effort. He went only rarely to meet his young friends at the café, and he even lost the will to react, even when he started to imagine that Satan had given another man the duty of providing him with an heir. His nightmares increased his unhappiness. His sin was in having sought an impossible creature. He had, however, said to himself that too good a seamstress would end up sewing the eyes of her husband together, and his wife slept peacefully while he writhed in a pit of snakes.

His friends became alarmed. They pretended to think he was ill. They pulled him from the pit, took him to the capital, to enjoy life again, and since he loved himself more than anything, he began to drink again, to eat, to play, to satisfy his desires, to do deals, and take long, solitary and dreamy walks, at night, when the city is empty and it can belong to only one man. The capital saved him.

He returned home. Two other friends had inquired after him in his absence and assured him that *no one had anything to feel guilty about*. Belkhodja believed them, clung to that belief. He felt better, but he hadn't taken the hammam into account.

What no one had seen in his wife, other women had finally noticed at the hammam. They had found, as they said, the roots in the fog, by getting the young wife to talk. All naughty stories go through the hammam, which is, for many, the place of perversion for women, just as the gambling den is the place of perversion for men, except that the hammam is worse than the gambling den, because the gambling den is known for being a place of dissolution and true pleasure, it isn't trying to be anything else—you go in and the whole town knows what you're doing there—whereas the hammam, with its burning stones and jets of water, is primarily the place where one goes to rid oneself of the impurities of life; but it is also there, in the steam, among all the naked bodies, that women come to exchange unhealthy recipes and where sins are prepared and revealed, including one that is among the most vile, hypocrisy.

"I have something to tell you from someone for whom you have become the only light."

"No! I forbid you to play that game with me, don't tell me anything."

"Alright."

"And you should be ashamed to tell me impious things."

"If they were impious words I wouldn't try to tell you, or show you the photo I was given."

"A photo at the hammam, in five minutes the steam will turn it into a rag!"

"No, I left it in my basket, at the entrance."

"Your messages are made to destroy the one to whom they are addressed."

"You're wrong, he's the one who is lost, because of you, and you know who I'm talking about."

"When your cousins claim that they are going to be lost, they never go very far."

"But he's not like the others, he's going to leave."

"Leave? Where?"

"He's desperate, he's going to join the French soldiers and go to the Sahara, very far away, where they die."

"He's incapable of doing that, he's a liar."

"No, he told me that he would join up this evening if I don't have an answer, and if you don't want to hear any more, I won't bother you with it."

And so on, between women with calm faces, and the impious message will finally be delivered, and will be the object of a response, negative, of course, but formulated in such a way that it, in turn, calls for a response, and above all not a departure for the Sahara. And so all the conversations will continue for the happiness of the hammam owners and for the anxiety of the women who go there with an urgency whose ardor is not only from the desire to be cleansed. They talk and the one who says nothing is also the one who has the most to hide.

Belkhodja's young wife was smiling but reserved. Her friends at the hammam had tried to get her to talk. After all, young brides, especially the girls who come from the country, who have lived a less cultured life than those in the town, and who have fewer words at their disposal, have a lot of things to tell, and they often do so with a naïveté that is the delight of those around them. This one had quickly become the target of the fanatics for whom a spoon can always extract what is in a jar. Without results. They had left the young wife with her friendly smiles alone, but the way she always seemed to be thinking of something else made them think that she must be doing a lot more than what a husband might ask of a wife.

And then, little by little, the newcomer relaxed, speaking innocent word after innocent word, and when you put such words end to end they always ultimately turned into something that was not completely innocent, from one confidence to the next, from exaggerations to rectifications. She wasn't exactly naive, the young wife who came three or four times a week to plunge into the steam of the hammam where they were beginning to see through the fog. When a friend talked to Belkhodja's mother, she had at first refused to believe what she was being told. She had taken her time. She questioned the women who had met her daughter-in-law about what she liked to do, her hours at the hammam, her activities, her outings, her encounters, about everything. She let them speak. She also threatened those who didn't talk enough. She questioned her daughter-in-law directly. She set traps and she finally understood, like all those who had already understood. The young wife wasn't naive. Oh no, the truth had come out: she was simple-minded.

Simple-minded, yes, a bit backward, as they also said. Other, more straight-forward descriptions had circulated. The dreamy young wife was nothing but a big dummy. The sly Belkhodja had married a real dummy. There was no risk of that one being perverted. The mother had defended her son. He couldn't have known. In such a situation men can be unaware for years. And she, herself, in-formed her son. She didn't tell him that he should have come to her instead of placing his interests in the hands of an unscrupulous matchmaker. She didn't stress that she would never have chosen for him a girl who had only a chickpea in her head. She was loving. She simply said and repeated that to repudiate that woman would be to lose face.

Belkhodja had become the laughingstock of his world. Some advisers told him: "Throw away the poker, it will take the smoke with it," but he followed his mother's advice. He was happy to send the simpleton back to the country, where that type of thing is noticed less than in the city. On the advice of Doctor Ber-thommier he decided not to have children with his wife, but he didn't complain to anyone about the misfortune he was enduring. He didn't want to be at the mercy of his confidants. He waited for them to forget all about it. He could then take another wife, when the anguish of perhaps making another bad choice would have passed. The little band at La Porte du Sud had enveloped him in their friendship. Those young men who were so ready to make fun of everything vowed not to make the slightest allusion in his presence. They had defended him against slander. They tried to distract him, to engage in great discussions in which they asked for his advice on questions of religion and politics, even if it was only to contradict him, and they forced him to spend time in the capital again. He did excellent business there and spent wonderful evenings drinking, laughing, and dreaming. Shame was easier to treat than jealousy.

One morning, at the beginning of the month of October, Raouf himself came to Belkhodja's shop along with his American friend. She was about to leave the country, and wanted to buy one of his most beautiful pieces, a Zerrour, a choice that lasted hours, the three of them in front of a copper tray, with two servants who unfolded the rugs, and another who at intervals changed the teapot, one of the most beautiful conversations that Belkhodja had had that year. Kathryn asked him many questions about each of the rugs he showed her, the stitches, the code of the colors. She knew quite a bit. What she asked Belkhodja was in addition to her expertise, wool on wool or wool on cotton? Or silk . . . "It's finer," Belkhodja said, "but . . . (he caressed his mustache, with a sad look), since it is finer the degradations of time are seen more quickly . . ." For the large Zerrour that Kathryn finally chose, Belkhodja asked such a low price that Raouf objected. Kathryn understood. She acted as if she couldn't possibly buy it, and Belkhodja agreed to increase his price. All three of them were happy with the bartering in the contrary direction. Money exchanged hands, but each had showed that money wasn't what motivated them above all else. They parted ways with their dignity, and Belkhodja dared compliment Kathryn: "Your eyes also know how to buy."

Belkhodja had wanted to take revenge on the matchmaker, but she couldn't be found. He ended up attributing that bad adventure to the realm of destiny, but he wasn't content with ordinary *mektub*: he sought something that was his own, which would show that above all he had overcome his misfortune, and sometimes, when the tableful of friends had laughed a lot, he quoted a saying that they had never heard before, but which seemed like the voice of destiny itself: *For each one who laughs there must always be one who cries.*

Between bouts of bitterness and resignation he began to endure his existence again. One day he learned that in the city people were saying that he hadn't married a cow of Satan but a donkey of God. He understood right away where that had come from. And that destiny had very little to do with it.

17

TROUBLED TIMES

It was that time of the autumn when ripe fruit would soon make way for dead leaves. In Nahbès this change wasn't greeted with sadness. The rains didn't come, but at least the temperature was less stifling. Work on *Warrior of the Sands* was progressing, but Neil was dragging things out, moving at a more human rhythm. No one wanted to go back to the States, though they were eager for news from back there. The telephone worked badly. Newspapers arrived weeks late. The Fatty Arbuckle case continued to cause damage in the world of film and performance. An actor, Wilbur Dutton, had had a picture taken with his mistress. His wife had called a lawyer. Yes, that happened in Atlanta, very far from California. He had gone all that way for nothing. His bosses had said to Wilbur, "If you break your marriage contract we'll break your acting contract," and in Hollywood and San Francisco or New York actors were forced, no, said Kathryn, felt forced every morning to declare to every journalist that their only values were God, America, and marriage, which didn't prevent the leagues of virtue from continuing to cry "shame" in front of movie theaters, and photographers from rooting you out wherever you shouldn't have been. Only Marion Davies, Hearst's mistress, was at peace. Even Hearst's legitimate wife didn't dare say anything. She knew what her husband was capable of.

"We've become a nation of hypocrites," said Neil, "but since prosperity is returning, it doesn't matter."

"Prosperity on credit," said Samuel Katz, "Credit is a lie, the banker doesn't *grant* you a loan, he's selling you a product, a very expensive one!"

They also talked about the election of the first woman senator in the States. Gabrielle congratulated Kathryn, who answered that it wasn't a change, but luck. And one morning Raouf disappeared from Nahbès.

Ganthier didn't seem to know. Kathryn didn't say anything. Neither did Gabrielle. But that same night Gabrielle in turn disappeared, and things became clear when news from the capital began to arrive, the stirrings of political agitation, asserted the French, a foreign influence, from Moscow, from Cairo, no hold over the country, it's going to fall again. Some pointed their finger at the Americans: your angelism, the rights of the people, what abstraction!

The Prépondérants of Nahbès demanded that a "preventative curfew" be imposed in the old city. Marfaing didn't want anything to do with that. When one has muscles one needn't show them. He continued to go to the bar of the Grand Hôtel, relaxed and friendly, delivered some news, censored, of course, to squelch the unfounded rumors by means of what he laughingly called founded rumors: Yes, there have indeed been demonstrations, but they were the squawking of crows, nothing more.

In Gabrielle's absence, Kathryn passed along the news to Rania. They also talked about Raouf:

"As soon as politics are involved, he drops everyone and everything. I'm sure he's forgotten the people who love him," Rania repeated *the people who love him* carefully, and the *people* being vague, Kathryn saying, "He's a spoiled child who only thinks of others when they are standing in front of him." She was furious not to have any news. Rania thought there was a bit of vanity in Kathryn and found it unfair, and in Kathryn's opinion he was behaving like a little male, who thought that women should step aside when things became serious, Rania trying to create a diversion: "Here, the peasants say that the legions of martyrs will descend from the heavens and attack France from the Sahara."

News came from all sides. The sovereign had demonstrated some remnants of pride. The people's attitude toward their sovereign was bizarre, a foundation of contempt—after all it was his family that had reduced the country to this—but as soon as he showed any sign of a spine, they sang his praises or they spoke of the crown prince, a classic scenario: the father is docile, but the prince is a good man, he often talks with the nationalists, assures them of his support. In fact, they said, the sovereign wanted to take advantage of the current uproar, of the coming visit by the president of the French republic. The French were planning to portray him as a sovereign, and now he wanted to play a real sovereign, so he fired one of his ministers who was too close to the colonists and met with the U.S. consul in private.

And in an editorial in *Présence Française*, the newspaper published by the Prépondérants, the editor-in-chief, Richard Trillat, demanded the rejection of "all these thoughtless native demands and a response reflecting our long-term interests," which meant the end of the protectorate and the country's alignment with the regime of Algeria. They spoke about it more and more, there could be no more hesitation, and some Prépondérants spoke even more directly: "We give them this, they demand that," with gestures accompanying the words, holding the right arm straight out, the index finger of the left hand placed at the base of the right index finger and then going up the arm to the shoulder, and they added, to be more explicit: "But we're not going to drop our trousers!" Richard

Trillat even demanded an actual policy for the Christianization of the country, re-Christianization, in fact, attracting the criticism of those who tried to be
more diplomatic. France owed it to itself to respect the Muslim religion, "which
we know," said the resident general, "has a taste for immobility," which was not
without advantages for French interests.

It was rumored that the sovereign had also made an explicit gesture in front
of the resident general, raising a hand to the sky and passing the other under his
throat to show the extremes to which he was ready to go if they imposed deci-
sions on him that were contrary to his status. He detested his ministers, assigned
by France, a question of principle, said his partisans, a more practical decision,
said those on the side of the residence, since some ministers had more access to
public resources than he did, and they also wanted to control his and those of
his son, which were prodigious, by the way, especially those of the crown prince.
As for the sovereign's wife, she sought to insure her future as a potential widow
by having one of her favorites made a minister.

And so the agitation was coming from the palace, some said; no, from the
nationalists, said others; and Raouf traveled through the capital, from meeting
to meeting, talking with friends who were communists, socialists, nationalists,
being called an eclectic bourgeois by some as soon as he showed the slightest
skepticism about what was going on; the people in the street proclaiming that
they were ready for anything: they talked to each other without knowing each
other, talked at intersections or in front of a pastry shop, gave looks of defiance
to the police or soldiers patrolling the streets, met in groups of ten, fifteen, or
more; it wouldn't take much, here, either, the world could be turned upside
down. Raouf ran into Gabrielle—they were worried about him in Nahbès, he
should send some news. Raouf replied that if he sent his friends news he would
have to send some to his father, and he didn't want to. He refrained from saying
that he had already been held several hours at a police station.

On the phone Gabrielle told Kathryn that she had seen Raouf and he was
fine. Kathryn went right away to see Rania, and that time it was Rania who was
angry: he was just a kid who didn't send news so he could appear important, to
frighten his father and family. The young widow got even angrier at Ganthier,
who had also left for the capital. He must be throwing fuel on the fire. If he
thinks that's the way to obtain his plot of land, he's mistaken! Kathryn found her
friend's trembling voice when she talked about the colonist bizarre. She almost
asked her why. Rania calmed down, returned to Raouf: You were right, most
men in this country are only little males, spoiled by women who get only what
they deserve. They spend their life at the beck and call of males, and the males
call the docility of those women honor because their own docility, toward for-

eigners, is without honor, little spoiled males . . . She fell silent . . . adding that
they were perhaps finally about to change . . . What she said about little males
reminded Kathryn of what Gabrielle had once confided in her: here women
ruin boys, especially the servant women. For them the male heir is sacred, a
guarantee that the house will survive, that their old age will be assured: I've seen
one kiss the penis of a newborn! . . . Gabrielle had told Kathryn that she wanted
to write a piece about it, but my boss would take out that paragraph. He would
talk about decency. He is capable of adding two lines to a story to describe how
a man condemned to death had to be dragged to the guillotine because he had
uncontrolled reactions, but this story of servants and newborns, he wouldn't
want it. He would look at me strangely, ask me if I had actually witnessed the
scene.

In the capital people were waiting for the spark. They talked about incidents
between the sovereign and France. The crisis also came from the poverty, said
the socialist militants, immediately taken to task by the communists: you talk
about poverty because you don't want to denounce exploitation; you cry about
the results but you don't blame the mechanism. For Raouf the communists
weren't wrong, but even so they took malicious pleasure in isolating themselves
and walking right into a wall. He, himself, couldn't manage to take sides. He
talked about it with Chemla, for whom the struggle would go on for many years:
they had to accept being in the minority, simply bide their time; this country
must first develop its own bourgeoisie.

In *Présence Française* the problem came from Paris, as usual, from the National Assembly, where the deputies of the left, the center, and some of the right
had just voted for a disastrous project, providing for a constitution, fundamental
liberties, and a representative assembly for this country which was absolutely
not a nation, and would not be one for a very long time, "You realize, it's Paris
that lit this fire, the carrot instead of the stick, they are weakening our North
Africa! And all this just when the Germans are signing a treaty with the Russian
Bolsheviks! We are facing a threat to the east, and they create one for us in the
south, not to mention those English bastards who are recognizing Egypt's independence!" Fortunately, there was the lengthy interview with the sovereign in
Le Vigilant, a very influential Parisian daily, and what the sovereign said in *Le
Vigilant* was a rejection of any ill-conceived reform, his horror of communism,
and his love for the protectorate. A nice touch, Marfaing confided to Daintree,
Marfaing's pride allowing his indiscretion, to stress the skill of the colonial authorities. It was the resident general himself who had dictated the responses
to the journalist. Yes, the journalist had indeed met the sovereign, not for very
long: My respects, Your Highness, thank you, Your Highness, good-bye, Your
Highness. The rest was good editing. They had perhaps thrown the *boules* back a

bit far, said Marfaing, because in reading *Le Vigilant* the sovereign had become furious—a corrupt journalist had made a liar out of him—but some nationalists claimed that the sovereign had perhaps not lied that much, he was used to playing both sides, and the sovereign was even more furious that they were making him the enemy of the nationalists, even moderate nationalists, and he decided to abdicate the day before the visit of the president of the French republic, a snub for a snub. And the news spread through the capital, Raouf watching the closure of shops, stoppages in transportation, factories, almost beginning to believe what was happening, the strike extending to the European city, the first marches, the police, insufficient numbers, the resident general bringing two regiments out of their barracks. In the middle of intersections in the old city, men climbed up on crates to improvise speeches.

One morning Raouf surprised himself by going to cheer the sovereign, who was standing on his balcony, a very mixed crowd, university students in theology, dockworkers, shopkeepers, office workers. He was with Karim and David Chemla. Even David had cheered. Raouf joked: "A Bolshevik cheering for the sovereign, now I've seen it all," and David: "Everything that sharpens contradictions is good." Karim had announced to his friends that he had given up his French studies and planned to enroll in the theology school in the capital: "They, at least, are fighting!"

The sovereign abdicated, creating a constitutional void. Paris was shocked by the abdication, the news traveling as far as Nahbès to darken the hours that Si Ahmed spent waiting for a sign from his son, and those of Rania and Kathryn, who wondered if that was going to unleash real riots, with deaths, especially of the young. "He is so clumsy," said the actress to Rania, Rania trying to think in spite of her fears: an abdication is perhaps the best thing that can happen to this country. Things will be clear, a republic, free of all superstitions, like in Turkey, and the colonists will be mere foreign owners if they want to stay. She was sure that Ganthier would stay. That evening the resident general had gone to the sovereign's palace and he had been received by the sovereign in his dressing gown, a sign of contempt. The sovereign had stipulated his conditions: the establishment of plans for a constitution as created by the French deputies—even Monsieur Maurice Barrès and Prince Murat signed off on it! With a legislative assembly, and the same laws as the French had for freedom of expression, association, and gathering! He also insisted that the corrupt and detested ministers be expelled. The resident general had left, told Paris, and agreed to receive a delegation of Prépondérants who had demanded the end of "humanitarian fantasies," Richard Trillat adding: "As for Paris and the National Assembly, we will do what's necessary!"

And the following day, the resident general paid another visit to the sovereign, a resident general with a cocked hat with white feathers this time, escorted by the African infantry, and, proceeding to serious things, suggesting the removal of all the sovereign's conditions, a refusal of his abdication, very simple, if not—no, he couldn't have said *if not*, a resident general from France in a protectorate country doesn't say *if not*, he says, "In the opposite event, with all the respect that I have for Your Highness"—then the country becomes a true colony. Very good "becomes," thought the general secretary of the residence, who was standing behind his superior, not *would become*. You must sense that we are already there, my little sovereign. This country *is becoming* a colony *attached* to Algeria, "and Your Highness will be deported, I did say deported, with your entire family, and not to Provence, we foresee Saint-Pierre-et-Miquelon, Your Highness, yes, a French territory, rather cold, but very calm, if that is the will of the All Powerful, of course," the sovereign giving in within a few hours. Enough false bravado from a weak mind, said the nationalists, a number also beginning to circulate, that of an increase in the sovereign's civil list, the resident general knowing well how to manage money without ever going overboard, the communists then calling for a boycott of the visit by the French president. For David Chemla it was henceforth "class against class." And Raouf: "You mean clay pot against iron pot?"

Some nationalists also wanted to boycott, as did the Bolsheviks: a quick meeting between the resident general and their leaders, and an equally rapid decision made by the nationalists, calling for participation in the general goodwill, an end to false nationalist defiance. The crown prince had responded, "They're caving in less than a day after my father did." "To convince my natives," said the resident general, "I tell them the story of the Greek man whose hands became stuck in the trunk of a tree that he wanted to open . . ." There were, however, voices in France bringing up the English example in Egypt: what we have refused today will be imposed on us tomorrow. The Prépondérants had won. Law and order reigned once again. The crowds disappeared from the streets. They had sent out the municipal hoses, and the nationalists were rendered "speechless," said the editorialists, using the phrase suggested by the residence. Some even demanded the reestablishment of the *crime of seditious whispering*, which existed here before we arrived, you know. And in *Présence Française* Richard Trillat demanded they go on the offensive "against the worst trouble-makers, those upon whom we made the mistake of bestowing our education! They should be on their knees, in a posture of the most complete humility, thanking us, instead of rebelling." Raouf, back in Nahbès, said to Rania: "I didn't believe in it, it couldn't have gone very far, notables don't like street fighting."

18

BIG PROBLEMS

The Americans went home at the end of October. They had promised to return in six months, to finish filming and perhaps even to start working on another film. In the European city, the rhythm of life had abruptly slowed down. This departure simplified the life of the authorities, and Marfaing wasn't sorry that Cavarro had packed his bags, even if Thérèse's sad mood annoyed him a bit, good riddance. The contrôleur civil had also said to Ganthier and Gabrielle that he found young Raouf quite serene for someone who had just lost the love of his life. Ganthier corrected him. Raouf had had his moment of great passion, of course, at the beginning, but Kathryn had put him in his place. He didn't tell me anything specific, but he turned into an escort, a nice role. Everyone found a use for him, including Neil, who used him to keep any real gallants away. Gabrielle didn't add much to what Ganthier had said. She had made a reflection about young people who prefer great ideas to warm skin and had informed her friends that she was leaving the country, yes, a big story on what was going on in Italy, lots of things to see, "even if I don't like that Mussolini."

In Nahbès they were still talking about what had happened to Belkhodja, a real blow from destiny, they said so as not to poison the story, but the term "the donkey of God" had circulated widely.

Belkhodja understood perfectly the role Raouf had played in all of that. He hadn't said anything but set out to find something that could really destroy the son of a caïd. In Nahbès too many people said that the merchant had slapped himself with his own hand, and they wouldn't have let him go very far in his vengeance. The demonstrations that had taken place in the capital had given him an idea. He waited for the return to calm, Raouf's reappearance in Nahbès, and then he took the train. Once in the capital, he sold a lot of rugs, refreshed his wardrobe, and one afternoon, he went to avenue Gambetta, to ponder scruples under the chirping of sparrows in the plane trees, seeking to establish, *ennya bennya*, intention against intention, the truth of his soul. He was going to indulge in vengeance. He was going to kiss a snake on the mouth and replace his lost pleasures with those of a bitter and dark fruit, but what was essential was to put the devilry of that passion to the service of good, by no longer crying about his unhappiness, the one who cries only steals his own time, and the hour was coming . . . A vigorous *bismillah* had finally given him the strength to open the door in a building occupied by some Frenchmen who were more discreet than others, who said "monsieur" and treated the natives with respect, but who knew how to hold them on a lifelong leash much better than any brute with a club could have done. He had a long discussion with them. At one point one of the men opened one of the cabinets that covered the walls, and Belkhodja saw a lot of small boxes, each with a capital letter on it. As he was leaving, the police thanked him and told him that the young subversive he had informed them about would be put out of commission for some time.

A few days later, in Nahbès, the contrôleur civil summoned Si Ahmed for a meeting at the end of which the caïd found himself even more attached to the French than he had ever been before, and obliged to act as quickly as possible to avoid great problems for a son who criticized him for being too connected to France, a son who immediately refused to do what had been foreseen for him, whereas in good families a son would always respond, yes, *na'am a sidi*, then he would kiss his father's hand and leave, with the freedom to go swallow his despair in one of the windowless rooms of the house. Except now, Raouf, an only child, had his *bac* and—the caïd knew this—did not have much respect for his father. Youth dreams of justice, honesty, freedom, equality, independence, rights, and it was one of the disadvantages of the French *lycée* and of certain Arab books that they made that youth want to freely respect estimable people.

In the past few years, the father had really tried to make his son understand that though he might not incarnate all those lovely ideas, that didn't mean he was absolutely corrupt. He received gifts, of course, but just what was necessary for the people who were above him to consider him a caïd of confidence, and not a puritan. The puritans were a threat to the balance of the country, and like the Spahis in full dress at the entrance of the caïdat, corruption was one of the attributes of the function, that's all, and then, as the adage says, "Power corrupts, but there have to be people to govern." Things almost took a turn for the worse when Raouf, in response to that paternal adage, had cited another, more popular one, "What the peasant harvests in a day" . . . his father himself completed it . . . "the caïd collects at night," and he had added: "You're going too far!" His voice was cold, that of a man who was giving up his right to anger because he had already gone too far for that, in a time when one loves nothing anymore, not because one has been disappointed but because those who should love you no longer do.

Raouf had said he was sorry, but his father tried not to find himself alone with him. That had made them unhappy, because they could no longer talk about what connected them, Jahiz, Ibn Khaldun, the authors that Si Ahmed advised

Raouf to read, and his dear Ibn Hazm, the Cordovan, which he had given to Raouf when he had told him of his enthusiasm for La Bruyère and La Rochefoucauld. And yet the caïd wasn't trying to remove the ideas that distanced them from the head of his sole heir. He had always behaved in a specific way with him, from the very beginning, a wife dead in childbirth, a newborn who shrieked in the parlor. He had taken the infant in his arms. He had swung his watch in front of him. He wanted to calm him, to get him used to the world, and he had the feeling, many years later, that he had always done that.

What had made the caïd's life even more difficult was that Raouf, when he was becoming an adolescent, looked for adversaries greater than his father, and he had quickly found them, speaking with growing violence against colonialism, domination, iniquity, hypocrisy, exploitation. He had read *Le Pays martyrisé*, had had the pamphlet read by those around him, and made pronouncements against the religious notables, "accomplices in all this for centuries." Si Ahmed did not, however, feel any animosity toward what his son was becoming, and he found consolation in saying to himself that no season is forced to respect the preceding one.

In response to his father's plan, Raouf repeated: "No! . . . Europe with Ganthier, no! If I leave, I leave alone! Or I'll go to prison, that shapes you as much as travel." The caïd sought the words, an appeal to reflection. Youth is happy when people think they can reflect. He offered Raouf a paradox to mull: "You will be much freer than if you were alone." He also knew that a strange relationship had formed over the years between Raouf and the colonist, like a fable, the fox and the wolf. They hate each other yet seek each other out. They like to talk together, compete for the best words. The wolf helps the fox become an adult so he can take advantage of his talents, use his strength and his wile on a fox who begins to develop his own, and the fox knows that it will be in his confrontation with the wolf, and not through respect for patriarchal rules, that he will invent his future life.

The day before, in Marfaing's office, Si Ahmed had spoken with Ganthier, calling him "my old friend." He had told him that since his success with the *baccalauréat* his son had been hanging around the Americans too much. He hadn't gone to the university and had probably begun to drink. Not only was the boy separating himself from religion and principles—you can always return to them, God knows how to be generous with the repentant—but he was also separating himself from the real world, which doesn't wait and never pardons. The caïd wanted Raouf to travel in the real world, and not the one you think you see in *Le Figaro* or *L'Illustration*. His son needed to go take some big knocks from the real world, and since Ganthier, his old friend, was planning a trip to France soon, would he agree to take Raouf with him?

Ganthier listened. "Old friend," it was a strange expression after all those years of venomous confrontation between them. He didn't respond directly to the caïd. He stressed how short his coming trip would be. He started talking about his own business, his farm. It is difficult to be gone a long time when you have a lot of acres to oversee, the eye of the master . . . And he reminded Si Ahmed that he was above all *a colonist*, wanting him to swallow the entire past all at once: border disputes, the seizing of land, all the squabbles, Si Ahmed's opposition to the extension of Ganthier's land, the pretext that they belonged to such and such a tribe, that they had such and such a religious or communal status, the caïd's leitmotif, "The colonists don't have all the rights, after all!" Ganthier had responded that the land wasn't worked, or very little, that he was going to make it yield like never before, that he would give work and bread to people who didn't have any, the caïd saying that for every franc given to his workers, Ganthier put fifteen in his pocket, Ganthier succeeding in his profits at the price of a baksheesh strongly negotiated with the caïd, and the bonuses paid to his own workers. "With an ordinary corrupt person," said Ganthier, "things would be easier, but that one also wants to improve the fate of humanity, that doubles the cost . . ." Yes, Ganthier took great pleasure in saying the word *colonist*.

Si Ahmed ignored the provocation. He even admitted that he recognized the weight of Ganthier's duties, but it was already winter; Ganthier wouldn't have any obstacles to prolonging his stay; and he, in the meantime, would go to Ganthier's land every Sunday with Monsieur Marfaing when he would agree to do him the honor of accompanying him. The contrôleur civil immediately picked up the caïd's words: "The honor will be all mine," and Ganthier understood that the caïd would offer nothing more, *He swallowed all my sarcasm, he will not lower himself to recall that France indeed owes him that.* Colonist or not, Si Ahmed treated Ganthier like a vassal, a great vassal to whom he was conferring his only son, but a vassal nonetheless, and he asked Ganthier to act as if the protectorate didn't exist, all of that in the office of Marfaing, the master of the region, and Marfaing, instead of remaining at least neutral, punctuated the caïd's words with a slight nodding of his head. He could have at least said, "The honor *would be* all mine."

It was warm. The large armchairs with carved feet were comfortable and clean, the coffee quite strong, but without too many grounds, the makroud fresh and crispy, the flies nonexistent, three men discussing calmly. What bothered Ganthier was the caïd's assurance, *He knows why I'm making this trip and that there is a good chance that I'll prolong it, who told him that? Marfaing? Marfaing always knows everything, it's his profession to know everything to the last piece of gossip.*

Si Ahmed continued to speak, hesitating as if he didn't know what he was going to say. He was a bit unclear, but at the third allusion Ganthier had understood: the caïd had high hopes that while Ganthier was away he could persuade a certain person to settle the matter between her and the colonist. The land doesn't like to be divided, does it? Ganthier realized that this issue of regrouping his land wasn't all that important to him anymore. He had even become used to spending two or three times a week, on horseback, on the path that went through the young widow's estate. He would see her in the distance, on her veranda, thinking that she was watching him. Si Ahmed continued: It would be a pleasure for him to know that Ganthier would be showing France to his son, and not only France, they could even go to Germany . . . Ganthier had reacted: *the Boches?* He had fought them for four years, he didn't understand the interest that those people awakened in the younger generation, and the caïd responded that what one didn't show to the young, they turned into a mirage. It was at that moment that Ganthier realized that he was trapped: by quibbling over Germany, he seemed to have given his agreement for the rest.

Before the caïd had arrived, the contrôleur civil had told Ganthier that Si Ahmed wanted to ask him something important—it was political—and France needed men like the caïd. Yes, it was Ganthier whom he had chosen for a confidential mission, yes, a colonist, and even the most reactionary in the region, he, and not one of the lovely socializing or Christianizing souls that hopped around the good natives whom they invented in their minds. Si Ahmed was not particularly sincere in what he called his friendship with France, but he wasn't a dreamer, and he thought that a move one inch to the left of his sovereign meant communism. He honored Ganthier and Marfaing with his confidence. He was preparing the future. He was giving them his only son to enlighten, "and you know, my dear Ganthier, that at this moment it would be better for young Raouf to go on a little trip. The police want to lock him up. The resident general is hesitating. I can still protect him, but he needs to make himself scarce, unless you prefer seeing him behind bars for some time."

Marfaing seemed to be enjoying himself. He knew that Ganthier would not endure the thought of seeing Raouf in prison, and Ganthier knew that if Marfaing had chosen him it was because his connections with the military enabled him to protect Raouf. And there was something else, the expression Marfaing used, "give us his son to enlighten." Ganthier and Marfaing belonged to the same Masonic fraternity, and in places higher up than theirs Raouf was probably considered a recruit for the future . . . Ganthier concluded by thanking Si Ahmed for doing him this honor, which he accepted as very high testimony to their old friendship, and while Si Ahmed was bowing once more with affection, the colonist for a fleeting solitary moment saw Gabrielle's Cheshire Cat smile floating in Marfaing's office. After all, young Raouf was an excellent reason to go to Paris. Ganthier wouldn't seem to be going there to chase after a woman who chose to wear trousers and still wanted nothing to do with him. He smiled, and the two men smiled at him.

As they were leaving, Marfaing said to Ganthier: "I'll take care of Kid . . ." Kid was an authoritarian and affectionate dachshund, Ganthier's hunting companion. Si Ahmed had continued to talk to the colonist while they were walking into the large hall of the contrôleur civil's residence: The youth of today frightened him, their contempt for their elders . . . an intoxication for learning . . . atheism . . . Could Ganthier remind his son to do his prayers over there? And may God be with Ganthier! An anxious Si Ahmed, paternal and pious, who squeezed Ganthier's arm: one might have forgotten his reputation for Machiavellianism and his penchant for strong alcohol. Ganthier suddenly wondered if Raouf would actually agree to go, and he realized that in a very short time he had actually taken to this arrangement. Gabrielle really liked Raouf. She loved giving him advice. Ganthier already saw himself in Paris with the young man as a protégé, a lovely trio, he had to be sure, especially since Raouf was as stubborn as a mule! As Ganthier was saying good-bye Si Ahmed admitted that his son might be a bit hesitant. He also wanted to go to Turkey: "That's what worries me the most, you understand, dear old friend, the bad example, so close . . . Those people, those Turkish officers, they are our distant family, today they unleash passions, and passions are daughters of death. Do you know what they found in one of my secretaries' desk? No, not the *Communist Manifesto*, and I'm counting on France to deal with the communists. No, they found the speeches of Atatürk, translated into Arabic. They're all looking for news from Turkey. There's a photo that is circulating now, the entrance to a village in Anatolia, a military blockade: when the peasants arrive they must exchange their turban of a believer for a Western-style cap, and at the same time they are shown what has been constructed in a ditch, a gallows . . . Do you want us to do that here? With an agrarian reform?" Ganthier laughed, and he began to look forward to having one of those discussions with Raouf during which each of them tried to paralyze the other, a discussion that would take them late into the night. He was already thinking of the argument he would use to convince him: "You don't want to go see how they create the world that is dominating you?"

Part II

THE GREAT VOYAGE:
WINTER 1922–SPRING 1923

19

THE *JUGURTHA*

At the harbor, looking up at the massive ship, their necks began to ache. Ganthier said:

"The *Jugurtha*, eighty feet high to the top of its funnel, four hundred thirty feet long, seven thousand tons, a lovely lady."

Then there were the usual arguments with porters, at the ticket window, passports, the swaying gangway, the warning horn, the passengers pressing at the poop deck for the farewell ceremony, and children still waving their arms as the dock became a thin line against the light in the distance.

Well before anyone else, Raouf gave the crowd a look that he decided would be his last, and went to stand on the bow, alone, waiting for the ship to be out to sea. Then finally he was looking at the open water, the last sounds of the horn increasing his impatience. His hands quickly became cold on the guardrail. He breathed in deeply, becoming dizzy in the finally open expanse, one that was completely different from that of the sand that his father had crossed in his youth, a parched expanse that opened up only onto increasingly poor oases, and when he arrived on the other side the towns were much poorer than Nahbès, an exhausting journey through sand and stones to arrive in a stunted land. "When God created the desert, he was so happy with the result that he threw stones into it," said Si Ahmed, who never understood the enthusiasm of Westerners for a journey that led to only one desire, that of returning home as soon as possible; whereas here, on the bow of the *Jugurtha*, beyond the waves Raouf was contemplating, there were wonderful cities for him to discover. And each time the bow fell from a wave he felt the violence of the energy that was carrying him to a world where true revolutions were still being prepared.

After a while he went back inside to warm up, noticing in passing someone who must have been watching him from behind a window in the salon, a young girl, dressed in clothing the colors of which he had never seen before: a dark green skirt, the color of a forest, with dots of cool red on it. As he passed by, she held his gaze, her eyes very light, transparent, brown hair under a beret . . . He nodded to her, a friendly gesture. Everything happened very quickly. He didn't even have time to note the exact color of her eyes.

He went back to his cabin and opened his suitcases so the steward could put everything away. The man was old, stiff, efficient. The drawers and cupboards smelled like furniture polish, lavender, and the bathroom like bleach and orange blossom. The walls were paneled with red wood, almost pink, and the copper of the doorknobs and the rims of the portholes reflected the slightest ray of light. Ganthier and Raouf both had first-class cabins, the caïd sparing no expense for his son. Marfaing had said to Ganthier: "Our dear Si Ahmed wouldn't have insulted you by offering to pay you for this, would he?" Of course not, and Ganthier would never have accepted. But two days before his departure he was offered thirty magnificent cows. "From Holland, but resilient, born in the country," said the vendor, who asked for scarcely two-thirds of what they were worth. Ganthier had understood, he refused. The man added: "If you don't accept I'll sell them to Pagnon." Ganthier accepted.

Raouf was one of the rare Maghrebis onboard to travel in first class, and the only one who wasn't wearing a djellaba. Other passengers looked at him like a curiosity: a native dressed European style is someone who isn't playing the game.

"Your compatriots aren't happy that I'm in a gray suit," he said to Ganthier, "They're friendlier to the two old men in burnooses. I even heard a woman say that she found them more handsome *in those* than in Western-style dress." Ganthier responded:

"The French don't like to be imitated."

"It's more that they don't like anyone to catch up with them."

"It's not a question of imitation or of catching up . . . They feel that you won't want them anymore."

"What's funny," said Raouf, "is that you can't stand it when they look down on me. Because I am one of your pieces of luggage?"

Raouf had promised himself never to appear gauche, but the first evening he arrived too early at the dining room. A pleasant and respectful maître d' seated him at a small table with a view onto the entrance to the kitchen. Ganthier arrived fifteen minutes later. He looked around for Raouf. The maître d' seated them at one of the bay windows looking out at the sea, at a table from which they could also see the entire dining room. When they were having dessert the captain came over to join them at their table. The conversation moved onto the port of calls where the ship would be stopping.

"I don't understand how French ships will facilitate our relations with Spain or Italy," Ganthier said, "and what's more, it makes the journey longer."

"Yes, but the direct route doesn't bring in enough money," the captain replied.

Raouf knew that some French people wanted to open the doors of the Maghreb to millions of Spaniards, Italians, and Maltese to increase the population and thereby achieve true colonization. Ganthier was against that, even though such a large number of Catholic immigrants should have pleased the former seminarian in him. Raouf refrained from mentioning that.

The second day, on the promenade deck, they encountered a group of four women, very flashily dressed, noisy. They spoke to everyone, and everyone spoke to them, but no one lingered with them.

"They are beautiful, decked out, lively, would you like me to introduce you?" Ganthier asked.

He had seen that those women had noticed Raouf and that irritated him.

"You think I'm incapable of recognizing coquettes?" Raouf said, "Your beautiful ladies are returning home after a stay at the court of my dear sovereign."

"Do you want one? I'm sure they would do it uniquely for the pleasure."

"No, thank you," Raouf replied, "but if you want to buy some ready-made love, you can count on my discretion."

Raouf had become friendly with a different female passenger, an Austrian girl his age. She was traveling with her parents; the father manufactured and sold windmills and electric motors throughout the world. Her name was Metilda. She was the one he had noticed behind the windows of the salon the day of their departure. She often played badminton on the deck. She was the best. Unlike many of her adversaries she was not hindered by excess weight; she ran and jumped gracefully. Since she won all of her matches, she played more often than others, until a young French girl, who was eliminated, refused to let her step in. The girl shouted: "This is a French boat. The Boches will have to wait!" The father of the young Austrian girl, looking upset, called her over to him.

Metilda later said to Raouf:

"My father is angry with me for putting myself in a bad situation."

"What is a bad situation? When you're right?"

"No, my father taught me a long time ago, it's a situation that you can't defend. I mustn't forget that I belong to a country that has been defeated."

"You're talking like my own father, but your country isn't occupied, you can live there peacefully."

"That depends. We also have to be careful at home. We're Jews, we are considered responsible."

"For the war?"

"No, for the peace, the conditions for the peace, like in Germany, the end of the empire, the end of the Habsburgs, *la fin des haricots*—the end of everything, as the French say . . ."

She smiled, then:

"Abroad I'm a Boche, at home I'm a mongrel."

"You speak French very well."

"For us it was the language of novels, poetry, free ideas, sensations. We said that German was for the barracks and bureaucrats, which isn't true, and today it's French that has become a language of the *diktat* . . . No, I'm not being fair, it's something else . . . Do you know Heine? Trakl? Georg Trakl, a poet who died during the war, I have a collection with me, his poetry is very beautiful, I'll lend it to you, *umschlingen schmächtig sich . . .*"

"They didn't teach us much about German literature at the lycée," Raouf interrupted, very happy to be talking about the lycée in the past tense, "but I'll read your poets, if you promise to read mine . . . and if you have translations." Metilda regretted her thoughtlessness: "*Umschlingen schmächtig sich die sehnenden Arme* . . . delicately the avid arms entangle . . . I'll translate them for you myself." Her eyes were very pale blue.

Later, Raouf gave her a translation of *The Muallaqaat*. He had added a poem that he had copied by hand:

"That's a French poem, the author isn't well known. It's very modern, 'May, lovely May floating on the Rhine' . . . It's more difficult than the others to learn. It's by Guillaume Apollinaire. He's dead, like your Trakl, wounded in the war, then flu." Metilda folded the sheet of paper and asked Raouf to recite the poem. When Raouf had finished she promised to learn the poem by heart, too:

"That way we'll be able to recite it together."

She had already remembered two verses, "The petals fallen from the cherry trees in May / Are the fingernails of the one I loved so much." She also talked about the voyage she had just taken:

"Mother made Father visit the old Jewish quarters in each city, and she told him, 'We should help them, but they must understand that they have nothing in common with us.'"

Raouf kept a remark on class prejudice to himself. Metilda also asked him why his friend Ganthier sometimes seemed sad.

"He's just a bit melancholic," Raouf said, "He left his dog, Kid, at home, and he's sorry he did. It's a dachshund, but takes up just as much space as a big dog."

"Does he love it a lot?"

"He says it's all that he brought back from the war, a gift from his men, but he will never admit that he loves it, he thinks that would be inappropriate, but I love Kid. He's a colonist's dog, but he doesn't bark at Arabs."

One morning, on the bow of the boat, Metilda looked Raouf in the eyes:

"I'd like to do what one of my cousins did, go to Palestine."

"I think we might fight about Palestine," Raouf said, coldly.

"Okay, let's talk about something else."

But Raouf smiled and Metilda added:

"Monsieur Ganthier told me that you know Francis Cavarro, and Neil Daintree. Have you really spoken to them?"

"Yes, and they have spoken to me, surprising, right?"

"You're mean . . . You're twisting what I say . . . I'm going to be self-conscious."

"I didn't intend to be mean, it's more of a reflex."

Raouf pointed out the horizon behind the boat:

"Back there I'm often forced to respond with bitterness, and where I'm going it will be the same, but I'm sorry I spoke to you like that. You're not the same, you're like my American friends. They ask me to really talk to them, and not just about rugs and palm trees."

"What about your school friends?"

"I have French friends, but I sense that when they're all together they speak differently. You're not the same."

Metilda smiled, she relaxed. Raouf also smiled, and continued:

"Admit that you shouldn't have brought up Palestine."

"Do you often do that?"

"What?"

"Let down your guard, smile kindly, but still go on the attack?"

"Can we make peace?"

"Okay, but for good this time, okay?"

She took his arm, and they began to stroll. Without looking at him Metilda said:

"Do you realize that we've just had our first fight?"

The weather was mild for the month of December. They ran into Ganthier and the captain.

"I don't like this temperature," the captain said, "Fifteen degrees down here, whereas up there (he pointed at the sky) it must be at least minus forty . . . We could be in for some trouble."

Raouf and Metilda began talking about a subject of great interest to many young people throughout the world: they began talking about movies. They argued, Metilda saying that Americans were too simple. Raouf defended them. He told her about Daintree; she had only seen *The Four Horsemen of the Apocalypse*. She knew a lot about German film, which Raouf knew nothing about, and she sometimes voiced harsh criticism—she said that film was three steps behind opera. She said that on purpose because Raouf had never seen an opera; then she regretted it and told him what she knew about the revolution in Vienna in 1918.

They were the same age, but she knew more. She smiled at him often, and in the evening, during their strolls, her voice filled with emotion.

"I love Stendhal," she said, "the quest for happiness . . ."

"I've read him . . . the little individual goals . . . I don't attempt to be happier than anyone else."

"Are you always so snide, so morally superior?"

He just looked at her, trying to seem friendly in spite of his refusal to say anything more. She pointed out a couple that had just met on the ship:

"You see, yesterday, during their first walk together they were hesitant; this afternoon they look like they've been together for years, and they're having more fun."

She invited him to have some tea:

"It wouldn't be appropriate for me to go to your cabin, but you can come to ours."

"Your parents are very open-minded."

"They want to be absolutely modern. Father would be horrified to be considered some sort of rabbi. He speaks Yiddish very well, but he hides it. He's very proud of his German and his French, and his atheism."

She had Raouf sit next to her, patted him once or twice on the shoulder, placed her hand on his forearm. Raouf didn't resist, but he didn't do anything. He became completely passive; he didn't even blush, nor did he seem to be shy. He perked up when they spoke of books and films, as if he were with an old friend. She had never had that feeling of complete equality with a boy before. Her Austrian friends also treated her as an equal, but she felt that the ones who were more in love already imagined her nursing a baby or giving orders to a servant. That wasn't the case with Raouf; he didn't see her as a housewife. Nor as a lover. She was a friend. She tried to find out if he had known other women, but he didn't talk about it, implied that there had been others, saying: "I really have a lot of other things on my mind."

He was a very pleasant traveling companion. He refused to play badminton because he didn't want to learn how, but he watched Metilda win while holding the towel that she used to wipe her face at regular intervals. As for what others thought, it was obvious: the young man who was holding a young lady's towel, damp with perspiration, could only be her lover. One of the mothers, with a large chignon, who was watching the young girls said of the couple: "Birds of a feather . . ."

Metilda was mad at herself for having made advances. She was even madder at Raouf for not responding. But he wasn't being coy; he simply wasn't doing anything. She wondered why. She finally concluded that she was dealing with a tormented soul, like the ones that one of her Viennese girlfriends had described to her, one of those young men who become so attached to their bad habits that they become melancholy and incapable of escaping that melancholy, which sends them right back to their bad habits, which then feed that melancholy; they suffer, but are incapable of changing. She had mentioned this in veiled terms to Ganthier, who had understood, and confirmed her fears, in veiled terms. Raouf was not an easy young man, yes, he had an American woman friend:

"I think he was in love with her in the beginning . . . It was rather literary, a way to experience what he read in novels and poetry, but the American woman was older, she turned him into her good friend. Yes, she went back at the end of October. He doesn't seem to be suffering very much, and there is another woman, a cousin, a widow, a *bas bleu*—do you know what that is?"

"Yes, that's what you call women who read books?"

Ganthier apologized. To continue the conversation he had brought up that other woman, the head of a large farm, an exception! A cultivated, energetic, stubborn woman! Ganthier surprised himself in singing Rania's praises . . . *And here I am talking to a Boche* . . . Metilda didn't resemble anything that he was familiar with or expected to find, there was something very free about her, a younger Gabrielle, but without provocation, who spoke to him as an equal, apparently without effort, without needing a purse that she could hold in her hands, which she sometimes put in her jacket pockets like a boy, but different from Kathryn, calmer, no doubt having had to fight much less than the American woman did. Ganthier also understood that Metilda suspected something other than just bad habits, and he disabused her. Raouf really was interested in women, but it would take him some time to become comfortable with them.

On their last night on board Metilda decided not to be appropriate, and she knocked on Raouf's door. Surprised, he asked her in, and for the first time he blushed. She had worn her boldest top, a rectangular neckline. He was in his dressing gown. They began by talking, then Metilda claimed to feel ill and asked to lie down a moment. She wasn't really ill, of course, but then the sea suddenly became very choppy, and she quickly did become nauseous. Storms in the Mediterranean are violent, Ganthier said later when he ran into Raouf in the passageway holding a yellowish Metilda, a towel at her mouth. She wanted to breathe as much fresh air as possible. The wind had picked up; the captain had forbidden access to the deck. From behind the windows of the salon, in the flashes of lightning, they saw the bow of the *Jugurtha* dive into the ever-higher lead gray waves.

"They're at least thirty feet high," said Metilda.

"Not as tall as that," said Ganthier, "but even so . . ."

When they arrived the next morning the two young people promised to write. Ganthier never really knew what had happened between them, and as she was shaking his hand Metilda said: "See you soon, perhaps . . ."

20

NIGHTS OF DREAMS

In Nahbès, before Raouf's departure, and by making even more promises to Marfaing, Si Ahmed had finally obtained the name of the one who had slandered his son. Yes, slander, that was the interpretation the contrôleur civil had given in his response to the letter from the general residence of France on the subject of young Raouf: slander, jealousy, a rather hot-headed young man, granted, but he reads and cites Pascal, Montesquieu, Balzac, had the best results on the *bac*. Youth rebels only against itself. They're basically good, if you know how to deal with them, and Marfaing knew how to deal with them.

The day after his negotiations with the contrôleur civil, the caïd had had another conversation, this one with Jacob Bensoussan, a very respected man in the world of loans in Nahbès and throughout the region, and Jacob Bensoussan had very happily agreed to Si Ahmed's request, as they had been friends for forty years. Then Si Ahmed had accompanied his son to the Nahbès train station. On the platform, he placed a white cardboard box in Raouf's hands: baklavas. Raouf said:

"I'm not ten years old anymore!"

"You're eighteen, and you've become hardened."

It was awkward. The caïd knew that Raouf knew the adage, "When you're hardened you can be broken." Before boarding the train Raouf kissed his father's hand, which didn't please Si Ahmed: Raouf thought he was feeling an emotion that he didn't want to feel. The train had started to move; smoke and sparks billowed out onto the palm trees around the station, and then it disappeared. The caïd had wanted to say, "I'm here, I'll keep watch."

Once his son had left, Si Ahmed did not seek out Belkhodja—absolutely not, that would have given credence to the slander. He had preferred to allow the merchant to carry on his business as he saw fit. Belkhodja, to survive his shameful marriage, increased his trips to the capital, spending lots of money on expensive things. Some criticized these new ways of a man whom up to then they thought was pious and said that the clothing of a good man is prayer. But for most of those who talked about him, Belkhodja's new vest, discreetly embroidered with gold thread, his immaculate jebba, his babouches of the best calf leather, changed at least twice a day, his extra-fine English socks, his elegant mustache, trimmed by a barber who visited him every morning, his silver cigarette case, his gold watch, and all his elegant ways, especially his calm, which separated him from all material urgency but left him full of attention for the requests of his clients—all of that was for business, an elegance of a great merchant, necessary for someone who had to stay in the capital frequently. A great merchant couldn't dress just any old way, eat just anything, sleep anywhere; he needed a style that mirrored the level of his business, business that brought him increasingly into contact with foreigners of quality: the French, of course, but also Italians, Egyptians, English, even Germans. Belkhodja was proud to send his rugs all over the world.

In Nahbès, elegance didn't cost that much, but with the money spent on a meal in an elegant restaurant in the capital one could live for a week in the provinces. Belkhodja was ashamed of his extravagance; he said that those expenses helped him in his trade. He wasn't wrong: that way of life put him within reach of very good opportunities, and he was able to grasp a few of them. In the evening, after meals with his buyers, there were also nightclubs—the Sphinx, the Miramar—the cost of champagne, and the bills that one slipped into the scanty bottoms of the belly dancers, quite an art, a gesture of discreet elegance but one that the other guests must notice in order to have an idea of the extent of Belkhodja's means. And after the cabaret, there were card games, the art of losing with good humor or of plunging back into risk after winning. Belkhodja's clients came and went, but Belkhodja was always there, every night. After midnight, there was also the white powder, a bit expensive to buy, but so much more effective than the kif pipe for staying lucid and agile. Granted, none of that was a sign of great piety, but Belkhodja felt that the unfair blow he had been dealt in his marriage earned him the right to the sins that he might henceforth commit. He dressed well, spent his money, sometimes told himself he was spending badly, like a donkey that scatters its barley, but his new accounting promised large profits. Belkhodja often went from one column to the other and paid himself in advance.

There was no one to voice a warning, even among his friends at La Porte du Sud. Almost no one in Nahbès knew about the debauchery that was being given free rein in the capital, hundreds of miles away, and those who did know said to themselves that the merchant had found in debauchery a means to soothe a soul prey to the violence of shame and hatred. Belkhodja could have pulled himself out of it, by controlling his expenses and not playing cards so often. What was most surprising was that he was not possessed by the demon of gambling; that was for the weak, and even the white powder for him was only something extra that helped him to see better in card games and business. It was also true that at the suggestion of the receptionist at the Excelsior Hotel, a Frenchman who greeted Belkhodja the way a European never would have done in Nahbès, at the suggestion of this receptionist—Monsieur Michel—Belkhodja sometimes requested a second pillow, to sleep better, a second pillow that the chambermaids, in the morning, among themselves, called a doormat to a brothel, a Russian or Italian pillow, of a very expensive blond; but Belkhodja didn't abuse that either because he came back most often to sleep at hours when even that type of creature must be taking a well-deserved break. All of that was basically very pleasant extras, but never essential. The proof was that he very easily did without all of it when he returned to Nahbès, though he returned less and less frequently, that was true.

And so Belkhodja had absolutely no reason to stop. He, himself, facing his conscience, recognized his sins, but he wasn't a slave to them, and the remorse he experienced even gave his prayers—he still did them at least once a day—the bit of guilt that went well with good piety. But the one thing Belkhodja could not do without, the thing he anticipated at the beginning of the afternoon when he was in the capital, a true drug, which turned him into a man outside of himself, an eater of time, was the night. Belkhodja had begun to love the night, and instead of going to sleep while devising plans as a diligent merchant would do, he plunged into the night, not that of Nahbès, which nevertheless had a few places suitable for causing a good man to err; no, the night to which Belkhodja was addicted was the night in the capital. And that passion for the night did not come from the vilest of what the night can offer, when the sky is veiled with black and bodies undress. If the night had been only gambling dens and brothels Belkhodja would have ultimately rejected it and, in disgust, fear, or fatigue, would have quickly returned south, to backgammon and fig alcohol. No, his passion had begun with aspects of the night that were more recommendable, the coolness of night, the depth of night, the night that awaits you when you leave a place of debauchery at three in the morning, as if the debauchery had been only a pretext for rediscovering the immaculate face of the night, the abysses of shadow and stars into which you could plunge while walking, with the clarity of one who is no longer tired, the night in which huge dreams could be dreamt, when you are the last human being to resist sleep, which you can face with all the strength of your imagination, when you dare, and it repays you by inspiring dreams that are far richer than those it grants to reasonable people who have ultimately fallen asleep.

Belkhodja loved those dreams at the end of the night above all else, dreams he savored while walking in the silence of the capital, dreams whose realization was held only by a thread, great deals that led him from the sale of rugs to owning a boat, then a real ship, then two, Belkhodja going from a merchant to a shipowner in a few dreams on the background of Ursa Major, Capricorn, and clouds. Like the French he launched his ships throughout the Mediterranean, and to enhance his dreams he walked toward the smells of the docks, the sound of the waves, or he returned to the center of the city, constructed the headquarters of his maritime company right on avenue Gambetta. He inaugurated it in the presence of all the authorities of the country. He invested in the farming of his native region, became one of the Mediterranean lords of olive oil. He didn't really like that oil, but knew that it could become liquid gold. He also bought a newspaper. He became its soul, defined great politics, took a plane, and with each of the great stages of his dreams he also had a new mosque built.

He walked in the night with great strides, to the point of exhaustion, and went to sleep in the morning, drunk on his dreams, and when he set off at the beginning of the afternoon to resume his activities as a merchant he had a tendency to be increasingly patronizing with people who were never at the level of his dreams. He took care of business, had dinner, and at the end of his dinner hurried to the cabaret, then to the best gambling dens. He ate, smoked, and gambled to accelerate the passing of time, impatient for the hour when he could leave, his head empty, to walk in the deserted night when you can talk to yourself because there are no passersby to think you are crazy . . . to launch his boldest activities at the moment when all others are interrupted . . . to have his successes file before his wide-open eyes, in the cool night air. And in order to plunge into his best dreams, those of a feverish night wanderer, he needed the expenses of the preceding hours to have put him into a state close to panic; he saw his capital dry up, he saw the time come when his shoes would be worth more than he, but he needed his dreams more and more, and never dreamt of grandeur better than when he thought he was on the edge of the abyss.

To maintain his lifestyle and his frequent trips to the capital, Belkhodja the lender began to borrow increasingly large sums. It was no longer a question of obtaining rugs from the starving Bedouins; the hunger had come over to his side, the hunger for dreams, and for the elegant life he had to lead to imagine what could be dreamt, and the debt that shocks you and launches you back passionately into the dream. One day, Jacob Bensoussan, his usual lender, gave him a veiled warning. He said to him: "When the party is over all that's left is the dirty linen," and shortly afterward for the first time he refused to help. It was from that moment that Belkhodja began to have serious difficulties. For a time his French police friends were able to calm his creditors in the capital, but his situation worsened; he absolutely needed money that Jacob Bensoussan now refused to sell him, while even demanding the reimbursement of what he already owed. In Nahbès people still didn't know a lot about Belkhodja's situation, but they quickly heard about Bensoussan's strange refusal. In the capital, too, the other lenders avoided him; Belkhodja had become their nightmare. The downward spiral accelerated in a few weeks and the merchant ended up going back to his house in Nahbès, where two or three relatives could at least feed him and help him save face. He no longer had any dreams; he had only one prospect, that of dishonorable ruin. And Si Ahmed watched all of that from afar.

One Friday as he was leaving the mosque, Belkhodja ran into the caïd. He feared the encounter, but Si Ahmed, unlike many people, greeted him kindly, even said comforting things to him that showed he was aware of his financial situation, and in a tone that also indicated he didn't know anything else. They had known each other for a long time. Belkhodja knew Si Ahmed was rich and discreet, had a great reputation as a negotiator, never refusing business if it promised to be profitable. Belkhodja had already been advised to approach him, but Belkhodja hadn't dared to give in to what his conscience suggested was a dangerous provocation. It is always possible to avoid the blows of a man whom one has harmed, but that's not a reason to place oneself within his reach. After their encounter, he did, however, decide to pay the caïd a visit. Their meeting was fairly pleasant. Si Ahmed spoke of his health problems, mainly his back. He had for a long time been proud to be able to carry the sheep of the Eid al-Adha feast, but now he was paying for that pride. Belkhodja took advantage of those confidences to bring up the difficulties he was having in his business, and he ended up "making overtures."

The caïd would not allow Belkhodja to sink to the shameful level of a beggar, and during the following visit, he himself jumped a few obligatory steps in this type of conversation, saying:

"I'm not a forest where one can come looking for wood. I also have my problems."

Coming from a man like Si Ahmed, that confidence was shockingly clear. Belkhodja even found it somewhat discourteous. He was afraid that the caïd had learned certain things; he attempted to feel him out:

"Yet you are not that bad off, it seems you have bought a new car, and in town they're talking about a trip . . ."

Si Ahmed raised his eyes to the heavens. Belkhodja was an old acquaintance. He forced himself to endure his remarks, then replied:

"Indeed, if I can't lend it's because I'm spending . . . The car is because one day I won't be caïd, and the trip . . . isn't for me . . ." Si Ahmed alluded to his son's voyage with no apparent bitterness. He continued:

"And it's when I'm spending my money that people think that I have some, but I am a caïd, not a banker."

Belkhodja hesitated, then jumped on the opportunity:

"I'm prepared to reimburse you at thirty percent."

"Yes," the caïd said, "and not at fifty, like for Bensoussan, who in any event no longer wants to lend to you. And be careful, it is not because he's a Jew that you mustn't pay him back; there are rules. And you know, on my son's head, I will never lend with interest."

There was no irony in Si Ahmed's tone, speaking of his son's head. He wasn't aware of anything. His tone simply indicated that the conversation had come to an end. As he was standing up, Belkhodja said:

"Si Ahmed, I am like a sailor who has suffered a great blow from the wind. I need help from a friend."

In the caïd's large house, a bordj at the edge of the city, there was a smell of olive oil, a heavy, fruity odor, a bit acidic, which infused even the red leather of the benches in the salon, vaguely nauseating. Belkhodja spoke of friendship; he had gone as far as he could go. He added in a voice filled with emotion:

"Thirty percent, paid in six months."

"You insult me! You take me for an apostate! Sixty percent in a year! You confer me to Hell! Is that your friendship?"

Si Ahmed was enraged. He cursed money, that instrument of the devil. He took Belkhodja by the arm, squeezed it, saying:

"Money causes debt, and debt is the millstone of friendship! And you still have your house, don't you?"

Belkhodja left without responding and without having received a response. He wasn't even sorry to be leaving, as the odor of the olive oil was oppressive, invasive, even if it was indeed a smell of the finest quality.

21

THE HAND

They arrived in Paris, and as they were going into the lobby of the Scribe Hotel, Ganthier gave a little shout of surprise: a few yards away, standing in front of an armchair, was a woman watching them with an amused, yet somewhat insolent look while she removed a pair of pale yellow gloves. He thought she was back in the United States with her husband and the whole film crew. Kathryn kissed them, yes, she was alone ... Neil wasn't with her ... He preferred to watch his rolls of film rather than his wife ... She was supposed to go to Germany ... Berlin ... I want to meet Mr. Wiesner ... Yes, the director ... a great artist ... He directed Pola Negri ... and I'm better than her, aren't I? ... It was wonderful what was happening ... Kathryn was taking advantage of the opportunity to visit Paris, a stay in Paris ... a longtime dream ... Yes, she was staying at the Scribe, like them. No, not exactly a coincidence—she knew they were coming to Paris. Raouf had written to her. He had been dreaming of this trip. I am sure that with you he is acting blasé, but he has been dreaming of this trip.

Raouf's smile seemed forced; Ganthier was carrying the conversation. Why had she chosen the Scribe? To see them, of course, and that was the upside of not being a big star, you could avoid the Crillon, the Meurice, the journalists, you had time to meet up with friends ...

"And I'm traveling light. Tess isn't with me."

"Did she stay in America?" asked Raouf.

"No, officially we're traveling together, but I gave her her freedom ... She rarely asks a favor of me ... She'll rejoin me when we return ... You'll have to do without her confidences ..."

Kathryn didn't add anything. Thoughts were turning very quickly in Ganthier's head. The actress's presence was going to simplify things a bit vis-à-vis Gabrielle. They were friends. Gabrielle wouldn't be able to refuse to go out with them, on the condition that the young American agreed to stay longer in Paris and that Raouf didn't get into a snit. At the moment he seemed happy to see his friend, but with him you never knew; he had to be starving for independence, not to be a tourist with two or three others.

The second surprise for Ganthier came a few hours later, when they met up for dinner in the hotel restaurant. Kathryn was seated across from him, next to Raouf. Suddenly, she threw her head back and laughed, without looking at anyone, nor at Raouf's arm, upon which her hand had landed. An octopus, Ganthier thought. And she left her hand there, as if it were the most natural position for it. Ganthier couldn't stand it, in Nahbès she had made Raouf her friend, one can take the arm of a friend to cross the street, but one can't do what one wants in a restaurant, even here, what right does this girl have to play with a boy who is in fact under his watch, a vulgar gesture, and which is going to cause damage, reawaken the desires and imagination in someone who thought he was master of himself, and who is six years younger than she, it's obscene, he's a virgin, didn't know what to do with the Austrian girl, who literally threw herself at him, and now Kathryn is keeping her hand on his arm, like that. A harmless gesture for her—she wouldn't do anything more—but it is going to panic Raouf, the audacity typical of an American woman: I'll touch you when I want to . . . Or maybe she did want to have him . . . But in fact those girls don't take, they light a fire and do nothing, American arrogance, showing their desire is enough for them, or else they go farther and it's worse! She is going to have Raouf after dinner, like a toothpick, a night in the hotel, then she'll send him packing and run off to Berlin. And Ganthier would have to pick up the pieces, and take them back to Nahbès, and give them to Si Ahmed, who had trusted him.

The hand was removed, a very lovely hand, by the way, Kathryn's perfume wafting between them, a light mixture of pepper and lemon, that woman allows herself to rest her hand on the arm of another when it is his arm she should be interested in, he should have put himself next to her, he hadn't paid attention, yes, he had chosen to sit here, to look into the actress's eyes, and in any case she could have then played footsie with the kid and I wouldn't have seen anything, I'm the one she should be squeezing like that, not a kid she is whipping into the throes of passion where he doesn't belong, not yet . . . Kathryn took her hand away, she must have realized what she was doing, she wasn't a femme fatale to that degree, oblivious rather, but one doesn't have the right to be so familiar when one is wearing such a low-cut dress! Raouf seemed upset, but not overly so, the kid is sturdier than I would have imagined, he's right, to act naturally is what you have to do when faced with this type of aggression, act as if an old friend is taking his arm, let her get excited for nothing, like the Austrian girl.

Kathryn was telling a story whose thread Ganthier had lost. She started laughing again, and her hand again landed on Raouf's arm. Ganthier's face remained friendly. He wanted to shout, "That's enough!" He couldn't even find the attitude that would have been appropriate to break up this teasing ploy. This didn't make sense! Did that woman, who was the most beautiful woman in the restaurant that evening, have to set her sights on an adolescent? She could have chosen another target, she was going to give Raouf a distorted idea of what a woman is: this is wrong, Raouf seemed to have control of himself, but it won't take long before he starts blushing up to his ears. Ganthier was trying to think of something harsh to say, an allusion to the refinements of a civilization whose rules are always difficult to master, but couldn't find his words, continued to talk about something else while trying not to look at the table.

Raouf had worked up some nerve and was now telling the story of the high-class tarts who were with them on the *Jugurtha*. Kathryn's hand wasn't on his arm anymore. He's practicing, thought Ganthier, he is disarming with youth, but he is talking about tarts to act like an adult . . . Raouf saying that it was Ganthier who had noticed those women first, they were returning home from a stay at the court of our dear sovereign, I assured him of my discretion, but I'm persuaded that he did not seek out their company.

And for revenge Ganthier started talking about the young Austrian girl: our young friend scored a conquest but he was bereft at not being able to deploy his Stendhalian knowledge; he didn't have time; she literally threw herself on him! Ganthier was having fun. Kathryn started to talk in a simpering voice, to parody a scene for Raouf: you don't have the right to have girlfriends other than me, not without asking my permission. A slap from a great friend on Raouf's hand, you understand? Another laugh, and the hand with the red fingernails resting on the forearm. Ganthier looked Raouf in the eyes. Raouf blushed. She might at least sense the kid's distress; she's going to drive him mad.

Kathryn kept her hand on his arm, now without simpering, she was going to have to leave that arm to pick up her knife, but she used her fork in her left hand for the *pommes sarladaises*, she wasn't even teasing, and Raouf didn't look at her much but didn't eat, for fear of freeing his left arm, is a potato sautéed in duck fat really worth removing the hand of Kathryn Bishop? Ganthier said to himself, she has a lot of nerve doing that in front of me, does she take me for a piece of furniture? or maybe she's provoking me . . . Yes, she's looking for a man for tonight, she's using the young man to excite me, maybe it's a game she's playing with Gabrielle against me, she might have written to Gabrielle, "If you don't want your colonist, would you loan him to me?" that sort of thing goes on a lot these days, in any event, her hand doesn't belong there, even to provoke me, or as if it's the arm of a little brother—he's gone beyond the age of little brothers! they played like that all summer long in Nahbès, it's over now, there are rooms above us, we're among adults now!

Kathryn took her hand away to pick up her knife, Raouf began to cut his duck leg, very calmly, and suddenly Ganthier understood: a true couple! He was sitting opposite an established couple who were meeting again! Kathryn wasn't provoking him, no, it was the familiarity of a couple! In a moment she would put her hand back on his arm and call him "sweetheart"! That's why Raouf disappeared for two hours this afternoon, a walk to cure his migraine before dinner, right! he cured his migraine in bed, he could pretend to be detached, there was no more urgency, an established couple who is back together, and in Nahbès Ganthier hadn't seen anything! For months! Raouf as a guide for the American woman, everywhere, all the markets, all the excursions, he spent hours and hours with her; no one had seen anything, he followed her like her shadow, people made fun of him, and there wasn't any gossip, no indiscretion, she was living at the Grand Hôtel, a place where a young Arab is noticed like a fly in a glass of milk, she couldn't take a step in the city without everyone knowing where she was going, there, then there, the caïd didn't see anything, either, or Marfaing, or anyone, the kid followed her like a shadow, not the slightest suspicion! A shadow is a eunuch. Kathryn had no more wine in her glass, she took a swallow from Raouf's while looking him in the eyes.

They couldn't have done that in the fields, now, could they? In any event there's always a peasant wandering around . . not in town, either, or else she disguised herself, wore a headscarf, and maybe he disguised himself as a woman, he must have been reliving scenes from *One Thousand and One Nights*, transforming himself into a deliverer of bread to enter any house of an obliging friend in an Arab town . . . not easy . . . Raouf as a woman, that must not have tricked very many people, love is blind, but the neighbors aren't, but who else, then? one of Kathryn's friends? maybe Cavarro, the discreet Cavarro? he had a villa, or maybe Wayne, the poodle, he adored Kathryn; he was capable of killing himself for her, then, suddenly, it was obvious: Gabrielle . . . Ganthier knew he had the explanation even before he could explain it, yes, Gabrielle, but how? those two often visited her at the house she had rented, they didn't hide themselves, the entire street saw them, the nose in the middle of the face, if he had asked the question, people would have responded: Yes, they came by, I think, they're often there, did they come back out? Maybe, they come by almost every day, you know. They saw them all the time, so no one paid any attention anymore; and once they'd gone in she would have put a bedroom at their disposal, the maid always left after lunch, maybe the journalist even gave them her own room, she would go to work in the sitting room, yes, that was the only explanation, she typed her stories while trying not to listen to the bedsprings, and when I would arrive she received me in the sitting room while those two continued to be the beast with two backs, in silence, because they had heard someone enter, in silence with imperceptible movements, it's even better, they were doing that

when I was there!! . . . and Marfaing might also have visited, Kathryn coming
into the parlor as if she had just been in the powder room, for everyone in the
town it was just a gathering at Gabrielle's place, around that American actress
who had become her friend . . . no, impossible, there must have been some
crosschecking, someone wondering how she managed it so that no one ever saw
her arrive, Marfaing did the same thing: he arrived, and then they laughed while
watching him watch the door, he was waiting for his Thérèse, okay, those two
were happy just to have tea, like everyone else, those people came to Gabrielle's
to indulge in some innocent pleasure while a young couple was indulging in a
less innocent one behind the wall, silently, with imperceptible movements, with
the extra excitement that comes from danger, he learned quickly, that virgin,
I'm not dreaming, he looks like he's been at the Scribe for a month, there must
be an education in bedrooms, or rather, the feeling of being happy, that must be
it, finished the mad desire for what one doesn't have, she is his, they are together,
that makes you placid, she must have told him promising things for him to have
such assurance right in a hotel dining room where he has never been in his life.

Ganthier started to watch Raouf with a different eye, telling himself that the
little scoundrel fooled them all, they aren't even petting anymore, a hand on
an arm from time to time, that's enough for them, they are used to each other
and it's still fantastic, a hand on an arm, he is hers and he likes that, he pulled
the wool over all our eyes, especially mine, whereas we've been spending our
time together telling each other personal things for years, and what's more, he's
made me his accomplice: "I don't want to leave, especially not with Ganthier,"
and I'm the one who insisted, I even invoked intellectual discoveries! and I must
have seemed really brilliant on the ship, asking him if he wanted any tactical
advice to seduce his young Viennese girl who thought he was melancholic, he's
been sleeping with one of the great Hollywood actresses for months and there
you were, scolding him for acting platonic with a nice young Austrian girl, you
spoke to him of Stendhal, maneuvers: wake up, young Raouf, prepare yourself starting now to receive the message from Europe, overcome your inability
to enjoy pleasure! He must have really laughed . . . Poor Metilda, she couldn't
measure up.

Ganthier felt alone, humiliated. The distribution of women had taken place.
His hands were empty; he was alone with his distress, with the melancholy he
had so easily attributed to Raouf when they were on the boat. On his left the
empty chair could have been Gabrielle's, and Gabrielle's hand on his arm.
Something the journalist had said came back to him: "I've never met a man
who truly knows how to love himself." He looked around the room so he would
seem to be doing something. At a neighboring table the conversation, which up

until then had been very discreet, rose a decibel, a woman saying to two young boys:

"Stop it now, you don't draw waves in your mashed potatoes with your fork, it's vulgar!" Her words having no effect, she then addressed her husband: "You might scold them! You can see I don't have any authority anymore!" and the husband:

"I'm not putting my authority in the mashed potatoes!" He was quiet a moment, then: "It's your fault, you give orders instead of making them respect you, you'll never change!"

Something else Gabrielle had said: "Men think marriage gives them the right to change their wife." Then there was the noise of a fork screeching on porcelain. One of the boys had discovered a new game. His brother responded with the same screeching, then repeated the noise of the fork while slightly increasing the intensity, the two children trying to see how far they could go without provoking a serious reaction. And the sight of the still young couple, encumbered by those two little imbeciles, made Ganthier even more depressed than the silent reflections he was having, nothing more than the hand on the arm, Kathryn showing Ganthier that she no longer had anything to hide, that's why she's come to the Scribe, "not exactly a star," right! She chose the hotel that the little scoundrel must have told her about a long time ago, the day I spoke to him about the hotel his father and I had chosen; an established couple, and how about me? And if she goes to Berlin, he's going to want to go with her . . . and Gabrielle still isn't in Paris!

What struck Ganthier was how natural Raouf seemed, he wasn't acting the innocent or the parvenu in things of love: that's life; there were people in the streets and lovers in hotels, Ganthier had only to accept reality, he might be able to recover something . . . Ganthier surprised Raouf looking at Kathryn's neckline, that little sneak feels the need to verify that they're still there, that they're the most beautiful, the most supple, the freshest, the most welcoming, and she has obviously worn the dress needed to feel the looks of her man, what am I doing here!

Ganthier was exasperated. He wanted to drop everything, to say, "You no longer need me, I'll meet you in a week," and then, finding an indirect jab:

"Did you see? The lady over there, the third table. It's really lovely, the red ribbon around her neck with a jewel in the center, very effective." Kathryn responded:

"Yes, given her age . . ." Looking Ganthier in the eyes, then: "You're not really going to tell me that I should wear such a thing?"

And Ganthier was forced to sing the praises of Kathryn's natural freshness in front of Raouf; he had let himself be had; a young person had gotten the better of him. Ganthier had never been interested in Kathryn, and here he was on the verge of a jealous outburst. Absolutely not, Gabrielle was going to come. He would need the American woman; in the end, two couples could be amusing. In the aisle of the restaurant an elderly woman wearing pale blue was advancing on the arm of a man in a black suit. Their shoes didn't make any noise, but the boards of the floor creaked one by one under their weight, attracting looks that were meant to be discreet, and which were thus all the more insufferable. The man and the woman blushed, trying to go faster by holding on to each other. Kathryn said to Ganthier:

"Guess who's going to join us the day after tomorrow?"

22

CROSSROADS OF PAIN

At dinner, it didn't take much. Ganthier began to tell about their meeting the Austrian girl on the ship, saying to Raouf:

"By the way, the captain told me that in fact Metilda is half-German. Her mother is German, born in Berlin."

Kathryn made a joke, but in her head there was a pang of concern. In bed, that afternoon, she had asked:

"How was the ship? Okay?"

Raouf, his head resting on her stomach, responded: "It was fine . . . I'll tell you all about it."

Later she said to herself, *That's what Neil says when he doesn't want to talk about something.* She wanted to forget, not go through with Raouf what she had gone through with Neil. Her moods went up and down during the next few days, and she fought them, caressing Raouf's cheek, he who in any event didn't sense what was going on, being too busy trying to regain his balance ever since he had seen through the window of the train bringing him and Ganthier from Marseille to Paris towns flying ever more quickly by, towns with their red brick train stations and houses with little yards, piles of wood, and clotheslines. And the houses turned into buildings that rose higher and higher, became thicker and thicker as they got closer to the city, and at one point, very far in the distance, the Eiffel Tower. A glimpse of a dream, then it disappeared. Then the sudden feeling that he was going to be swallowed up. He had envisioned something like "the two of us in Paris," from atop a rise in the city, perhaps not that tower, nor the cemetery where Balzac had Rastignac speak, but at Sacré Coeur, for example. He had seen a photo of Paris taken from the steps of Sacré Coeur: "My heart at peace, I climbed the mountain from which one can contemplate the city in all its breadth." But now, in the train, he wasn't contemplating anything. He was being shot through the blows of a whistle into a world that would force him always to do what he had begun to do ever since the buildings began to get taller: raise his head. The city forced you to raise your head, and when you lowered it you saw the train tracks that increased in number, Ganthier saying: "We're entering hell, the entrances are becoming larger!" Raouf silent, in his head a memory, "We will enter splendid cities," and soon the train rolling in a sort of ditch that ran between walls like cliffs on either side of the tracks, with buildings on top of the cliffs, and more buildings, the walls covered with advertising posters that became increasingly gray and dirty, not the city of peaceful squares and streets that you saw in photos, but a city of maws of blackened buildings, all piled together, "Hold your step . . . We will enter the splendid cities," a single gray cloud over everything. Finally the great station, getting out of the train and fighting the surge of passengers, Ganthier saying: "Be aware, son of the caïd, here we are only anonymous travelers!" Outside, at the entrance to the station an omnipresent smell of coal blended with that of manure and the exhaust of vehicles, black dust on all surfaces, all the growling, plaintive, sometimes hateful sounds pouring out of the people and machines in a commotion of tramways, automobiles, buses, and carts, clacking, bellowing, under a network of tramway lines that crossed one another in every direction in the sky.

They had begun to go on walks with Kathryn the day after they arrived, and to annoy Ganthier, Kathryn said that she found Paris *pretty*—no vulgar comparison with New York or Chicago, no, *pretty* was the right word—she adored Paris, caught Raouf, who was looking at a woman passing by, and said:

"Close your mouth, she's going to think you're an idiot." Raouf laughed, without at all feeling he had done anything wrong. Kathryn laughed in turn, and the story of the Austrian girl and the ship came back to her. That's the worst, she thought, when they do things without realizing it . . . He never talks about that girl. I have to drag the words out of him one by one, like I did for Rania, but that Austrian girl is more dangerous. Maybe he's not thinking about her anymore, maybe, but if we go to Berlin she'll be there, after all, she's half German, unless Ganthier refuses to make the trip; I'll be in Berlin, she'll be there, not Raouf, true, but she could join him in Paris while I'm not here. Why wasn't I really jealous of Rania? Because I decided that she and Raouf weren't possible? A cousin who loves him, no more.

Kathryn forgot about Metilda for a while. Then there was the happiness of being together and of life as a couple, without hiding anymore, choosing a hat before they went out: "Yellow looks best on you . . . No, everything looks good on you," Raouf also in agreement about a change of dress at the last minute because he could see Kathryn in her slip again, and sometimes she changed her slip.

"You know, not every woman is as shameless as I am." They kissed. Sometimes she would take the towels and clothes out of the bathroom so Raouf would have to come out naked.

"Raouf, how do you do it?"

"Do what?"

"You eat twice as much as I do, you could have a bit of a stomach," Raouf kissing the slight beginning of Kathryn's stomach:

"This is what I find most delicious about you." She laughed, called him clumsy:

"I don't have anything more delicious than that?"

Kathryn didn't dare ask Ganthier what had happened on board the *Jugurtha* and Ganthier didn't dare ask her questions about Gabrielle, who had appeared at the Scribe two days after they had, splendid. She had just returned from Italy; she was nice to Ganthier, acting as if she were his contemporary, saying "the children," referring to Kathryn and Raouf; she took his arm in the street; they made a handsome quartet. At the end of the day Ganthier was almost happy. At night, at the hotel, he heard Raouf leave the adjoining room to go to Kathryn's, and he didn't dare go to Gabrielle's apartment a half hour from the Scribe. He was waiting for an opportunity, knew he would be incapable of creating one, invented one in his dreams, couldn't fall asleep, and in the morning forced himself to appear the way he should to carry on in the quartet.

When he was alone with Kathryn for a moment, Ganthier made an offer of an exchange, an exchange of information:

"Raouf is growing up quickly. On the ship he was still just a kid."

Kathryn said: "How old was she?"

"Who?"

"The Austrian girl, I've already forgotten her name."

"Metilda? The same age as he, and she acted like a debutante."

"But Raouf seems older than he is!" Kathryn didn't add anything, waited for a response that didn't come, decided not to say anything to Ganthier about what he was waiting for in turn, then, seeing his face:

"Sometimes, in Nahbès, I would get tired of Gabrielle, always talking about you."

Ganthier blushed, Kathryn thinking: Austrian, German, Berlin, the same age as he, a debutante . . . in New York the rich kids go to debutante balls. Then she said to Ganthier:

"*Debutante,* we also use that term back home. I really despise the French word. People want to sound snobbish, but it just sounds stupid."

"It just describes what it's meant to describe."

"How?"

Ganthier was happy to elaborate:

"To 'debut,' in the game of *boules,* is to knock your opponents' balls away from the *but*—goal—*debutantes* are the girls who come to knock away the girls from the year before."

Kathryn didn't say anything.

Some evenings Raouf would sometimes disappear after dinner, or even before.

"Raouf out enjoying himself!" Gabrielle said. All three of them knew. Once, seeing the young couple come in after midnight, Kathryn disguised as a man, Ganthier had warned Raouf:

"Your revolutionary meetings are at your own risk, but if Kathryn is caught, her career is over."

Raouf then started going out alone, Kathryn wasn't jealous of those outings, saying to Gabrielle:

"I have my marriage, he's wedded to politics."

She was watching for something else, a letter . . . One day, at the hotel reception desk, looking at the mail slots, she surprised herself by saying:

"Nothing for us?"

That was to keep Raouf from asking the question again, and she started doing that even when she was alone in front of the man with the golden keys. No letter from the Austrian girl, but Kathryn knew what happens on a ship when there isn't much time . . . And Ganthier didn't dare say anything about the last night and the storm. He regretted his earlier indiscretions but waited in vain for Kathryn's about Gabrielle, *Why did she tell me, "She likes to take revenge"? But they must share confidences* . . . Regarding the ship, he had said:

"It was amusing . . . an enterprising young girl, Raouf, who seemed not to understand anything, but now I understand everything." Looking at Kathryn, then:

"Metilda didn't stand a chance."

Ganthier told her only innocent things, and for Kathryn it was perhaps worse, a boy and a girl who had experienced such pleasure in being together that they didn't even consider going farther . . . *He must regret it now, no, I'm stupid, they fucked, I've taken the boat enough times to know, and if they didn't do anything she'll try again, I wouldn't have given up, she's going to try to see him again, I would write, when you want a man you don't let him breathe.*

Kathryn lived like a time bomb, alternately on a ship she had never taken, sometimes on the edge of a catastrophe that she averted by asking Raouf nothing. Then she calmed down, took back her persona as a lover, and Raouf's arm, and the pleasure of walking as a couple in Paris. From time to time, without looking at him, she squeezed his arm, said in a low voice:

"Put your hand on mine," or there was the shouting of a concierge who caught them kissing in a doorway:

"Are hotels meant for dogs?"

Kathryn was once even called *a cheap hooker*, and immediately went to the concierge's window to confront her:

"That's not true! I'm very expensive!"

And later, to Raouf: "What am I worth, in your opinion?"

"Standing up or lying down?" Raouf had asked.

She liked to surprise him, kiss his hand right in a salon de thé, say to him: "You're my sweet pastry," cause a false scene when he pulled his hand away: "You're ashamed of us!"

She also did more discreet things, such as when he went in front of her as they were entering a café or restaurant and she would sometimes put her hand on his behind.

During their walks the entire city pulsed with a joyful rhythm, the flowing of the Seine, its banks, the beautiful arches of the bridges, Raouf saying:

"'Shepherdess, oh Eiffel Tower, the herd of bridges is bleating this morning.'"

"Who wrote that?"

"A poet, Apollinaire."

The *bouquinistes*, Raouf's vertigo in front of them, take a step and Michelet rose up, then a complete collection of Balzac, and Shakespeare, and Dostoyevsky, the journals of Stendhal, André Gide, sometimes the Tharaud brothers.

"Who are they?" Kathryn asked.

"A colonial cliché, with some truth from time to time."

They left the *bouquinistes*, walked into the Tuileries gardens, stepping lightly on the path of fine dirt. Kathryn started walking around Raouf while laughing and repeating, "I love you." They passed by girls, their heads uncovered, observed for a moment the people who were trying to warm up by pressing their backs against the wall of a sun-filled terrace, gardeners with copper badges, a curate in his robes walking in a straight line. There were many iron chairs with star-shaped openwork, and skinny women moving around, gathering a few coins in "rent," and when they saw the skinny women, young working girls in white caps got up quickly. Next to the large basin a mother was saying to her child: "I told you so!" in a triumphant voice, the crying child carrying a large sailboat, useless: the water had frozen. Farther, a dog was getting excited over a large balloon. In front of them they could see the Arc de Triomphe. Sometimes it was the time of day when the shadows in the large garden became longer and began to climb the trunks of the oaks or plane trees, the sun leaving behind a red light that became darker and darker. Raouf stood with his back against a tree; she put her back against him; he wrapped his arms around her; she held onto his hands, pressed them against her. There were still some light clouds, and a momentary red reflection on the windows on top of a building.

The *bouquinistes* were closing. Raouf quickly bought a copy of Apollinaire's *Alcools*, which he gave to Kathryn; the river was becoming paler and paler, abandoning its paleness for darkness, the depths of the streets became darker and darker, the buildings transformed into black cliffs with jagged lights that they watched coming on one after the other. They also liked taking the elevated metro, the illuminated iron caterpillar that moved above the boulevards alongside bedrooms and dining rooms up in the apartment buildings; a child was doing his homework at the corner of a table that was already set for dinner; the apartments became bigger and bigger as they got closer to Passy, Metilda was no doubt there, in one of those apartments, *This time I won't let it happen, one never knows when you have to say, "That's enough," If it's too early, you're crazy, or you make them discover what they hadn't seen,* Kathryn once confiding in Gabrielle: I would even sometimes point women out to Neil and tell him I found them attractive. Maybe I did it on purpose. He pretended to be unmoved; he found defects. To hear me sing their praises, you never know when it's time to stop, and when it's too late there's no longer any point: you just have the wrong role. Metilda entered and left Kathryn's head like a faceless passerby. Kathryn was mad at Raouf. He must have read in one of his books that jealousy stokes desire. He's not saying anything on purpose. He could say just one or two words, "She was nice . . . a bit much . . ." Raouf didn't say anything, *because he has nothing to say, I'm being stupid, he's not thinking about her anymore, he never thought of her, nothing happened, nothing, but why am I so upset? Pain always tells the truth.*

Kathryn became a crossroads of sudden pain, Paris the hiding place of a debutante, and alcohol didn't calm anything. They were on a bus, laughing out loud at a passenger who was knitting a huge pink sock; then, without warning, the city would shoot needles of pain into Kathryn's chest. The bus stopped, they got off, decided to walk from Passy to the Trocadéro, Kathryn saying to herself, *no questions, no lies,* and kissed Raouf's neck. The streets were silent, their steps in harmony, a sign in front of a door, "Rooms by the hour," and then fifty yards farther Kathryn's face became white. Raouf was concerned:

"What's the matter?"

"Nothing . . . a stitch in my side, it's bothering me!" And to the lie she added some truth:

"I hate being in pain!"

He sensed Kathryn's mood by her voice, didn't look at her. She calmed down. They reached the Arc de Triomphe by avenue Kléber, walked down the Champs-Élysées, some pressure on the arm she was holding, *Put your hand on mine.* They jumped into a taxi, met Gabrielle and Ganthier at the hotel.

"Raouf was introducing me to poets." Kathryn recited: "'Shepherdess, oh Eiffel Tower, the herd of bridges is bleating this morning.'"

"I don't hear any rhyming," said Ganthier, "I see a ludicrous image. That's called poetry, now?"

They changed clothes just as the night was beginning to take over, and the four of them, to rid themselves of any hint of moral uprightness, went to a supper club, the band playing in the middle of the room, the clinking of jewelry, place settings, joyful noise, brutal, competition from the other couples, and bursts of laughter from girls with splendid breasts when an overweight man tried to arch his back during a tango.

"Cinderella has gone home," Ganthier said to the maître d', who was about to refill Raouf's glass. Gabrielle got up to avoid an invitation to dance by Ganthier and threw herself in the arms of a partner whom she seemed to know. Ganthier asked Kathryn so she wouldn't be asked by anyone else.

Raouf was in a taxi, heading toward the rue de la Grange-aux-Belles, or to the thirteenth arrondissement, to other places, smoke-filled and humid, where skinny men spoke in trembling voices of a world beyond the seas.

"We are not backward!" It was a representative of the Intercolonial Union who was speaking, an Indochinese. He added, "And Europe is not the cradle of humanity"—short, with protruding cheekbones, his eyes sunken with fatigue—"Nor are we the reserves for your revolution."

"That comrade is uncontrollable," said a Frenchman speaking to someone next to Raouf.

The little man with sunken eyes was called Quôc. He retouched photos to make a living, translated Montesquieu into Vietnamese, and wanted to write a book that he would entitle *The Oppressed*. Raouf was ashamed that he didn't have such an ambitious project. Quôc had been traveling the world since 1911; he had gone to America, central Africa. He said, "I learned French in Saigon, English in London, and Russian in Montparnasse." Ganthier had warned Raouf, "The police are watching your Annamite. You're going to be in their sights, too." Gabrielle told Raouf that she would protect him.

On rue de la Grange-aux-Belles they had warned Quôc against the bourgeois Arab who dressed too well. Quôc responded that he had been recommended by several North African comrades, and that a police informant would have changed clothes to join them, he trusted him: "He thinks the way I did when I was younger. I was like him, the son of a notable, don't you trust me?" Raouf had tried to interest Quôc in his country. He discovered that Quôc knew almost as much as he did about the Maghreb and central Africa, and when he spoke about Indochina it was always very precise: "Do you know that back home there are official outlets for opium? Licensed shops, like for alcohol, distribution insured by the colonial state. For a thousand villages France opened in my country a thousand opium shops and six schools; it is in the process of building a seventh." He didn't need to assume a sarcastic tone, and continued: "We also had volunteers who signed up for the mother country in 1914 . . . The French officers held ropes across the street, one at each end of a village, and all the young men who were in between the ropes were volunteers . . . There were even some who didn't want to exercise that volunteerism, so they rubbed their eyes with pus, or lime." He told Raouf that he had begun by wanting reforms. He had sought the help of enlightened people in Paris, but imperialism is an octopus. You can't negotiate with an octopus. You cut off its tentacles, and then you negotiate . . .

Raouf also ran into Quôc in more bourgeois gatherings, like the Club du Faubourg or the Amis de l'Art. When Quôc saw him, the Indochinese man excused himself and introduced his new friend to a corpulent woman who spoke magnificent French while rolling her *r*'s.

"Madame is a great writer!" Raouf bowed respectfully. He soon found out that in addition to Colette, Quôc also knew Léon Blum, Marcel Cachin, and Marguerite Moreno.

And the next day, at breakfast, Raouf asked Gabrielle for more information. Yes, Marguerite and Colette were more or less together, but Colette also liked men: "No, Ganthier, she isn't sleeping with Marcel Cachin, let's be serious!" Kathryn's laugh interrupted them. She was reading the *Daily Mail*, with the headline "Mobbed in London." Raouf asked what "mobbed" meant; it was something like "crushed by the crowd." In the photo they recognized Mary Pickford and Douglas Fairbanks, *mobbed* in front of their hotel, with a crowd of admirers. Kathryn read: "Douglas was forced to evacuate his wife by carrying her on his shoulders . . ."

"Carried on Douglas Fairbanks's shoulders. I'd love to be Mary Pickford for fifteen minutes," said Gabrielle.

"But no longer than that," said Kathryn, "Afterward he starts drinking again."

Gabrielle tempted by the shoulders of a man: Ganthier felt a wave of relief pass over him.

23

BROTHER AND SISTER

The doctors at the large French hospital had said that it was due to very bad health overall. But they were nonetheless able to bring Rania's father, Si Mabrouk, back from where his ailing body had wanted to take him, for the time being, they said. What came next would depend on a very strict diet, and they were sure that, in spite of the heart attack, he had many happy days ahead, or generally happy days—that is, with all due respect for your excellency, days without alcohol or sugar, no fat of any kind, cooked or not. Yes, lean fish, white meat of chicken, no salt, either. Yes, that does mean no fried food. Your body is fat, your heart is fat, your arteries are fat. The fat is weighing down your blood. You must lose weight, both visible and invisible fat. Just because the patient has survived doesn't mean he is out of the woods. The woods are still full of danger, said the head of the department of cardiology with the chuckle of a reed-thin man, a true reed, not an ounce more than a six-foot-tall reed. A strict diet: you must fight the good fight, your excellency!

Si Mabrouk had forbidden anyone to tell his daughter about his condition, but among those who are alarmed, those who are saddened, and those who rejoice, news of this type travels very fast, and the same day she had been, as they say, stricken by the news, Rania went to the capital: "I'm going to take care of you!" Then, seeing her father's reaction, she corrected herself: "You're going to take care of yourself and I'm going to help you, you'll see, you'll be fine."

"But I'm already fine," said her father from his hospital bed, striking his chest warily. Rania said:

"The doctors don't exactly agree, but you will be fine, with some self-discipline!"

She quickly invoked the help of God, and seemed happy to be able to incarnate discipline. She had written to Gabrielle asking her to send some medical books, which hadn't yet arrived.

Rania's brother, Taïeb, found it scandalous that a woman would start talking about the human body in general, and about that of her father in particular. Si Mabrouk didn't want her to stay: If you're here that means I'm not well at all. Is that really what you want me to think? I have two European nurses. They take good care of me (he pointed to his lunch). I swallow only lettuce leaves, boiled fish, rice, and water; I'm not even supposed to eat a grain of couscous, and if you're here, Taïeb is going to continue to come every day, to watch us. I'll get upset. That's very bad for the heart, and then there are things I don't want to discuss with you, as you know, also so I don't get upset, or be concerned. Just think about it, my only concern is your situation vis-à-vis your brother. It would be better to do things while there's still time. You could choose your husband. Taïeb will not even let you choose. For him the family is only a court. Decide . . . But if you choose too quickly I'll be worried. What do the doctors think? Are they any clearer? They talked about improvement? In any case I don't want to know, but if the . . . delay . . . is really very short I'd prefer to continue to eat things that taste of life. No, never mind. I'm determined to keep to that diet. You have my word.

Si Mabrouk was thinking out loud in front of his daughter, his gaze fixed on the rays of light reflected by the steel posts of his brand-new bed. A bottle of oxygen was placed next to the bedside table: If you want to keep the Nahbès property, you must find a way, and it isn't easy, Rania saying: I won't need that, I won't need anything! Which was the most upsetting response she could give, the father and daughter each playing the game of upsetting responses, Si Mabrouk continuing: I could sell it to a man of trust. Rania didn't say a word, the father continuing: And you could buy it back from him with the money I give you, Rania saying with a laugh: A farm like that isn't easily returned, it would take a very trustworthy man. She was tempted to say to her father that it would be useless, then realized that the calculations he was doing were helping him to forget his hunger, because he was hungry. I'm dreaming of méchoui, he kept saying, I keep dreaming of méchoui, tagine, couscous, baklava, that never happened to me before, I would give my soul for some honey, almonds, the crust from half a baklava, well browned in the oven . . .

Some people stoked that hunger with the remarks they made in front of the invalid: You've lost too much weight, Si Mabrouk, that's not good. An old friend even told him, "An empty bag can't stand up," the former minister asserting: I'm not sick, I'm convalescing, I will soon be able to cheat a little. He wasn't permitted to smoke, either. Among doctors that was the new thing: tobacco is the enemy, along with alcohol and fat, sugar. "They're starving me, and they're forbidding cigarettes that calm the hunger!" Rania had given instructions to the servants and nurses: filter the visitors, he needed rest. But among civilized people, an invalid was to be visited, and that invalid was bound by the laws of hospitality, he must welcome them; and a visitor, especially a relative, must bring a cake, a homemade cake, made by the most respectable person in the household. What can you do in front of a nephew who tells you: grandmother made it?

Rania put a stop to all that. The response to every visit was that the master was napping; they could come back a bit later. Of course they could leave the cakes; he would be delighted. Or she allowed an hour for a group visit, upsetting people, and her father ended up having the reputation of a bedridden sleeper, "I can neither eat, smoke, or talk to people!" It wasn't true. They greeted friends who respected their instructions, and not the one who was scolded by Rania because he had brought cigarettes even so, a former minister, too. An assassin, that's what the young widow had called him, adding that she would make his behavior known in high places. The man left. Si Mabrouk had laughed after his departure: He wasn't trying to kill me, he just wanted to cheer me up, but it is a bit true that he's an assassin. He must have thought you knew a thing or two, or that I told you something . . . you know, for the farm. I know people who keep their word, at least one man in Nahbès, Si Ahmed. The best solution would be to give you the amount in cash. You'll buy the farm from him. You'll have it in your own name, and when I will have closed my eyes for the last time you'll be able to stay there, but that won't prevent Taïeb from trying to marry you off to a man of his liking, and if you possess a lovely property that will increase your suitors and the pressure.

Sometimes Taïeb would come into the room. He kissed his father's hand, greeted his sister, a good, affectionate boy. He said: Don't let me interrupt you, what were you talking about? Already furious that his sister didn't leave when he arrived. He was the elder brother: she should have even called him *sidi*, as was the rule in respectable families. She never did it, or did it only to mock him. It was against nature to give so much freedom to a girl, but his father had always done that. One day he had heard him say to a friend, "She was born, and something happened in my heart, and since then it hasn't changed." For Taïeb she was a spoiled sister. His father had always been enthralled with her, with what he called her intelligence, her precociousness in speaking, reading, writing, counting. She was the only one in the house who could stand up to him without immediately having a crop come down on her head, and there was also a sign that made things clear — now that his father no longer drank he realized it — never had Si Mabrouk been in a state of inebriation in front of his daughter, whereas in front of him . . . without any dignity . . . *as if I counted no more than the rug on which he ultimately vomited.*

Taïeb had seen his sister gradually begin to talk as an equal with his father, who was ecstatic with his daughter's audacity. The world was upside down; it was the Western world. It regained its hierarchy only in the stern reminders that Si Mabrouk gave to his son. A girl who liked books; Taïeb had rejected them as soon as he had seen that she liked them. He had kept only one, which he cited constantly, a collection of hadiths, and he had become furious when his sister had begun to criticize the use he made of them. The worst was the day when she had insulted him, had said to him: You want to return to the old law because you think that you will pay fewer taxes, not even three percent of what you earn in your rotten brick factory off the backs of fifty poor fellows that you make work as if God didn't exist! She had been to that brick factory once, such gloomy men. Sometimes people laugh when they work; it's a sign that poverty hasn't won. Raouf had said to her one day: When they laugh it's because they sense that the world could be better and that can make them want to transform it. In Taïeb's brick factory, no one laughed. In response to her insult Taïeb tried to slap his younger sister. She blocked his arm; she was a head taller than he. He had tried to kick her. He had seen the triumph in his sister's eyes, typical of her: to force him to make spurious gestures when he was just defending the True and the Right. She didn't say anything. She knew that he was aware of what he was doing, that he was suffering from it. He had tried to hit her again, without success.

Their father had separated them: "You're not children anymore, shame on you!" Taïeb had noticed that in pronouncing the word *shame* their father had looked only at him. Since then he never tried to hit his sister again. He had discovered that it was better to use a cold power. He told himself that after his father died, he would be able not only to have himself immediately obeyed by his sister but also to prevent a too-advantageous marriage for her. He had suffered too much in the presence of the dead husband who had almost become a second son to Si Mabrouk, and the favorite one. In the beginning, his father enjoyed calling him when he was with his son-in-law, and Taïeb said to himself that his father wanted to lean on him, to give to the other not only his opinion but that of his son, that of the men of the family, and then he had realized that Si Mabrouk spoke with his son-in-law of things that he didn't understand, or less and less as the discussion advanced, points of law, ways of calculating risk, hypotheses for investment, loans that would enable them to make investments that would earn much more than they had cost. He told himself that those were things against religion, one was not supposed to earn money with money: that Paris stock exchange was only a place of perdition.

His father was always kind to him during those discussions. In reality he was doing it to humiliate him. Taïeb had wanted to protest but said to himself that it was better to continue to appear as if he didn't know anything. After all, his father could think what he wanted, but he could never challenge his place as the eldest son. He didn't really want to do so, in any event—Taïeb was sure of that—it was just the custom: treat his son like a dog, to teach him, to harden him. One day that would come to an end. He wondered what would be better:

to marry off his sister now, see her go under another authority, leave the house; she would leave him free to live his life, but with the risk that she might marry a powerful man; or wait for death to carry off his father's body, and organize a marriage with a good man, of course, but of moral goodness, a man without influence, a man who throughout his life would need Taïeb's help, and a man of tradition, who would bring Rania back to the right path, through the necessary means. He had to act carefully; he had found such a man. For now he preferred to keep him in the shadows.

Rania wrote to Gabrielle regularly. Letters from her followed, from all the places where the quartet stopped, in France and Germany. Rania had told her about her father's illness, without mentioning the concerns she might have about her own fate.

"She doesn't talk about it," Gabrielle said to the other three, "She must think that taking care of her own fate at this time would be inappropriate. I'm afraid one morning the sky will fall on her head."

"That Taïeb is a monster!" Kathryn said. Raouf agreed. Only Ganthier pointed out that the brother had law on his side. He said to Gabrielle:

"The same law as that of the rioter you once presented as a Christ figure to the readers of *L'Avenir,* and also that of the people your Rania supported not that long ago by feeding their families, they were ready to die for that old law, which assigns females the place you know about . . ." Raouf's face was solemn. Ganthier added:

"Our dear revolutionary is discovering the omnipresence of contradiction. It doesn't have only a positive role. Sometimes, instead of nicely going beyond itself for the better, it crushes people."

"Her father won't allow it," said Raouf. Ganthier smiled, then:

"Do you mean that former minister, an 'enemy of the people' and 'valet of colonialism'? Are you counting on him to save your cousin? You're beginning to make progress!"

In her response to Rania, Gabrielle tried to be reassuring. She didn't doubt that Si Mabrouk would be able to protect his daughter, which hardly reassured Rania. *When what your friends say rings hollow, that means you're in trouble,* she had thought. At the bottom of the letter there was a note in Raouf's handwriting, just as hollow, and a surprising "Cordially," from Ganthier. Rania looked out the window. It was raining on the capital. She missed her fields, her walks, and the wind of the sea that ruffled the clumps of grass on the sides of the path, and someone else with whom she would have liked to have walked, talked, close herself up in . . . *He will come and I will allow him, no, he will allow me,* she hesitated between different pleasures that were only in her head . . . *ghadi sayu-*

jadu amsi, my tomorrow is only yesterday . . . She came back to herself. Her father was doing better. He kept to his diet without cheating. He pressed her to return to the farm.

"Don't let your people get used to your being away."

"My people like me . . ."

"Yes, but apart from laughter and tears, they can't do anything, whereas Taïeb, with his will . . ."

Sometimes Rania wondered how a brother and sister could end up detesting each other so much. She realized that her father suffered from not having been able to prevent it.

24

A NIGHT AT GABRIELLE'S

"I'll walk you home, Gabrielle": that statement was running through Ganthier's head. He was with Gabrielle at the Daumas's house on avenue Mon-
taigne, it had taken him some time to get to that simple five-word utterance. He
just had to find the right tone. Place some tenderness on *Gabrielle?* No, better
to give her a reason, "I'll walk you home, it's not safe to walk alone." No! That's
too long, and it sounds like I want to be her protector! Act as if we had already
decided to leave together: "Shall we go?" She would be speechless, success! No,
she would be furious, and would say, "I'd rather go home alone," looking around
the room as she says it, so don't act superior with her, not casual or protective,
something like "May I accompany you?" But I can already hear her say, "That
won't be necessary." Don't say, "May I," take control! But "I'll accompany you?"
is dangerous. She could respond, "There's no reason," or even, "That's very kind,
but you must be tired." She's fifteen years younger than you. She's capable of
saying that while looking you up and down, just when you forget to hold your
shoulders back, she never misses an opportunity for revenge. That will teach you
to talk about Monsieur Seguin's goat, on the evening you hope to seduce her,
the battle between the goat and the wolf, the entire night. You shouldn't have
kept going on, you should have just enjoyed the profiteroles, but they seemed
to be interested in what you were saying—that Ganthier, just as brilliant as ever.
She smiled: There's a proverb in Avignon, *A woman who smiles is soon underneath.* But when a woman like that listens to you while smiling, it means she's
letting you dig your own hole. She doesn't like men. She watches you dig. And
you talk about the night of the little goat, the struggle, the pleasure the little goat
puts into that struggle, the happiness of being a wolf in front of such a goat. She
must not have liked the metaphor of the goat. Three glasses of champagne, a
couple glasses of white, a Bordeaux that made you want to go lie down under
the barrel, and for the red a Burgundy, an indescribable Gevrey-Chambertin.
Glass after glass you were inexhaustible on the little goat, idiot, with cognac at
the end. You have to forestall the "no thank you," just a hint of a request, out
of courtesy, but with words that must force her to say "yes," or a mute acceptance—that would be best, mute acceptance.

Ganthier was much in favor of mute acceptance, it made the body speak: She gets up, she doesn't speak, she answers with her eyes, her body, she pulls in her stomach — if she does that while she's speaking to you, you've won. Place her in front of a dilemma. She accepts with her entire body or she affronts you, but she wouldn't dare do that. She knows what the Daumas would tell everyone: Can you imagine, yesterday evening she refused to let Ganthier see her home. She doesn't want to be seen in a taxi with a man: she would get in trouble with the girlfriends! You must make the "no" impossible. Act forceful, but force wrapped in velvet, "I will accompany you," to make it a fait accompli, with a question in your voice, and then a way out, offer her a way out. That's good: "I'll accompany you to your door." She must be able to imagine herself saying thank you to me in front of her door, and turning her back on me.

At the last minute Ganthier removed "to your door" and added a bit of hesitation: "I'll accompany you . . ." Gabrielle agreed, her eyelids closed for an instant. Yes, like you will close them when we're at your place, my little goat, that's what you always have to do with women, challenge them, that's what they like about us, and I was right about the goat, a *yes* with closed eyelids . . . As for her stomach, Ganthier had forgotten to look.

In the taxi, they continued to talk very naturally, about the Daumas, politics, Europe, the crisis between France and Great Britain. She knew more than he did, had more details. He listened to her, he watched her lips, her shoulders, then forced himself to look at the street, to listen to the noise of the motor. Sometimes, in a turn, their shoulders touched.

When they were in front of her building he was bold, supple, and precise. He didn't give her time to take his hand to say good-bye. He was in front of the outer courtyard door, ringing the bell to alert the concierge, opening, stepping back to allow her to enter. She muttered something while passing in front of him. He thought he heard *If you'd like* . . . didn't ask her to repeat it. It was a lovely, new building, near the Trocadéro, with an elevator, two large mirrors on facing walls in the lobby on either side of the elevator, mirrors that multiplied their reflections to infinity, a couple returning home, it was wonderful. While the wooden cage climbed in luxurious silence he breathed in the young woman's perfume. It wasn't an overly sweet scent. He had heard a name mentioned during dinner, *Mitsouko*.

They went into her apartment. He still wondered at what point he was going to take her in his arms: I should have done it in the elevator. She took off her coat, took his, said to him: "Have a seat." She poured two glasses of cognac with authority, then: "Please excuse me a moment."

She slipped away. He relaxed. He was sure of what was going to happen.

His best moment was right then: a lovely parlor, with sound-dampening rugs, very light, warm colors, not many knickknacks, a splendid vase of birds of paradise, large lamps, space. She had probably gone to remove her girdle—no, she doesn't wear one—touch up her makeup, maybe put on a more comfortable dress, more supple, more relaxed than her suit.

He was sitting in one of the armchairs, the mistake of a rookie. In an instant he was on the sofa. He sighed in relief. The sofa was wide, beautiful yellow leather, supple, deep. He imagined Gabrielle with her legs tucked under her. It was warm . . . Across the room there was a wooden sculpture, an enormous Buddha sitting on an elephant as if it were a footstool, more than three feet tall. The Buddha was smiling, his eyes lowered . . . The sofa wasn't really the most obvious choice. What will you do if she thinks you're coming on too strong and she sits in an armchair? He went back to the armchair, reflected, and saw what he should have seen earlier: the side table to the left of the sofa, with cigarettes, an ashtray, a book. That was her place. He went back to sit on the sofa, a very Napoleonic maneuver, advance from the right. He moved to the center, no, that was too much. He moved back toward the armrest, realized that even though the apartment was warm, his hands were icy. Not now! He put them under his thighs. He imagined Gabrielle in a half-open dressing gown.

She came back into the room. She was naked, a glass in her hand, and completely naked, her hair undone, she walked toward him. He had a moment of panic, took refuge in a thought, she practiced dance . . . She moved to the left, placed her glass on the side table, opened a large phonograph. She had two lovely dimples on her lower back. He took his hands out from underneath his thighs. They were just as cold; this wasn't the time . . . From the phonograph there came the voice of a woman, German, a wrathful woman. He didn't know how to look at Gabrielle. He tried to summon his desire, glanced at the Buddha, who must have seen a thing or two. He looked back at Gabrielle. She had turned around. She was smiling like the Buddha, but her eyes were wide open. He couldn't hold her gaze. The singer was singing Wagner, *Willkommen ungetreuer Mann*. She had put that on on purpose. He didn't dare look at her breasts. He looked high up on the wall behind her, telling himself to stop looking at the wall. She was naked, anything but that. He wondered what was happening to him, the height of intimacy and you're not doing anything? Stand up? Go to her? Wait for her to come to you? *Welcome you disloyal man*, the anger of Venus in *Tannhäuser*, who was that singer? You could ask her since you are here, and the name of the conductor with—that nude, it was insane, Wagner, she had done it on purpose, the guy who is not impressing his Venus. How do you seduce a naked woman? A hooker would already be in action. Get up, take her, bend her, that's what she's waiting for, but you don't even want to, never done such a thing, too much light, all these lamps, it's like daylight, I'll have to undress. What the hell is she doing? Gabrielle had gone behind the large vase of birds of paradise. They left traces of orange and purple on her white skin. She picked off a wilted flower using her nails. He realized that she had been talking about flowers for a moment, about the fragility of plants in the winter. She's mocking me. Venus's anger had come to an end. She went to remove the needle from the phonograph, went back in front of the vase. He forced himself to say something, about plants. I'm a moron. Leave, leave telling her you are at the wrong address. Gabrielle naked. He had no desire, and cold hands. She passed next to him. He almost took hold of her hand, but the time it took him to decide to do it, the hand had disappeared. Gabrielle went back to the bathroom. Two dimples on her lower back. Join her? He shook himself. Naked or not, I'm getting up and taking her. But I feel nothing, nothing I can do, or it's too quick.

Gabrielle again in the doorframe, with a basin of steaming water in her hands. She placed it in front of the other armchair, turning her back to Ganthier, the dimples, firm buttocks, fleshy, the *royal rear guard in the battles of pleasure*, Verlaine. I don't feel a thing. She stood up, turned, sat down, slowly put her feet in the water, saying, "It's boiling," with a moan of pleasure. If she asks me if I want a basin, too, I'll slap her. He felt himself blushing, which happened only very rarely, and never in intimate moments. He was angry at himself, blushed even more. Leave while blushing, that would look great. He heard the voice of a woman saying, "He was afraid, he ran away." She's playing with me. She's beautiful, don't sneak looks at her, like a schoolboy: look at her the way I would look at a statue. There, the breasts, the beautiful areolae, breasts held high, hanging gently from their weight, a pretty weight, a beautiful springboard. He followed the beautiful springboard with his eyes to the nipple, then the roundness back around, joining the thorax, she knows all that.

After an eternity she pushed the basin away, wiped her feet, tucked her legs under her, and started talking about the weather, the cold snap, the rise of the Seine. She shivered: "Be a dear, would you mind getting my pajamas? They're hanging in the bathroom behind the door," Ganthier got up, happy that he was being told what to do. He heard her voice behind him: "They're light gray, and my slippers should be in front of the bathtub, they have white fur trim!" He returned. She was standing up. He helped her put on the pajama top. She stayed for a moment facing him. He placed a hand on her shoulder. She pulled away to put on the bottoms. She looked at him sweetly. She slowly tied the cord of the pajamas. He felt better, the pajamas looked good on Gabrielle, they were a bit big for her. His desire returned. Playful, casual, he wanted to untie the cord of the bottoms. He followed her, placed his lips on her neck. She turned around: "So, it's back? Is it my pajamas? Do you want to keep them for the night?" In the same tone he said: "I'm sorry, I'm forgetting myself." He looked at her in the eyes, took one of the brown locks of hair between his index and middle fingers. She didn't react. He let go of the hair. His hand descended down Gabrielle's back. She took his hand, brought it back between them. Her look was cold. He was afraid of a "now leave." He went back to sit on the sofa, assumed a humble air, held his hands out to her: "Can we make peace?"

She sat down on the sofa.

"I'm very clumsy, a true king of bad timing."

She smiled. He took her hand. She pulled it back, asking:

"Why did you come to Paris? Business or politics? In Nahbès you appeared to be the most perverse colonial in the country." She was teasing him. Perverse colonial, it certainly describes you this evening, but good, she wasn't throwing him out. He didn't know how long the confrontation lasted, a struggle of so many seconds, a hand that he took, that didn't resist, but Gabrielle used the hand-holding to block any attempt to go further, a kiss on the forehead that brought him no reprisals, but Gabrielle permitted no others. She resisted, but without throwing him out. She was very strong, but didn't use her strength. She preferred to say "no" dryly, but she allowed him to put his arm around her shoulders, like a friend, talking about everything, and in a moment he was face to face with the evidence. They were confronting each other, the goat and the wolf. She was making him pay for the jokes at dinner, a series of gestures, without conclusion. She sometimes accepted the progression of a hand, then blocked it. The pajama allowed him to feel the suppleness of her body. He tried to untie the cord. She blocked his hand, and in doing that it landed on her stomach: it was warm. Each time he tried to undo the cord she increased her pressure, and she resisted at the same time with all the strength of her muscles, the stomach of a gymnast, and her eyes fixed with the same hardness, but not chasing him away, all of that without animosity, without ceasing to talk.

At one point he needed to take a break. He leaned back slightly, onto the back of the sofa, stretched. She'll end up giving in; she was looking at him kindly. That was it; he wasn't going to fail. He was worn out, but now he was sure of what was coming. He just felt very tired . . . He kept her hand in his, scolding himself for having drunk so much, the alcohol making his head heavy . . . He closed his eyes . . .

When she awakened him with a cup of coffee there was daylight. She was dressed, perfumed. He made a grimace as he stood up. She asked him if it was his back, adding: "Sofas are always terrible." She didn't talk about age; her tone was neither sarcastic nor upset. He saw himself in one of the mirrors in the parlor, his suit wrinkled, his face wrinkled, his shoulders drooping, his cheeks already gray, his feet swollen in painful shoes. He tried to act naturally, to leave like a friend who has spent an impromptu night; he could have cried out of rage. She allowed him to save face, asking: "What are we doing this afternoon?"

"Kathryn wants to go to the movies, she wants to see a German film, *Müde Tod* – 'Tired Death.'" Gabrielle almost burst out laughing, then:

"Great, you'll take care of it? Then I'll pardon you!" Then in a dryer tone, "Well, maybe."

She closed the door. One day he would find out what Gabrielle had confided in Kathryn:

"I showed him that women are not condemned to modesty. He couldn't get over it."

25

A TASTE FOR WEALTH

Despite the smell of olive oil that pervaded the house, Belkhodja continued to visit Si Ahmed, whose door was always open to him. Belkhodja told himself that if the caïd allowed him to come in it was because negotiations hadn't ended: it would be better another time; it was written in the rhyme of the adage *kheira bigheira*, like a necessary link between "the best" and "the next time." He stopped looking for another lender. And Si Ahmed continued to say no. He could have had a servant say he wasn't at home, but that was Si Ahmed's strength. He let Belkhodja in. He listened to him. He told him no, sometimes revealed his bad mood, but he listened to him . . . The one who speaks sows, and the one who listens harvests. And Belkhodja returned because he said to himself that in Si Ahmed's refusal, a door remained ajar. He was confronted with a no, but he remained master of the comings and goings, and of time. Normally, in business a good interlocutor ultimately proposes a solution, because it isn't right to say no to someone when you've known him for a long time and when one has means, he loses his dignity before you; it isn't worthy to leave him in that state. And it can bring bad luck. "When I say no, it's no," is something the French would say, whereas a man of tradition always finds some sort of compensation to offer to balance his refusal. He can as a last resort send you to someone else, with a letter of recommendation. That doesn't cost a lot, and once you have done that, the one asking can no longer ask you. But Si Ahmed didn't say a thing. And that could indeed mean that his refusal wasn't definitive, that he must have several solutions in mind. Sometimes, when there was a lull in the discussion Belkhodja became aware of the chirping of a cricket. He would sometimes say, "It isn't far away," hoping Si Ahmed would have a servant get rid of the pest as he would have done at home. But Si Ahmed did nothing; one day he even said: "I sometimes find it annoying, but when I'm alone and it's too quiet, it's like the silence of death."

Some days, when Belkhodja seemed to be about to give up, the caïd asked him for details about his business, just like that, as if for a negotiation to come, as if it were enough to wait for things to finish happening, and Belkhodja became patient again while telling himself that the one who waits already has more luck than the one who hopes. Then he became worried again, because Si Ahmed's procrastination was making him more and more upset. The caïd showed no irritation. He opened his door to the merchant, but his face was closed. And Belkhodja began to be afraid. Si Ahmed must have serious problems; he might be ill or ruined. In the end, his business was a closed book. People said he possessed this or that farm, shares in this or that business, a flour mill, fishing boats, livestock, a phosphate company, but no one really knew, and most of his business didn't go through a store where one could assess the clientele or the merchandise. They thought Si Ahmed was rich because caïds have the reputation of never forgetting themselves. It was even said that his skin had a yellow tint because he slept with his gold, but he could be in dire straits, and the truth, a serious truth, was that the caïd, to refuse a favor to a friend, must have, as the French say, problems.

There was something else, which Belkhodja hardly dared to admit to himself: Si Ahmed's son, Raouf . . . Raouf's problems must have become Si Ahmed's problems. Money problems and political problems must be coming together. Belkhodja had gone too far in his denunciation of the son; it was badly played. He should have been content with vague accusations, a young man with nationalist tendencies, who late in the night spoke careless words, but the merchant had wanted to shine in front of the police in the capital. He had spoken about communist sympathies: the caïd's son was the friend of the man named David Chemla, a Bolshevist student, and Raouf read *L'Humanité* at the home of his former teacher, another communist, but untouchable, wounded during the Great War.

The police had remained unimpressed. To wake them up Belkhodja had added that Raouf also frequented people who regularly went to Egypt and Turkey, and that seemed to be of interest to them: Were those people received in the caïd's house? And David Chemla, did he happen to meet up with nationalists? With Raouf? Belkhodja responded that he didn't know but that he was going to find out. One of the French police had then wondered if there might not also be some double-dealing going on by the father of the young man, a Francophile caïd in the morning, a vicious nationalist in the evening. Belkhodja regretted not denying that last hypothesis, not simply responding to other harmless questions about Si Ahmed, and now everything was coming back to haunt him, the fruit had broken the branch! Si Ahmed—and not only his son—must now have some real problems, among which money wasn't the most serious. A caïd is appointed and removed with the stroke of a pen, and he can be the object of an investigation into corruption, with the confiscation of his property. The day was perhaps near when Si Ahmed would say to Belkhodja that it is difficult for a dead man to help a sick one.

For a few days, Belkhodja was really afraid. If the French in the capital really went after the caïd, he would no longer be able to help him. He was, however, Belkhodja's only lifeline, that's what he had been told repeatedly. He was ashamed of the place where he had been told that, of the person who, in the shadows, had pointed out Si Ahmed to him as his last resort, a piece of advice that was well worth the money he spent to get it, "your one and only lifeline." To obtain that advice Belkhodja had gone sixty miles north of Nahbès, in the very heart of the medina of Ghouraq. He had crossed a space filled with huge nettles that revealed the stelae of forgotten graves. He found himself in a room with walls covered with flags of faded silk from mosques, amulets, talismans, dried and blackened toads and chameleons, and others that were still alive, attached to strings, and there, in an alcove strewn with pillows, an enormous woman, squatting, facing the door, had greeted him. On a tray in front of her several rag dolls were lined up: potbellied sultans, black-skinned genies, houris with well-rounded hips, warriors with their throats slit. These were the messengers who would put the fortune-teller in touch with the good or evil spirits of the astral plane, and that woman, after an hour of incantations, fumigations, turning of cards and manipulation of dolls, had told him: "It is in your town that your one and only salvation resides, an old acquaintance and a powerful man." Nothing else. And yet Si Ahmed, the powerful man, refused to help Belkhodja. He was clearly going through a rough patch. Belkhodja remembered the caïd had himself mentioned the time when he would no longer be caïd. A rumor of political disgrace must have reached certain creditors; it might be debts that were weakening the notable.

While going over these overwhelming hypotheses again and again, Belkhodja ended up seeing a less somber side to them: Si Ahmed in dire straits, that meant that Belkhodja should be able to get what he wanted from him. If the caïd agreed to the loan, and he must still have something to lend, even if he in turn had to borrow from Bensoussan, if he agreed, he could then display the loan as a sign of his solvency. A borrower is always suspect, not a creditor! When he developed this hypothesis, Belkhodja felt better, but Si Ahmed, in his oil-infused parlor, spent his time repeating that he didn't have any money, and that, even if he did, he wasn't a banker.

Belkhodja tried in vain to break this cycle and became lost in the thoughts that Si Ahmed gave him all the time in the world to ruminate by making him wait alone in the parlor where their meetings took place; and one day Belkhodja had understood that the smell of olive oil that bothered him wasn't coming from the back of the house, from the place where meals were prepared, but from behind a door in a corner of the parlor, from a place from which also came the sound of the cricket. He dared to open the door a crack, and the cricket fell silent. Cans, eight rows of ten cans, twelve-gallon cans, a strong smell of extra virgin—Si Ahmed was stockpiling a thousand gallons in his house? For what occasion? To sell at a profit on the eve of the next Ramadan? It was a very dense odor, a luxury oil. Belkhodja went back to sit in the parlor. If the caïd put so much oil in a room next to his parlor, he must have a good quantity stockpiled elsewhere. That day Belkhodja didn't say anything, but the next time, he began to talk about the oil, just like that, in small increments. The smell, it was a good smell. He complimented Si Ahmed on it, and Si Ahmed said to him: Don't talk to me about my oil, it costs me a great deal! When he accompanied Belkhodja to the door, the conversation centered no longer on a request for money but on the olive oil, and it was Si Ahmed who now voiced a request, and who sweetly asked Belkhodja not to speak to him about his oil, a true sin, and Belkhodja felt that he had to honor that sweet request, which promised indulgence in the days to come.

Belkhodja was a king of rugs, but didn't know much about olive oil, except that it could be very lucrative. Si Ahmed had begun to tell him the story: the Romans, the region covered with olive trees, then ruin for centuries, and the reconquest, trees more than a hundred years old. Did you know that a tree gives its best harvests between fifty and a hundred and fifty years old? And the pressing, the cold pressing . . . Si Ahmed clapped his hands. A servant entered. Si Ahmed gestured with a hand. The servant returned with a plate and a small dish that contained salt. He placed the plate and the dish on the low table in front of Si Ahmed and Belkhodja. He took a silver ewer from a corner of the room, as well as a basin and a napkin. "Set that down!" said Si Ahmed, who wanted to pour the water on his guest's hands himself. Belkhodja did the same for him while the servant went to get a round loaf of bread whose warm odor had invaded the room, and a bottle filled with an oil of such pale green that it was almost golden. He put everything on the table. "Leave us!" Si Ahmed ordered, contemplating the table with a sigh of satisfaction. "Now you are going to understand," he said to Belkhodja while pouring a large pool of oil onto the plate, then taking a pinch of salt, scattering it over the oil, breaking the round bread, detaching a piece, crust and bread, dipping the piece of bread in the oil, and he held it out to Belkhodja. The bread smelled good, the warmth spread the aroma of the oil, and Belkhodja had in his mouth a taste that could become that of his wealth, Si Ahmed saying: You can even smell the quality of the mule that turned the grindstone to crush the olives, a patient beast, well fed. Not as strong as an ox or a camel, you don't need that, the grindstone isn't too heavy. And you can't put too many olives into the crusher at once; the right crushing must be fine but remain consistent. The quality of the mule, and then the quality of the press cloths, my friend, the pressing filters, the fine quality of the esparto grass to make the press cloths, and the quality of the arms of the men at the press, men worthy of creating liquid gold, and I almost forgot: picking by hand, not with a stick. You must never harm the tree, or the fruit will remember.

Si Ahmed told about his oil the way storytellers told stories at the marketplace, when everyone is in a circle around them, and they have to know how to hold the attention of all those people, prevent them from going to another teller. It isn't easy to talk about oil the way one would talk about the adventures of a hero or a lion, but Si Ahmed was able to do it. Belkhodja complimented him, without mentioning his money worries. Then Si Ahmed left the oil aside. He changed the subject. They spoke for a long time about what some of their friends were doing, their successes, failures, especially deaths, which makes one aware of the fragility of all one's joys, the unexpected nature of the blows of destiny, unexpected for humans. Of course, Si Ahmed said, humans discover only too late that which has been written forever, and then Belkhodja spoke of oil again, of the pleasure that it brought. It wasn't an ordinary oil, not a simple odor; when you breathed it, it really tickled the palate, the back of the mouth; it was so strong that it was a taste even before tasting it. And Si Ahmed became softer and softer under the compliments paid to his oil. He had come to its fabrication belatedly, an olive grove that he brought back, that he had enlarged, and now he sold the best oil in the South, *ghemlali* oil, of a purity . . . You know they even ask for it in Paris? Do you know how much a bottle sells for in Paris? Even the Transméditerranéenne orders from me for its hotels and ships!

Si Ahmed sighed, rubbed his palms together, and went back to describing his oil: They bought it without even tasting it. Si Ahmed could have doubled his production by using certain processes, but he wanted only the best quality.

Belkhodja said to himself that it was too good, all that oil, right there, waiting to be sold, the oil in the room next door, and above all the oil that must be stored elsewhere, where? It was too good, no, it was a sign—Raouf and his father— God had sent him the wound and the remedy. And what Belkhodja didn't see, in Si Ahmed's darkened parlor, was the shine of a wood saw, the shine that it has when it is newly purchased in a store, the black shine of the blade of a saw in the caïd's eyes.

Belkhodja began to calculate the difference between what he would have to pay Si Ahmed for all that oil in cans, and a retail selling price, perhaps even by the quart, half at least by the quart, the rest by one or two gallons—it was as if the devil himself had decided to buy all of Si Ahmed's stock by using Belkhodja— how much would he have? Enough to fill a truck at least, that was certain, a very large truck, probably two. Si Ahmed had become Belkhodja's prey. He couldn't lend. He must also be in dire straits, much more than Belkhodja. He had no more money, and he kept his oil because he couldn't sell it anymore, because he already owed money to buyers whom he knew. That's why he wasn't keeping it in a warehouse in the town and was hiding it right in the middle of his house. Otherwise his creditors would have taken his oil. Raouf's trip to Europe must have ruined Si Ahmed. What Belkhodja had said to the police about the caïd's son hadn't been a blunder. Things were in order. It was thanks to that denunciation that Si Ahmed was now struggling and at the mercy of Belkhodja. The son's trip to Europe, and probably the baksheesh to the French to be left alone—the French rarely took bribes, but when they did they were always big—to save a son, all this oil in a house, in the dark, thousands and thousands of gallons, a true fortune, that one could increase, a truck, two trucks filled with the best quality oil, twenty, thirty thousand francs, maybe not that much, or by mixing a bit, at least twenty-eight thousand.

26

GREAT MURMURINGS

While visiting Paris they also sometimes stopped to catch their breath, in cafés with red banquettes, copper railings, and walls covered with mirrors that multiplied the lamps and faces. Gabrielle discreetly took note of a patron who was saying to his neighbor: "The cocktails are expensive, but when you've had four or five you don't feel like dinner anymore, and that's something." And that other man who seemed to be looking at nothing: they had seen him come up from the stairs leading to the toilets in the basement, seeming in a hurry, but constrained, a waiter pushing him from behind with the flat of his hand. They were in a brasserie on a square opposite the Jardin du Luxembourg. The waiter, his teeth clenched, was muttering a few words, "Asshole, you're going to see what you'll see!" The owner, behind the cash register, as calm as his employee was agitated, started to talk on the telephone. They couldn't hear what he was saying. "They look like Laurel and Hardy," Kathryn murmured. The man whom the waiter was now holding against the bar was fairly tall, fat but big. He could have gotten away from the waiter with a simple movement of his hips, but he didn't do anything. He stood there, placid. His red eyes went from the bar counter to the dining room. His chin trembled as if he were going to cry.

The owner hung up the phone. He looked at the man, then turned his head toward the large windows that looked out onto the square. Everything was calm. The other patrons hadn't seen anything. At the bar, the presence of the large guy, the waiter, and the owner seemed natural. Raouf asked Ganthier what was going on. Ganthier didn't know any more than he. Gabrielle asked: "Are you going to continue to play the innocents?" They couldn't respond. Gabrielle, in a harder tone: "You're not going to tell me you don't understand!" Kathryn started to laugh. It echoed around the room. She was leaning back, her back pressed against the leather of the banquette, her hands holding the edge of the table, a hearty laugh, aimed at the hypocrisy of men. The owner and his employee seemed worried. Kathryn became serious. Gabrielle said to Ganthier and Raouf that she was going to take them to the women's toilets to show them what gentlemen did at the right height in the walls and doors, a Parisian specialty Kathryn said, and she pointed at what they hadn't noticed, a small, hand-cranked drill that the man with the red eyes was holding, yes, in the left hand, behind the folds of his raincoat.

"The instrument of the crime," Gabrielle said, "We call that a *chignole* in French!" Kathryn added that in the States such things were rather rare: the men are more impulsive; they're not content simply to watch.

While they were talking, two police officers on bicycles arrived at the door, kepis, dark blue capes.

"Note the capes, young Raouf," Ganthier said, "They are weighted with lead. When you roll them up they make a very effective club. Now you know what awaits you if you continue to frequent your dear friends!"

"The police are involved in everything here," Raouf had replied, "They target men with ideas as well as men with drills."

"Are you sure your friends have only ideas? And nothing with which to follow up their ideas? Not strikes, violent ones?"

"Maybe . . . That would be great, a large, anticolonial strike, over three continents."

"One can always dream!"

Raouf sighed: "At least we would stop being the voyeurs of our plight."

The policemen parked their bicycles against the front window of the brasserie, the owner frowning with displeasure. They came in. The owner and the waiter greeted them, a four-way discussion, voices low. The man with the drill didn't say anything.

"What a sad sack!" said Kathryn.

After a few minutes the officers left with the man. One of them took the bicycles; the other handcuffed the defeated man to his arm. The three of them stopped in front of the roundabout where the cars and buses were slowed by careless pedestrians or a carriage whose cracking whip brought to mind a circus parade around a basin in which a nymph and a bronze triton were gripping a huge shell. Kathryn and her friends were watching the officers and their prisoner, who were now going up rue Soufflot, Gabrielle saying:

"Poor guy!" And Ganthier:

"Well-cut clothing, not really ugly. He should have a wife like everyone else, but no, no wedding ring. He doesn't like women, he just likes his torment."

Kathryn, her heart suddenly clinching from Ganthier's words . . . *Torment, that's not true, one doesn't love one's torment.*

Then they, too, left the brasserie, continued their stroll . . . One doesn't love one's torment, one tries to know, one has the right to know, and to look for a letter . . . A jealous Kathryn saw herself going through the pockets of a coat, a jacket, a mad curiosity, and the fear of being caught, one is already mad, no, one is ill, that's all, you're afraid of losing him, searching since it doesn't

mean anything. During that time the other Kathryn joked with her friends, discovered the city, walked briskly in the cold, kissed Raouf. Everyone was there;
calm returned in the noise of their heels on the pavement. Raouf sometimes
trotted to keep up with his lover, and the shop windows were the best. She forgot Metilda. She was no longer with her torment. She looked at coats, dresses,
purses, scarves, shoes, more dresses. She had converted Gabrielle to shopping.
Raouf and Ganthier followed.

The women had been on war footing since the morning, the time when
crowds surged out of the large mouths of the Metro, streams of people of all
sorts, beautiful clothes that had gotten off the red first-class cars, and others, employees, secretaries, switchboard operators, clerks in department stores, delivery
men, accountants, milliners with round boxes.

"They aren't paid much," said Gabrielle, "but it lets them say, 'I work in Paris
near the Opera.'"

They saw a world of tense faces go by.

"Yes," said Gabrielle, "they're in a hurry, that's the modern rhythm," and she
told about newcomers who stood in front of their bosses, stopwatch in hand,
giving each person the time he was entitled to. Yes, they do say, *you're entitled to,*
and if you don't want it, that's your right. You can always go back to your slow-
rhythmed province, to Lure or Mombard: I work near the Lure train station,
would you really want to say that?

Kathryn and Gabrielle went in, looked around, bought or left without buying, Gabrielle saying without embarrassment:

"I should buy more often, instead of always waiting to lose a few pounds."

At Bailly the saleslady opened a box of pumps while singing Kathryn's praises,
her slender ankles, her high arch, "You have a Greek foot," Kathryn thinking, *I'd
be surprised if the cow of Tyrol has one.*

"Raouf, is Tyrol in Austria?"

"Why are you asking?"

"I don't know, I can't remember."

At the cash register Kathryn paid while looking at the staircase leading to the
floor above along a wall covered with a large mirror. In the middle of the mirror
were two incongruous warnings, "Watch Your Step," and "Hold onto the Railing." Kathryn asked the clerk:

"Is the staircase that dangerous?"

"It's not the stairs, it's the mirror . . . The customers watch themselves going
down and they forget they are on the stairs, we've had some serious accidents,
and it's the same with men."

They left. More clothing stores.

"Hey, the fashion is coming back!" said Ganthier sarcastically, he pointed at a large window, three dressed mannequins, massive figures, long, black skirts, dark green vests.

"It's a Swiss shop," said Gabrielle, "not German."

"German Swiss!" said Ganthier. It could also be Austrian, the hems of the dresses were decorated with red and gold embroidery, as were the busts and vests, Kathryn caught Raouf looking at a bust, she must have large breasts, likes to have them held, Kathryn suddenly seeing a Metilda lying in the window, a bus passed behind them, a depressing dark cloud, *I'm crazy, no, I'm ill, and now she is everywhere, he has to talk to me about it, I don't ask much of him, tell me what he did, just one night, probably, the last one, I'm tired of being crazy.*

The quartet started off again, Kathryn holding Raouf's arm, looking at their reflection in another window, *I look younger than my age, he looks older, we make a nice couple, we don't need a cow from Tyrol.* She decided to dress Raouf; Gabrielle enthusiastically supported her: an entire afternoon at Old England, between mirrors and laughter, Raouf in tweed, velvet and cashmere, Ganthier surprised to see that it looked pretty good on him, but still calling him a dandy. They then went into a Félix Potin. The food came from all over the world. Raouf stopped and said:

"Look, that bottle of olive oil, it's fifteen times more expensive than in Nahbès, I'm going to become an oil merchant in Paris," Ganthier congratulating Raouf:

"A nice conversion to capitalism, young man! The future is to the intermediaries."

They went back out, looked for a taxi. A sudden shout, a young girl hitting a sixty-something-year-old man on the head with her umbrella, a bowler hat rolling on the ground, the woman shouting at people to be witnesses: "He pinched me!" The man picked up his hat and left, very dignified. Kathryn felt sick: Is that how men end up?

They heard the cries of the newspaper sellers, like gulls in a storm, each shout trying to overpower the others, "Woman from Auvergne has throat cut in bed by a Russian!" or "New lies from Germany," or "Polish are arrested for stealing children," some very ugly faces on the front pages, and then "Crisis in Berlin!" Farther away, the sound of an accordion coming out of the entrance to a building.

"Traveling musicians, they must be in the courtyard," said Ganthier.

"They are paid less and less," said Gabrielle.

"Why?"

"Because of the radio and record players."

One evening Kathryn decided to accompany Raouf again to the rue de la Grange-aux-Belles without telling Ganthier. They first went to Mokhtar's, a friend of Raouf's and Chemla's, Kathryn wearing trousers, a gray jacket, a cloche, no makeup. In Mokhtar's room a cold wind came in through the gaps in the door and windows, drops of humidity on the walls, Raouf saying to Mokhtar:

"You know, I don't think like you do . . . ," and Mokhtar:

"Since you're not a Social-Democrat . . ."

A slap on Raouf's back, then:

"A progressive bourgeois, that's worth all the social traitors."

A bed, and a mattress on the ground: Quôc was staying with Mokhtar, who was helping him survive, did the cooking for him.

They went into the great murmurings on Granges-aux-Belles just as a voice at the podium was saying:

"It isn't possible to think like our invaders, nor is it possible to think and act as we did before."

It was the auditorium of a music hall. There was a bar at the entrance, separated from the room by a guardrail, and an area with some hundred bistro tables, and a passageway along the walls. People were listening to the speakers or talking in more or less low voices. The balcony was also filled with people, a cloud of smoke on the ceiling, very few women, apart from those who, on the left, at the corner of the bar, were keeping a few silent and attentive men company.

"Annamites?" Kathryn asked.

"No," said Mokhtar, "Chinese, they are the only ones who come with women, and who talk to them."

"Do you know them?"

"Not really, Quôc introduced me to one of them."

"The short, fat one, the tall, thin one, or the average, distinguished-looking one?"

"The distinguished-looking one."

The Chinese were in sharp contrast with the rest of those in attendance, their factory worker uniforms and a calm tone and subtle gestures, Mokhtar pointing out:

"Student workers."

One of the Chinese went to the podium, the tallest, a softer voice than those of the other speakers, but he spoke very clear French. He spoke of a country-continent to overthrow, of justice to be had, was called a reformist by one of the Frenchmen present, responded by asserting his desire for total revolution, and for another Frenchman China was only a peasant reserve, which should wait for the revolution in the cities:

"Let the bourgeoisie have its day, you can settle things with it afterward. Otherwise you'll have fascism, like the Italians!"

The Chinese man defended himself:

"We already have fascists!"

Kathryn was intrigued by the presence of the young women whom the men were apparently treating as equals.

"Because they are bourgeois like Raouf," said Mokhtar, laughing.

"No, it's because they are in advance," said Raouf.

Quôc had joined them. He introduced them to the Chinese, who bombarded Kathryn with questions about America. The tallest, who had left the podium, answered before Kathryn had a chance to respond:

"Aggressive politics, division of the working class, big club politics."

Kathryn didn't understand much, preferred the questions of the short, fat one. He was called Deng; he loved factories, machines, and department stores. The most distinguished was named Chou. He also asked a lot of questions, smiled while saying:

"We came here to explore the heart of the monster." He also said that France had helped him to progress:

"When I arrived, I was a young reformist."

"Like him," said Mokhtar, taking Raouf by the shoulders. And Quôc:

"We have all been reformists . . ."

Chou continued: "I've been here three years, I've finally understood the enemy, we have to forge a weapon of steel," and Quôc, in a cheerful tone:

"That means they have become communists!"

"And that we don't need a master . . . ," added Chou.

The young women looked at Kathryn, both fascinated and distant. They asked her questions and responded to her questions. Yes, they were cable women in an electrical factory, Kathryn avoiding asking them if it was difficult. One of the women was called Fan. She wanted to become an engineer in radio transmission.

"In China it's impossible, but since everything seems impossible, it can become possible."

She had attended a demonstration of an experiment at the Sorbonne. It was in the Descartes amphitheater:

"I thought it was wonderful to have it in that amphitheater, we really like Descartes. The man who did the experiment was called Belin. There were images he was able to transmit through a telephone, Édouard Belin, he called that a wave scene, he put a drawing into a big machine, and the drawing reappeared in another similar machine, thirty feet away, without a cord, a wave scene!"

The distinguished-looking Chinese man, pointing at the young woman:

"She knows how to build a radio!" Raouf noted that he hadn't said *even knows how to* . . .

The next day, at the hotel, Kathryn wanted to know everything about the world of politics. She had newspapers brought to their table at breakfast and said to Ganthier and Gabrielle, "Explain France and old Europe to me!" pointing to *Le Figaro, L'Avenir, Le Temps* and (to Ganthier's displeasure) *L'Humanité*. When the maître d' handed that paper to her with obvious disapproval, Ganthier assumed the same air, and then was mad at himself for being on the same side as a flunky. Gabrielle commented on events with an intelligence that Ganthier didn't like, but he reserved his arrows for Raouf:

"Reading the newspaper is the morning prayer for modern man, but that is no reason to neglect your own, with the rug, faith, intention, and all that . . ." Raouf smiled sweetly, without answering, and his good mood bothered Ganthier. He told himself that it came from the night before, *and that little bum is still being pleasured by watching his girlfriend swallow her toast and jam!*

They also commented on the Saharan raid by the French half-tracks. Ganthier liked the expeditions, the space, the future. Raouf remained silent. Ganthier demanded admiration. Raouf finally said:

"Your expeditions serve above all to show that France is at home everywhere."

There were also the tensions in Europe, the question of the war reparations to be paid by Germany. For Gabrielle the French had invented the concept of a war that cost nothing:

"The bourgeoisie gave their sons, but not money." Ganthier responded:

"The defeated must pay!" And Gabrielle:

"But not until 1980!"

They stopped arguing and opened their mail, a letter from Nahbès for Ganthier, Gabrielle asking if it was news of his dachshund, and Raouf saying that Ganthier didn't need news of Kid by post because he got it every day by phone. The letter was from Si Ahmed. He informed his *old friend* that all was very well on his property, but he regretted to tell him that he hadn't made any progress on the question of land consolidation; the opposition was stronger than foreseen. Ganthier said to himself that he would take care of all that when he got back, *I will ride my horse right onto Madame's veranda, and I will have a discussion with her, I should have done that a long time ago.*

Si Ahmed's letter didn't ask any questions about Raouf; it would have been inappropriate. Ganthier was annoyed. Gabrielle noticed:

"Rania is making you mad . . ."

"Do you know her as well as that?"

"She's a true friend. We write, I even have a photo."

Ganthier had watched the young widow grow up; he had always found her a bit boyish. In the photo he saw the face of a beautiful woman with large eyes, high cheekbones, slender lips, a long and powerful neck. He dared say:

"A lovely artist's print . . ."

"You're an ass," said Gabrielle, "There's no retouching."

"I don't recognize her."

"Because a photo is something other than a habit."

Ganthier frowned. Gabrielle:

"I've even seen photos of you where you aren't too bad."

They continued to talk about Rania; for Ganthier she was a fanatic, anti-French.

"You don't understand anything," said Gabrielle, "For her, theology is a weapon," Raouf adding:

"She is far from being credulous," and Gabrielle:

"As for being anti-France, you say that as soon as anyone states that a protectorate is not a colony."

Raouf was having fun. Ganthier was more patient with Gabrielle than with him. Ganthier wondered what that meant, "You aren't too bad," *a way of putting me in my place, or an invitation . . . One day, when all this is done, I will discover that she was in love with me, I have to go back to her place . . .*

Kathryn had plunged into a newspaper, then, laughing, she showed them a full-page ad in the *Petit Parisien*: "Arthritis sufferers, defend yourselves!" and Raouf, looking right at Ganthier:

"That's the new 'Arise, Ye Dead' of the bourgeoisie." Ganthier had had enough. The kid was making fun of him, *I put him into the modern world and he calls me an arthritic bourgeois!* On the other side of the Mediterranean Ganthier incarnated the new civilization; here, a son of a notable dreamt of the red dawn and turned him into a relic of history.

Later, during a stroll in the Jardin d'Acclimatation, Ganthier slapped a man he had just passed on the path going in the opposite direction. Raouf, Gabrielle, and Kathryn, who were walking in front, turned around. They didn't understand. The very pale man was holding out a card, saying: "Sir, I beg of you . . ." Ganthier interrupted him: "Pistol? Sword?" The man had seen the ribbons in Ganthier's buttonhole, and he left without saying anything more. Raouf asked what had happened,

"He bumped into me, that's all."

Ganthier was on edge. As they were leaving the park he muttered: "An arthritic must defend himself!" And a few days later, this confidence to Gabrielle:

"I don't know what came over me. The guy had just passed Kathryn, and when he got to me I heard him say, 'Arab-fucker.'"

"Be careful," Gabrielle said in an amused tone, "You're going to find yourself siding with the anticolonial left."

"Never! All that I want is a France of a hundred million inhabitants, a great nation of equal citizens."

"That's not exactly what your dear Prépondérants are hoping for . . ."

"Do you know that in 1915 the antiaircraft defense of Paris was commanded by a black graduate of the polytechnic . . . from Guadeloupe . . . the son of slaves?"

"We can always dream . . ."

27

A LIBERATED COUNTRY

They left Paris for Alsace. It was a Sunday. It had begun to snow early in the morning, an increasingly thick coating on the pavement, the sidewalks, the awnings, the streetlamps . . . the sound-deadening white of snow . . . sometimes a lull. The snow was waiting for the snow, which returned in bigger and bigger flakes, covering the black of the soot and coal around the Gare de l'Est, then was dirtied anew by the greasy exhaust of a bus or the cloud that escaped a locomotive, the flakes then coming to bury what the soiled snow revealed to be an unbearable spot, and after the train departed it continued to snow much more heavily over the landscape. At one point Raouf saw barges similar to those on the Seine, immobile in the middle of a field of snow.

"The Marne-Rhine Canal," said Ganthier, "They're not going anywhere, it's frozen, it must not be very warm inside."

The trip took more than eight hours, with alternating fields, hills, and an increasing number of jagged woods, large cemeteries under the snow, villages often in ruins. In the curves they could see the magma of heavy smoke in the locomotive's wake. The train stopped often, in small villages or larger towns, where sometimes a church bell rang the hour like a lamentation. On the platforms, Raouf and Kathryn were surprised to see so many travelers in black, women traveling in twos or threes.

"They're still looking for the grave of a husband," Ganthier had said, "or of a brother, son, father . . ."

Gabrielle added: "And the hotels make them pay as much as on the Côte d'Azur." After a moment, then: "Rania never wanted to . . . ?" She interrupted herself, and no one continued.

They then traveled through forests, the trees sometimes beating against the window of their compartment; then the snow drifts became taller and taller, the train tracks seeming to enter an igloo; then a long tunnel; then there was the plain again, an expanse of white.

"The snow that falls fattens the earth," Ganthier said, as if to reassure himself.

Beyond the Vosges the countryside was cleaner, less devastated than that which they had just traveled through, and at one point Ganthier, who was looking out the corridor window, pointed at something like a break in the line of the horizon, a dark object, "The spire!" he said, "The spire of the cathedral, it's different from the Eiffel Tower, the spire of Strasbourg!" A moment of silence, then: "We didn't say so out loud, we didn't want to be called vengeful, but that was what we fought for. They said it was for civilization, but it was for that, a piece of our fatherland. That's what stokes righteous fury, not civilization!" With Ganthier one never knew how much of what he said was meant to be sarcastic.

In the streets of the city, Raouf and Kathryn were surprised to hear a strange sort of German spoken, whereas every balcony, almost every window, displayed the French flag. It was snowing even more than when they left, a windless snow, large flakes that fell straight down one after the other to cover everything, settling thickly everywhere, more heavily than in Paris. And on the roofs of the smallest houses one could distinguish superimposed layers, representing the snowfalls that had followed each other for several weeks. In the evening it was even more beautiful. Kathryn wanted to take a walk after dinner. They abandoned the warmth of their hotel on place Kléber, very few people in the streets. They walked in the virgin snow, more than eight inches on the ground, walked down a street with arcades that led into a long, newly restored square.

"What is that statue?" Kathryn had asked.

"It's Gutenberg," Ganthier said, "Let's take the street on the left."

He let Raouf and the two women go in front of him, then there it was again, abruptly rising up some forty feet before them, blocking the street they had just taken, four hundred fifty feet of cathedral climbing into the dark sky, with snow-flakes that fell on their eyelashes while they looked, the enormous portal, the spire on the left, the pink stone and the snow that danced in the drafts along the facade, in the light projected by a lamp. Raouf was dumbstruck.

"It sucks you upward?" Ganthier had asked.

"Magnificent," Raouf said, "and a purely aesthetic magnificence, like for you."

"Nothing else?"

"No, like you . . . that is . . . like the you of today."

Ganthier turned toward the two women. He hadn't liked Raouf's allusion to his past as a seminarian:

"I suspect that our dear Raouf has a small tendency toward atheism . . . an atheism without alcohol . . . That's rare among Arabs."

"You don't know anything," Raouf said. To ease the tension, while they were getting nearer to the front of the cathedral, Gabrielle spoke to them about Goethe's discovery of the cathedral, Alsace, and a certain Friederike:

"He was seduced by a frilly skirt that allowed a pretty foot to be seen up to the ankle!"

The next day they had to go to the prefecture, for passport control, and waited in a corner of a large room. On the other side of the room Raouf noticed a man, seated by himself at a table on which was placed an inkwell and pen-holder, probably some sort of low-level bureaucrat who wasn't entitled to the four walls of an office and who was put anywhere, in a hallway, a common room, or even on a landing as in Nahbès. This one had the same melancholic look of a chaouch; all administrations were the same. The man had responded to Raouf's stare with a smile. He seemed to be at loose ends. Then another employee brought him a pile of papers, and he began to make little marks with his pen on each sheet. He was slow, applied, you might have said, a schoolboy who was watching his downstrokes and upstrokes. Raouf asked Ganthier what that man could be doing. Ganthier didn't know.

Raouf stood up, as if to stretch his legs. He went over to the man, said hello, showing the right degree of respect: "May I ask . . ." The man was affable. With the tip of his pen he pointed at the sheet of paper he was working on. Raouf heard him say: "I am the *et mèn'che*." He didn't understand, hesitated. Pretend that he understood? And wait to hear more? He often did that in school. Or ask again, outright? He asked what "*et mèn'che*" meant. He heard the worker respond, "The man of the *ets.*" He didn't understand. The man added: "Like this!" And with his pen he put an acute accent on the first *e* of the word *République*. The man straightened up, looked at his work, leaned over, put another accent on the last letter of *Liberté*, raised his eyes to Raouf, "The Germans don't have our accents." That was his work, to add the grave, acute, and circumflex accents on all the French vowels that needed them.

"There are also cedillas!"

Before the astonished look of Raouf, the man added:

"You must understand, most of our typewriters are still German. The Germans introduced us to many modern things, they stayed for close to fifty years, and it must be said" (the man lowered his voice), "German typewriters are better. The only defect is the absence of accented French vowels, our dear accented vowels . . . So I am the 'é man,' the 'é *Mensch*' in Alsatian." He also said that no one was permitted to speak Alsatian in the administration anymore; for the French it was a Boche thing. Yes, he put all the accents on all the documents. His task was official; it was included in the list of positions in the new public administration.

"And believe me, it is an important task. Each time I add an accent I am helping our dear Alsace to return to the bosom of the motherland!"

Toward the end he spoke mechanically, with the air of not really believing it. Raouf had not, moreover, immediately understood, because the man had pronounced the French word *giron*—bosom—as *chiron*. He caught himself, then: "Accents are easier to correct on paper than in one's voice, perhaps because we're attached to our voice. We are a great plain that many people have always crossed over, we keep in our throats the trace of that which has happened in our history." And to be pardoned for seeming doubtful, Raouf had carefully looked at the man's work, a lovely calligraphy, he said as a connoisseur. Each accent began with the stroke of his pen, and loosened, ending with a light touch. The man's rhythm was efficient, precise, with a dip into the inkwell every eight or ten accents, just what was necessary to have the right amount of ink without risking a blot.

"If you're here, it's probably for a passport," said the man, "You'll see, it's the same thing over there, in the Rhineland, wherever we have our occupation troops: the *é Menschen*, a profession of the future for Alsatians!"

He was being both sarcastic and proud.

"No, I haven't always worked here. Before, I was a German teacher. We need fewer of those today."

Once the formalities had been completed, Raouf and his friends went to treat themselves at a salon de thé. There were even more pastries than in Paris, and according to Gabrielle that was intentional: the government wanted the return to the motherland to be done under the best of conditions. Raouf told them about his conversation with the *é* man.

"What machine do you use?" Ganthier asked Gabrielle.

"A Remington," Raouf immediately said.

"He's more observant than you are," Gabrielle said, and Ganthier:

"Another foreign brand."

"Yes, but adapted to the French language and 'made in France.'"

"In any case," Ganthier said, "with a machine it's not the same French, you're not writing, you're typing!"

There was condescension in Ganthier's voice. Gabrielle defended herself: on a machine you can't go back and correct yourself; it required writing without needless embellishments. For Ganthier it was the end of style.

"No," said Gabrielle, "it is a return to the classics, direct order, essential words, and a quick phrase, like a watercolor."

"But the clacking of the machine . . . a pen lives, not a keyboard!"

"Do you know what Joubert said? Music has seven letters and writing has twenty-six notes . . . I love my keyboard."

From time to time Raouf looked around the room, which was filled with massive furniture. Not far at another table there was a young woman, alone, seated on a banquette, a very powdered face, bright red lips, a very soft, black leather jacket with a fur collar. She was concentrating on her movements, her spoon moving slowly above the assortment of red fruit accompanied by cookies that filled the large bowl placed in front of her next to a cup of steaming chocolate.

"Are you still here, Raouf?" Kathryn suddenly asked. Raouf looked at her without understanding. Kathryn waited a moment, as if she was waiting for an answer, then:

"Because if I'm cramping your style, I can leave!" Her tone had become hard.

"And on my way out I can ask her if she'd like you to join her. I'm sure she'll be happy. You might even be able to put your hand between her legs."

Ganthier and Gabrielle looked at each other, ill at ease, Ganthier not even daring to turn his head toward the other table. Kathryn had become pale. It was a true scene, in public. Raouf felt lost. He had simply wanted to see what the girl was eating. He was maybe going to order the same thing, that's all, he hadn't realized . . .

"That's what drives me crazy," said Kathryn, "He doesn't realize, he was really looking at what she was eating, and he didn't see the way she had been looking at him for ten minutes!"

Then, with her voice scarcely any lower:

"That . . . bitch knows that he's with me, that doesn't prevent her from . . . with her eyes . . . do you have a verb in French?"

"*Zyeuter*—to eyeball," said Gabrielle.

"*Mater*—same thing," said Ganthier, "but it's slang."

"It's the same thing as *zyeuter*?"

"It's stronger, it's when a man possesses a woman with a look."

"But that's what that bitch is doing, she was possessing Raouf."

"But it's not Raouf's fault," said Ganthier.

"That's it, defend him."

"I didn't do anything, nothing," said Raouf. Gabrielle also defended him, he hadn't seen anything . . . For Kathryn that was the worst:

"One day, without seeing anything, he'll find himself in bed with a bitch."

"That's a bit much, isn't it?" asked Ganthier.

"If he loves me he should be able to recognize women who want to harm me!"

Ganthier thought that would be a lot of people to watch, but refrained from saying so. While they were talking the woman had left the salon de thé. Kathryn calmed down. She stroked Raouf's hand. Later, Gabrielle to Kathryn:

"You've dressed him up like a dandy, and now you're furious that women are noticing him."

Ganthier had spent the hardest six months of the war on the slopes of the Vieil-Armand, above Cernay. He wanted to see what it looked like now. They made the trip by car through the plain, then the vineyard. In Ribeauvillé they stopped for lunch at an inn, a nice chicken with cream sauce. They were the only customers and the owner spoiled them.

"We make French fries here, like in France. Even when the Germans were here I made fries. They never said anything to me. They were happy to come and eat them."

She was a woman with a nice face and round body, a good-looking fifty-something. She appeared to have a crush on Ganthier. She kept coming over to their table, carefully moved her hips when she went back to the kitchen, in a trot if she wanted them to appear lively and ample. She spoke to them a lot, even sat next to Ganthier on the banquette, stood up, expressed her admiration for his hair, couldn't hold herself back, and passed her hand over his head, saying, "*S'esch a guete Kerl!*" in a throaty voice that she tried to make sound chirpy, and everyone burst out laughing at this good woman's attentions, Ganthier as a "good boy," the seducer at the inn.

They were spending the night at a hotel at the top of the Grand Ballon of Guebwiller, a large wooden chalet. They ate off plates painted with scenes from daily life, farmwork, walking, a dance with tuba players. The beds were tall, narrow, covered with red duvets. Kathryn was sweet. In the morning it was very cold. It was still snowing. "Star Lou beautiful breast of pink snow," Raouf had murmured in Kathryn's ear, awakening her. Later, Kathryn wanted to put some protective cream on Raouf's face, but he didn't allow it. They continued to play. Outside, it was a world of silence, of pine trees, larches, cloudy, with blue openings between two rounded mountain peaks. Raouf liked walking in the forest, more silence, the noise of shoes on the powder, observing the prints on the ground, the same marking repeated at almost a yard apart until the entrance to the woods, two paws close to each other, and behind the paws, a longer print, deeper.

"A large rabbit," said Ganthier, "It's also called a variable hare."

"Why?" Raouf asked.

"Because it changes colors with the season, from brown to white, to avoid being seen."

"A true rabbit of the protectorate," Raouf had concluded.

They found themselves facing an expanse of snow, barred in the distance by a curtain of pine trees, and behind the trees, very far, other peaks. Log cabins were wearing huge white hairpieces. A path suddenly veered off from theirs, marked by snowshoes, disappearing behind an escarpment in the terrain. On the horizon the snow blended with the lead gray of the sky. White powder fell from the trees whenever a gust of wind moved the branches. They heard the cries of rooks. Raouf loved to feel the burning of the snow in the hollow of his hand. Sometimes the sun slid between the clouds and a spot of light appeared on the snowy mounds.

"Let no one utter the adjective 'fairylike,'" Gabrielle said. Raouf and Kathryn went up to bed very early. Gabrielle and Ganthier talked for a long time in the hotel parlor. Ganthier had the feeling that Gabrielle was getting used to him; one night they would naturally find themselves in the same room.

The next day they got back on the road, climbed the Vieil-Armand, which the locals still called Hartmannswillerkopf, Ganthier saying:

"We called it *La Mangeuse*—the eater . . ."

Raouf stopped provoking him. They were walking on the scorched mountain, between bunches of rock and cement, pieces of rusty beams, a trench suddenly widened by a shell hole. Ganthier was surprised to have so few memories, a man wounded in the stomach who had asked for the canteen and almost inhaled the metal . . . He started to talk to forget the black blood that smelled like tripe, a few words, *potholes*, mortar shells, one hundred thirty pounds, those damned *potholes*, you could put ten men in the holes that they made, and the flame throwers, the gas, but not often, the fronts were too close to each other, sometimes scarcely sixty feet, you could even hear them talking over there, "and the two crests that went down on our left and our right. We didn't call them crests. We said the left thigh and the right thigh, exciting, right? The worst was December seven years ago. We had gained a quarter of a mile. Those idiots in command hadn't bothered to send us reinforcements in time. The reinforcements were for the ones across from us, and they even came up behind us. The command had forgotten to clean up the fortifications that had been breached. The Boches came out at our backs. The entire 152nd was obliterated—excuse me, I'm boring you." Farther, among the graves, a few women were sharing a watering can.

They went back to Strasbourg. In the lobby of the train station Raouf bought some postcards. Kathryn didn't ask for whom, but in the taxi that took them to the hotel, her mood darkened. Raouf refrained from asking her why and asked Ganthier:

"Is it true that after 1870 the Germans supported your colonial conquests to turn you away from Strasbourg? They would have paid for your defeat? And in 1918 all of the Germans really left to go to the other side of the Rhine? After all those years in Alsace? Even those who had bought land, built buildings, factories? Left without compensation? Now that's good decolonization!"

Raouf was quiet a moment, then, looking out the taxi window, at a massive building just below the violet sky:

"Everything they built is beautiful, the Rhine Palace, the courthouse, the opera, the museum, even the train station . . . My favorite is the university, and the library, it's huge . . . Do you think you'll do the same for us one of these days?"

28

THE SUITOR

Rania finally agreed to leave her father's house and return to Nahbès. She took the train accompanied by two servingwomen, under the watchful eyes of European travelers who could perhaps accept that a native dressed in silk and wool might travel in first class, but the two servants, she could have put them in third: Was she really that afraid of being alone? Some people even looked at her hostilely in the waiting room, when they noticed that she was holding a book—that seemed bold, and a French book, literature! She's even holding her book the right way. It seems it is one of their favorite authors, but even so, she's doing it on purpose: she could have chosen the Comtesse de Ségur, or *Sans famille*. Did you see the faces of the other two natives when they saw a woman of their religion with a French book? She could have propositioned men and it would not have been worse! Rania and her servants found themselves alone in their compartment.

When they arrived things were different because Si Ahmed and Marfaing had come to meet her to get news of Si Mabrouk, a French traveler confiding in his wife:

"For Marfaing to have accompanied the caïd, she must be the daughter of a great family, but I still don't see why: one, she is traveling without her husband; and two, why would that husband allow her to read Rousseau?"

"I've always been told not to read him," the wife said, "Apparently that *Nouvelle Héloïse* is full of vice."

At the farm it was cold. Rania couldn't stand the smell of gas stoves. She read in front of the fireplace, wearing a camel-skin burnoose whose hood she even sometimes put on. She only raised her head at the onset of dark ideas. She chided herself . . . It's the lack of activity that's making me cold, *tala layli min hubbin man la arahu muqaribi*, my night is getting longer, the one I love is not beside me . . .

She went out as often as possible, walked in the countryside, in front of the cart, remembering that Gabrielle had once told her, "Walking just to walk, without obligation, is an invention of rich Europeans." She was often on the verge of tears. Then her breathing became deeper. She was absorbed in the plants she saw, but it wasn't a mere spectacle. Everything reminded her of things to be done: weeding, pulling, righting, taking out stones, digging, especially digging irrigation ditches. They had been left without care for two weeks under the pretext that it was winter, and they were filled with dirt and sand. A peasant had been putting off the task until the next day for centuries, and so on, and the country had died from it, for centuries. Not completely: they had done enough to survive but not enough to launch themselves into true work, due to the religion, Raouf often said in his most critical moments, the fault of the Turks, the fault of tyranny, the fault of the peasants themselves, the fault of no one and the fault of everyone, and someone always ended up saying that it was written in the great book of immutable things. She remembered something Ganthier had said to her uncle (some memories made her hate Ganthier): "In this country they haven't even been capable of inventing a broom handle, as if a woman bent over to the ground, a whisk in her hand, was the height of human innovation!" Her uncle had called him a racist while laughing:

"You took centuries to invent the halter, and you're criticizing us for being slow!"

After a month Rania went back to see her father. She immediately asked one of the nurses if she ever thought about changing her uniform, and pointed out to the family doctor that he was coming by only every third or fourth day: You know my father, he has to feel like the police are coming! The doctor was accompanied by a young man with a red face whom he introduced as the assistant to the cardiologist. The young man remained silent. One of her father's servants came in with tea. Where is the sugar? Rania asked. In the tea, the servant said. Rania tasted. It was syrup. She spoke in a cold voice: There were instructions, the tea should be served unsweetened, and my father can put a half-spoonful in his glass, no more. The servant lowered her head. You know that in addition sugar makes you hungry, *hchouma*, Rania added, content to shame the servant. She raised her head, looked Rania in the eyes, and Rania understood perfectly what was in that look, and in the two seconds it had taken her to look at her, it was no longer a matter of sugar, but of an unveiled face in front of two strangers . . . Later Rania had taken the servant aside, she said: Those men are doctors, they see many things other than faces . . . and you're going back to your village! Si Mabrouk tried to defend the servant. Rania asked what that woman was doing in the house: "I can find out very quickly, you know. When one tries to teach someone a lesson one often has something to hide. She's going back to her village, and if she ever returns I'll know about it very quickly. You have to recover your health, not tax it."

In twenty-four hours things were back to normal, and she was able to start talking to her father. She had perhaps found a suitor.

"You? All by yourself? So quickly?"

"With the help of a woman from around here, one of Raouf's aunts, a distant aunt."

"Did you use a matchmaker? Don't tell me you also went to make offerings to a marabout!"

Rania hadn't responded to any of her father's sarcasm. She continued: He was a man from a good family, thirty-six years old, yes, still a bachelor.

"Not married at thirty-six?"

Si Mabrouk thought he might have a hidden vice. This very careful girl was going to end up with someone who went to brothels, or . . . He remembered a story that had gone around in the capital, a father who didn't want a son-in-law chosen by his wife, and who had found an infallible means to get rid of him. He had demanded of the man a medical certificate swearing that he was not a passive homosexual. Si Mabrouk refrained from telling his daughter why he was smiling. She saw it as indulgence, took advantage to say that at thirty-six men have history, and in this case it was perhaps a story of a failed first marriage, the bride's lungs.

"Engagement or marriage?" her father had asked, "they're not entirely the same thing!"

Rania realized that she didn't really know. That surprised Si Mabrouk:

"I thought you were more thorough . . . Okay, go on!"

The man hadn't been stricken by the illness, he was in good health, and . . .

"And you must be careful," Si Mabrouk said. The next day he started asking around: a businessman from the capital, importer of French agricultural machines.

"A profession of the future," Si Mabrouk said, "Each machine puts thirty families into poverty!"

"But they increase the yield," Rania said, "They create more food for people, so . . ."

She was interrupted. Her father didn't require a lesson in economics, and he knew what was coming next: If you wanted to survive you had to farm like the French did and do it even better; you could call that a curse or damn the curse and make progress. Rania forced herself to think of practical things, which held her tears at bay. She wanted to take advantage of her stay in the North to buy some livestock from the White Fathers, the French monks who were creating hybrid cows that people were beginning to talk about. She had seen an animal that weighed almost a ton, a zebu with a beautiful light gray coat, very lively eyes. It had made its skin vibrate with such force that no horsefly had been able to stay on it, and it walked away with the majesty of a wild beast. Rania was interested in three things: large livestock resistant to drought, grain machines, and the manpower needed for the olive trees, almond trees, fruit trees, vegetables, all of the best quality . . . In the capital, demand was increasingly high. If the White Fathers were surprised to be doing business with a woman, they didn't show it.

The suitor also had the reputation of being authoritarian and eager to succeed. That had surprised Si Mabrouk, his daughter's interest in such a man. In veiled terms Rania had said that it was time she accept the world as it was, "and you know that I like progress." The father talked to Taïeb as if he had himself found the man, but Taïeb had quickly understood. This came from his sister; he didn't like this plan. This suitor was a modernist. He had already tried to marry a modern woman. It had been a catastrophe. He wanted to begin again. They would make the worst sort of couple, with the worst consequences for the reputation of the family. Taïeb had tried on purpose to question the man's health, tuberculosis . . . or maybe something else. He seemed delighted to be telling that to Rania. In any case, she replied, a third of the men in this country are syphilitic, and then she left their father's room.

Taïeb met the suitor as if by chance, at the barber's, an Italian who had settled in the busiest spot in the European city, a commercial strip inside a block of buildings. It looked like the ancient city, the lack of sky, the narrow passageways, but with the brilliant effects of electricity and French-style shop windows, a good place for a chance encounter, two men talking seated side by side in a corner at the barber's.

"You know what a widow is, she'll claim to know more than you . . ." Taïeb had also stressed that his sister wouldn't bring a lot to the marriage: "You're going to spend a lot for her, but she will not bring much, we're not rich, and when I become head of the family I won't be in a position to help you."

The man didn't give in, and Taïeb told his father that the suitor thought only of money:

"He thinks that you're going to wrong me to set up my sister. Tell him that's false!"

Taïeb avoided adding, *Anyway, you don't have the power to do it.* Aside from Taïeb's inconvenient intervention, things weren't said directly. They were reported by the matchmakers, who went back and forth between the families. The suitor was undecided, and the brother and the sister confronted each other while taking care not to bother Si Mabrouk too much. That suitor had been had in his first marriage—everyone knew it—and as soon as the second marriage would be officially announced, they would ask why Si Mabrouk would accept a used man, as the French say, for a son-in-law.

"You know people," Taïeb said to his sister, "For the time being they're not biting, but as soon as they're sure, they're going to be rabid, they're going to put you on the same level as the one before, they're going to say that the man has a habit of women . . . (Taïeb looked for a word, frowning) . . . imperfect women," and he continued rapidly before his sister had time to react:

"Is that what you want people to say about us? That we have sold off an imperfect woman cheaply?"

It was clear he was enjoying those words. He wasn't claiming them for his own, of course. He even regretted having to use them, but that was life. He spoke while taking care to stay at least twenty feet away from his sister:

"You must understand. Don't think that I'm insulting you, I'm saying that that is what people will say, what you will become in their opinion. If you marry a man without reputation you will lose yours. He won't need to cloister you. You won't dare go out anymore. Do you really want people to talk about it to our father?" Rania's defenses started breaking down, then she resumed defending the importer, and Si Mabrouk was worried.

To counter his sister, Taïeb quickly spoke of another suitor, whom he had been keeping in the shadows up to then, a theology professor, a good reputation in his neighborhood, often called to lead prayers, but not at all a backward-looking imam, sometimes even dressed European style, speaks French well, but intransigent on the true religion. And Rania in turn asked around about the man, and she quickly had a lot to worry about. He was truly virtuous, no alcohol, no adventures, a man born in the country, a believer, honest. How had her brother managed to discover this rare species? She ended up attributing Taïeb with the intelligence that she had denied him for years. Seeing Rania's eyelids become heavy with boredom, the matchmaker said to her: "I'll continue to find out more about that man. I will find out, my girl, I will find out. All camels have a hump."

29

KINDER DES VATERLANDS

The four of them left by train for Germany, into the Rhineland that had been occupied by French troops since the end of the war. In Baden-Baden they stretched their legs while waiting to change trains for Mayenburg. The main street in the city was a mixture of beautiful store windows and a half-starved populace. From time to time they saw a line of people waiting in front of a store, drawn faces, a few vocal outbursts, but not for long, as if no one had the strength to continue a conversation. "Or rather," said Ganthier, "as if hunger isn't capable of destroying their sense of discipline."

A bit later, when they were returning to the train station, they saw a group of men marching behind a flag; a new nationalist emblem, Gabrielle said, the swastika. A patrol of French soldiers appeared and the demonstrators dispersed. To the left of the station, in a little street, there were a dozen or so women with laced up boots.

"They all have the same boots, why?"

"The boots indicate their specialty," Gabrielle said to Raouf.

"I don't understand . . ."

"Their specialty is cracks of a whip."

And Ganthier, without looking at Gabrielle:

"They, at least, do it for money."

On the pavement the snow had turned into dark gray soup. In front of the station some grooms were picking up a horse that had fallen in front of its cart. They finished unharnessing it, tried to get it onto the flatbed of a truck. The horse found some energy, resisted.

"The truck must smell like the slaughterhouse," said Ganthier. One of the grooms managed to put a ring around the horse's ear. He pulled it, and the pain kept the animal from rearing up.

They were back in the train. They arrived in Mayenburg on January 10, in the Rhineland under French occupation. Their hotel looked out over Schiller Platz. At the end of the afternoon they took a walk in the neighborhood, rows of large homes, between maples and pines. Ganthier pointed to the facades with two balconies:

"And they say they're too poor to pay their war debts!"

Passersby looked at them coldly. There were a lot of French soldiers in the streets. Some officers forced the Germans to get off the sidewalk when they went by.

"They exercise preponderance here, too?" Raouf asked. Ganthier didn't say anything.

They had dinner in a large brasserie on the square. The maître d' told them that because of shortages, themselves due to a series of causes escaping the good intentions of the country, and from which they couldn't really see how they would ever recover, there was unfortunately, at noon and in the evening, only one dish that could be served. Gabrielle and Ganthier translated, Ganthier commented:

"A single dish, potatoes and meat sausages! Everything is sausages in this country . . . Their women are sausages! Even their sentences are sausages!"

Ganthier knew that Gabrielle wouldn't like that sort of comment; he said it on purpose. At the table next to them three men, in their fifties, were talking with beers on the table in front of them. Noticing that Ganthier and Gabrielle spoke their language, they tried to explain Germany to these nonmilitary invaders:

"Welcome to the country where the sky, the earth, and hell have finally united!"

The conversation was slowed as translations were provided for Kathryn and Raouf. The three Germans enjoyed looking at Kathryn while she was being told what had just been said. Then they continued cheerfully: To understand us you must first understand what the *Gemüt* is (two of the men put a hand on their chest, the third pointed at the ceiling). It is the heart, the heart naturally tending toward good, to the ideal, *Gemüt*, and *Gemütlichkeit*, the state of what is good and calm, which you find at home, in a nice home. Never forget that one of the first stories we tell German children is that of a house made of gingerbread!

Ganthier kept his thoughts on German sweetness to himself . . . But sweetness, continued their interlocutor, carries a risk, doesn't it? The risk of getting soft, laziness is just waiting to overtake us. The proof is that we have several words just for laziness, *Bequemlichkeit*, *Müssigkeit*, *Untätigkeit*, and apathy, *Gefühllosigkeit*, and above all . . . *Leidenschaftslosigkeit*. Yes, it's when they get to six syllables that our words get to the heart of things, *Leidenschaftslosigkeit*, a lack of passion . . . with the understanding that passion is suffering, *Leiden*, which you experience in passion, but for us the lack of that suffering is more painful than the suffering itself! Fortunately, when faced with that lack of passion, we have something in the depths of our being that we use to stay alert, something you would translate on the contrary with some half-dozen different words, said one of the Germans who spoke French better than he had at first wanted to show: *inquiétude, anxiété, affolement, nervosité, agitation* . . . various words, whereas in German . . . the man made a fist and held it up in front of his face, for us it is a root word, *Unruhe* . . . the great upset, the great emotion, which battles the lack of passion, and which is one of the two indissociable beasts of the team with which we set off to encounter *Wirklichkeit*, reality. Yes, you're right, *Unruhe* is not a root word—the root is calm, *Ruhe*—but that's our German paradox: the compound word has become like a root, because what comes first for us is *Unruhe*, and *Ruhe* we obtain only afterward, thanks to the other beast of our team, which is thus inseparable from *Unruhe*. That other beast is *Ordnung*, of course, the other half of life, order. *Ordnung* is also the rule that enables things to be put in order, *Unruhe und Ordnung* . . . And we set off behind that team to confront reality, the shock of which awakens in us, guess what . . . *Streben!* Hope, pursuit, quest, ambition, in a word? Drive! But not just any drive, not anarchic, *Streben nach Vollkommenheit*, drive toward perfection . . . We're complicated, aren't we?

The conversation lasted a long time. Ganthier defended what he called French clarity against the great German tumult: all your words that end in *keit* or *heit* . . . You're confusing rhyme with reason. French, on the contrary, is the language of reason. Ganthier cited Antoine de Rivarol, clarity . . . subject, verb, noun . . . direct order . . . Passions may move us, but French syntax is unbending!

Replies and opinions flew back and forth, in the headiness of a shared between-two-worlds, which was suddenly more attractive than either world taken separately: one discovered oneself a stranger opposite the other, a moment of vertigo, and Kathryn ended up confiding that her maternal grandfather was born in Kiel. The Germans congratulated her. She answered that it was like all births, chance, and one needn't congratulate chance. They changed the subject. They continued their convivial exchanges, made warmer by rounds of beer. In the back of the room a short round man was beating out a tune on the piano.

In the morning Raouf woke up with a start. A din outside, shouts that reached the windows of the fourth floor, words in German first, then more words in French, short, and to the point. He started to open the shutters. Kathryn came over and put her hand on his, saying:

"Be careful, I don't like this."

He opted for glancing through an opening in the shutters. Gabrielle joined them. She also dissuaded Raouf from opening the shutters:

"Random bullets love spectators."

But Raouf was able to see people who were gathering around the statue of

Schiller. They weren't in uniform. Their numbers grew, a mix of bourgeois hats and worker or student caps. There were also women. In front of the group there was a large void, then thick lines, rows of soldiers, with helmets, in blue coats.

Someone knocked on the door, and Raouf went to open it. It was Ganthier, dressed for the day, whereas the other three were still in their pajamas. At first Ganthier seemed suspicious; then he also started to look through another window. The day before the colonel commanding the French garrison had told him: "Tomorrow, sparks will fly, so your little *bicot* will stay in his room, or else we'll bring him in, and the American woman, too, whether or not they are authorized. You shouldn't even be here." Then the officer's tone softened: "If at least you could . . . at least a bit . . . control . . . Madame Conti, we would be very grateful." Ganthier had nodded his head. Soldiers don't like journalists, especially women journalists.

The colonel's "sparks will fly," came with the announcement that the French army, at the beginning of January 1923, was no longer content with occupying just the Rhineland but was now taking possession of the entire Ruhr, including its mines and steelworks. The officer had added: "You know their saying? 'You have to let rot that which you hold not' . . . Well, they signed a treaty in 1918, and they're going to honor their signature, without complaining!" When he had stopped speaking he had almost hit the top of his boot with his switch; he often did that with civilians, but then he remembered that Ganthier had also spent four years in the war.

On the square the shouting became louder and louder, isolated shouts, then chants, in a chorus. They were able to make out a few phrases, "*Soldaten raus! Franzosen raus!*" and Gabrielle translated others, *Besatzung*, that meant occupation. The demonstrators were all pressing together.

"These people are used to demonstrating," said Gabrielle, "They are making a bloc."

"Yes," said Ganthier, his mouth thickened by the beers from the night before, "They've been spending their time at this since the end of the war. The soldiers should immediately go in with the butts of their guns; otherwise they'll have to shoot into the mass!" Raouf in a neutral tone:

"Like back home?"

There were other orders in French, the soldiers taking three steps back.

"Maybe they're going to calm down," said Gabrielle.

"That would surprise me," said Ganthier, "and our soldiers shouldn't have stepped back."

Commands continued to be shouted out, the sound of rapid steps. Other soldiers had erupted onto the square, occupying the space freed by the first row, facing the demonstrators.

"Here comes the best part of the show!" said Ganthier, and Raouf:

"Those are the Spahis." Ganthier continued, in a dark voice, "Yes, the Germans adore being struck down by colonials, and when we really want to annoy them we send in our Senegalese, but this morning they must already be in the Ruhr."

On the square, the Spahi officers were walking back and forth in front of the men who had been commissioned whether they liked it or not from a mountain tribe in the southern Mediterranean, and who were now standing, carrying weapons on the line where for centuries the descendants of other tribes had confronted each other, themselves coming not from the south, but from the north and the east, the next to last to arrive, the Franks, having turned against the following wave, the Germans, Kathryn saying in a shaky voice:

"They're not actually going to shoot, are they? Those demonstrators don't have weapons. If they fire on them I'm ready to testify that they didn't have any weapons!" And Ganthier:

"And then you will also be able to explain to some twenty or so American journalists what you were doing in this hotel . . ."

He was watching the square, imagined himself standing next to one of the officers in the first row, two great tribes, the Franks and the Germans, the Franks themselves ancient Germans who above all no longer wanted to hear about that common origin, two groups who over the centuries had refined their reasons to massacre each other—border, throne, church, reformed or not—to the point of each rallying behind two words that struck louder than all, the *Patrie* and the *Vaterland*, Ganthier adding:

"Of course, the people who are shouting are patriots, but there are moments when patriotism means accepting one's defeat," the two words *Patrie* and *Vaterland* then ceding the main role to idols judged to be more effective, *Kultur* for the people from the northeast, and *Civilisation* for their adversaries in the west, idols in the names of which the last massacre was carried out, Raouf looking at the statue of Schiller:

"And those people, there, would you say that you're here to civilize them?" The two tribes finding themselves again on the banks of the Rhine, five years after the peace, in a face-off. Gabrielle commented dryly:

"It's Poincaré who wants this . . . to force the Germans to pay . . . and they aren't able to pay . . ."

Ganthier didn't say a word. In any case, he couldn't have cared less about Poincaré at that moment, Raouf and the two women in pajamas in the same room . . . A glance at the large bed, which looked made up, the comforter smooth, Raouf and Kathryn, yes, of course, and it was even stupid to pay for two rooms, but Gabrielle? What was she doing there? A dressing gown on one of the armchairs, hers? Put on to walk down the hall and come here? Then taken off? Gabrielle's pajamas were light gray, the same ones as in Paris. She still filled them very well. Ganthier saw her in profile: tempting, she is still on the edge of being overweight, but never goes beyond it, how does she do it?

Gabrielle stuck her head through the gap in the shutters. She sensed Ganthier was looking at her, turned around, smiled at him, as if to make peace, returned to the spectacle in the square, taking notes all the while, like an eye without lids, the crowd of shopkeepers or office workers in suits, people in gray aprons, those out of work. How did you recognize someone out of work? By his gestures? More violent? A mother and four kids, one in her arms, workers, people still waking up, a crowd that could become a true testimony not in the eyes of the French and the Belgians whom the French dragged around everywhere with them to be able to talk about the "allied troops," but in the eyes of the English and Americans who didn't want this invasion . . . the Anglo-Saxons whose stock markets in London and New York would lose no time making the French understand that they had made a mistake . . . as the German newspapers had been saying for several weeks, adding with sinister joy that then the mark wouldn't be the only currency to plummet.

The slogans and the chanting made the panes of the third window that had remained closed vibrate even more. A perfume floated in the room. Ganthier hesitated: Was it Chanel, Kathryn's? Or Gabrielle's? Gabrielle must have put on some perfume in her room before coming to join these two. Yes, but she might also have borrowed Kathryn's . . . Given how close they had become they could very easily share their perfume. That little runt must have been their plaything all night long. He has learned to live with his times.

Songs had followed the shouting, a cacophony, no song louder than another.

"I would have thought that they would know how to sing in chorus here," said Kathryn. As if in a reply to the songs, the shouts of the officers provoked a clanging of metal, bayonets placed on gun barrels, shouts of indignation blending with the songs, the demonstrators tightening their ranks. A song suddenly rang out above the others. Gabrielle said:

"It's 'Die Wacht am Rhein,' 'The Guard over the Rhine' . . ." In the background they also heard snippets of "L'Internationale." Ganthier stepped back, he saw Raouf and the two women from the back. He took a piece of paper from his pocket:

"The Boches are acting brave, but it's skin-deep courage, they know what's coming!" He folded the paper. It was a bilingual proclamation from the French command, in large, bold type, the promise of summary shootings for any gathering, and the death penalty for any act of sabotage, with or without victims, and curfew at five in the evening. Ganthier chuckling:

"*Ach!* Gone are the five-to-sevens, you realize, the lover excited by what he's going to do with his sweetheart, he rings at Frau So-and-So's, at five after five, and bang! He gets shot in the back, like a vulgar saboteur!" Ganthier's voice was set against all the lovers in the country. He again looked through the shutters, and muttered: "We are going to create a few cadavers . . ."

And suddenly there was only one song, which silenced all the others, a tune that was even more militaristic, "La Marseillaise." The French soldiers were responding, the beautiful four-count rising of "La Marseillaise," a true chorus. The *Patrie* was silencing the *Vaterland*, "*Allons enfants*" . . . No . . . It was the Germans, not the French soldiers who were singing, but the civilians, what could resemble "La Marseillaise"? A song from the nineteenth century?

"No, it really is 'La Marseillaise,' in German," said Gabrielle. She had begun to translate, *Kinder des Vaterlands, enfants de la patrie, Tyrannei blutiges Banner . . . l'étendard sanglant . . .* The Germans had already sung "La Marseillaise" against their kings and princes in 1848, but this time they were singing it against the French, loudly, in voices that became increasingly harmonious. The people didn't advance. They sang while stomping their feet on the paving stones. Raouf started to laugh:

"A song against tyranny? Today? In the great French empire? They have to stop it right away!" Facing the civilians, the soldiers were becoming agitated. A voice shouted, "Bastards!" another, "We'll stick your 'Marseillaise' up your ass!" An officer shouted in turn. The soldiers were quiet. Opposite, the demonstrators were at the refrain, *Zu den Waffen* . . . while stomping on the ground even harder. The shouts of officers, followed by mechanical sounds, then a rumbling, a sort of huge, gray metal coffin appeared, on four wheels, mounted on the back with a wall pierced with two horizontal slits that framed a black tube aiming forward, an armored car similar to those that one sometimes saw emerge from the barracks in Nahbès used for patrolling in the south.

"This will be our greatest success," said Gabrielle, "Germans who sing 'La Marseillaise' five years after victory!"

She looked outside, a hand resting on Kathryn's shoulder, Raouf saying that she was trying out phrases for her article. She continued:

"The Germans are singing the revolution that we are no longer fighting for!"

Raouf asked her whether she believed that the Germans were really going to revolt. Ganthier responded:

"They better not . . . and by the way, why do you find them so interesting?"

"They are resisting a foreign occupation . . . Will you denounce me if I admit that this morning I feel a bit German?"

"Oh, if you'd like, you can even go down to the street, shout with them. Do you know how they say 'an impossible task' here? They say 'washing a Moor,' we'll see what kind of fate they have in store for you!"

From the square there now rose up the sounds of a clarion, and Ganthier, while watching through the gap:

"Don't forget that you will also be a great agent provocateur!"

The soldiers were advancing, one, then two steps. Gabrielle was writing in her notebook. Opposite the soldiers, the demonstrators were pressed even more tightly together. Raouf didn't understand. The soldiers were going to shoot; those men should be spaced apart.

"Yes," said Ganthier, "but in battle the shoulder of a comrade helps you to stay."

"They're going to get themselves killed, why?" asked Kathryn. Ganthier responded that it was to forget that they had been defeated.

"No," said Gabrielle, "It's because they don't want to be the only ones to pay for a war that everyone wanted."

"You can demonstrate when you're powerless. At home in Nahbès it's called a valiant last stand!" Ganthier had made a point of saying *at home* to upset Raouf.

They had to prevent Kathryn from going down to the square. Another song rose up, the "Deutschland über Alles." Ganthier saying:

"Look, they're stepping back, they're singing their hymn to be able to retreat. Your resisters are leaving, they're disappearing like water down a drain!"

"They're right," said Gabrielle, "The living are becoming rare."

The civilians were leaving the square while singing, some waving their fists at the armored car. Raouf said to Ganthier:

"This occupation is more pleasant for you than war. This time they don't have an army."

"Yes," Ganthier responded, "and that cost us a great deal, now they have to pay!" His hand had cut through the air. He wasn't looking at Gabrielle, but he knew that she was listening. While talking to Raouf, it was she whom he wanted to confront.

30

FOR AN ORCHARD

In Nahbès, Belkhodja had long believed that Si Ahmed would be his lucky charm, and now he himself had become the lucky charm of Si Ahmed: he could state his conditions. Si Ahmed was happy to tell the story of his oil, like a devotee of love tells of the body of his sweetheart. Belkhodja didn't dare shake his head; rather he did it in small movements, as a sign of well-meaning surprise, but for him it was impossible to imagine devoting as much time and as many scruples to details that no one would notice, the finesse of the crushing, the weight of the grindstone, the quality of the mule, the pressing filters, and the quality of the arms of the men at the press! The French have an expression for that, and in his head Belkhodja asked pardon from God for using such an expression, but it described well what Si Ahmed was making, "jam for pigs." In fact, he didn't use those words in front of the caïd, or in front of anyone else, he just thought them, just before excusing himself before God, and that gave him the contemptuous strength to do all the calculations that resulted in Si Ahmed always being the loser, a loss that earned him his title of pig provider. While listening to the caïd Belkhodja reflected, *Buy all that oil, a six-month note, he'll agree, he needs the money, just like me, more than I do, he has to pay for his car, if he gives it up he'll lose his financial status, whereas today he is a man who can still buy at auction with a fluttering of his eyelids, and then there are his son's problems, the trip to Europe so that jackal can return with a new coat, that takes money.* Belkhodja held Si Ahmed in his hand. He just had to negotiate the note well.

One day he dared ask the caïd if he expected to sell his oil; Si Ahmed's strength lay in not letting a response wait too long, for there is always a moment in business when you must give the other a foretaste of victory, so that he doesn't become tired of his dreams and begin to do real calculations.

"Perhaps," replied Si Ahmed, with a distracted look, "Times are difficult."

It was a half-admission. Belkhodja's hypothesis was correct. If the caïd sold in the wholesale market he wouldn't make a large profit, and he probably already had one or two creditors in that market. He was tired; he wouldn't have the patience to sell retail. He had to pay for his son's trip and the baksheesh to the

French police, and the car, and if he started to sell retail everyone would say that his affairs were not going very well.

Belkhodja had spent several days researching the market, wholesale oil, retail, how much the best oil sold for in stores, in one-gallon cans, how much it would cost to put one gallon in cans. How much would a grocer pay for twenty cans, or even bottles, a gallon, no three-quarters, like wine, the price of a gallon: how much did a bottle cost? The bottle was more complicated but had a much better return, and why not go up north, to Ghouraq, two trucks. He could do some very good business, two large trucks of *ghemlali*, put it into bottles in Ghouraq, or go directly to the capital, with the stock, put it in bottles there— Si Ahmed had said so—the prices there were excellent. One or two months of selling it retail in the capital and Belkhodja would pay off both his debts and Si Ahmed, or even conclude a deal with the Transméditerranéenne. Sell it all to the Transméditerranéenne, with a decent commission to the head of the kitchens: that was even better, yes, and why not sell in France? Belkhodja returned to see Si Ahmed. He was excited. He had begun to act like a French businessman on the continent; he had jumped some steps, with the excitement of the crazed. At the last moment he had shortened the period of reimbursement, a note for three months, and brought up a friend's price. Si Ahmed acted as if he hadn't heard a word.

A few days later Belkhodja came back to renew his offer. He sat across from Si Ahmed. He had decided not to watch the caïd's face and most often stared at one of the white walls of the room. He forced himself to appear as someone who lets his calculations argue for him. He was indeed going to spare Si Ahmed any concerns—a note at zero percent, between good Muslims, and his house as collateral, it was good collateral—and Si Ahmed had the strength to respond:

"No, I will never accept the house! When one takes the house that means there is no confidence!"

And in the silence that followed, Belkhodja understood that he was going to win; they were talking about confidence. Si Ahmed had the rope around his neck, but suddenly he said:

"Cursed is he who deprives a family of its roof!"

Another silence, and Belkhodja was afraid. He stopped calculating. Si Ahmed had repeated *cursed*, and he didn't sound like someone who was going to calm down and conclude a deal. He was leaning on his fear of punishment from On High to refuse him. Belkhodja began to panic. The caïd didn't have the reputation of being a pious man, but when an impious one begins to fear God he fears him ten times more than any honest believer. Si Ahmed was suggesting that he make the pilgrimage:

"You should return to what's essential, purify yourself, vis-à-vis Him (pointing at the ceiling). No one will be able to take aim at your business during your pilgrimage."

Belkhodja found the idea of a pilgrimage insulting; he wasn't that old. He was angry at the caïd. He decided to speed things up. He brought out his final proposal: his orchard, half his orchard, an orchard of one hundred acres, planted in squares, well-spaced trees, two wells, ample irrigation that not a piece of ground escaped, and the large hedge of poplars that stood guard against the wind from the sea, the last thing that still made him a man of worth. He had sworn to his father that he would never give it up, but collateral is not a sale, not the house, but half the orchard, four times the worth of the house.

"You're really ready to put up the family trees?"

There was concern in Si Ahmed's voice. Belkhodja didn't like that. He stood up. There was nothing else he could do, too bad. At least he was going to stop being shaken around like the tail of a rooster. He was going to sink into his debt. They would seize all his property in any case, house and orchard, and the caïd would fall, as well. They would both find themselves begging, whereas a well-concluded deal would have enabled each of them to escape, *mektub!* Si Ahmed accompanied Belkhodja to the door of his house, doing nothing to hold him back, adding on the threshold, his face somber:

"If I helped you it would be . . . Can you swear to me that it would be the last time?"

Before realizing what he was doing, Belkhodja swore on the head of his ancestors whose trees he was putting up as collateral, and he was finally able to come to a price, the quantity of oil and total price, strike hard, something between the wholesale price and the retail price, and Si Ahmed's face darkened, his chin moved, from left to right. He didn't say no. He spoke about his oil again, the first pressing. Belkhodja asked how much he had. Si Ahmed didn't know exactly, two hundred fifty, three hundred cans, but he would count them that very evening. Belkhodja asked if they could plan on four hundred fifteen-gallon cans, all at once, six thousand gallons, the supply for all the ships and hotels of the Transméditerranéenne at the highest price for two years.

Si Ahmed didn't say no, but he became as slippery as a fish covered with his oil, and Belkhodja heard himself proposing a note of twenty-two thousand francs. "No!" Si Ahmed said. Belkhodja didn't know what to do. At twenty thousand it was already too much; he would have to go to Paris to make enough profit; he had offered that sum while regretting it. Perhaps Si Ahmed's hardness was a sign from destiny, a door that destiny opened to Belkhodja to pull him from the trap into which he was falling, because at the moment when he had proposed those twenty-two thousand he knew he wouldn't be able to reimburse that debt with the profit, even if he sold by the bottle, at the best price, and by mixing a little. Even someone who did the accounting all alone could see a flash of truth, and it was a crazy offer. Any number above seventeen thousand was crazy, or the Transméditerranéenne, long negotiations, and he would have money for himself only by not reimbursing his smallest creditors. Belkhodja had as quickly as possible to get out of this madness, but he saw himself in the capital, with new clothes, doing new business. Of course the oil wouldn't be enough, but it would open the doors to business again. He had to count on the profit that would come from other business, Germans, great buyers of rugs: he would get out of his debt through them. He had to get to the capital as soon as possible—the Transméditerranéenne, or an agreement with Marseille, no, Paris, directly, a half-wholesale sale in Paris, the Paris fair! That could increase his profit twofold, almost, but there were all the uncertainties of transporting it. Twenty thousand, that could be doable. No, it was still too much: why had he offered that sum? The merchant sensed his ruse escaping him. He had to renegotiate. He stood up, said good-bye. He had to let a night go by and start afresh on new foundations, six thousand less, and Si Ahmed, on the threshold, took him by the shoulders and said:

"Okay, agreed, twenty-two thousand! You know why? Because we've known each other for close to twenty-two years, and also because you were there at my son's birth!" Si Ahmed's eyes were shining with emotion. The sheep had walked into the oven by itself.

Belkhodja had been afraid to lose, but now his victory frightened him. He almost didn't react when Si Ahmed pointed out that the collateral would include the entire orchard, so as not to tempt the devil, he had added. Belkhodja understood that in Si Ahmed's mind the devil might whisper to the debtor that he wouldn't need to reimburse him, that taking half an orchard was not that serious. Si Ahmed also hastened to admit that he had to be careful, and so it was a good deal. He wasn't lying, but he was selling high, not really that high, the best oil; Belkhodja now only felt the end of his efforts. By selling carefully he would have a good price, not to mention the profit that he would then earn from the sale of rugs.

The desire to get back into commerce and resume his dreams won over Belkhodja, as did the desire to sell as soon as possible, to be in the capital without further delay, good sales of oil and rugs on the first day, the feel of new bills in his hands, and at night, walking in the darkness, dreams and ships to launch on the seas, for real this time. He above all needed money. Even if, in Nahbès, even on the retail market, oil, even of that quality, didn't go above sixty centimes a quart, he needed money as soon as possible. Belkhodja thought only of victory, not its cost; he took away Si Ahmed's cans in the night, two trucks, and he sold several dozen cans in Nahbès, at the auction the next day, enough to pay for renting the trucks to quickly go up north and make a splash, and he was about to set off with his trucks when a buyer proposed to buy the whole lot, wholesale! He showed his wad of cash to Belkhodja. He lived in Ghouraq, a city to the north of Nahbès, fifteen thousand francs, in real bills that rustled in the hands of the man from Ghouraq. Belkhodja started dreaming again, decided to gain a month by not having to put the oil into bottles, eliminate the cost of storage, the haggling, chasing down buyers. This was a gift, to be done with that oil and return as quickly as possible to his rugs and his dreams. What was essential was to pay off the worst debts. As for the rest, if he could get his head above water he would be able to swim to the shore.

He sold the oil to the man from Ghouraq, and that same day, he went to the capital with the fifteen thousand francs in cash. He paid back the most pressing creditors, found his best buyers. His business quickly picked up. He spent a lot. The old dreams returned, as did the new debts he had to take on to stoke them. Things moved along. Belkhodja had some good sales, then some losses, heavy. He still felt the bills rustling, but he had fewer and fewer of them. Catastrophe was slowly arriving. He refused to acknowledge it, and he liked his refusal. He might have been able to react if he hadn't been tempted by an enjoyment stronger than that of drugs, gambling, dreams, and anguish: that of the imprudent shepherd, the victim of an inundation that he could have prevented, who, himself, tries to drown the last of his animals.

At the end of three months Belkhodja hadn't paid back the note to Si Ahmed, who told him in a sad voice:

"Success is a climb, ruin is a descent."

The caïd gave him an additional month but added the harvest from the trees. A month that Belkhodja spent in nocturnal reveries at the harbor in the capital. At the end of the month Si Ahmed took possession of the orchard, one of the most beautiful in the region, an orchard worth thirty thousand francs, at least. He took it right before the harvest. He wanted the harvest because of the French navy: it had a lot of ships to show the Italians and the Spanish that it was the strongest, and it needed oranges and lemons or else the sailors' teeth would fall out. Si Ahmed sold the harvest to the French navy, a net profit of three thousand francs, four times the price at auction, but real citrus fruit, on the verge of maturity, and then he told the French that they could come pick the fruit themselves, and the sailors came. At the end of the day they were even offered the opportunity to go into a large wooden shed that had been hastily constructed outside the orchard that was guarded by police, five minutes for each man, with wine and the sounds of women. The shed could be seen. It could have been hidden in the orchard, but for Si Ahmed there was no question of sullying his property.

When the whole story came out, the people of Nahbès said that morality had been saved. Belkhodja was nothing but a leaking bucket. He had even lost the money put aside for his pilgrimage, and since he was diabetic, he didn't know if God would leave him enough time to recover that sum. God could one day decide that he had done enough for people like Belkhodja and allow the final creditor, death, to demand its due. It was Si Ahmed who stepped in, while Raouf was still in Europe. He came to Belkhodja's aid. He paid for his doctor; he allowed him to survive. People said that it didn't cost him very much, hardly a fraction of his profit from the oranges and lemons sold to the French—alms are only a condiment for the rich—but everyone still showed admiration at that gesture. Si Ahmed had saved a soul with the money taken from the Christian sailors, the soul of Belkhodja, a habitué of evil places in the capital, a drug addict, a man who was falling into paganism. He had even been seen in Ghouraq at the home of a Maltese woman who performed fumigations, and the rumor that the former merchant had had dealings with the French police spread even faster. Si Ahmed had given Belkhodja much less than the percentage he should have given through the simple duty of charity if he had been a true believer, said some, but for Si Ahmed, what counted was not the amount of the alms but, like oil, the quality.

The man from Ghouraq who had bought Belkhodja's oil at the wholesale market for fifteen thousand francs in bills that rustled in the hand never returned to Nahbès, and Belkhodja didn't need to know that the man was only an agent of Si Ahmed. No one told him. He had absorbed all the bitterness of the story; he didn't need to vomit it back up.

31

IN AN OCCUPIED COUNTRY

Red and black on white, it was cold at the steelworks of the Ruhr, with sometimes an anemic fire outside on the snow, something elementary, and crowds, gray and black, in front of the doors, picketing, French troops, sometimes a salvo, then calm. Some evenings Gabrielle typed out her reports, Ganthier asking: "May I?" and Gabrielle: "Of course." Ganthier expecting to read a story and falling on a list of measures taken by the French occupation authorities to regulate customs duties, taxes on wood, the circulation of barges, alcohol, tobacco, people, and iron, and bans on traveling on a given road, unless one had a safe passage signed by such and such an authority, with all the special powers of the allied mission.

"In fact, we don't have any more allies," said Gabrielle, "The English and the Americans are against us, we have only the Belgians."

There were also regulations about unions and associations, the press, trains and tramways, and French laws on German laws, civil rights, penal law, traveling, newspapers, waterway locks, currency . . . And Ganthier:

"Isn't it a bit mad to put all that in an article?" His tone was peaceful, to make the word *mad* go down. Gabrielle had smiled:

"You know that my mad list is going to please the military censors, don't you? And it will be successful . . . not only in Paris."

Gabrielle's articles were sometimes published in translation in the States. She continued, in a sort of dark joy:

"Can you imagine the people in New York, seeing all these taxes and regulations? They're going to think that Poincaré is installing communism in Germany!" And Ganthier:

"That's not very honest . . ."

Kathryn came out of her silence, her voice tense, saying that the French press was no more honest with Americans:

"When you read *Le Figaro* you have the impression that we spend our time fighting about contraband whiskey with gunfire! Just because we don't support this invasion . . ."

Ganthier refused the confrontation, turning instead to contemplate an etching hanging above the table where Gabrielle was working, a charge on horse-back, one of the riders with a bow, another with a sword, another with the scales of justice, and a fourth, a thin, old man armed with a trident—Dürer, *The Four Horsemen of the Apocalypse*—then he went back to Gabrielle's article, names followed by professions, doctor, lawyer, professor, journalist, pastor . . .

"What's this?"

"They're hostages, they're put on trains. By order of the command, they will be the first victims of sabotage."

"Hostages are something the Prussians do. A French officer would never do that, that's false!"

Then Ganthier said to himself that it was probably true, and the Paris press would even brag about it. Kathryn added that the day before, a French officer had told her that he was there to repair the mistakes of President Wilson.

They had spent a few days between Duisburg and Dortmund. They dined early, in loud places where smells of fat, onion, and beer prevailed, odors made enjoyable by their walks in the cold air. Afterward they met in one of their rooms to talk, sometimes seated on a large porcelain radiator in the shape of a corner banquette, for which the coal was sold to them on the black market at triple the cost. Each porcelain tile represented either a young man or a young woman, sometimes a couple, peasants, three motifs that were repeated over the entire surface, in blue and white.

They left the next day, getting out of the car at regular intervals, walking carefully on the ice, mixing in with passersby, lingering in front of a poster before a patrol came to pull it down, France as an ogre crouching over the factory smokestacks, Gabrielle sometimes taking a photo, to the great disapproval of an officer who was watching them from a distance but who always let them carry on upon a nod from Ganthier, Raouf saying:

"I wonder where that discreet power you have over them comes from . . ."

And Ganthier: "You're not going to start complaining now, are you?"

He pointed at a group of thin, tired-looking workers:

"Look around you, do you really believe those people are going to stage a revolution?"

That was Ganthier's goal, to get Raouf to wake up, to act like Kathryn, to teach him about life, "I should be at least as capable as an American actress, in politics, I mean," he confided in Gabrielle to make her laugh. It also happened that he defended Kathryn, excusing her harsh treatment of Raouf, her fits of jealousy: she was suffering, and she was fragile. Gabrielle responded:

"Fragile? Did you see her nails?"

"What about them?"

"They never break."

Kathryn had received a letter from Paris. Raouf saw the envelope but didn't say anything.

"It's from Tess," Kathryn said, "She's in Montparnasse and is very happy."

Since Raouf was still not talking, Kathryn told him the unknown story behind Tess's being sick in Nahbès, what she knew about a pursuit in Louisiana, where Tess was from, when she was called Lizzie. No, it wasn't she who was being pursued, it was a man. He was running fast in the woods, and a pack of dogs was chasing him. It was almost like in a film, you know, you can imagine. He outruns them, and because he senses that he is outrunning them he runs even faster, until the dogs start barking, and he understands that it's going to be harder, but he continues to run, until he realizes that the dogs aren't behind him but are moving up on the sides. And the rest of the story, as reported or imagined by Kathryn, was one of biting, then blows with a stick, and an order that had stopped everything, and they put the runner in chains. Perhaps a voice had even said, "with iron, no surprises," and that had made everyone laugh, and the rest was in the newspaper, a photo, the newspaper that Tess who didn't know anything about it had opened two days later. This type of thing was so common that it didn't appear on the front page but inside, a photo with the name of her cousin, the body of her cousin, what remained of it, on a bed of ashes on the ground, a ditch with a bed of ashes. The photographer had even captured the smoke, and all around there was a crowd of onlookers, policemen, and a caption underneath, "The rapist ends up on the ashes of hell," and the following week they discovered that the cousin was innocent. People didn't even attempt to deny his innocence. They said "he was in the wrong place at the wrong time," adding, "during a moment of legitimate anger by the population"—those were the words of the prosecutor when he had refused to pursue the matter any further—Kathryn saying: "'Legitimate anger,' you can imagine what Tess must have felt." Later Raouf dared say: "I know Tess's writing. It wasn't on the envelope." Kathryn said that the rest of the story was too difficult to share.

All around them the currency and life were deteriorating, while their francs and dollars bought them every privilege. Sometimes Gabrielle disappeared. One evening a French commander took Ganthier aside. He was very upset. They were going to have to take Gabrielle back to France, "Your friend the journalist, five years ago I would have still had the right to put twelve bullets into her. She spent part of the afternoon with German Bolshevists and a French man. That type of contact with the devil should at least suffice to put Madame Conti on a train back to Paris!" Ganthier responded coldly to the commander, who calmed down and gave a few details. The French communist was called

Péri. His leaders had sent him to encourage fraternization among the French soldiers and German workers: that association was a crime! Ganthier asked the officer if he had had a look at Gabrielle Conti's service records during the war, his voice was shaking. Across from him the commander began to smile; without a doubt this civilian was screwing the journalist. Ganthier was getting angry. He was furious at being suspected of doing something he had been unable to do for months. He really wanted to slap the man:

"You well know, commander, where Madame Conti keeps her napkin ring when she's in Paris, the ministers like to be informed . . . Arrest your Péri if you want, but my friendly advice, regarding Madame Conti, is to leave her alone."

They finally arrived in Berlin. That city was a bordello, Ganthier had warned them, down-and-out, Raouf said, surprised to see such sunken faces in a European city, a famine in a garden, Kathryn said when their taxi was going along a third large park. Gabrielle allowed the city to pass before her eyes, a blur of images, like that line of amputees in front of a dispensary, even thinner than ordinary passersby.

"They won't all die . . . ," said Ganthier, pointing at a huge convertible with a chauffeur in livery and, in the back seat, a man with fat cheeks, a fur hat, wrapped up in traveling blankets; in the distance a crowd was coming out of a church. Raouf remembered something his former teacher, Montaubain, had said, "The war has brought God back, along with gangrene." Even farther away a procession of men was going by, hard faces behind a fanfare and flags, a city of trucks, traffic jams that were even worse than in Paris, and suddenly the calm of a lake, woods, and then scaffolding, cranes, rolling cranes, factory smokestacks, sites of halted construction, a door in front of which a long line of angry-looking men was waiting. "*Rass al-'atel* . . . ," said Raouf, "The out of work man's head is full of demons," a leprous city in places, and impossible to know if the leprosy was advancing or retreating. They moved along, Kathryn with her fits of crazy love and her unpredictable anger, Raouf with his dreams and his maneuvering, Gabrielle with her notebook, Ganthier with his sarcasm, a city even blacker than Paris, entire quarters with facades with closed shutters, dirty windows, blinds falling down, people around a brazier, each person holding a potato on the end of a stick, patrols of helmeted policemen. "The police seem to be dreaming," said Kathryn to Ganthier.

"Do you know what they're dreaming about?"

"Food?"

"No, look!"

A policeman had bent down by his shoes.

"See, he's picking up a cigarette butt!"

A woman went by. Gabrielle said, "The women in Berlin are more often bare-headed than in Paris." An accordionist was alternating tender melodies and martial tunes. A dozen healthy-looking cows came out of a large doorway, a farm right in the city, red and white animals in the streets, going to the fields. The four friends relaxed while watching a baker's apprentice wearing a smock go by, a cheerful servant girl, her black dress and light hairband, a straw basket on her arm, an army of mailmen, too, and schoolchildren, a lot of little girls with their backpacks, many more than in France, said Gabrielle. They stopped in front of a building to watch a huge sparkling steel grill slowly sink into the ground, without a sound.

"The people here have a cult of perfection in their mechanics, for the perfect gearing," said Ganthier, "Fortunately the Versailles Treaty forced them to inscribe *made in Germany* on their products, that protects us." As it disappeared into the ground the grill revealed a large window filled with watches and clocks; one out of two items was used. They left, and soon Raouf said:

"I sense that the women here are different from Parisian women, but I can't put my finger on it." Kathryn didn't say a word. He's making progress, Ganthier said to himself, he's trying to provoke her, then, laughing:

"German women pay less attention to men, here they have an inner life!"

In some streets the people were cleaning, in others, no.

"They've lost the habit of doing things together," said Ganthier, "All the better for us!"

And Raouf: "Is that what you'll say in your report to military intelligence?"

A driver raised his cap just as his boss was arriving, and the boss also greeted him by raising his hat, a very serious look on his face. In the salon of their hotel, a talkative German man explained to them:

"Since the beginning of the republic we have introduced a respect for all, and seriousness in that respect, the rest is unchanged. We are a very serious people, but during the war a Herr Doktor was able to sell to hundreds of thousands of my compatriots a recipe for making bread by replacing flour with hay. It was very convincing, he believed in it!"

Later Ganthier added: "That's one of their problems, they themselves say that a German can't tell a lie without believing it himself."

At Raouf's request one morning they went to walk along the Landwehr canal.

"Would you throw in a rose?" David Chemla had written to him. It was to honor the memory of a revolutionary, Rosa Luxemburg. The canal was deserted, the banks, as well, Raouf had forgotten the rose, promised himself to return, but didn't do it, probably because Gabrielle had in the meantime informed him that for Rosa Luxemburg nationalist struggles were not true struggles. At the hotel, the same German man told them:

"We are a generation full of despair and contempt, but we have rediscovered the cult of grandeur. We now want the largest brasseries, the largest hotels, the biggest movie theaters, the largest brothels in all of Europe!"

And suddenly, in the street, Kathryn noticed a large advertising poster, the same poster several times along the avenue, *Goldfarb Motors*. In Paris Ganthier had told her:

"The father is an industrial motor manufacturer, a Jew from Vienna, Goldfarb." Since then, Kathryn hadn't thought of the father again. It was a shock. Metilda was there, with her father, her Berlin mother, not a Tyrol cow, but a girl of the city, with all the freedoms and intelligence of the city. She knew that it was going to happen, and the following days she saw the name of Goldfarb in the streets, in magazines, in movie ads, a great Berlin campaign for Goldfarb motors. Metilda was there, the same age as Raouf.

Kathryn read the gossip section in the newspapers, didn't see anything. That girl also knew how to hide. Kathryn decided not to get angry anymore; anger only made him stop talking. She needed to laugh, love, flatter, disarm, question. She also imagined falling ill, seriously ill, from her torment, and Raouf at her bedside, finally responding to her questions: he never loved anyone but her, Metilda was only a mistake, a single time; he was crying, yes, he had encountered her in Berlin; Kathryn surprised herself telling him in a final breath that she wished them all the happiness in the world, he no longer controlling his sobbing . . . She awoke from her reverie, shaking her head, telling herself, *She is here, he's screwing her, no, he's in love with me, but that's just it, that excites him, but he never goes out without me . . . or rarely, he must tell me if she has contacted him, I don't ask him much, admit what he's done.* Kathryn invented a dialogue:

"Did you tell her you were my lover?"

"I didn't dare."

"Didn't dare?"

"I would seem to be bragging, wouldn't I?" Raouf was lying. The real reason was that he wanted that girl to think he was free.

"I must send her a photo of us!" Yes, a photo. She would force Raouf. Both of us in our coats, smiling in the snow like elves at a party. Let her see that we want to go back and get in bed. She'll understand, and it will hurt her, and she will drop him, and he will also be hurt. He will beg for my forgiveness and at that moment I'll leave him. Kathryn didn't like some of the aspects of the role she assigned Raouf. She couldn't talk to a whiner. Raouf stopped whining, and there was no need to send a photo. There had to be a meeting, to really hurt Metilda, a K.O. The scenario pleased Kathryn, a meeting at teatime, the three of us, and why not with Gabrielle and Ganthier? And perhaps one or two German filmmakers, so a dinner, a lovely table, we'll talk about everything. I will talk movies with the Germans, I will tell them about America, they will listen, Gabrielle will support me, Ganthier will take care of Raouf, I will be nice . . . Metilda, you're not saying anything? You mustn't let us intimidate you like that, tell us about Vienna, is it true that the girls' schools are very strict? That they forbid you from touching your hair in public? While laughing Kathryn would put her hand on that of a director, Raouf pouting, Kathryn would be winning, and suddenly Raouf would no longer interest her: You have your little Austrian girl, go screw her and don't interrupt the conversation of the adults, Raouf would beg her with his eyes, Kathryn wondered what the director would look like, the one she had come to meet wasn't currently in Berlin, she had to wait a few days, he'll know how to revive my characters, he's a master of the chiaroscuro, when shadows become an appeal, even on a face, my chiaroscuro, which Neil never wanted to film — he says that my strength is to be sharp and clear. She imagined herself ever more clearly in front of the German director. She became his favorite actress. I'm too hard on Raouf: what's wrong with me?

Kathryn stopped daydreaming. She was suffering in this city, but she liked it. Berlin was the noise of wind in the trees, mixed with the sounds of birds, four or five times Central Park in Berlin, and Berlin made her love Raouf, the golden light of Berlin on the snow, one morning, and Raouf:

"In German they say that the morning has gold in its mouth . . ." Kathryn didn't dare ask who had taught him that expression, and furious with herself at not daring, and suddenly stricken with cold anger at Raouf, who didn't understand a thing, Kathryn saying, "Kiss me!" in a flood of tenderness, to erase her anger, gold in the mouth . . . The other one must have told him that in bed! Another morning, right in the middle of the Tiergarten, a woman started calling, "Greta! Greta!" some annoyance in her voice. The woman was in front of them, a hundred feet away, on a wide path. She repeated, "Greta!" Anguish, a lost child, a city of gardens and a city of crime, and they saw a red spot in a thicket, on the right, almost next to them, a coat, a little figure that was up against the trunk of a large oak tree, a little girl, hardly six years old. The woman's voice was getting desperate, and the little girl was letting her mother be desperate. "There's one who already knows a lot about pleasure," Gabrielle had said. The voice repeated, "Greta!" cracking. Over there, next to the mother, passersby were beginning to look around. Two riders had stopped. "The rascal, I want to turn her in," said Ganthier, and Gabrielle, "No, maybe the mother is mean. You never know what goes on between a mother and her daughter, let's leave them alone, come on!"

"Wait a minute," said Kathryn, "I want to see when she decides to come out."

"She's going to laugh like a jokester," said Raouf.

"Or she'll say she was lost," said Kathryn.

The mother was shouting at the top of her lungs now. The little girl in the red coat left the tree and made a detour through the thicket crying, "*Muttie!*" before coming out onto the large path, crying.

"Sincere tears," Ganthier said, "She's crying out of real fear of getting a good thrashing."

"They're like the tears of an actress," Kathryn said, "She's pretending she was afraid when she was lost."

"And what's more, I'm sure the mother is going to feel guilty at letting the daughter wander off," Gabrielle added, "Look at the kid, she's not even running to her mother . . . It's the mother who lost her, it's her place to go get her."

"All's well that ends well," Kathryn said, "but I'd like to see the same scene with a boy."

"Boys don't do that," said Raouf with all the sincerity in the world in his voice.

"Boys don't learn early on how to lie and escape? So how do men do it?" Kathryn asked.

"Mothers," said Gabrielle, "never let a boy out of their sight, because they know that they think only of escaping."

"I didn't have a mother," said Raouf.

Kathryn became tender, but she couldn't stop thinking about what Gabrielle had said, *He thinks only of escaping.* She remembered what Gabrielle had told her in Nahbès, the servants, the nanny, what they did, Metilda leaning over Raouf . . . And the next day as they were walking down the street, sounding completely natural:

"Your friend on the boat, is she the same one as the motors, in the ads?"

"Yes."

"Do you think we could meet her? That would be nice."

Raouf found that amusing. He would write to see if that would be possible. Kathryn was sure he had already done it. Police strolled by, two by two. "There really are a lot of them," said Kathryn, and Ganthier: "Don't forget that scarcely a year ago there was an insurrection here." A man-sandwich appeared in front of them. Only his head and boots could be seen. He was covered with newspapers, with headlines about a demonstration organized by the party of a certain Adolf Hitler, "a small party of excitables, and not the only one," said Gabrielle, translating, adding: "If France were one day treated like Germany, we would soon have our Adolphe Duponts!" Ganthier wondered if she really thought such things, *In fact, she only likes paradoxes, the headiness of thinking to think, that's what's worst, it's not surprising she sympathizes with this country.* Raouf managed to translate another headline by himself: "The German people are not yet colonized by France."

They were shivering. And the sun, when it appeared, was icy. They went into a café to warm up. The café had large, colored mirrored balls that gave the customers very thick lips, sunken eyes, long ears, and a yellow or blue tint, as if life were only an ill-fated farce. The customers seemed to like it. When they left Raouf burst out laughing:

"Look at that lovely duo, *Unruhe* and *Ordnung!*" On the road two skinny men, wearing white shirt fronts, morning coats, and top hats, were pedaling a tandem bicycle that was making a disturbing clanking noise. The one in front was leaning over the handlebars, grimacing, gesticulating, twisting himself while keeping his head straight so his hat wouldn't fall off, and the other was sitting up very straight, his chin up, with no other movement than that of his legs. Where were they going?

32

THE SMILE ON A GRILLED SHEEP'S HEAD

One morning, Taïeb came to his father's house with a lawyer friend: no, I just want to introduce you. I have every confidence in your lawyer, but mine is a friend. He has lots of contacts. He knows everything. He knows people's pasts. Taïeb's goal was to frighten his sister. It was enough that she know that a new lawyer had spent some time with her father, and if her suitor's business wasn't spotless they would quickly know. Did she really want everything to come out? The suitor himself began to grow tired of it. He had people say that it is never good for a man to be the object of conversations in the capital. And in the evening Taïeb, in a calm voice, asked Rania to talk for a moment:

"I'm not doing this for me, but to avoid anything bad happening to you." This time he wasn't seeking to break his sister. He was trying to surprise her with his arguments:

"What does this importer want by marrying you? It's not money, it's your beauty, of course, and your intelligence. I could tell you that it's to rule over you, but you already know all that, it's in your books. To subjugate a woman like you is more satisfying than marrying a housewife. You see, I also know how to think like they do today, but that's not what's most important, and you already know him, you have done your own research. You have even had a few discreet conversations with him, that's normal, you are modern. A simple question, then, has he for even a single moment seemed to have even a tenth of the qualities of your dead husband?"

Taïeb was careful not to say anything offensive. Rania was surprised at this new tone. She responded prudently: the man was interested in her life, her life in the country. Taïeb continued, "You know, you could keep the farm." Rania was both wary and confident, saying that the "future one" had admired the way in which she kept the books. Taïeb smiled, don't force anything, his sister was reasoning. He just had to let her be, and slowly the bits of reasoning would be put in place in Rania's mind. Taïeb in passing repeated the word *accountant*, a reliable accountant, she must understand, a wife condemned to doing the books, Taïeb saying that the affairs of that importer had gone through difficult times, as she knew well, and you can guess how some businessmen get out of difficult situations . . . You will spend your life with numbers, trafficked numbers. Yes, he trafficks, otherwise he wouldn't earn all that money. At one point Rania looked at Taïeb coldly: "You know all about cooked accounts!" He didn't react. He continued: "You won't be the slave of a husband, you will be the accomplice of an embezzler. In the end it will make a great tale, like the ones you read in your Egyptian novels, and our father will be the father and father-in-law of people who are brought before the judge . . ."

Taïeb had let those ideas sink in, then he arranged a meeting in his father's office with the suitor of his choice, Si Bougmal, and that day his father looked wonderful. Rania's perfume still floated in the room, *She must have tried to wage her final battle,* thought Taïeb, *She has lost, my father wouldn't have received us like this if it were only to show Si Bougmal the door.*

Si Mabrouk welcomed him warmly. Si Bougmal was a thin man, thin lips, short hair, slow movements, a smile meant to show that he permanently received a light that didn't come just from the material world. Taïeb was proud to introduce his father to a man of this sort, and Si Mabrouk had congratulated the suitor at length:

"You lead a model life, Si Bougmal. I have the means to know everything and I know that you drink very little, and only in order not to stand out among your peers when you're with them. You are feared by your students, little liked by your colleagues, but that is not necessarily a bad thing, and your situation is prosperous, very prosperous. You have the respectability of a theologian and a good income—no father could be indifferent to that—and you are calm, not like a man who is holding himself back, but like one who never needs to resort to violence, and no one has ever accused you of going to or of being taken to bad places, which makes you a remarkable man among us. You are a blessing, Si Bougmal . . . a blessing with income from real estate, a true comfort for the soul (Si Bougmal raised his eyes to the heavens), a comfort for the soul of a father who is concerned with the future of his daughter and the children she will have . . . and you . . . are the owner of the largest brothel in this city!"

Taïeb jumped out of his chair, indignant at what his father had said, a father who made a gesture with his hand, and who continued in a mechanical voice:

"You don't practice vice, Si Bougmal, you are content to live off of it, and the money is paid to the overseer of your farm, as if you were doing excellent business with wheat, almond trees, the gifts from God . . ." Si Mabrouk was tapping with a hand whose veins were very apparent a gray file that was sitting on his desk. Taïeb glanced hopelessly at the suitor who remained silent, even continuing to smile. Si Mabrouk stared at the suitor coldly, saying to himself, *Are all crooks like that? When I read Badi'Ezzaman I really like his hero, a crook, imam, pimp, jokester, drunk, but this one is as motionless as a merguez . . .* Then, out loud:

"Do you enjoy yourself in your brothel, or are you content with the pleasures of hypocrisy, dear Si Bougmal?" The word caused Si Bougmal to react. He objected in a very controlled voice. He wasn't the owner, not exactly, he was part of a group, itself . . . Si Mabrouk interrupted him: "A group in which you are 90% owner." Si Bougmal said that it wasn't forbidden, by any law, and with an instinctive gesture he showed the palms of his hands. Si Mabrouk said: "One can have clean hands and a disgusting soul!" Taïeb looked from his father to Si Bougmal. Si Bougmal was still smiling, but with the smile on the head of a grilled sheep. Taïeb stood up again, took the suitor out of his father's office, to the front of the house. He returned to his father, awaiting the worst of his anger. It was Si Mabrouk's turn to smile. He was very calm.

Rania was also in the room. They allowed Taïeb to explain. His speech was feverish. He hadn't known a thing, he swore, on the Holy Book, everyone can make mistakes. Rania herself had been mistaken about her suitor, a profiteer!

"Yes, but you almost had me locked up in a brothel! I wonder why you didn't check him out . . ."

Taïeb couldn't speak, he had understood that in the *I wonder* she was hiding another response . . . His sister knew more than what she had told their father . . . *She knows about the two thousand francs that Bougmal loaned me, she could have told our father what she had discovered a lot sooner, he would have stopped everything, she let me get involved as far as possible, and now my father thinks I'm an idiot, she could make me out for a scoundrel, talk about my debt, talk about a plot, she prefers that I be only an imbecile in my father's eyes.* Taïeb was torturing himself. He had acted too quickly. If there hadn't been that importer he would have gone more slowly. Rania certainly had proof of his connections with Bougmal. They were in the accounts at the brick factory. He had stolen from the receipts and put back into the accounts what he borrowed from Bougmal, who was to have been paid back by the marriage, but he didn't know anything about the brothel—Bougmal didn't tell him anything about it—that money was money from a brothel . . . He felt dizzy. His sister was holding him hostage, and she was escaping from him. At any moment she could ask him, "Why did you want to give me to that man?"

The days passed, and Si Mabrouk finally said to Rania that in the end she never really wanted her importer of agricultural machines: "You didn't really want to marry him, you wanted to force your brother to present his champion, to be able to make your own inquiries, and now you have him, you've had a good laugh, my daughter, I'm feeling much better."

Si Mabrouk tried to negotiate a relaxation of his diet with the young medical assistant who came to see him, but the man was even more terrorized than the servant by the look Rania gave him.

All these events had tired the young widow. Her father was doing much better, and so she returned to Nahbès. She told Si Ahmed that she refused to conclude the land exchange with Ganthier, but in the colonist's absence the situation actually interested her much less. The caïd did not seem to be impatient, in any case, as if he had other fish to fry. She took comfort in taking care of her land. She missed her foreign friends, and not just them, she closed her eyes to envelop a figure in her arms, desire, tears, and the constant hope . . . *I could beg him . . . What I feel is a poison, I don't exist for him, I can't help it, but I don't want anything illicit, I'd like to marry him . . . It seems marriage for love is a Western invention, not even a century old, yet my first marriage . . . No, it wasn't a marriage for love, he had asked for my hand, I wanted to enter into life, he was handsome, already rich, full of energy and the future, a true match said my father . . . Love came very quickly . . . Is love simply the means to make a match agreeable? No . . . When he was fifteen minutes late I trembled, and when I was upset he was sad, we invented each other . . . Do I not love him anymore?* She dreamt of a living man while thinking of what a dead man had made her feel. It was up to life to decide, marriage for love, why had they told her about it? She also thought of the other woman. She was sure that in reality there was nothing, *I'm going to find the right moment to tell him, or to show him, what will be the right moment?* One day she would decide. She would disguise herself as a European. She would surprise him, a small veil over her face. She tried on dresses in front of a big mirror, announced herself in a sharp voice, "Madame de Wolmar," and burst out laughing.

33

OTTO

They were at a restaurant with Otto, an officer in the former imperial army who was trying to reinvent himself through literature. They had said to Ganthier: "You're trying to understand Germany, he's trying to understand France, that should work." A model Prussian officer, shaved head, thin mustache, as dry as a sword, and blue eyes. The first time he proved very friendly with everyone except Raouf, to whom Gabrielle had said, "For him you're closer to a cannibal than to a European."

"The biggest cannibal of all," Raouf had replied, "is Europe."

Otto knew French authors admirably, the classics. They complimented him. He became bolder:

"At thirteen I spoke French better than German. We had beaten you in 1870, we could admire you, maybe you'll do the same thing now. My favorite author is La Rochefoucauld. I know his work by heart, very critical of war, but indeed, a true warrior must confront La Rochefoucauld's criticism!"

Otto was happy to preach to the French, criticism of valor, courage in combat, his finger raised to support the quotation: "Perfect valor and absolute cowardice are two extremes at which one rarely arrives," smile. Raouf looked at his glass, seeming upset. The others praised Otto. They urged him to continue, and suddenly Raouf, in a hard voice, said:

"Cowardice absolute!" and Otto:

"Pardon me?" There was contempt in the officer's voice. This dark-skinned dandy wasn't actually going to put his two cents into their conversation. Otto had been told that Monsieur Ganthier and Madame Conti had influence, they could be interesting. Otto wanted to talk to those people, not to just anyone, not to that one! He sought Raouf's gaze the way a duelist seeks a weapon, to kill. Raouf kept looking at his glass. Ganthier sought a means to break the tension. Raouf then said:

"Not 'absolute cowardice' but 'cowardice absolute,'" and Otto: "It doesn't matter!" but not violently. That dandy was perhaps correct, Otto was no longer very sure, kept repeating, "It doesn't matter!" Raouf still looking at his glass: "No, the order of the words is important, a-b-b-a, 'perfect valor and cowardice absolute,' it's a chiasmus!" A lesson in rhetoric now, thought Ganthier, he's upping the ante in pedantry. And suddenly Raouf was looking Otto in the eyes: "Do you understand why?" And, after a silence, "a-b-b-a, valor and cowardice are next to each other, they touch, they rub, because basically they are of the same nature, and too bad for valor! A nice presentation, isn't it?" Raouf had assumed a melancholy air, without the aggression Otto was counting on for the fight. The officer bowed: "You have finesse, sir," and Raouf, as if to excuse himself: "I had good professors." Gabrielle to Raouf, later: "He must be saying to himself that beneath your skin color there must be something, but be careful, he didn't like it when you stole the show . . ."

Otto became more reserved. They spoke of everything and nothing. Softly, Ganthier told Otto the anecdote of the men in top hats and tails whom they had seen go by on their tandem that morning. Otto responded that they were most probably employees at a funeral home, they often do that, they don't earn enough to take the tramway, Otto finally asking Raouf if he knew *a little* German literature, and Raouf: "They never talked about Germany in the French lycée, but I know two poets, Heine . . ."

"Obviously . . ."

"And an Austrian poet."

"Austrian?"

"Yes, Trakl, Georg Trakl, a young Viennese woman told me about him."

Otto then looked almost affectionate. He pointed out that Trakl died during the war, after the battle of Grodek.

Kathryn was like a statue. Two days earlier, Raouf had introduced her to Metilda. She had never seen a girl with such pale blue eyes, and just the opposite of a cow. Metilda had immediately said:

"I was afraid of this meeting. Raouf told me that you are very jealous, but I believe that women shouldn't be so hard on each other, don't you?"

She considered herself a woman. A long skirt, boots, and a white blouse, tie, dark jacket, belted, at the right place . . . They tried to appear natural. Metilda spoke of the ship, and Kathryn of the mistakes one can make on the last day of a crossing.

"The last day," Metilda said, "I spent in front of a bowl, in the middle of a storm."

She knew how to make fun of herself. That had worried Kathryn, but she ultimately told herself that nothing had happened, the idea suited her, and now, right in the middle of the restaurant Raouf admitted the poems. It wasn't a simple traveling encounter, poems were worse than a kiss. Fury overcame her. She asked in a joyful voice: "Did you also recite Arabic poems to her?" And

Gabrielle at that moment: "Look!" A man was entering the room, bare-headed. Suddenly he was the only one there, a tuxedo, monocle, a pink parasol on his shoulder, in the winter. They were expecting a woman behind him, but he was alone.

The man pointed the closed parasol at a table. The maître d' rushed over to pull back a chair. The man with the monocle waited a moment, then sat down. He placed the parasol on the table, opposite him, and he put a hooligan's cap on his head. At the other tables some patrons were laughing, an actor who was putting on a show? With the snap of his fingers the man was served champagne, didn't touch it, plunged the parasol next to the bottle in the bucket. Another snap of the fingers, a word to the waiter, who returned with a large plate of French fries and a jar of mayonnaise. There was murmuring in the room as the fries went by. The man showed no emotion. He took a fry with his fingers, dipped it into the mayonnaise, ate it, drank a mouthful of champagne, and continued while looking around the room.

"That's not an actor," Otto said, "He's a filmmaker. He lost an eye, but the other one is a true camera, it seems that his wife makes him do things like this to battle his shyness. His name is Wiesner, Klaus Wiesner."

Ganthier said that he must not be a very great filmmaker. When you do great works you don't need to act the clown.

"Oh yes, he's a great one," said Kathryn, "Do you remember in Paris, that film *Extenuated Death*, it was his, he's the person I'm here to see." Otto didn't seem surprised by Wiesner's eccentricities:

"He's a unique character, I know him, they say he's done much worse things than what he's doing here."

None of the four friends risked asking Otto for details. If he wanted to tell about *those much worse things* he would; if he didn't, nothing would compare to the sly joy he might have in leaving an audience of well-bred listeners hungering for some malicious gossip. Raouf avoided Kathryn's eyes. He knew she was furious. He shouldn't have talked about the poems. He had met a young girl on a boat; she had become a friend, only a friend; and the poetry was only friendship. Kathryn was angry, but not like usual. An anger with pinched lips, Gabrielle said to herself, a desired anger, a week ago she would have made a scene, right here in the restaurant, regardless of Otto, and now she is angry only because she thinks she should be, in fact, what she's interested in is that crazy person with his parasol, and Raouf will soon miss the time of true jealousy. Otto asked who the young Viennese woman was, and Kathryn said, quite naturally:

"One of our friends, very modern. She told us that in her generation no one wants to die at war anymore, or love people who sacrifice themselves for the fatherland." Her voice was dry. Otto was paying for Raouf's sins. Before the Prussian could react, Gabrielle asked him a question:

"What does Herr Wiesner's wife do?"

"She's a screenwriter, a great storyteller, one of the best! The husband deals with impossible stories, but the wife can tell captivating ones." Otto didn't seem to want to say anything more. A moment of silence, which Ganthier broke:

"You've still not told me where you were."

It was an abrupt change of subject, with no details, as if such a question, asked by a man who was approximately the same age, could involve only a single place, a single time.

"Most of the time on the Meuse front, in Les Éparges . . ." And Ganthier:

"I was there, opposite you, with many others." Then looking at the man with the parasol:

"Him, too? Is that where you met him?"

"No, he is from Austria, like Trakl (looking at Raouf), he was hit with shrapnel on their Russian front, now he is German, and ready to defend the *Vaterland!*" A silence, Otto continued: "He retained a taste for firearms . . . And he was married before." He didn't say anything more.

When Ganthier had introduced them to Otto, Gabrielle told him that she didn't understand his interest in such a fellow:

"Or is it the extreme right that connects you?"

"Let me point out, dear friend, that in public *such a fellow* gets us through customs, especially these days." Raouf asked:

"Do they dislike the French less if they frequent fascists?"

Ganthier didn't respond, simply adding that Otto was navigating between several roles, the front lines warrior when he was with his friends, the gentleman in social life, the enthusiast of French literature, in the tradition of Frederick the Great, not to mention other borrowings from *Faust* and Wagner.

Regarding the man with the parasol, Otto continued:

"We like him a lot, not long ago we even came to his aid," and he went on to tell what happened, a whole whirlwind of hypotheses that got carried away with their sixth bottle of champagne. "Herr Wiesner's first wife is dead, people talked about it a lot at the time. They say she shot herself in the chest, with her husband's pistol. That was immediately thought strange. Yes, between the breasts, probably because she wanted to keep their beauty in death, or maybe she thought at the last moment that in the chest it wouldn't be too bad—thanks to the war our surgeons have become experts in bullets to the chest—an alarming wound, from which she would have recovered, better loved . . . But, unfortunately for her, a lot of time passed before they called for help, that was also bizarre. That was two and a half years ago, approximately. There are so many things happening these days that we forgot all about it. It's difficult to be a wife in the film world, if you aren't an actress you're a woman in the shadows, thus very quickly a shadow of a woman," Otto was very happy with his chiasmus. He looked at Raouf. Raouf didn't react. Otto continued:

"And under the lights there is always another woman, even if she herself is married, you are the legitimate one, you're jealous, but if that other woman sees your husband more often than her own, it's because she works with your husband, a work very useful to the art, not like you, you have to let artists do their work as artists, and the other husband is anything but jealous, he's a good husband, official and placid; the other woman works more and more with your husband in the editing room and it's always a stupid scene, the one where the legitimate one falls upon the adulteress in midaction, in an editing room . . . And this is where there are conflicting hypotheses, on the details of the activity in which the lovers were indulging, and even on the place, the famous booth or a salon, with the eternal salon sofa, and the question of knowing who is on their knees," said Otto while looking at Raouf, "and for the rest of it, there is a hypothesis of a somber romanticism. The cheated wife plunges into the clouds of despair, locks herself in the bathroom, and shoots a bullet between her breasts, or she has a more . . . southern reaction. She attacks the couple, the gun in her hand, they struggle, and in the melee the shot is fired, a conjugal brawl, and an accident, but they say that the other woman, who doesn't deny her presence with our director, only the modalities, asserts that the wife really did go into the bathroom, and that she, the collaborator, can testify that she was always at the husband's side, a husband who thus could never have hurt his wife—a way of speaking of course—and there is an even darker hypothesis: the lover overwhelmed by the scenes that his wife is making has an empathetic gesture, as in film; empathetic gestures are very dangerous when they're done in real life, with a real pistol, in front of a wife and a lover. The lovers can then become . . . in French they call it 'diabolical,' right?"

Otto turned toward Kathryn:

"In America, this sort of thing, how do they deal with it?"

"There's a trial, and even several, but the results are usually the same, the man escapes!"

Otto adding, "Here it's not always useful to have a trial when very honorable citizens, decorated officers or a very great filmmaker, for example, assert that nothing criminal occurred, they can testify to it. The police really believe any testimony that has social weight, even if the very great filmmaker or the decorated officers were not strictly speaking on the scene. We are in a time of

. . . 'skinny cows,' as you say in French, so we have confidence in weighty testimony. That has created a lot of discussion on the subject. At the time there was a true competition among opinions, for what would become . . . the common opinion." There was a silence. Otto smiled at Raouf. Raouf was like a statue, and Otto:

"The common opinion today is that there was a tragedy in the life of that man with a monocle."

"It would seem," said Kathryn, "that he's a prince of light and rhythm."

"He is our greatest filmmaker," said Otto, "He causes a lot of jealousy, thus a lot of malicious gossip, especially because it was his own pistol, the weapon of tragedy, a war souvenir. It's pitiless, the souvenirs we bring back from the war, we always end up using them, in a conjugal brawl, or when faced with a traitor."

Otto didn't say anything more. He now allowed his new friends to take aim at lovers and mistresses, true desire, dissimulation, and vengeance. Those French were full of goodwill, wanting to understand what was happening, Ganthier, a respectable adversary, but French troops were in the Ruhr, behaving like an ax in the forest, nothing respectable about it. Otto smiled. The French as usual weren't capable of exploiting a situation. They've fought with both the English and the Americans. That was like them: cut themselves off from allies who had helped them win, they thought they were the sole victors, they had to be allowed to believe all that, one day the scales will fall off their eyes. Otto wouldn't say that he had just returned from a training camp run by his organization, two days spent in manoeuvers in the countryside with high school, university students, veterans, bureaucrats, the upper class, aristocrats, or workers—that was the most exalting, the presence of factory workers who came with their bosses, behind the flag, and since the arrival of the French in the Ruhr, more and more of them showed up at the organization's meetings, the true German people, reformed, and who stopped pouring ashes on their heads, a true victory in defeat. One of his friends had imagined covering four tractors with a camouflage cover. Consider those assault tanks, he said: from then on the war will go very quickly. The infantry soldier must learn to run behind an assault tank. They didn't believe him, but running was good for you. The path would be long. Otto was confident. Ganthier asked what became of Herr Wiesner's lover.

"She's his second wife, of course, she has him wrapped around her little finger, and from time to time she sends him off to battle his shyness in public places."

The next day Gabrielle said to her friends: "I'm persuaded that Otto knows people who assassinated Minister Rathenau last year."

After the restaurant Otto declined to accompany them to a cabaret: "Do you really want to see a man in a pulled-up nightshirt being whipped to the sound of a bad tango by two whores in evening dresses? I'm sure that in Paris they do that with more chic." Raouf took advantage to also decline, in spite of Kathryn's looks, where was he running off to? With Otto? Kathryn and Gabrielle had insisted that Otto stay.

"If I agree, you'll come, too?" Otto asked Raouf. Raouf wondered who Otto looked like. The champagne was affecting his memory. He was sure he had met someone who looked like him, in a book he had thumbed through on the banks of the Seine, not read, I should have bought it . . . an officer, aristocratic manners, cultivated and casual. In the book he had a monocle, was walking across a room, and the author said that he was letting his monocle fly ahead of him.

The large boulevard where the restaurant was located, the Kurfürstendamm, in the evening became a kingdom of wine, women, song, and the dollar, especially the adjacent streets, with girls with crops and whips who also offered you cocaine and shows "with the forbidden!" Otto was now talking about the transvestite balls of Berlin where hundreds of men in women's clothing and women dressed as men danced under the benevolent watch of the police. The wildest were the bourgeois participants, "the cradle of our puritanism!" said Otto, "My young cousin told me that, in her school, to be a virgin at sixteen was shameful, to be successful, to be a true leader in her class, you had to have a lot of specific things to tell your . . . *friends* . . . about what you knew how to do with your body and with the body of a man, and the body of a woman, and with several bodies at the same time." Kathryn asked Raouf while laughing if Metilda knew that much. "It's not nice to talk like that," Raouf replied. He was happy to have shown some resistance.

They ended up going into Papagaio, one of the chic cabarets on the Kurfürstendamm. Two men in tuxedos, pink vests, white bow ties, bright red lips, and powder on their faces greeted the clientele and seated them in a universe of men with little hair and young women with brilliant jewelry. On the stage the girls were thinner than in Paris. One of them turned her back to the audience, bent over, passed her head and her chest between her legs, and looked at the new arrivals with her head upside down while singing "Willkommen." They applauded her. Half of the girls, said Kathryn, wouldn't have survived a casting in a New York club. She saw that Raouf didn't seem disturbed by the show, much racier than in Paris, is it because of me? Or Metilda? It must be Metilda, he seems somewhere else. Otto drank the most. He tolerated alcohol the best, and was the most talkative. He greeted with small nods of his head several men scattered around the room, Gabrielle saying to him: "You're not the only officer to come into a cabaret this evening." He smiled. Those were his friends. They were there like he was—to have fun and gather his strength before the great festivities. He didn't say anything more, and it took a question from Gabrielle to learn that the great festivities were the ones that would allow the purging of the country and the restoring of the individual, against decline, against democracy, the bourgeoisie, liberalism, the modern world—he almost said the American world. He added:

"But we're not reactionaries. We want a revolutionary, imperial, and socialist order. Germany will ensure the restoration of the West!" Ganthier, aside to Raouf: "They don't have enough to buy an ounce of butter and they want to restore the West!" Raouf replying:

"Compared to Otto you could pass for a leftist."

Otto was no longer in a conversation. He was allowing his words free rein, and they let him carry on to try to learn a bit more: politics are not preferable to war, "politics today are war, and *besser eine eiserne Diktatur . . .* better a dictatorship of iron than anarchy of gold. I marched, two years ago, in a putsch that turned out badly. We didn't have speakers. Today there is perhaps someone whom we can use for a time, that Herr Hitler, a former corporal, another Austrian. His only quality is that he knows how to speak," and Ganthier, annoyed: "What does that mean, knows how to speak?" For Otto it was to say to desperate people to look at the foreign tanks in their streets: "Those who don't dare attack those tanks with their canes will never amount to anything!" Otto repressing a laugh, continuing: "So people give you an ovation. Everyone knows they can't attack tanks with canes, Hitler foremost, but that gives them the strength to dream, and with that strength they look at the tanks in a different way. We are not nihilists, we want the future of the worker, while keeping capitalism. Marx was right, it is the most powerful form of creation in the world, but first you have to do away with democracy, and nationalism is the explosive with which Monsieur Poincaré provides us in large quantities, with each sound of foreign boots in our streets!" Otto, a bottle of champagne in one hand and a cigar in the other, filled their glasses while proclaiming that there should always be light at the bottom of the bottles.

Later, Gabrielle said to Ganthier:

"That guy would blow up the planet to reach the moon, and he is inviting me over! He wants to show me a *Strandkorb*, do you know what that is?"

"Yes, a beach chair, a large armchair made of wood and wicker. He put it on his balcony, two seats. He told me that it reminds him of the beaches of his occupied country, yes, 'occupied,' the corner of Prussia that they had to give to the Polish, the Danzig corridor. It's always risky to live in a place that can be transformed into a corridor. He says that it's the land of Kant—in fact Königsberg is more to the east, after Danzig. Those are the two great specialties of the country, Strandkorbs and Kant. The armchair is ingenious, a retractable shelf on each arm to hold your beer, another shelf under the seat that slides out and becomes a footrest. I'm sure that Otto dreams of spending an afternoon sitting on it with you."

"I don't think I really interest him. I don't think he's interested in women."

34

FASCINATION

Kathryn was able to arrange a meeting with Wiesner: "It's not because you're American that I'm seeing you, it's because I saw you in a film by your husband, *The Rose Merchant*, it's very good, very well done." Kathryn was ashamed of that film. It had earned a lot of money but it was an easy story, a tearjerker, with two alternate endings, a happy marriage or a tragic death. The producers had demanded a happy ending, believing that only intellectuals—that is, people capable of reading a newspaper—would like a tragic one, but the tragic ending was as successful as the marriage of the heroine, and they asked the managers of the movie theaters: do you want death or marriage? Or both? In any case, it was a tearjerker. Neil didn't like the film either, and he was counting a lot on his future *Eugénie Grandet* to regain the admiration of artists. Neil was like that, always in advance of a film that would reestablish everything, and always in advance of a woman, Kathryn said to herself: He must be having fun back there, I don't even want to know whom with anymore, I even wonder why we're still together, because we see so little of each other? Because that pig Arbuckle was too much and the studios don't want any divorces . . . because we don't care enough about each other to have the energy to break up, because we don't have any more vanity, because the situation is convenient . . . Before we arrived in Nahbès I never lived on the other side of cheating, it was by cheating on Neil that I've learned how easy it is, and so Raouf was payback for Neil? My jealousy scenes . . . Metilda must have seemed much easier to live with. That's what men look for, easygoing women . . .

Kathryn wondered if there was any irony in Wiesner's admiration for that *Rose Merchant*. The filmmaker spoke to her in a friendly voice, but she sensed that at any moment he would become the master. She needed him. A great film shot in Berlin—that made you someone special in Hollywood. She knew that she would never be a true star, but she could be someone special. Berlin was her chance. Wiesner knew it, too. He was already using that knowledge to dominate, but what he wasn't saying and what she knew was that he also needed her. To have a well-known American actress was a true passport, whereas in the States films that came from Berlin were still forced to be called "European." During the war, in school courtyards, a lot of American schoolchildren had burned their German books.

You know, said Wiesner, I'm interested, if you'll allow me, interested in a different sort of acting than what you did in *The Rose Merchant*, which you perhaps still do a bit, we will try to change some things, if necessary . . . That was it, he was criticizing the film. Kathryn was reassured about Wiesner's tastes, not about his honesty; she would stay on her guard. The following days, in the studio and on the set he was unexpectedly sweet with her, but not at all with the others. "Yes," he had fun saying, "Our society is becoming anarchic these days, it has some good sides, you must free forms to be able to create, but if you want the work to be done, nothing's better than the good old *Kasernenhofton*, the 'barracks yard' tone." Later, she heard him say something that hardened all the faces: yes, he had indeed said *Hundsfötsche*, a makeup artist translated, dog vagina? Whom did he say that to? They didn't know exactly. Why didn't anyone react? Because what was essential was that the work be done, and for the people on the set that wasn't his worst insult, a tangled cable, a bad lipstick job, and the worst came out, in the original language, *travail français!*—French work! For Kathryn, Wiesner installed a halo of calm, friendly and specific instructions, but violence and fear pervaded, and she felt it was circling her. Wiesner's hand brushed her shoulder, her cheek. Kathryn was flattered. Once she saw Wiesner's wife watching them, very cold, a blond with short hair.

What Wiesner asked for was difficult, contradictory. For him actors were colors that should be able to change in an instant; great theater actors did that very well. Wiesner didn't say anything else, didn't ask her if she had done theater, or if she was a great actress. He had a very directive concept but demanded the natural. He often had a scene repeated, even when he seemed satisfied, and the more he repeated one, the more he asked Kathryn to appear to be improvising. He raised her chin while making her pivot her head, asked her to keep the pose to test the lighting. She started to have a sore neck, didn't dare say anything. He had her act with another woman, one instruction, suddenly, "Seduce!" The actress put her hand on her chest, "Perfect!" Wiesner said, "A lovely moment of surprise! We must keep it, with less expression . . . The opposite now, place yourself against her back, slide your hand, no, don't try to look complicated, a simple gesture of breaking and entering at the opening of her dress, but with the look of an ingénue, you've never done that? You're not like my actresses, they say they have to be drunk to enjoy men . . . And now, more complicated, you look chaste and sated, yes, both at the same time, not easy, the mark of the greats . . . We'll get there, with a lot of work." He was silent a moment, dove into his notes, thinking, *These actresses who think that the egg is more intelligent than the chicken, you still have to show them everything!*

Wiesner's wife often joined them during breaks. She complimented Kathryn coldly. Once she showed her husband a newspaper article. He laughed, pointed at a column:

"A teacher has written a letter in which he does an inventory of his career. The man kept accounting books, thirty years in his profession, you know what that amounted to?" Wiesner translated while reading: "Four hundred thousand blows with a cane, one hundred twenty thousand whipping sessions, one hundred thirty thousand blows of a ruler on hands, ten thousand two hundred punches on ears, he is very happy to have trained youth!" Wiesner mocked the teacher, but they sensed that he agreed with him; the teacher was just a bit extreme.

"Were you beaten a lot?" Kathryn dared ask him. She was also thinking of Raouf's early years, of what he called his two schools. "At the Linz boarding school," said Wiesner, "we had to recite our lessons for the next day before going to bed. A stick was more effective through the fabric of a nightshirt." Kathryn said that she had never been beaten, by no one.

"Really? It's because you're not a boy."

"In America people are beating children less and less, it's called democratic education . . ." Wiesner and his wife looked at each other. Kathryn wanted them to respect her. She added in a suave voice: "That's what allows us to beat others . . ." Wiesner didn't respond. That girl was trying to escape her collar, and she was enjoying it! He got up to go give some orders. His wife followed him. Kathryn started thinking of Raouf again, *He could have come with me, he doesn't want to, he's playing shy, that allows him to go see his Austrian, I didn't know we were so modern.*

Later, Kathryn said to Wiesner that the teacher's list could make a superb comic montage, short sequences, a lively rhythm. Wiesner nodded in approval: What was that girl thinking? She was there to go in front of the camera, not behind it, she wasn't her husband. He said, smiling, that it would show criticism of good education, but so much the better, "when, in a film, I distance myself from my opinions, it's the sign that I'm inventing; for Chekhov an original story in the twentieth century would be that of an honest banker . . ." Wiesner wondered what he was going to be able to do with this American. Her face wasn't thin enough, she wouldn't catch the light, but she held it as was rarely done . . . *Not the allure of a star, she will never be a precipice, rather a woman with whom one would like to live, beautiful, but placid, she's a very good supporting character, or a victim, perhaps . . . The symptom of the crisis of values is that this woman is a victim, innocent, or she could commit a small sin, like all of us, but for her it would turn tragic, I'll have to make her die, but first go through infamy, because of a small sin, she could tie her own rope in the chiaroscuro . . . and before dying, a great hope.* He assumed an affable air, asked her: "Dear Kathryn, what little sin would you be capable of? Little sins, you know, that's what connects the audience with the character."

Basically, Kathryn did not find Wiesner very interesting, and she began to tell herself that she had made a mistake. Neil regained a few qualities. He would sometimes shout on the set, but no one cared, and they had fun. On her request Wiesner had shown her one of his films, a riot of blacks, whites, light and shadows. On the screen there appeared in succession an insurrection, a putsch, an assassination, a man and his disguises, playing cards, a master letting his valet take drugs to control him better, a master of the hour and of well-held traps, pitiless with delays, a train flying by—suddenly she was no longer mistress of herself—and the stock exchange clock, and sixty miles an hour, *I've never seen a drunk so well filmed,* a false drunk, a forger in his lair, the lair full of blind workers, and false news at the exchange, and rates that collapse, a crowd at the exchange; in the middle a man is alone, like a pillar, he's crying, he's scratching his head, puts his hat back on, shouts, wipes his face, shakes some papers; twenty-four images a second, and in each second at least ten gestures by ten different characters; and the scene is suddenly more vast, at least a hundred characters, and never the same movements; the lowering of the rates, the fall, the crisis, the rates go back up, the crook now a millionaire, *How does he do it so I don't leave this tumult? He must have cut at least half of it, each cut creates a tension, and events don't follow each other, they move, he is more American than Americans,* the winner at the exchange becomes a psychoanalyst, promises to heal all the sick through dialogue, *Not even time to smile, I'm suffocating, it's been at least twenty minutes since it started,* a light that doesn't illuminate, which is threatening, that pierces, that creates a shock, which attacks like a thief, *Almost a half-hour now without breathing and I don't want it to stop,* and now a woman, on the stage, like a burst of fresh air, *To be that woman, to be filmed like her, as a burst of fresh air, you don't need a princess costume, in this rhythm one is royal, and I disappear before they have seen me enough, I become a regret.*

The film was crazy. The best way to make a good film, said Wiesner while they were changing the reels, is to burn one's vessels, take the example of a man who cheats at cards and who ruins someone else, it's awful, it's for the everyday audience! My character, the crook, he also earns, but . . . he decides not to put away his gains, why? You see, that intrigues you, it's because I first decided to have him give it up, even before knowing the reason. You have to put yourself on the edge of the unknown so that the viewer also has the sensation of the unknown, and after I found it, why is he doing that? Because he is not a simple crook, he's a man who shatters morality to feel his instincts. For him that's what's essential, not money, and that's what film is. It makes the never-seen rise up, even if it's infernal . . . That's not very American, is it, two hours of illusion to leave the audience with no illusions?

It was superior to anything she had seen up to then. It was all that Neil wanted to do, that they didn't let him do—to be an actress in such a film! She listened to Wiesner. Everything changed as soon as he started talking about his films. He said that you needed life in the illusion. Others were wrong in wanting to produce the illusion of life: I'm trying to put life in the illusion, and life in the illusion is a snag, a blip, but that relaunches the rhythm! When, in a film, a clothing designer presents a fashion show, for example, he holds by the hand the beautiful girl who is wearing the dress. She walks on the podium, three feet above the ground where the designer comes up. That just means, "Here fashion is being shown." For me, at a certain moment, the designer leans over the girl's shoe and brushes it with his finger, not at all to remove a speck of dust—there can be no motive, just a sign, a bit incongruous, but that's it, life that surges in the illusion, that's all. Or a king who is stuffing himself, a medieval king. He's not content to take the meat in two hands. That's what you would expect, because you know it already: here's a medieval king! If the film imitates what you're expecting, that's not film. You need something else. For example, the king cuts a slice of the meat—you could also expect that, it's everywhere—but for me, then, he takes the slice in his whole hand and wipes the dish . . . And when my hero cheats human lives, it's not a common story. It becomes a work of art because he cheats himself to taste ruin . . .

One day Wiesner asked her:

"Does my glass eye bother you?"

She said no, then added that it must be twice as hard to truly measure a space. Yes, he replied, in the beginning I was forced to fight against my vision, less depth perception, it was good for me, I learned to compensate, and what I see I owe to myself, not to nature. Nature provided the means, life inflicted the loss, and I re-created it!

He smoked a cigar constantly. One day he made fun of her habit of chewing gum (but she never chewed when she was on the set). She said that it was to avoid having those close to her find themselves opposite a mouth that smelled like cigarettes. Since then he didn't smoke around her. She told herself that she was in the process of betraying Neil. It was more serious than loving Raouf. Neil was the profession. He had let her go to Berlin, but she knew that he was not at all in favor of that German experience, and she sought reasons to hate Neil. She had plenty. There was one she preferred, Neil looking for a letter, saying that he was sure he had left that letter on his desk, he couldn't find it, who had moved things around on his desk? A police investigation! Or a jealous wife, it was the same thing, incompetence! Incompetent even in jealousy! He had repeated the word three times. She had responded that the mess on the desk was his doing, the same disorder as in his head, the disorder that the studio owners complained about! She knew that she was hurting him. The producers were criticizing his *Eugénie Grandet* screenplay for lacking unity. He didn't want a screenwriter; he wanted to do everything himself; he couldn't. He was suffering; he was going to become a veteran of failure. Someone had messed up his papers, the work of a jealous weasel—then, more direct, right in her eyes: I don't give a damn if you read my mail, but put it back where it was after you do. She felt nauseous: I don't need to rifle through your papers, I know everything, is your mistress jealous? If you want I can calm her down, tell her you were with me . . . He became mean: Don't act the martyr . . . not with me . . . Anyway, you don't know how to act . . . Kathryn responded that's not what they tell me, saying nothing else. But that wasn't the first time she had gone through his papers. After all, it was her right . . . She finally understood the reason for his anger. She told him: What makes you crazy is that you think I'm trying to read letters that no one writes to you! She left, laughing. Why should she stay with a guy like that?

Now Wiesner was showing her the boards for his great project, a mythical story. He himself had drawn a giant dragon, mechanized, and sketches of a landscape.

"I don't want a landscape, standard scenery. I can't stand postcards. I want the eyes of a landscape, and not many words."

"You don't like words?"

"When there are too many words it's like when I have too much money in my pocket." He was getting excited while he was talking. They were in a private screening room. Wiesner had put an arm around her shoulders. She was afraid that his wife would come in. Wiesner understood, said in a low voice: "She's making sure we're not disturbed."

35

THE RETURN

Raouf looked back. Behind them, in the middle of the road, a headless rooster was turning around and around.

"Is it okay?" asked Ganthier.

"If you like, but the peasant won't agree."

Ganthier stopped the car and backed up. A man came out of a thatch-roof house. Ganthier got out, greeted the peasant, told him that he shouldn't let his animals wander on the road, and held out a bill. The bill disappeared into a pocket. Ganthier shook the man's hand, got back in the car. They set off again.

"I bet you gave him enough for two roosters."

"Four or five," said Ganthier, "For us it's an incident, for him it's a scandal . . . and perhaps he won't throw stones at the next car."

They had been on the roads in France for several days, speaking little. Kathryn had gone back to America. Gabrielle was in Russia, with a friend she had introduced to Ganthier at the train station when she was catching the Berlin-Moscow, a slender girl with red hair, brown eyes, clumsy movements, an Englishwoman. Gabrielle has found someone to protect, Ganthier thought, I didn't fit the bill. The young girl was verifying that the porter indeed had all their luggage. She interrupted Ganthier's gesture and said to Gabrielle: "Give me some change!"

"I don't have any," Gabrielle responded, in a timid voice.

"I told you to get some! You never listen to me! As if I were nothing!"

Gabrielle was distraught. Ganthier, instead of enjoying this role reversal, did what he had wanted to do: he paid the porter. When he turned around he saw the young girl pass her handkerchief under Gabrielle's eyes while murmuring: "I'm sorry, so sorry . . ."

There was a moment of calm. The young girl thanked Ganthier in an almost friendly tone. He offered her a cigarette; she refused. He held his case out to Gabrielle, who glanced at her friend before refusing. Ganthier put his case back in his pocket. The young girl looked him up and down while smiling sweetly. Then she stared at Gabrielle, who quickly held her hand out to Ganthier to thank him, suddenly seeing in front of her a friendly and tender man, very dif-

ferent from what he had been up to then, and who was suffering. It was too late.
The young girl in turn held her hand out to Ganthier, a hand that was both slender and hard at the same time. Ganthier turned around and left along the platform, leaving the two women to talk in front of the door of their sleeping car.
He didn't dare turn around.

And a few days later, in the train from Berlin to Paris, he had been surprised
not to see Gabrielle in the reflection of the window, not to be able to observe
her the way he did during their travels. Sometimes their looks would cross each
other in the reflection, and Gabrielle smiled like a hunter who has just surprised another one. He closed his eyes . . . Their discussions . . . the articles she
gave him to read . . . the Tiergarten . . . the ruined night in Paris . . . He again
looked through the window and she appeared, naked in her armchair, her feet
in a basin of hot water. He had gotten up to go into the corridor, leaving Raouf
alone in the compartment. He looked out at a distance at the landscape while
thinking: *Pain is a desert island*, then: *I am the king of fucking idiots*.

In Paris Ganthier decided to make the trip from Paris to Marseille by car, and
had immediately bought one.

"I want to drive it myself, and learn how to repair it. I don't want to be at the
mercy of mechanics!"

He chose a Peugeot, a convertible, a large four-seater to replace the Panhard
that was aging in Nahbès, and he spent six days at the garage taking it apart and
putting it back together, under the watch of the mechanics.

"Your friend is a real grease monkey, can't you leave him with us?" the owner
had said to Raouf.

"What's more, I'm paying to work, a nice deal for you," Ganthier had added.
This fantasy had cost him a lot, but he was happy. Raouf, too: he had had free
rein while Ganthier was learning about his car, and spent it in discussions with
his Maghrebi and Asian friends, and especially with David Chemla, who had
decided to do his studies in Paris while working for the Communist Party. They
hadn't seen each other for months, since before Raouf left for Europe. Chemla
had become harder, and Raouf sensed that a world separated them. He, himself,
had decided not to get his card from the party, even clandestinely. David hadn't
reproached him, but Raouf sensed that he no longer judged him worthy of their
serious discussions. He had cut himself off from the avant-garde; he shouldn't
be part of the debate; he had the right only to stock responses. It hurt him. He
had, however, willingly told about his trip to Germany, the thwarted revolution,
the nationalist demonstrations.

"The hope that must be protected now is the Soviet Union," David had
said.

The day before they left, Raouf had gone to find Ganthier at the garage. Ganthier was sweating. He had changed a drive shaft and finished putting a tire back on. Raouf said to him:

"A car like that replaces many things."

"Do you know why I really like your conversation, young Raouf? Because you take care of all the clichés, it's comforting."

Ganthier continued to tighten the bolts, looked up at Raouf:

"What about you, is all well, have you remade the world with your Chinese?"

He had a smile that Raouf hadn't seen before, then, in a low voice:

"We both need to keep busy . . ."

With his back turned, he continued: "Except that you're becoming an adult, your days are not yet cadavers!"

In truth, Raouf was suffering less than Ganthier imagined. Certain things had come to an end, by themselves. Others had started again, also by themselves, and had also come to an end. Kathryn had brought an end to their relationship. No, that wasn't entirely true. Anyway, nothing had been said. One night she hadn't returned to their hotel on Kurfürstendamm. Raouf hadn't asked. He had realized that for some time he only thought of Kathryn when he was with her. The following days they had continued to talk, to walk. He had come several times to the studio to pick her up with Ganthier, who avoided making any reflections on the rather platonic role of escort. Kathryn still considered Raouf a part of her life, but in a different place. She had even once insisted on taking him to Metilda's parents' home, where he was having dinner, and she had left with Ganthier in the car that Wiesner put at her disposal. Ganthier seemed sad. She knew why and she had told him:

"I don't like that Englishwoman Gabrielle managed to dig up . . ."

Ganthier hadn't responded. Another time, Raouf, by himself, had gone back to the room he had never been in, without knowing if he was doing that of his own volition or if he had sensed that Kathryn was going to ask him to. He returned from Metilda's apartment. He considered it very modern not to have spent the entire night together.

To provoke Ganthier Raouf had gone to visit a competing garage, at the Ford dealership. He got behind the wheel of the latest model, the "T," and he rolled the car down the avenue Foch, his cap in the wind, in the company of Ganthier and the Ford mechanic. That had shocked Ganthier. The kid looked like a Californian. Raouf had seen his face:

"Do you realize, if we started buying American cars in the Maghreb? The short-circuit?"

"You should stay to your right."

"You'll have to teach a lot of natives French if you want them to continue buying from you in the twentieth century." Raouf's driving was alarming.

"I'm not refusing to listen to your wild imaginings," Ganthier said, "but you should concentrate on your driving."

"And when you will have accomplished that noble task and your dear natives will have all read *Les Misérables* and *The Social Contract*, they will nicely show you the door . . . to go get things from the Americans."

"That will be progress, the protégés of France who become flunkeys of the dollar!"

"Except if we have a revolution!" Raouf had said, laughing.

"Keep to the right, slow down, and don't go onto the roundabout at the Arc de Triomphe. You're stricken with the arrogance of drivers!"

Raouf had accelerated, and found himself turning around on the place de l'Étoile. The madness came from everywhere. Sometimes a policeman blew his whistle. No one paid attention. You must above all not stop. Raouf went around for a while before being able to get out of the infernal circle.

"That's the modern world, Raouf, if you stop you're lost!"

Raouf had managed to get onto the avenue de la Grande-Armée, concluding:

"In the end, I prefer the fantasia . . ."

"Are you talking about that horse race that ends only in shooting blanks? That's revolution? That suits you!"

They finally left Paris in the hum of cylinders, goggles over their eyes, coats and gloves of black leather.

"We're going to be taken for secret service agents," Raouf had said, "and in your case it's not completely false."

Sometimes Raouf became sad. He preferred attributing it to the inexplicable, working a memory in silence, the first time, a hand that had suddenly taken his in Nahbès, one day when they were both at Gabrielle's, waiting for her.

"No one is here, come on!" Kathryn had said to him, her lips against his ear. And in the bedroom the hands and mouth of Kathryn had continued to explore Raouf. He had remained silent. She spoke only a few words, in a tone of sweet statement: *You've never had sex before* . . .

While he was driving, Ganthier spent his time regulating the carburetor of the motor with the help of a button on the dashboard, happy as a kid with a new toy. From time to time he tapped on the steering wheel, as he would have patted the neck of a horse. He breathed with ease in seeing a nice curve up ahead or, better, a tight bend. The road became more and more beautiful. Sometimes it was bordered by plane trees, and some mornings they saw white frost on the grass of the fields, like the haze of a dream.

"We have time," said Ganthier, "The boat leaves in six days." He let some geese with large behinds cross in front of them. They were hurrying to cross the road while sticking their heads and necks out in front. "It's a counterweight," said Raouf, laughing.

The car slowed down to enter small towns dozing in the middle of the day.

"In Germany people always seemed to be doing something," Raouf had once noted, "Here you might say that time has stopped."

"Yes, with all the dead from the war things now only happen in the rhythm of parents and grandparents."

In an issue of *Le Petit Parisien* Raouf read an article out loud:

"Nationalist troops marched yesterday in Munich . . . Hitler declared that they constituted a national army destined to deliver Germany . . . complete equipment . . . hostile shouting at France and the Jews, crossing the city with a band in front of them . . . They call Hitler the 'Bavarian Mussolini.'"

"Gabrielle was right," Raouf had added, "Three months ago that guy was nothing, and now every time a civilian is killed by the French he gains thousands of supporters."

"Maybe, but in another three months he won't be anything anymore, he's just a donkey with horns."

"Do you think Otto is now one of them?"

"Otto was born to be shot, by someone or other," Ganthier said.

Raouf couldn't understand Otto, a revolutionary and a conservative, and capable of spending entire nights having fun in places that he wanted to get rid of. That was Berlin, everyone was changing, it just took a stay in the city to change. Berlin was reinventing the world! The passions of the old world had given death. Metilda's generation no longer wanted to hear about the old world but instead about free minds, free love, liberated bodies. One morning she had taken Raouf in a car to the banks of a lake where men and women were running out of large saunas, running naked into the icy water, then coming back out onto the banks and whipping themselves with birch branches, laughing, before going back into the sauna. Raouf had ended up agreeing to join them with Metilda in one of the steamy sheds.

Raouf didn't drive. He took care of navigating, surprising Ganthier. He was almost never wrong.

"How do you do it?"

"A visual memory."

"We're going south and you don't need to turn the map around. You never confuse the right and the left?"

"I'm good in geometry."

Raouf didn't point out that in the evening he worked on their itinerary. It is good that mature men continue to believe that youth is a miracle.

When Ganthier was able to reserve a hotel room by phone he was happy to drive until eleven at night. He liked to drive in the light of his headlights, swerving the steering wheel to avoid a rabbit or, worse, a cart without a lantern. Raouf watched the Michelin billboards. Silence settled between them. Kathryn returned to Raouf's thoughts, or Metilda. He tried not to feel vain. Kathryn's scenes of jealousy didn't seem like bad memories to him. He told himself that she had only anticipated, that she had become intolerable, and that his meetings with Metilda had then become much easier. Anyway, in Berlin that jealousy had quickly lost its energy. He was getting ready to see Kathryn again in less than six months. Neil had confirmed that the whole team was coming back to finish *Warrior of the Sands*, and to start a new film. "To be able to work again in calm, without producers spying on and photographers stalking us," he had written, "that's priceless."

Sometimes the Peugeot broke down, to Ganthier's great displeasure, but up to then he had always been able to repair it and concluded with: "And this is work!" They had easily gone over the hills of Burgundy. One evening they went to a village dance. The musicians were either old or very young. In a too large room many young women were dancing together; others, themselves not yet thirty, danced with a bored or sad child, while looking toward the door of the room; the music was slow. People stole looks at Raouf and Ganthier, who didn't dare leave the bar. They observed the room in the mirror above the counter, and Raouf: "You wouldn't say that we're in a country that won the war."

They usually left early in the morning. On the straightaways the Peugeot became a race car, Ganthier and Raouf became race drivers, from head to toe, in their nerves, hearts, muscles, those in the abdomen especially. Raouf was afraid, would never have admitted it, but had realized that, when he spoke of Ganthier's farm, he never went above an honest twenty-five miles per hour. Then the headiness took over, acceleration to close to forty miles per hour, and the trees flew by.

In Berlin Metilda had been surprising.

"In Vienna I am Viennese," she said, "Here, I'm a Berliner, we don't know what is going to come, the old ways of loving are dead and we must try everything. I'm not angry with you about what didn't happen on the boat, I'm angry that you didn't talk to me about Kathryn, to have preferred to pass for a virgin, whereas you know a lot," she said, laughing, under Raouf's caresses, "I'm not jealous of Kathryn, I'm very grateful to her. You know a lot of things and you give the impression that you invented them, but your error is in considering women as trophies." In love her movements could be quite violent—but first she folded her clothes.

After 12:30 in the afternoon Ganthier lost all interest in driving. He started looking for a restaurant. "Not here," he often said. When Raouf showed surprise in front of a promising facade, Ganthier said the same thing to accompany his refusal: "They'll have today's sauce but yesterday's meat." They ended up finding a suitable place. Ganthier took time choosing, discussed with the owner, changed his mind during the discussion. Then it was a question of the wine, Raouf saying, "I won't drink any, or a half-glass, choose for yourself." Ganthier ate slowly, Raouf like a wolf. Then they left. The weather was good. After an hour Ganthier slowed down, drove into a field, climbed into the back seat, time for a nap. He was as regulated as a musical score. Raouf read, dreamed, lost himself in observing the flight of swallows, or wrote to Metilda. When he had said good-bye to Kathryn they both knew that they would be seeing each other again soon. With Metilda it was different, true adieux, but she had said: "We're not going to dissolve into tears, are we?" Raouf missed the Metilda of the boat, the one who spoke of hunting happiness, but he proved to be as strong as the Berlin Metilda, and they each wished the other many good encounters to come.

After a forty-five-minute nap Ganthier got back behind the wheel, stopping around 5:30: We're not going to miss an opportunity to relax, look at that shadow, magnificent! They settled in the magnificent shadow, under an arbor surrounded by trees. The branches seemed to be moving amid the clouds. Ganthier ordered pastis, began to think about the place where they would spend the night. When they arrived at the hotel, his first concern was to have a trunk filled with what was most precious to him taken to his room: a toolbox, air cylinders, a stock of candles, a spare clutch, and even a new cylinder.

One afternoon they were going through a village. "Look!" said Raouf. A dozen or so boys between fifteen and twenty years old were sitting in the sun on a stone wall. They were singing while clapping their hands.

"That's it, we're in the south," said Ganthier.

In Marseille, Raouf was happy to see the *Jugurtha*, which seemed smaller to him. He sometimes went alone to the bow, thinking of his two female friends, dreamed while making them talk to each other. In Berlin such occasions had been too rare, and when Metilda proposed organizing a dinner with Wiesner, Kathryn, Raouf, and her, Kathryn became sullen. The dinner never took place.

The crossing was storm-free, and at the moment when the *Jugurtha* entered the harbor, Raouf said to Ganthier:

"They traveled, they knew the melancholy of ships . . . they returned . . ."

Ganthier laughed: "I don't want to think about that anymore. I need to take care of trees and livestock out in the open air . . ."

"And you're going to see Kid again, do you think he'll recognize you?"

"You're getting on my nerves, young Raouf . . . And you, what have you decided? Where will you do your studies, there or there?"

Ganthier had pointed at the bow, then the stern.

"I don't know yet," Raouf said and, changing the subject, "This trip didn't work, you didn't succeed in converting me to the Great Empire."

"*Mektub*," said Ganthier.

"You don't believe in it anymore?"

"In what?"

"The France of a hundred million inhabitants . . ."

"Nobody wants it, especially not those who talk about it."

"And your preponderance?"

"With a generation like yours, it's going to be difficult. Ultimately I don't believe it anymore, what interests me is not to weigh on people, it's to create more French, we must defend the Mind!"

"Your Catholicism is returning . . . with age."

"You're bothering me, young Raouf."

"Yes, master!"

"And the revolution?"

"Revolutionaries don't want it to happen at home. They want to leave the primary role to the bourgeois, and since there aren't enough of them yet, it could take a long time . . ."

"So we're going to continue to talk in Nahbès, eh? You should marry your cousin, we would be neighbors."

"I know her. If she is thinking of someone, it's not me."

"You don't know anything about it."

"Nor do you."

Part III

ONE YEAR LATER: NAHBÈS, JUNE 1924

36

A TRUE FOX

The Americans didn't return in six months, rather the following year, at the end of June, and this time without McGhill, the producers' snitch. In the meantime, Neil Daintree had filmed three successful westerns. He was now back to finish *Warrior of the Sands* and counted on this stay to find a subject for a film that would be more distinctive than the endless stories of sheikhs. When they arrived Raouf had just returned from Paris, where he had completed his first year of law school. Neil was extremely friendly toward him, and they began to give each other lessons in Arabic and English. Gabrielle Conti was also there because she had decided that summer should be spent in the sun with people who liked you fairly well. Something had changed in her relationship with Ganthier. "What's going on with you and him?" Kathryn had asked. Gabrielle found the question very American and managed to dodge it. In any case she didn't really know, herself. She was discovering many more qualities in Ganthier, but she was savvy enough to realize that it was because he was showing less interest in her, and perhaps because he was more muscular than the men she met in Paris. Rania was happy to see her friends again. She kept repeating to herself, *I am beautiful . . . I have rights . . .* and became angry with herself for having such pitiful thoughts. Kathryn found Raouf's features to be more drawn, his voice hardened. In Berlin they had managed to part with a smile, and neither of them wanted to bring up Metilda or Wiesner. There was some distance between them, but it was good to see each other. Kathryn still would have liked to know how things stood between him and Metilda.

Raouf and Ganthier resumed their confrontations, which were no longer as harsh. Ganthier seemed less "preponderant" than before, and Raouf seemed to have given up revolution for the time being. "Law school is to blame," said the colonist, "It makes you patient, so many things that have to line up just so if you want them to work." Raouf found Ganthier melancholic, and he refrained from telling him that he seemed to have aged. "I'm at that age when you reread things," said Ganthier. He had also started reading a Muslim mystic, and he was even trying to translate the text, which led to more discussions with Raouf. "No," said Raouf, "don't translate *qids* as 'saint,' that's too cloying, too pietist. *Qids* is foremost the 'sacred,' Hallaj isn't a curé at Saint-Sulpice!"

To celebrate their return to Nahbès the Americans offered to arrange a free outdoor film screening for everyone in the town. Marfaing found the idea interesting. One had to move with the times, "The natives, you understand, if you inject them with small doses of modernity, electricity, cars, movies, they will end up working with you. Some, at least, the modern ones, they'll break with the fanatics who prohibit images, and that will keep the moderns from being supported by the fanatics!" As soon as they heard about the screening the leaders of the Prépondérants, Pagnon and Jacques Doly, the lawyer, made it known to the contrôleur civil that they were not in favor of it, and Colonel Audibert, the local commanding officer, was also reticent, the crowds . . . overflowing . . . Marfaing responded that overflowing crowds when you know how to control them are fine; a few knocks on the head with rifle butts by the greatest army in the world are a wonderful preventative measure. Marfaing emphasized his cynicism to show the officers that he was not just a bleeding heart. The colonel said that Daintree was wilier than he seemed, that they were playing with fire, and Marfaing replied, pointing his finger upward, his eyes wide open: "I'm stealing the fire! And I'm making history!"

In making history he was also making his mistress, Thérèse Pagnon, very happy. She was dying to see a film with Francis Cavarro in it. Daintree had one, which took place during the French Revolution, *Scaradère*, an odd name. Yes, Daintree had said, the producers felt that if they mixed *Scaramouche* and *Lagardère* that would bring in more people. Marfaing was hesitant, the Revolution . . . Daintree said that it was the first part of the Revolution, 1789, the Bastille, the people united, and the message that great France is sending to the entire world, Liberty, Equality, Fraternity, the Enlightenment.

"So, dear Neil," Marfaing had said, "a film to enlighten, not to encourage fanatics, correct?"

Neil had liked that idea. He showed excerpts to Marfaing—stupid landowners, an apathetic and spineless king, young people filled with good intentions, lots of love scenes—that might work, with a majority of Europeans in the audience, handpicked natives, a nicely contained evening, the Enlightenment, the first revolution, the one that Édouard Herriot, the new head of the French government, liked. Marfaing would show that he could be a good servant of a government of the left, perhaps even replace the resident general, whom Paris had never pardoned for the events of 1922.

They gave themselves a week to prepare. As a distraction, Ganthier took Neil some twenty miles out of Nahbès: Let's go where there aren't any tourists, or women, a "man outing." No, we're not going to a brothel, but I'm not going to tell you, you'll see. They drove at a good clip under a sun that turned everything gray and ocher. There was no vegetation except for a few ashy plants; it was geology in a pure state. At one point an enormous structure in the shape of a broken arch arose out of the ground, parallel to the road.

"Keep looking," said Ganthier, "In ten minutes we're going to see the other piece. They were separated a long time ago, but you can tell they were together once . . ."

Their conversation was filled with innuendoes, Neil trying to find out what had happened in Germany, without asking too many questions about Raouf, or about Wiesner, some jovial questions that fooled no one. Ganthier thought: What bothers him is not that his wife slept with a German filmmaker, it's that she wants to work under that guy's direction, and that she adds, as she did yesterday in front of everyone, *It could be a true work of art!* And does he know about Raouf? He might suspect something, or he might not want to know, no, he must know, what's ironic is that he must have found out just when it was over, and our two lovebirds don't seem to have resumed their habits at Gabrielle's, a page has turned, perhaps, or maybe Kathryn went back to France this year, two lovers under the roofs of Paris, and if I ask Neil about what trips Kathryn took that will give him ideas, Raouf should still be careful, jealousy doesn't have to be right to explode.

They finally reached their destination, Ganthier's car rolling into a douar with houses low to the ground all bunched together. They had to park, get out, walk in a mixture of sand, dust, and loose stones to a deserted square. Neil realized that in fact people were around, but on rooftops. The village chief greeted Ganthier, who said to Neil:

"I brought his youngest son to my farm. He can't leave much to him, so with what he is learning with me, the boy will be able to have a small farm of his own one day, he's a good worker."

They were seated on a rooftop protected from the sun by an awning made of reeds. The square remained deserted until a camel, preceded by baleful cries, was suddenly led in. In fact, said Ganthier, it's a female camel, in heat. The man who was holding the camel by its bridle was walking it around the square. They heard more cries in the distance. Yes, the cries of a camel, there are males close by, Ganthier said, but for the moment they're making them wait. Neil asked, laughing, if they had driven through the dust for two hours to watch camels screw. Ganthier said you must be patient, it isn't exactly what you might expect, you'll see, it's educational. Their host came to sit down on the banquette next to Ganthier. He served them steaming, frothy tea, which they drank down, talking about the harvest, livestock, difficult times for honest folk, the Master of the two worlds who holds everything in his power, and the village chief made a gesture with his hand. Another camel entered the square, larger, stronger, and the female camel was already placing her tail on her side.

It took several men to hold the male camel. He bellowed, reared up, an almost uncontrollable mass, and all around people were also shouting. Then the men tried in vain to drag the male outside the square. They took the female away, and the male finally gave up under the blows of a stick. Around the deserted square only the shouting of humans could be heard. The female camel returned. She tried to follow the scent of the male but was held back. "Do people really enjoy watching frustrated animals?" Neil asked.

The male returned to the square.

"No," said Ganthier, "That's not the same one, he's smaller, they shouldn't have chosen a smaller one." And again the female moved her tail, the smaller male proving to be just as difficult to handle as the bigger one, and shouting from all sides, shouting like at an auction, bills and coins going from hand to hand, the male then led out of the square, the female remaining alone.

"That sack that's hanging out from the males' lower lip," asked Neil, "Is that a wound?"

"You're observant," said Ganthier, "No, it's the sack that stores water. Normally it's on the inside."

Neil asked if it had been pulled outside. Ganthier said:

"The people aren't as sadistic as you're implying! It comes out naturally, do you hear that noise? A real balloon . . . There is only air inside, there's no more water, a sack that expands and contracts, with that strange chirping. The sack moves up from their throat through the larynx because it's dry. No, they aren't prevented from drinking. In fact, the camel doesn't want to drink. He could if he wanted, but that idiot over there doesn't want to swallow a thing until he has satisfied a need more pressing than thirst. You saw how they were also drooling, like sick animals, and their eyes are baleful. Yes, all of that comes from the need to screw, the sack, the baleful look, drool, the noise of a balloon. Those lovesick idiots go on a true thirst strike until they've found a female. It's good old Mother Nature who has perfected this to force camels to perpetuate the species. Do you want something to drink? First you screw. And that makes them violent. They lash out, they bite, they are muzzled; that makes them even worse. With humans it's when they drink that they become violent; with camels it's the opposite. Yes, they will fight, thanks to the genius of men, because normally camels don't fight just for the sake of fighting. English dogs will kill each other at any hour of the day, but not camels. The camel is not a wild beast, he has to have reasons, and good ones, and he doesn't have to be whipped into a frenzy the way dogs do. They bring it to him on a platter. They present the female to the first camel, then take him aside, just enough to get his blood heated, etc., and then they bring in the second camel, present him to the lady, who is beginning to get impatient, and presto, they bring in the first male again, who is also full of ardor, and it will begin. This is when the owners and the bettors can lose their burnooses. Watch, it's getting serious, the two males both in front of the lady. The second one is really smaller, that's not normal, yet this isn't a village that has the reputation for rigging fights . . . You can see how things are heating up between the rivals. They're sizing each other up, making noise, and now the lady is gone; our two males are face to face." Ganthier dared to say: "In the same situation two modern men would find a way to work things out . . . every other day, for example . . . a compromise." Neil added, without laughing:

"Compromise is what distinguishes us from animals. It enables us to continue to work together."

"There—they've begun!" said Ganthier.

On the square it was like hand-to-hand combat, shoulders knocking, chests pounding, hooves kicking . . .

"That's to intimidate," said Ganthier, "There's more, watch, the big one is trying to grab the other's neck, and the other one is breaking away, biting. Yes, a camel bite really hurts, and you see how the sack is becoming purple? And the gushing foam? Oh, his neck is caught again, clearly the big one is the strongest in this contest!"

The smaller camel was biting from below to prevent the other one from catching hold, and was bitten in turn, another neck hold by the big one, missed, the two animals backing off, then charging each other, their crashing bodies making dull thuds. After a while the smaller camel gave up, lowered his head, accepted the other's domination. Was the battle over?

"No," said Ganthier, "He isn't giving up, he's staying. He's weaker but he's not a coward!"

"Do they fight to the death?" asked Neil. Ganthier didn't reply. The weaker camel was still in the fight, but its neck was lowered toward the ground.

"It looks like he's submitting," said Neil.

"Yes, but he isn't. When it submits it leaves the square. It's crazy, this is the first time I've seen something like this. Those neck holds are their main weapon: supported by the legs, all their strength goes through the chest and the neck; the neck is both an arm, a trunk like an elephant's, and a snake, there you go!"

The bigger one stuck out its neck, wrapping it like a trunk around the other's neck.

"He's trying to choke it, he's going for the kill," said Ganthier. The other wasn't even trying to bite anymore. His knees buckled under the attack. In the audience very few people seemed unhappy; most must have bet on the bigger one.

"This is unusual," Ganthier said under his breath.

Then, using all the strength in his camel legs, the small one suddenly sprang up and tossed the big one into the air, almost a ton of huge camel six feet off the ground, and it fell on its hump, legs in the air in a cloud of dust. The strangler then became the strangled.

"Now it's the big one who has taken a fall," said Ganthier, "He has fallen on a true fox!"

The true fox now fell onto the body of the big one. He dug in a hoof, his head, his jaw. The other's cries became louder and louder; blood flowed out of his stomach. He kicked his hooves and threw his neck in every direction but couldn't find a hold.

"A camel without purchase is finished," said Ganthier.

"Why is the smaller one standing up?" asked Neil, "Does he think he's won?"

"No, a ruse within the ruse, look!"

The small one had placed the big one's head between its hooves, and the big one's blood began to spurt out of its ears and nostrils. It kicked its legs, in vain; its movements became weaker.

"He's going to finish him off," said Neil.

Death cries now, it was over. Men rushed over, pulled the winner off.

"They won't let him die," said Ganthier, "A nice big male costs too much!"

The defeated one got up shakily onto its feet and limped off, dripping drool and blood. The winner was celebrated, a silk blanket, ululations . . .

"He couldn't care less about the ululations," said Ganthier, "He's only thinking about the female. He'll drink only afterward, and the sack will go back into his throat."

Around them money was again circulating. Neil tried to pick out the losers by their faces.

"I won," said Ganthier.

"I didn't see you make a bet."

"The village chief bet for me, not a lot, but it allows him not to feel indebted to me, and I accept his money so as not to offend him."

"And that doesn't bother you?

"No, it doesn't even pay for a can of gas, he knows that, and he knows that I know, *hakda l'hayat*, that's life."

On the way back to Nahbès, Neil told Ganthier that he would like to stage a camel fight in his next film:

"If I find the right subject . . . That fight, those ballooning sacks, those bets of a few francs, it's both dramatic and grotesque, difficult to do, but it would be worth it," he added, thinking, *I also know why you wanted me to see that fight between males, but you don't have to worry about your friend Raouf.*

After a while, Ganthier took a side road on their right, a narrow road that suddenly pitched downward, turning into a path with ruts and large stones. They had turned onto a rocky, narrow path, and suddenly there was a coolness of greenery and shadow, large palms opening up the landscape, banana trees, lots of grass, a network of small irrigation ditches, an occasional pool with white lights on the surface of the water and on the wings of the dragonflies. There were also pomegranate trees and plants low to the ground, tomatoes, melons, barley, a few men working on the ditches, a man slowly coming down from a palm after cutting a bunch of perfect, brilliantly brown dates. They greeted the man from afar:

"Let's not go any closer," Ganthier said, "He'll feel obliged to give us his dates."

Neil sat down on the edge of a water tank, took out a notebook, a box of paint, a brush . . . He was sorry that Kathryn wasn't there. It was in such moments that he felt he was still in love with her.

After some time he joined Ganthier and said:

"This is rare!" And Ganthier:

"The watercolorist is a thief!"

Not far away there were some low houses the color of the earth. They greeted another man who was working in the sun. He was kneading a damp mixture of clay and straw, and was putting it into small, horizontal wooden frames.

"For bricks of dried earth," said Ganthier, "They're fragile, crumbly, have to be replaced all the time. Here they never stop making them, and making more of them, as they did twenty centuries ago. That man learned the profession from his father, who himself . . . They say these people are lazy, but they work all the time, if they stop they starve, come on!"

They arrived in front of a circular basin, partly carved out of the rock. The back wall had a mosaic on it, a banquet scene, but the central part was missing.

"Hot springs," said Ganthier, "The Romans made baths out of them, and maybe something else. On the left there's a phallus engraved on a low wall, that's what attracts tourists . . ."

As they were leaving the oasis, they encountered a group of English tourists who were enchanted with the faces and eyes of the children whose photo they were trying to take. A slightly older girl forced the others to go into one of the houses, and as she was going in behind the others, she turned around and spit in the tourists' direction.

37

SCARADÈRE

The following Thursday, everyone gathered in the public park in the European city, several hundred people. In the first rows were the Americans, the French, and local notables, Marfaing, Si Ahmed, high-ranking officers and bureaucrats, then the colonists, important European merchants, Jews and Arabs, lower-ranking bureaucrats, and the group of young people who were studying in the capital and who already had a taste for film, and the middle class in djellabas who hesitated between progress and tradition, and Italians, Spanish . . . On the left, separated by chevaux-de-frise, were the lower classes who had come out of curiosity or had been rounded up by the Spahis.

The projection truck was parked behind the audience, and Wayne was standing next to it with a megaphone, ready to translate the film's title cards into French. Marfaing had taken precautions; a company of Senegalese reserves were standing in front of the chevaux-de-frise. He had also summoned some veterans. They would channel emotion and keep an eye on any anti-French in the audience. The caïd had deployed his neighborhood bosses and his informants. And people began to talk as soon as the first images appeared, in French, Arabic, Berber, Spanish, Italian, pidgin. Some asked their neighbors questions, others answered, some answered that they didn't know, others' answers were wrong. Some commented, others argued, intellectuals who looked down on everyone else, sometimes without understanding, and the uneducated whose instincts were spot on, the locals talking out loud, the Europeans in softer voices. Karim said to Raouf:

"There are quite a few old turbans here. They are against images but they still came." And Raouf:

"They're taking advantage of the opportunity. They will say that they were forced to come."

Neil was carefully watching this partially virgin audience. That's also why he proposed the screening, to observe people who were watching a film for the first time, their reactions before they learned how to pretend, and Raouf felt ill at ease, torn between his reactions as someone familiar with film and those of the novices, who were teased by others who were more familiar, happy to be able to practice the condescension of a progressive petty bourgeois or a colonist. He was angry at everyone, at Marfaing, Neil, Ganthier, and the little group from La Porte du Sud who chuckled every time a first-timer reacted.

". . . Why does the American have the right to talk and not us?"
"Because he's reading the words written on the sheet."
"That's not a sheet, it's a canvas."
"Look! In France there are also shacks, they're poor."
"What are the French saying? Civilization? With shacks?"
"That's because it's in the past."
"What past?"
"Their past, we have a past, they have a past."
"The road isn't paved, and their windmills are made of wood!"
"Mine is made of iron, it cost me an arm and a leg!"

"You can see right away, my friend, that what these Americans do is less refined than French culture."
"Yes, they don't have theater, that explains everything! That said, for the audience this evening it's perfectly appropriate."

"And the guy in France with the rifle, he's beating a poor guy with the butt of his gun!"
"Is the poor guy dead?"
"Yes, he's dead, look, the woman is crying."
"And the one with the rifle, what's he saying?"
"He says that's what happens to poachers."
"How do you know?"
"Because of Wayne, he's reading the words on the canvas, just listen."
"In France it's like here, only the rich have the right to steal."

"What's more, dear friend, I'm not sure it's best to show violence. It's like in the theater, it should take place behind the scenes. Racine does it perfectly."
Other voices called for silence. The murmuring calmed down, started up again, the crowd cheering for a young man in black, a lawyer. On the screen he was consoling the widow: then a cry from the audience, a woman's cry, a French woman, no manners? A shopkeeper? The cry again, sharper, echoed by other cries from Frenchwomen, it's Cavarro! The man! Behind the lawyer, it's Cavarro! The audience now recognized Francis Cavarro. They applauded him. Then a carriage arrived on the scene.

■

"Who's that?"

"Wayne's saying it's a marquis."

"The marquis has powder on his face, like a Christian woman."

"*Hchouma!*"

Then Wayne's voice: All men are born free and equal under the law . . .

"What's that?"

"Wayne said that men have rights."

Wayne repeated: *The lawyer is reading the Constitution.* Some applauding in the audience, a few shouts, "*Yahyia l'dustour!*"

"What are the Arabs yelling?"

"It's the nationalist slogan, *Long live the Constitution.*"

The officers and gendarmes were watching the crowd, especially the natives in European dress. A shout, *Silence!* Other shouts, *Yahyia l'dustour!* And other voices, softer, in reply, *L'Qur'an dustourna* . . .

"Now what are they saying?"

"*L'Qur'an dustourna,* they're saying that the Koran is the Constitution. Those are the old turbans, they're against the ones who are shouting *dustour.* They're saying that the country doesn't need a Constitution, the Koran is enough."

Raouf also shouted *yahyia l'dustour* with Karim and their friends from the little band. The officers were asking for orders. Marfaing said to the colonel:

"No, let's not do anything yet, we mustn't cut off the hand of the thief before he's stolen something! And listen to them, they are divided, the devout against the supporters of a constitution, we can keep score!"

On the screen, the marquis threw the Constitution on the ground, the lawyer slapped the marquis, and in a duel the marquis killed the lawyer with the thrust of his sword . . .

"What is Wayne saying?"

"He says that the marquis is saying, *Justice is done!*"

"That's not justice, the French say we must have justice, but they don't have it there! The peasant poaches and the guard kills him . . . The lawyer slaps the marquis and the marquis kills him . . . Is that French justice? It's worse than what the peasants dole out!"

Someone asked what Cavarro had just said . . .

"Cavarro?"
"Yes, the lawyer's friend."
"So you mean André! In the film Cavarro's name is André. He says he will avenge his dead friend."

The crowd applauded André. The screen went black . . .
"They're changing the reel," said Marfaing.
"I know that," said the colonel.

The voice of Thérèse Pagnon behind Marfaing, talking to a friend:
"Francis is very elegant, the frock coat is flattering, and the trousers are very well cut."
Marfaing didn't like Thérèse being interested in Cavarro's trousers, or her calling him by his first name. At the back of the park Tess was taking advantage of the darkness to help a veiled woman get into the projection truck, and Rania was able to sit on a stool to see everything, the audience and the screen, and the image that the lamp projected on the screen in a beam of light filled with dancing dust that Rania was surprised to discover was so dense, covering the group in which she thought she recognized, but as if in a cloud, the back of Raouf, those of Ganthier, Marfaing, Si Ahmed . . . *To see without being seen . . . and to prevent my being seen, I am forbidden from seeing.*
The film started again. Wayne's voice: *After the lawyer is murdered by the marquis, André goes to his godfather's house to seek justice.* A murmur in the audience, a name running through the rows:
"Kathryn! Look, it's Kathryn!"
"The American woman? The one who walks around town with the caïd's son?"
"Yes, that's her!"

Applauding for Kathryn Bishop, what was she doing on the sheet? Wayne said that she is the godfather's daughter . . .

"And the guy with her, is he the marquis?"
"Yes."
"Did you see her chest? *Hchouma!*"

"No, she's not showing everything."

"It's still shameful."

"She's very pretty. *Rani fuqha, ya rabbi!*"

"What did the Arab say, behind us, with his *rani fou* something or other?"

"*Rani fuqha, ya rabbi* means My God help me to be on her."

"He better not try! They're interested in our women, now?"

"Ah, you're not fooling anyone, dear friend, American women are now your women! That's why we see you so often in the Grand Hôtel!"

André's godfather was saying that he was going to have his daughter marry the marquis. The people grumbled their sympathy. Poor André, he came for justice and he lost Kathryn. And those who were listening carefully knew that Kathryn's name was Séverine. On the screen she was leaving in a carriage . . .

"And where's the marquis?"

"Wayne said he left earlier."

"Why didn't we see him leave?"

"Because it's a movie."

The marquis reappeared and also got into a carriage . . .

"I don't understand it, the marquis is leaving, when he already left?"

"In a movie at first you don't understand, then later you understand."

"Do you understand it, captain?"

"No, these Americans will never have natural order, French clarity . . ."

"And there, now Séverine is in the chateau but she already left it!"

In the first row, Neil turned to Kathryn:

"That moron put on the wrong reel. We need to tell Wayne to get in the truck and fix it."

Kathryn got up, "I'll relieve Wayne for the reading, I like doing it."

And Raouf saw her walk up the side aisle. I'd like to join her, *They'll see me get up, I don't care, do I really want to join her?* He closed his eyes so he wouldn't see her, opened them. She was moving slowly, *She's giving me time to join her.* He closed his eyes again, *A bed . . . Paris . . . Berlin . . . fights, walks . . . Who is she with now?* He shook his head. It had been more than a year since his heart had beaten that hard . . .

Kathryn was reading: Like many people of his time André was hoping for revolution. A shout from the audience, *"Tahyia atthaoura!"*

"What did the Arab back there say?"

"He shouted *Long live the revolution,* my colonel."

"Get rid of him, before he spawns more revolutionaries!"

"What's written? Wayne isn't saying anything anymore?"

"No, it's a woman who's saying the words on the cloth."

"It's Kathryn's voice!"

"No, she's called Séverine! Now I know, in the film, it's Séverine!"

"No, it's Kathryn who's talking. Look, she's standing up, behind the big funnel, next to the truck with the light, where Wayne was."

"Kathryn is reading, and she's in the film at the same time, how does she do it?"

"Look carefully and you'll understand."

"And Cavarro, he's on horseback, like a peasant, when he has a Rolls!"

"That's because that was a long time ago."

"A long time? Before the war?"

"Yes."

"I was in France during the war, it was already a lot more civilized."

A large square on the screen, an equestrian statue . . .

"The guy on the pedestal, next to the horse, with people all around, is he reading a paper?"

"It's the Constitution again!"

"Yahyia l'dustour!"

"And who's on the horse?"

"It's a king."

"The French always say they cut off the king's head, and the one on the statue has his head, when did they cut off the head?"

"After the film, I think."

"What do you mean, *after?*"

"That means in the film they're going to make the Constitution and after that they're going to cut off the head."

"You can cut off a head with a Constitution?"

"First you vote, then you cut."

"Yahyia l'dustour!"

"Look, all the people in the square, they're cheering."

"*Yahyia l'watan!*"

"Now what are the Arabs shouting?"
"They're shouting *Long live the nation.*"
"They think they're a nation?"

On the screen a soldier was killing a demonstrator. People threw the soldier on the ground and killed him.

"It's like here, the cow that falls, it attracts knives."
"Look, Cavarro is on the pedestal, *yahyia* André!"

Marfaing to the colonel: "You see, they shout and they applaud, whom? A French hero! I was right! Why panic?"

Now the cavalry was attacking the crowd, André escaping, *yahyia* André! A stone came out of the audience and struck the canvas at the height of the cavalry who were pursuing him. Two Spahis seized the one who had thrown the stone. Voices grew louder. A sign from the colonel, commanding the officers, soldiers with guns at the ready. Everything calmed down. A couple began to fight in the fourth row:

"No, I'm not going home! You wanted me to come with you so you would look good with Marfaing, I'm staying! You can very well protect me! Look at Thérèse and her husband, they're perfectly fine!"

"Pagnon has nothing to fear. He's opened up half these Arabs' bellies. Even the orphans thank him! It's not the same for me, I'm the tax collector!"

They were now at the home of André's godfather, Séverine taking a wounded André in her arms. In the truck Rania was filled with emotion . . . *These are shadows on canvas, and a stupid story, why am I crying?* Her gaze stopped on one of the figures in the audience, *I see him without him seeing me, but the world in which I can sit next to him exists only when I close my eyes . . .* bakaytu min hubbin man yuba'iduni, *I cry because I love the one who keeps me at a distance, I would do better to go back to the farm, I'm only good for kicking my blanket.*

". . . *Hchouma!* Séverine stuck to André when her father is marrying her to the marquis!"

"When you're wounded French women do that."

"Who's that sleeping in a chair?"

"That's her father."

"Séverine's father is sleeping? Then it serves him right! When you have a daughter you act like a shepherd, you don't sleep."

"Séverine has two men, she's lying to her father about the first one, and she's lying to the first one and to her father about the second one!"

"She's not lying, she has pity."

"Be quiet, what did André say?"

"He told Séverine that he was going to kill the marquis!"

Raouf listening to Kathryn's voice, remembering the times she would speak in his ear . . . the warmth of her mouth at his ear, at night, when they told each other things, *We don't sleep enough*, said Kathryn. *It's your fault*, he answered, kissing her. On the canvas the gendarmes were arriving. André disappeared through a door, "*Yahyia* André!"

André fleeing into the countryside, taken in by a troupe of traveling actors, the Illustrious Theater.

"Their film, my friend, there is no unity of place, no unity of action, no unity of time, no unity of interest. This will never be a form for a beautiful work of art!"

The veterans remembered the theater in the army:

"I saw theater, too, they are on a platform in the back of a room and they tell a story."

"Like in the film?"

"No, in the theater the actors are real people, you throw a stone and they get hit, and if they throw them, you get hit."

"Are they people like us?"

"Yes, but you can't touch them."

The story continued. André was pushing away a large actor who was trying to hit him with a cane . . .

"Who's the big guy?"

"Kathryn says he's an actor, his name is Binet."

"Binet is an actor and André has the right to touch him? I don't understand, so André is also an actor?"

"No, the actor is Cavarro, he's playing André."

"Why does the big Binet want to hit him?"

"Because André fell off a haystack onto him."

"That haystack isn't real, it is too big."

"No, it's real, it's hay from back there, a French haystack."

"We have big ones here, too, at Ganthier's, and at the Belmejdoub daughter's farm."

"Is she still refusing to exchange land?"

"She still is, she has the courage of a man."

"It seems that Ganthier is going to threaten her in her house."

"No, you can't go to a widow's house like that."

"People say that this year they've seen him."

"People will say anything."

"I don't understand, there's André, he's not an actor, and there is the big guy and the others, they're actors?"

"Yes."

"Then where's the platform?"

"They don't need one, they're not acting, they're resting."

"I understand: they are actors, they're not acting, so they're real."

"No, they're in the film."

"In the film they're acting, but there they're not acting, so they're real?"

"No, they're actors."

"I don't understand anything."

"Listen, I'll explain . . ."

Raouf, noticing a wink between two men in the audience. They were pretending not to understand anything to drive the one explaining crazy. They had understood it all, and were having fun at the expense of the one who thought he knew it all. Fair enough, Raouf said to himself.

". . . Now listen! Kathryn is saying that months have gone by, André has also become an actor."

"You see, I was right!"

"Be quiet and watch, it's Paris!"

"Months go by like that in the movies?"

"Yes."

"And whose house is that?"

"That's not a house, Kathryn says it's a theater!"

Kathryn adding: The actors have become famous and André is suffering from not seeing Séverine anymore:

"It's beautiful, all those well-dressed people."

"Look, it's the marquis."

"Where?"

"On the right, at the edge of the balcony in the theater, he's watching."

"Kathryn is saying that André is wearing a big nose and is playing Scaradère."

"Why is he kicking fat Binet? Because he hit him with his cane before?"

"No, it's to make everyone laugh."

"And why is the theater stopping?"

"Because they're changing the reel."

Marfaing to the colonel:

"This is going well. The nationalist shouting is not that bad, and those Americans, they can really tell a story! Will André find Séverine again? They even turn the Revolution into a screw-fest!"

"You call *that* a screw-fest, monsieur le contrôleur civil?"

On the screen André is with another woman. Kathryn gives her name, *Climène*. She is Binet's daughter. They were getting lost. Is that André's house? No, it's in the hotel.

"In France when you go to a big city you go to a hotel."

"You don't go to your family's?"

"No, in Paris they don't have families, they go to a hotel."

"People without families, those poor people."

"They aren't poor, they are people who sleep with everyone, they don't know who their family is anymore."

Climène gave André a stony look.

"What is Kathryn saying?"

"She says that an incomplete conquest wounds a woman's vanity."

"What does that mean?"

"I don't know."

"I know, Climène wants André, so she goes to his room."

"That's not vanity, it's shameful!"

"You saw them, on the mouth, he's kissing her!"

"Climène has won!"

"You know, dear friend, that in America, a kiss takes ten feet of film?"

"Yes, but for foreign showings they make it longer."

"Basically Francis doesn't get much out of it, you can sense it's purely professional, but I'm sure that in real life . . ."

Thérèse chuckled. Marfaing didn't like that.

". . . Now Climène has gone, and who is that one?"
"It's Séverine! She's also at André's house."
"He has all of them, *cheitan lakhor*, he's a devil."
"No, look, he doesn't have Séverine, he's on his knees in front of her."
"Séverine says that she's marrying the marquis, the marquis is rich."
"They've had a revolution and the marquis is still rich?"

Raouf forced himself to take stock, André and two women, the marquis and two women, Séverine and two men, Climène and two men, a nice geometry, four triangles . . . Kathryn and me, Wiesner and Kathryn, Kathryn and Neil, Metilda and me, Neil and someone else, who? Metilda and who? He chided himself, the calculations of an old man . . . Séverine had disappeared. André was looking for Climène. Climène was with the marquis.

"The marquis already has Kathryn, is he taking two wives at the same time?"
"No, look at the house, one is going out and the other is going in."
"And Papa Binet during this time he's eating chicken with his hands! The French tell us to use a fork, and at home they eat like that?"
"But Binet is not just in France, he's here, too."
"No, look, he's never been here, he doesn't know how to eat with his hands, he's eating like a pig."

Climène leaving the marquis, joining André at the inn, telling him that she would not leave a marquis for a little actor like him, and in the following image Séverine telling the marquis that she had seen him with Climène and she never wanted to see him again . . .

"Good for her. The marquis killed the lawyer, he denounced André, you don't give him a woman."

38

A MASS UPRISING

Scaradère was again on the theater stage, talking to the audience. And suddenly they were lost in new images: the countryside, a duel, the marquis . . .

"Where is the theater?"
"Look, it's the field we saw earlier when the lawyer was killed, the marquis is killing someone else."
"No, not someone else, it's the same guy, he's going to kill the lawyer."
"I'm lost, the lawyer wasn't dead?"

Thérèse Pagnon: "It's the wrong reel again!"

Kathryn speaking slowly: André is telling the theater audience about the assassination of his lawyer friend by the marquis six months earlier.

". . . André is showing the past? When people show the past they're crazy."
"Watch out, lawyer! The marquis is going to kill you!"
"Shut up, that won't help, he's going to die, *mektub*."
"A man can't show the past, that's God's eye, I'm leaving."
"Now the people in the theater are attacking the marquis."
"In the army's theater you couldn't."
"When there are a lot of you, you can, we could have."
"You mean this evening we can beat up the colonists?"
"Yes, and the soldiers will shoot you in the stomach, and no one will come off the canvas to help you."
"Where's the marquis?"
"You talk and you're not watching: he left with Séverine."

Rania said to herself: Those two women are right, they're making fun of them but they're acting . . . they're taking! I, too, have the right to love . . . but what if he doesn't love me? He responds "no" to me and I've exchanged my dream for wind, I hate men who force you to declare your love, but I prefer to lose everything than to wait anymore.

An argument between Ganthier and his neighbors. One of them was outraged: How can we allow the natives to talk so much during this screening? This is what they call culture, isn't it? And Ganthier:

"No! For them it is above all the revolution they will fight against us one day."

"You're still the provocateur, dear friend, all your land, but it would make a good Soviet farm!"

On the screen André has become a deputy . . .

"Yes, he's talking to the great assembly of Paris."

"The *djema'a* where we can't go?"

"Yes."

"But if we have a *dustour* we can have our own *djema'a*, like the French."

In Paris the marquis and the other nobles were challenging the deputies of the people to a duel and they killed them.

"Why?"

"Because André and his friends want every man to have a voice, and the others don't want that."

"It's the same here, my voice is worth nothing next to a colonist's."

"That's because the French say they have preponderance."

"What's preponderance?"

"It's when you preponderate."

"What's that mean?"

"It's when you have the machine guns and the Senegalese."

"The French say you are preponderant when you are more civilized."

"More civilized? They eat chickens back there like pigs."

"And the killers, with those nice clothes, are they preponderant, too?"

"Kathryn says that the noble just said that he will kill those who aren't civilized."

"André isn't civilized?"

"*Yahyia* André!"

"Preponderant, the French say that it's when you're ahead."

"So the Americans preponderate the French?"

"André has also become very strong with the sword. Every day he kills one or two rich people."

"Soon only the poor will be left."

Raouf listened to Kathryn's voice and wondered why she and Neil were still together, to avoid causing a scandal in the newspapers? Or because *it's really hard to break up when you don't love each other anymore?* That would have made another good discussion on La Rochefoucauld with Otto . . .

". . . What's the marquis saying?"

"He wants to kill André."

"And Séverine doesn't want that. She's telling the marquis that she'll marry him if he doesn't have a duel with André."

"She's wrong, a guy like the marquis, you don't marry him. The woman should open her eyes before doing that."

"Yes, afterward all she can do is close them."

"And now, where are we?"

"At the duel!"

"The marquis has lost his sword. He's up against the wall, kill him!"

"Why is André letting him get his sword?"

"Because André's a true nobleman, with a heart."

"He's wrong, you don't give a rabid dog its teeth back, you kill it."

The wounded marquis, unable to raise his sword; André turns his back to him, disappearing; the marquis limping, sword in hand, to his carriage; Séverine, seeing him, thinking he killed André. She begins to faint. The marquis holds her up. André turns around. He sees her in the marquis's arms . . .

"You see, colonel? Not a single subversive cry! Two men, one woman, the magic of the movies!"

"You mean a feuilleton! Little Arthur thinks that Little Gustave has stolen Little Bonemine from him!"

The film stops, reel change, starts again, Kathryn saying that several weeks have gone by. On the screen a crowd, an orator, a large chin, like a fist, Danton! Kathryn adding that the revolt is growing . . .

"Did you see the teeth on Danton?"

"Yes, like the poor."

"Then the poor will trust him."

"Where's André?"

"There, on the left, Danton is giving him a piece of paper."

Kathryn's voice: *Danton orders André to organize the Revolution in the prov-inces!* In the streets a crowd armed with sabers and knives . . .

"Did you see the grinder's millstone, as tall as him!"
"I don't understand why the movies make such a big millstone, just to sharpen, it takes up the whole canvas, it's turning really fast!"
"If it comes apart it will come right at us!"
"And the grinder, without a shirt on, and a woman next to him, *hchouma!*"
"The woman is thinking about revolution."
"That's not good, revolution with women."

Cries in the audience, *hchouma!* The colonel, worried,
"Maybe we should stop it here . . . If there's a riot on the screen . . ."
"You hear their cries, *hchouma*, for them revolution is shameful."
Rania couldn't care less about shame, I refuse to live with a stone on my heart, I'll stand in front of him and I'll speak, and if he speaks of our differences I'll call him a coward, a man is obliged to respond to such a word, no . . . Men don't feel they are obliged to respond, they turn their backs and they leave . . . Turn their backs, it's their right as rulers!

". . . Look, all those people in the street, they're breaking everything."
"It's going too quickly!"
"The day that happens here, you'll see how fast it goes."
"The people with knives and guns are coming from all directions."
"Kathryn says they're going into the king's house."
"And the king is still sitting down, he's not a real king, when that happens a real king gets on his horse and fights."
"Okay, the king got up."
"Is he going to fight?"
"I don't know!"

In the countryside now. André at the home of his godfather, who tells him that his daughter Séverine and her friend Madame de Trégastel are in danger in Paris. André decides to go get Séverine . . .

"André is showing a piece of paper to his godfather, what is it?"
"Kathryn says that it's his orders, signed by Danton."

"It's like in the army, with that André can go anywhere."

Kathryn saying that André wants to save Séverine, but not Madame de Trégastel.

"Who is that Trégastel?"
"I don't know!"

The godfather telling André, Madame de Trégastel is your mother!

"Long live the seventh art, Monsieur le contrôleur, Little Arthur learns that the friend of Little Bonemine and Little Gustave is his own mommy!"

The rhythm accelerates. André is in a house in Paris. Séverine discovers he's not dead, and Madame de Trégastel takes André in her arms, crying, Kathryn reading, *My son, my son!* André shows his orders . . .

"Watch out, behind you, it's the marquis, he has a pistol."
"The marquis is everywhere! How does he do it?"
"Watch out, André! The dog has returned!"
"The marquis wants the paper and André refuses."
"André has a pistol, too."
"And Trégastel is putting herself between them."
"She's telling André that the marquis is his father."
"What?"
"The marquis is André's father!"
"Their eyes are crazy!"
"Trégastel is crying."
"Everyone is crying."
"Even the marquis is crying."
"He's asking for peace from God."

"Those scenes, my dear, I dare say it's a bit much."
"Would you like a handkerchief, Madame Pagnon?"
"Useless. In these situations my wife doesn't need a handkerchief, she needs a full sheet!"

"Peace from God, you can't refuse that."
"André is giving his orders to his father, why?"

"So he can be saved from the Revolution."

"And the marquis is refusing!"

"André has taken out his sword."

"Is he going to kill his father?"

"Look! He's giving him the sword!"

"The marquis is going outside with the sword? Against the whole Revolution?"

"When you have lived like a dog, you can die like a man."

The crowd now attacking the marquis with axes; André in a carriage, going through a gate out of Paris with his mother and Kathryn; the crowd is very agitated . . .

"The people are doing what they want in the streets now, they are killing the rich, they all have a bottle of wine, *hchouma*."

"Revolution with wine, it's shameful!"

The colonel asking Marfaing for the order to intervene, Marfaing not responding, This is going pretty well, but Daintree has fucked me, his film is showing the Terror! These Americans, always ready to create a mess! Right, while he's denouncing the revolution of women and wine, the Muslims are forced to be against that, but it's best to stop it.

"Neil, that's going too far! We're stopping it!"

Raouf regretted that he no longer wanted to shout, "Long Live the Revolution," Today, it means nothing to me, that's the disadvantage when one has ended up as a mere observer . . . David and Karim will both now call me a bourgeois who waits and sees!

Scenes of pillaging on the screen.

"They're carrying women off under their arms!"

"They shouldn't have been in the streets."

"They're stealing everything, even from the store selling pots and pans."

"*You* have a store that sells pots and pans, do you still want a revolution?"

"There, what's that woman doing in the street?"

"She's sharpening an ax."

"Everyone's taking an ax."

"We could do the same."

"Kathryn is saying that the crowd is shouting *Long live the nation!*"

"*Yahyia l'watan!*"

"What does that mean, a procession of rioters?"

"It's like it was here, ten years ago, when we killed Christians in the central market."

"Are the French doing like us? We can do like them?"

Danton on the screen, Kathryn reading the message that is brought to Danton.

"Danton says that Prussia is attacking France."

"Prussia is the Germans?"

"Like in Verdun?"

"Yes."

"Why is the piano playing military music?"

"Monsieur le *contrôleur*, I'd like an order!"

"Just a second, everything is still under control!"

Mass uprising in the streets of Paris.

"It's the war, the Germans are attacking."

"Like they did in '14, we must go!"

"And Danton is shouting to take up weapons!"

"He's shouting *Long live the nation!*"

"*Yahyia l'watan!*"

"The Boches are attacking. You're a man, you'll go."

"*Nemchiou*, let's go to war!"

"Stop fighting for the French."

"No, he's right, we're going! It's war, *l'harb*, you're a man, you'll go, and you'll shoot the Boches!"

"Look on the canvas, the soldiers are marching pressed together. They have bayonets, like we did."

"And we also sang against the Germans! 'La Marseillaise.'"

"And the pianist, Hector, he's playing the same thing."

"And everyone is singing, look, the Senegalese are singing, *Form your battalions*, only the Italians aren't singing, and all our veterans are singing like at Verdun, even the wounded, and our soldiers, too, everyone."

"Look, next to Danton, André is holding Séverine, they're singing together, *yahyia* André! And Rachid, he's also singing because he sells them oranges, and M'hammed is doing it, too! *Let's march, let's march,* we're going to beat the Germans!"

Marfaing wasn't saying anything. He was singing, standing up, looking sideways at the colonel, Don't gloat, some of the natives are singing "La Marseillaise," I was right, they applaud a hero of the Enlightenment and the war for human rights! And Thérèse can very well wait . . .

On the sidelines there wasn't any singing. A few stones were thrown at the audience and the projector truck. People were taking advantage of the images, and taking revenge. Shouts, commands, the Senegalese opened the chevaux-de-frise and charged with blows of their rifle butts. Groups of poor people dispersed into the ravine, running down the slope like madmen. Two soldiers who were faster or more excited than the others were suddenly surrounded below, on the edge of the wadi. More shouting, shots fired . . . In the public park people were getting worried. It was farther away, but still. The gendarmes started evacuating the park calmly. No more shots were fired. And Marfaing didn't talk about it in his report to the residence; he wrote about what he called a lovely demonstration of Franco-American friendship and progress, "which enabled the more modern element of the local population to demonstrate its attachment to France and the enlightenment of its protectorate!"

39

THE PRÉPONDÉRANTS

For Pagnon and the other Prépondérants of Nahbès—that is, Doly, Laganier, a half dozen officers, as many bureaucrats, many colonists, as well as merchants and artisans (who, Doly noted, would never have been admitted to their
high-quality Cercle if we had been in France)—for all those people the film
screening had been, as they said, the last straw. Marfaing and his *enlightenment*, Marfaing and his Americans, Marfaing and his liberal wind blowing over
Paris, his little games with the left, and the caïd's double-dealing, and the triple-
dealing of Ganthier, said Pagnon. Ganthier seems to be one of us: in fact, he is
always glued to the Arabs, and when it's not the Arabs, it's the Americans. The
residence doesn't want to hear about it, and when we try to alert Paris, they say
he's untouchable. Military intelligence, my ass!

Pagnon was holding a grudge against Ganthier. It wasn't just political; it went
back to the Bellarbi affair. Bellarbi was a peasant, as brittle as nettles in the
month of August, who owned thirty acres, olive trees, wheat, some livestock. His
father had been able to live off all that. Bellarbi could have continued living off
it, but then Pagnon had wanted that land. Pagnon wasn't dishonest; he offered
a decent price. Bellarbi refused. So Pagnon went up to a normal price, but Bellarbi continued to refuse. So Pagnon offered the price he would have offered
a French person. Bellarbi still refused. Pagnon took it badly. He said that with
those people honesty was useless. His wife tried to rein him in, she didn't like
trouble, and then she said to herself that anything that could keep her husband
occupied wasn't a bad thing.

In general those sorts of issues were dealt with in the civil administration, in
the evening, among the initiated, and the next day an administrative measure
would be taken. The meeting took place. Marfaing didn't refuse, but he dragged
his feet. He forced Pagnon to start over, ask again, and to ask again is annoying.
Then came the day when Marfaing again told him that it would be done, of
course, but, dear friend, don't get upset . . . It upset Pagnon when he was told
not to get upset. He told others that Marfaing was an ass, that they should force
him to act, and then a grenade exploded on a path that went through Bellarbi's
land—no, not to frighten him, not some cretinous threat, it was more subtle, an

explosion at the wrong moment, at dusk, just when the gendarmes were passing by on patrol, very close, because they were just frightened. They didn't put
their fear in their report, but they put in enough so that Marfaing was forced to
sign off on it and Bellarbi was sent away, an attack against authority. The penalty
for that was the seizure of his property, which was to be resold right away, and
if Bellarbi didn't cause too much trouble, his prison sentence wouldn't be too
long. He was lucky, because an attack, even without victims, could mean the
guillotine.

But Bellarbi didn't go quietly. He caused trouble. He spoke of being set up,
demanded justice. The nationalists got involved. Si Ahmed finally asked what
was going on, and that's when the gendarmes found a grenade in front of their
door, this one defused, with an anonymous letter, typewritten, which said that
there were many grenades like that in a shed on Pagnon's property, with the
detonating cord used to explode them from a distance, very good cord, strong
and supple, modern, cord bought in France, not Arab cord. The gendarmes
went to see Marfaing. Marfaing had received the same letter, without a grenade, but with the cord. The gendarmes were upset: Your crazy doctor could
have killed us for a few acres; he could have at least warned us! Marfaing had
Bellarbi released.

The gendarmes wanted to go to Pagnon's farm, but things settled down before they went any further. To calm the gendarmes Pagnon had six months'
worth of vintage burgundy wine delivered to them. He also gave up on Bellarbi's
land. He wasn't happy. He acted as if it were he who was the victim of a plot. He
kept repeating that someone had really tried to blow up the gendarmes, but he
didn't know who it was. He even said to people he trusted that the day he found
out who had written that letter there would be blood in the street. There would
be consequences. He would find out: there was a traitor in their midst! Thérèse
told him to be quiet because people were going to wonder what the traitor had
betrayed. Pagnon didn't insist, especially since one evening, at the Cercle, Ganthier pointed out to him in front of everyone that by threatening with death the
one who had sent the anonymous letter, he was going to provoke that person
into taking initiatives against him. Pagnon scowled, Ganthier even joked: "And
you risk finding yourself in your cemetery." That made everyone laugh, because
the cemetery next to the hospital was called "the Pagnon cemetery." The doctor
calmed down. He offered champagne to all present and said to Ganthier that it
was a pity, if he had obtained that land they would have been neighbors. Ganthier didn't reply.

Since then, Pagnon didn't say another word about that affair, but he hadn't
forgotten Ganthier's joke, and when the Prépondérants began making plans to

unseat Marfaing, Pagnon made sure Ganthier was quarantined. No need to talk about this with someone who talks to everyone. He repeated his phrase "triple-dealing." Some members of the Cercle told Pagnon that that was when one returned to one's original spot. He didn't find that funny.

They began to discuss seriously an idea proposed by Laganier, the high-ranking bureaucrat in the *contrôle civil*, Marfaing's closest collaborator, who thought only of getting rid of his boss, so he could fill the post in the interim, at least. The incidents at the outdoor film screening had made him think; he spoke of the roots of their grievances. This was his great idea, the natives are unpredictable? Then let's set them on the right course! The Cercle mustn't wait for the moment, they had to create it, and fight, no, administer a vaccine, as Marfaing does, but a true horse pill: drain the abscess for ten, twenty years, and settle things with Marfaing in passing, and maybe even with the Americans. Those discussions between Arabs and Americans are no good, it makes our Arabs pretentious!

Laganier didn't like America. He spoke of decadence, of new barbarism lighted with electricity, of mechanized plutocracy. The others let him speak. All of that wasn't important; what was important was land, measures that would enable them to seize more native land when the Arabs will have calmed down. They had the right to do it; it was even an old leftist slogan, "Land for those who work it!" That's what several Prépondérants told Gabrielle when they learned she was writing an article on them and on the history of the colonization. Their fathers had arrived on this land wearing black clothing, with only a bundle of belongings, and what they knew how to do; knowledge that came from very far back in time, Gabrielle had written, men with empty hands but who had strength within them. It wasn't the richest who crossed the Mediterranean, or the most clever, but they had some of that knowledge that takes centuries to settle in the minds of men, and they arrived in an uncultivated place—a former garden, however, Ganthier had told Gabrielle, the Numidian garden, but that was perhaps a Ganthier legend, a gilded legend, with its fruit, vegetables, olives, almonds, melons, a garden that was later transformed into a wheat machine by the Romans, the wheat that killed off the other crops; they didn't know anything about that at the time, so beautiful was that wheat, and because no one's eyes were good enough to see beyond the scarcely more than thirty years that at that time made up the life of a man.

Ruin had come without anyone anticipating it, a long-term ruin, they now knew, bitterly, but this time it was perhaps a black legend, drought and famine throughout the Mediterranean basin, and people thought it was a curse, the fault of the stories they told about their single god, or on the contrary the vengeance of a single one against idolaters, but in reality it was the fault of the wheat, which puts so much joy in men's hearts when the ears are heavy. The Romans needed it for their plebeian cities: a million bushels a month for the Rome of Augustus and his successors, free bread for the people. Northern Ifriqiya became the breadbasket, where they tore out the vineyards, even the olive and citrus trees; and when everything was submerged by the blond tide they went farther south, to even more arid lands, with even less rain, smaller yields, over larger areas; the nomads were chased away. They also captured the wild animals—lions, panthers, and others—they were sent to Rome, and they cut down trees for wheat; carnivores became rare, and the paradise of wheat became a paradise for herbivores, a land that became even more stripped by the grazing of goats, gazelles, and sheep, and there was nothing to fertilize the land—one year of wheat, one year of rest with weeds for the herbivores; they thought that was enough—and the land flew off in the wind. There were fewer plants and so there was less rain, but they didn't know, and when it rained it carried off the land. The plants began to creep to survive, and it became a country of Roman ruins on a ruined land. And when new conquerors arrived it improved; then it fell again, for centuries. Then other conquerors arrived, with a single god, not the same one, but always only one, conquerors who were not farmers, said some, having on the contrary the cult of water, said others. And the country sometimes improved, then fell again, improved, and the colonists in black clothing arrived from Europe to a land where farmers still used a plow made of burnt wood, and the newcomers had in their heads and in their arms a more efficient knowledge: it was like their weapons, a blunderbuss against a Lebel rifle and a seventy-five-ton cannon, the conditions in a slow country, centuries of "Turkery," said some, of bigotry, said others, so that in the end they lost their energy. And it wasn't clear when the great progress had started, over there in Europe? Or how, perhaps by chance, a warmer climate, or a better grade of iron, for the scythe, much better than the sickle they still used to harvest here, bent over, singing; with the scythe there is more hay, more animals, more manure; the plow replaced the swing plow; they invented the harrow, the shoulder collar, the roller . . .

And everything that had taken centuries to settle in their minds, in their tools, and in their bodies, the newcomers were now suddenly attributing it to their genius, the natives for them being only backward-looking. They were the moderns, they had understood, and the ones who have understood have a right to the land, and they took it: first the fallow land, then the land of the nomads, tribal land that soon had no tribes. The nomads folded their tents, put them on their donkeys, and left, *qifa nabki*, let's stop and cry, said the other, *min dhikra . . . manzili*, on the remains of an encampment; they are used to it; and this time they left them their tents and a few goats, whereas before, the sovereign's people confiscated everything for taxes and they couldn't even change grasslands; all they could do was pull it out from between graves on the outskirts of cities. They were now allowed to keep their tents so they could go farther away, and when they left, great estates were created, hundreds, thousands of acres. The estates were profitable, especially when the expropriated nomads were brought back to work them. Those people, when they are kept under tight control and aren't left alone, are fine, and they are very frugal! And the colonists also brought all those who go with them: artisans, masons, mechanics, employees at the post or gas office, bakers, teachers, curés, laborers, restaurant owners, foremen, people who were hard workers and led hard lives, intolerant and prolific, having believed in this land the way some had believed in America, but on a smaller scale, forgetting how much time it had taken them to get there, calling racial genius what centuries had enabled them to accumulate, designating themselves holders of a natural superiority, and the cleverest among them choosing a word that was better than *superiority*, superiority could be de facto, so let's say *preponderance*, there is righteousness in that word, value, legitimacy; and in Nahbès the Prépondérants hadn't immediately gone into action. Laganier first wanted to have the backing of their spiritual leader and man in charge in the capital, Richard Trillat, the editor-in-chief of *Présence Française*, even if not everyone agreed about Trillat, a man who was a bit crazy. His favorite saying was, "The darkening is the cross that is raised in the crossroads of today's society, between fallen verticality and triumphant horizontality." They found that rather insane, the most irreverent calling Trillat "the marabout." Nor did Trillat endure the slogan "the greatest France" of a hundred million . . . It was silly nonsense, a white is a white, a black a black, an Arab an Arab. "For me, a guy who continues to call himself Mohammed or Mamadou will never be a part of France. The whole problem comes from giving them education!" Trillat didn't even like France very much. During one of his trips to Marseille the customs officers thought he was an Arab in the French line. He had lived for a long time in Lebanon, had dark skin, brown hair, thick lips. A customs officer called to him: "Where are you from?" Trillat responded, "Corrèze," holding out his passport, with the guttural sounds of the Levantine in his voice, and the bureaucrat wondered if he might be dealing with a disguised Ben Something or Other, with that rosary in his hands. That was what raised his suspicions, the rosary. They sometimes saw Christian Arabs from Beirut pass through, but they went directly into the line for Orientals. They didn't claim to be from Corrèze, not like this Trillat, who was perhaps from Corrèze. The customs officer gave him back his papers, from the tips of his fingers. It might have ended there, but Trillat began to yell at the bureaucrat, and the more he yelled, the more his voice resembled that of someone from Beirut. The customs officers dug in, went through his suitcases, and strip-searched him. That's to give you a reason to complain—a *profound* reason! Since that day Trillat thought that France was rotten because of its bureaucrats. Of course, he didn't tell that to Laganier, who was a bureaucrat, and he showed enthusiasm for the plans of the Prépondérants of Nahbès: Very good, a fixation abscess; they were finally moving to action; you should also catch a few sons of Zion in your nets, and some wops, they're getting ideas; we mustn't let Mohammed or Mardochee or Pepino get the upper hand! Our slogan should be "Maghreb for France and France for the French"! My paper will support you! Laganier left Trillat with what he called a true papal benediction.

40

THE STORM

Elsewhere, there were those who were less concerned with plotting than with living agreeably together. Kathryn and Raouf took walks that were more natural than before, because this time they really were what they had for a long time pretended to be: good friends . . . each of them now hiding what he or she wanted, having only one fear, that of showing a desire that would put him or her at the mercy of the vanity of the other, who would then try hard to sacrifice his or her own desire to that vanity. Raouf was afraid of being asked to talk about his relationship with Metilda and what might pass for dissimulation, and Kathryn didn't want to be questioned about how she had become Wiesner's mistress in only a few days of filming in Berlin. And so they were happy to be together without adding anything more, in an ambiance that even allowed them to laugh about the past and to continue to enjoy shared emotions, like the day when they had been attacked in the street by dogs. Careful, said Raouf, they often have rabies, and that means a month of shots in the stomach! He gave the parasol to Kathryn: Stay behind me! Then he slowly put his hand in his pocket, and took it out just as slowly, one of the dogs, the biggest one, came to within fifty feet, his teeth bared, and with surprising speed Raouf threw the stone he was hold-ing; too short, Kathryn thought; the stone landed just in front of the dog, which hadn't backed away, but it ricocheted on the pavement and hit the dog right in the mouth, a dull sound of stone against bone. The dog took off yowling, fol-lowed by the other members of the pack.

"Do you often have stones in your pockets?" Kathryn had asked, her voice tense.

"When I'm walking, always."

"There are plenty of stones on the ground. All you had to do was bend down and pick one up."

"I really like having time to choose the right one. The stone has to be big enough, fairly round, and since the dog doesn't see me bending to get one, he can't get ready."

"Was the ricochet on purpose?"

"What do you think?"

Then he explained: "A dog watches direct trajectories, it can't calculate. We learn to throw like that very early here, even before we play marbles or *mechmeche.*"

"What's that?"

"Apricot pits, you put four on the ground, in a pyramid, and using another pit, from six feet away, you try to knock over the pyramid. You have three tries, or only one when it's a 'sudden death' match. The one who knocks over the pile gets the pits. You can make the game more difficult by putting the pyramid farther away in front of a wall, and you have to hit it by first ricocheting the pit against the wall. If you miss your throw you have to give the owner of the pile the pit you used to throw. Not just any old pit—the throwing pits are true jewels. They are painted; the owner puts his own personal mark on it. You dig out a hole in it and pour in melted lead, to weigh it, make it heavy or somewhat heavy. They make wonderful projectiles; they hit hard. A good throwing pit is worth a hundred ordinary pits, or even more, even money."

Raouf's ramblings on *mechmeche* had had the desired effect; they had calmed Kathryn. They set off through a residential quarter, along streets bordered with eucalyptus and jacarandas, their leaves drenched in beautiful pale green and purple, a few carriages, no cars; from time to time a gray bird came to hop in front of them. The houses belonged to people who had had an ambitious vision, no doubt more ambitious than they were, and who wanted to show where they had come from: houses from the Basque country, Alsace, Brittany, Savoy . . . The architecture wasn't very adapted to the land; the owners named this quarter Little France.

"They have property to defend, and are bitter because they don't have enough," said Raouf, "This is the Prépondérants' turf."

The quarter was calm, peaceful. The natives were there only to serve and went back home in the evening, except for the guards, who lived on the street in shacks. Behind the houses the gardens often gave directly onto the countryside. Passing in front of a house with Provençal roof tiles, broken shutters, flaking paint, Raouf and Kathryn heard a whinnying. They glanced over through the screen of reeds that covered the front gate: an old servant woman was putting a bandage on an old horse, which still had some energy left.

"I bet she's also the nanny, the maid, and the cook," said Raouf, "and her master goes out strutting on the horse on Sunday afternoons among all the beautiful people, at the stable riding ring where they look down their noses at him. Luckily for him there are Arabs he can look down his nose at . . ."

"You don't know anything about them," said Kathryn, "I think you sound bitter."

"I have trouble sympathizing with a guy who has his horse bandaged by an old servant woman."

They arrived at the front door of Gabrielle's house. The metal doorknob was a bit shaky. Raouf said to Gabrielle:

"You're settling down in this country."

"Why do you say that?"

"Last year you would have had that doorknob repaired within a day."

Gabrielle laughed: "I'm beginning to enjoy taking my time."

Raouf: "*L'ajala min echcheitan . . .* haste comes from the devil!" And after a moment: "Here we respect time, we even think it's capable of repairing door-knobs."

Gabrielle hadn't dared ask Raouf if he knew a workman. Ganthier ultimately recommended an Italian to her, Mazzone. Mazzone was good, but he charged a lot, especially to the French and other foreigners. He knew how to add things on that left the client with no means to protest or barter. When he had to put a screw into a wall he charged for the drilling of the hole for the wooden peg into which the screw would go. He charged for the cement and the making of the cement that was used to set the peg. He of course charged for the peg and the whittling he had to do to adjust the peg: he called that "fashioning the peg." The clients were stuck. One couldn't haggle about a detail costing a few coins—it would have been obscene—and his entire bill was made up entirely of details costing a few coins, and if one raised an eyebrow at the exorbitant total of all those few coins, Mazzone's finger would slowly begin to go down the list of his materials and work while, with his light blue eyes of a Piedmontese who has con-fidence in divine harmony, he watched for the moment when the client would find an error that didn't exist. That was Mazzone's strength, he was honest in the details, but the final bill made you want to scream, and his best defense was that his work was excellent, and everyone knew it. His only employee was Hassan. Hassan was proud of his boss, the best in the region, and Mazzone was proud of his employee: "He's not like the others, he doesn't steal!"

Hassan was apparently satisfied with his somewhat unusual situation, be-tween *the others* and *m'sieur Mazzone*, the one the French called "the maca-roni" when they were among themselves, or only with Hassan, in the kitchen where he had come to unblock a pipe. They knew that Hassan would repeat the word to his boss and they said it on purpose, to emphasize the existence of a hierarchy that good manners forced them to ignore when "Monsieur Maz-zone" came to their homes. Hassan didn't take offense at hearing his boss called "macaroni"—that was the way of the world, a world in which Hassan knew that his boss didn't take offense, either, when they told him on the telephone: "Be so kind, if you can't come right away, at least send your wog . . ." A world in which, when they spoke of some good clients, Mazzone and Hassan would say "that Frenchie dog" or "that French bitch": such was life.

At the bar of the Grand Hôtel, they had resumed their habits, and so as not to spoil the ambiance, Gabrielle and Kathryn hid their anger at not having been invited to the camel fight. Gabrielle said that in the Middle East one could see even worse things. But according to Ganthier the Middle East was more puritan than the Maghreb, so it should on the contrary be less spicy.

"You won't get me to talk by provoking me," Gabrielle replied. The others begged her, and Neil asked in which country did the worse things take place. It wasn't exactly a country, she said, rather a zone, ever-changing, unstable, straddling several of those countries that we created out of the Ottoman Empire by dividing up the oil wells: a region of assassins, or *haschichins* if you prefer, a land of drugs. I spent two weeks in their villages. They haven't abandoned hashish, but they don't kill as much . . . and for entertainment they have their old cults . . . The most famous one happens once a year, at night, not just any night, it has to be a cloudy night with no moon, when you can't even see the path in front of you, but that's not good enough, there is always a bit of a glimmer, so they create darkness within darkness, a large, sealed room in a big house . . .

"Were you there, or did you hear about it?" asked Cavarro. Gabrielle smiled . . . A large room, all the adults in the village, men and women, including the sheikh and his wife, there could be fifty people; no one is allowed to speak, you can only move; there is only the sound of breathing and the rustling of fabric, the sound of sequins on fabric . . .

"That means you were there," said Ganthier, laughing. Gabrielle continued: Not the slightest glimmer of light, a true cult. They begin with invocations, and then they chant, and continue to chant. You can't get used to the darkness, you can't see a thing, it's hot, and you start feeling dizzy. They keep chanting and then there's a great silence, and someone says something; it is repeated in a chorus; something else, more chanting; and while chanting each man takes a woman in the darkness and has her . . .

"Fantastic," said Cavarro, "We did the same thing in Hollywood before Fatty's shenanigans. They were great orgies!"

"It was like that, up to a point, if you wish," said Gabrielle, "but there's something that makes it truly unique, a detail that changes everything!"

She interrupted herself, gestured to the waiter, two ice cubes, please.

"They've made progress with whiskey, don't you think?"

"If your story is really good, you shouldn't keep us waiting," said Neil.

"The detail changes everything," said Gabrielle, "It's a rule of the game, which you probably don't have in Hollywood . . . an absolute rule: the sheikh's wife must be . . . respected. And to avoid any mistakes, they put a little bell around her neck."

Gabrielle also resumed her habit of visiting Rania at her farm. Kathryn and Raouf often joined them. Rania surprised Gabrielle; she routinely wore her glasses. Gabrielle asked her about that.

"It's to show that I'm not just someone who rolls couscous," Rania said, "That said, I roll couscous perfectly."

Once, from the veranda, they saw Ganthier in the distance going by on horseback.

"You really should settle your land issues with him," Raouf said to Rania, "It's becoming grotesque!"

Kathryn joked: "If you accept the exchange, you will no longer be able to watch the elegant rider go by."

"I'll find another way," Rania replied, happy to be able to joke with her friends. When they were alone Kathryn asked Gabrielle: "Where do things stand with you and our dear colonist?" This time the journalist replied: "He is, as you say, giving me the cold shoulder."

Raouf also told them about a scandal that was rocking the capital. It happened during a reception at the general residency of France: a young lawyer, the youngest son of an important family in the region, the Baghdadis, had dared to appear with his wife, and the wife wasn't wearing a veil! Gabrielle was delighted. Rania approved the bold move, but not the choice of demonstrating it at the general residency. Raouf said that he agreed with the move, but many of his friends thought it would be better to wait to have independence to do such a thing . . .

"If we want to liberate men, it appears we need the support of those who want women to remain prisoners," he added, laughing.

"While we wait," said Rania, "our dear modernists will always have the possibility of marrying European women."

And Gabrielle said to Raouf: "Are the women who marry Europeans here any freer?"

"There aren't very many of them," Rania said, "The European has to convert, that makes them hesitate . . . That's why things usually remain secret."

Then there was the storm, huge masses of dark gray that came from the sea and suddenly covered the entire horizon, with lightning that broke the sky like the blows of an ax, a massive storm, a river pouring down from above, a godsend, moreover, because the land was very thirsty, and people wanted the rain.

In the city, the first drops that crashed down onto the dust were already the size of bottle caps, and people thanked God. Then the water started falling in sheets and flowed everywhere, like it does when it won't last long. It carried away the lightest things, the sand in the streets, the stones, paper, then dry bushes that one pointed to, saying: "It's the great washing day!" It continued to fall harder and harder. With the help of the wind it carried away all that carelessness had left for it: chairs, tables, stalls, watermelons from the market, children's carts, parasols. It was violent; throughout the city people ducked their heads and began to run like chickens. Some found shelter under a doorframe while waiting for the end under a purplish sky. This was the height of the violence and it was going to leave as it had come.

People began to get very worried when, in the lower part of the city, they saw a cart floating without its animals, then two donkeys, on their backs, swollen like balloons, and a panicked rat, clinging to one of them, the growling water carrying it all away, toward the ravine, toward the wadi, where the water was rising faster and faster as if in a hurry to meet that which was falling. In asking too much for rain they had awakened the waters of hell, which had also come from the sea, knocking the boats in the harbor against one another, and it wasn't the worst thing to be a boat in the harbor because, in the distance, other boats had begun to disappear between two crashing waves, rendering back to the depths the thousands of fish they had taken from it, and the worst wasn't saved for the feluccas: there was one out of two chances they'd survive and right themselves while being baled out as quickly as possible. The worst was saved for a few trawlers with motors because a trawler with a motor is a shell constructed around a block of cast iron and steel, a motor that is more than half the tonnage of the boat and that has but one desire, to escape as quickly as possible and return to the bottom of the sea, to the rocks and minerals, the raw matter out of which it was made. It took only two or three big waves more violent than the others: the luck of the sea, that's what they say.

And on the land they congratulated one another for not having to confront the waves. On the land there were only gusts of wind, but all the same, those gusts began to pull down walls, for they were the most destructive of gusts, backlashes of a whip from the fight among the winds. They even pulled up houses, those on the ravine, that then joined the tons of detritus flowing from the discharge of the open sky, and the brickwork, and the cement sentry box at the entrance to the bridge between the Arab city and the European city. Everything was carried off in whirling torrents, for hours. Sometimes a man struggled, died, with or without shouting. Some tried to save others, right in the street, with water up to their chest, in both cities; others huddled up under eaves. Night fell. It didn't change a thing.

In the morning the rain stopped. The clouds thinned out, and then disappeared. The surface of the sea was once again smooth. Misfortune had stopped moving; it could now be observed; they called that taking stock. People began cleaning up the mud, and buried some twenty dead, also mourning those whom the waves hadn't returned. And there were a lot of people in the church of Nahbès for the funeral of the assistant harbormaster, killed during the storm by falling beams. He was well liked. All the employees, all the dockworkers, one after the other, remembered owing something to him. He hadn't always been like that, but he had lost his two sons in the war; he had become emotional. He couldn't abide suffering, and suffering had taken revenge. In fact, the entire city was there, in front of the church, in the church.

"Can you imagine, Arabs coming into the nave with their bicycles!"

Ganthier was next to the man who had said that, and he had replied to his indignation:

"Rest assured, they won't be bringing their bicycles to your funeral!"

A hearse with six horses then went through the city on avenue Gambetta to the gravesite of the assistant harbormaster. All the metal parts of the hearse and the carriages in the procession, anything that might have shone, had been covered in crepe. Even the whips had black ribbons.

In the days that followed, people started to get back on their feet, and life got back to normal under a sky that was once again immense and vacant. There hadn't been any flooding on the film set, only gusts of wind, nothing serious for Americans used to the climate of the Pacific. The heavy machinery had held up fine, the rest a bit less so, nor did the local scenery, especially the tents. So there was some delay in resuming work. But no one was unhappy, and the damage was even covered by the insurance policy.

41

THE HUNT

Three days later, in the middle of the countryside, twenty miles from the city, the water was still flowing in the wadi, churning and bubbling, but the dog still dove in eagerly before Ganthier had time to shout, "Stop!" Raouf, Ganthier, and the other hunters saw the dachshund disappear into the yellow water. Raouf heard himself shout, "Kid!" and Ganthier gestured to him to stop shouting. Raouf understood: Let the dog go ahead, it was his only chance now, but a slim one. A human would let himself be carried by the current, try to swim on the diagonal to the opposite side, but Kid didn't want to go too far from his goal.

Up until then it had been a fairly routine hunting outing. They were trying to renew a passion, after the catastrophe, but it was like the beginning of a lot of hunting parties: a long, discouraging walk, a few quail that were scarcely worth collecting after they were shot, a young rabbit. They were ashamed, and the majestic nakedness of the landscape increased their shame.

"This makes you happy?" Raouf had asked. This was his first hunting trip. He didn't like it, but Ganthier had invited him to come with the group. Without a gun. Raouf had understood: It wasn't a proposal to convince him to come, but a condition set by the other hunters: An Arab? Why not! Especially the son of a notable. But no gun. "You'll see," Ganthier had added, "It's seductive. It will be a change from your books, your ideas." Those ideas aren't doing so well these days, are they? The shock of Europe? Sheikh 'Abduh and Lenin, all that stuff, can you still manage? And civil rights in Paris, and Gandhi, and the newspapers . . . in Arabic, French, English maybe, always the mixture, revolution, the pillars of religion, the nation, the glorious past, defeat before the foreigner, and then independence, to come, if you're good, equality, the evil colonist and his school, and university in the mother country now, of which you know so well how to take advantage. Come on, let's get a taste of pursuits in the open air, and if you want a gun, we'll see what we can do.

"You're not afraid a gun will give me ideas, like those Rif mountain folk who are shooting the Spanish so well right now?" Ganthier didn't respond.

Raouf had agreed to go because Jules Montaubain was a member of the group. Montaubain had gotten rid of his rifle in 1915 when he returned from the war, but he accompanied the hunters with his pointer. He had begun his career as a primary school teacher in Nahbès, then he became a French and history teacher in the little *lycée* in the city. At least half the hunters had had him as a teacher; that's why they invited him, in spite of his Bolshevism, and also because he had left an arm in the trenches. Every time Raouf encountered the man who had been his teacher for five years, he was delighted. With Montaubain you could be certain that when you entered his class you would learn something important, the use of the imperfect, the structure of chalk, proofs using nine, the Battle of Valmy, the poems of Lamartine . . . Those were happy years, during which Raouf had competed with David for who could know the most things the quickest. Montaubain found that amusing, and was careful not to show favoritism between two kids enamored with learning and reasoning. The best moments were when he read *François le Champi* and *Les Misérables* to the entire class. Some parents said the teacher should do less reading and more dictations, but all the former students agreed: those readings were what they remembered the best.

They had left the cars at the head of the path, under the watch of two auxiliary soldiers, and after an hour and a half of exasperated walking, the group had finally managed to sight a covey of partridges. It had taken a bit of time to walk around them, and the birds flew off before they were within shooting range. No one understood why. Rather, no one had sought an explanation. They weren't going to start arguing about some random noise. Using the binoculars they could see the birds landing at more than a mile away. Another walk around them, wider this time. The terrain was climbing, slightly, but the sun made it seem steeper, a rocky terrain, no trees, not really any grass apart from clumps of esparto, and bushes gray with dust plunging their roots more than thirty feet into the ground in search of water. They held on to the dogs to keep them from overexerting themselves. Ganthier had wanted to carry Kid under his arm. The dachshund would have none of it. He trotted between his master and Raouf, sometimes turning toward Ganthier, waiting for his liberating "Go!" An hour to get where they were going, against the wind. The other dogs, big, speckled, long-legged pointers, who were also becoming impatient, and who were finally liberated by a whispered "Go look . . . Go on, look . . ." advancing close to the ground toward the bushes, their legs bent, progressing by inches, noses full of living smells, stopping, interminable, a voice that said, "Careful, we're close," and suddenly the sound of panicked wings, flight into the sky and salvation, and each bird standing out on the blue background, violent with light, shots fired. Of all the hunters only Ganthier hit two birds with both barrels. Eight partridges fell to the ground, seven on the hunters' side of the wadi, the eighth on the other side. The big pointers stopped at the edge of the water. A survival instinct. For Kid, the retrieval instinct was stronger. They didn't see him anymore. The yellow of the water was a thick clay that could only make the dog's coat heavier. They saw the top of a fawn-colored head, then nothing, the tip of a snout, or an ear, it wasn't clear, then nothing.

And then, there was the dachshund, almost a hundred yards downstream, finding just what he needed to gain a purchase on the opposite side, climbing out, shaking himself off, running through the grass along the wadi, grass that was taller than he, tail sticking straight up, yapping made hoarse by the water. He quickly found it, the partridge that had fallen on the opposite side.

"Fucking rifle!" said Ganthier. He was talking, not about a weapon, but about a hunter whose lead shots had left the bird with strength enough to fly off.

"Kid, sit! Stay!" shouted Ganthier, "Stay!" But Kid dove back in, the partridge in his mouth. Everyone knew that it was going to be even more difficult than before, because a partridge held in the jaws ... It's not just the weight, even for a dachshund, it's because it lets a lot of water into the dog's mouth, muddy water. Someone said: "All that water, bloody hell, where is it coming from?" After a few seconds the voice answered itself: "And more important, where is it going? There won't be a drop left for the wheat ..."

From time to time a hunter glanced at Ganthier, whose face was livid. Kid was flailing in the raging water, disappeared, reappeared, without letting go of the partridge. Ganthier started walking quickly downstream. Kid wasn't trying as hard to fight against the current. The group followed Ganthier. A man said: "He's drowning, he's not going to make it." Raouf thought Ganthier was going to jump on him. It was the man at whom the "fucking rifle" was aimed, a fat man, with multiple chins that fell under his mouth, Jacques Doly, the lawyer. The man shouldn't have mentioned drowning; he should have kept quiet; but he hadn't dared respond to Ganthier earlier, and now he was managing to do even more harm than with a response, while seeming only to be making a statement, because saying, "He won't make it," is not just a statement about the disaster; it was a summoning of it. Ganthier controlled himself.

They saw Kid less often now. At one point there was a bend in the wadi. It brought the dachshund closer to the shore. He put a paw on a root. Ganthier ran to him, but Kid was sent back into the current. One of the pointers barked, its voice broken; another whined, as if he, too, knew what was happening to Kid; he didn't howl at death because dogs know that that bothers the masters, but it was as if he were. And his master shouted: "Shut the hell up!" Some hunters stopped, out of breath. They didn't really know how Kid was doing it. Going over, okay, it was the hunting instinct, the desire for the prey. Maybe also a dachshund desire, to show the other dogs, the pointers, the aristocracy of hunting, what one can do when one is small, with large ears and a ridiculous voice. It was perhaps for that reason that Ganthier hadn't restrained his dog. He knew him; he knew what he was capable of. It was dangerous, but something in Ganthier perhaps couldn't resist the idea of letting Kid show what he could do. Hunters are proud of their dogs, and the dogs are proud of their masters: that's why some of them dive in when they shouldn't. But the return? Why? It wasn't fear. Some masters beat their dogs if they're late retrieving; they turn them into cringing lackeys; but no one had ever seen Ganthier beat a dog, or a worker, either, for that matter. And he was crazy about his Kid.

Later, when they talked about this story, people said that the dog was stupid to have tried to cross again, that Ganthier would have stayed for days on the opposite side waiting for the waters to calm. No, Montaubain said, Kid wasn't stupid. Ganthier had spent years training him to retrieve, a foam ball when he was a puppy, then his first baby bird, exchanged for effusive petting, and his first quail, a bit chewed up. He had learned quickly, and it turned into not only his duty but his joy, to return to his master with his mouth full, and he wasn't going to give up that joy for some silly wadi whose water was still violent, even at the cost of drowning. Death in joy, even dogs can experience that, Montaubain later said, because otherwise death is really too awful. Others sensed that he was thinking of something else.

When he finally reached the bank of the wadi Kid dragged the partridge to Ganthier, then collapsed in a single movement onto his side. He vomited yellow water in jerky movements with gagging sounds. He couldn't get up. Ganthier threw the partridge aside. Raouf looked at it a moment. It was lovely, almost a pound, a red beak, white neck circled with black, the chest grayish lavender; the feet were also red. The guy who had killed it badly didn't dare come closer.

The hunters left along the wadi. Raouf and Montaubain stayed with Ganthier, who was kneeling down. He was talking softly, caressing Kid's side. Kid still couldn't get up and breathed with difficulty in between bouts of vomiting. Montaubain's pointer was whining. "Shh!" said Montaubain, and Ganthier:

"No, it's good that he hear him, too." Ganthier repeated: "Come on, my friend, don't give up!" His voice was becoming increasingly resigned. Then the tone changed. Raouf and Montaubain understood that Ganthier was now speaking to them. Ganthier spoke of Kid while caressing him, a sort of funeral oration: Kid came to this country when he was three months old. He is incredibly resilient. He goes for miles around the property every day, the ground, the stones. He's the only dog who never comes back with bloody paws. He was very good with the partridge, as long as you don't ask the impossible of him. I didn't ask, I didn't want him to cross. Ganthier picked up some stones, showed them to Raouf and Montaubain, slate. Poor earth, that makes the wild game calculating, hardy . . . That partridge . . . it knew that it had to put the wadi between it and the dogs . . . It knew . . . Half-dead up there, it still found a way . . . Ganthier's voice cracked. He looked up at the sky until his eyes hurt. They could hardly hear Kid breathing. It was now very hot, a burning air, without the tension of the hunt.

"Let's go home," said Ganthier, picking up his dog. He left striding briskly. Raouf picked up the partridge—its warmth surprised him—and he and Montaubain followed behind Ganthier. After a moment Ganthier began to stumble as if he couldn't see in front of him. Raouf understood: tears. He gave the partridge to Montaubain and took Kid. When they arrived at the cars Raouf looked at the two soldiers who were still standing guard, giving them a steely look. He put himself in their place, in their heads, *The caïd's son is carrying the colonist's dog.* He searched in his memory for an elegy for a hunting dog, a poem by Ibn Rabi'a, *ghodfan dawajina qafilan a'samouha,* dogs with drooping ears, thin sides . . . and who can die under the horns of gazelles. That's what he was going to recite to the soldiers, a tribute to dogs written by a lord, but he wasn't sure they would understand that fourteen-centuries-old Arabic. He didn't say anything. For those men, the dog was a bad animal, one that attacks angels sent from heaven. Ganthier said to Raouf:

"They're not happy, but they are regaining some pride at your expense."

He took his dachshund back. He always had this reflex: as soon as he felt that some distance was settling between Raouf and the common people he made him feel it. Raouf was a bit mad at Ganthier, but he didn't respond. Montaubain put his hand on his shoulder, for a moment, then he joined the chauffeur in front with his pointer, who was still whining. Raouf and Ganthier got in the back, Kid between them on the back seat, half-wrapped in a towel. "Let's go!" said Ganthier to his chauffeur. The car took off quickly. Kid was now having silent convulsions.

42

AN EDIFYING SPECTACLE

In the capital, after his meeting with Trillat, Laganier paid a visit to his colleagues at the Renseignements généraux. He told them of his interest in their informant in Nahbès. The colleagues said to him: "Belkhodja? We can even give him to you. He's no longer of any use to us!"

Belkhodja had become poor, a poor man who didn't appear to be but who depended entirely on the assistance he was given. He went only rarely to the European city. He lived deep within the medina of Nahbès, where a servant of Si Ahmed came every week to pay his tab at a cheap restaurant. Belkhodja had to survive. He was the living testimony of what it would cost someone to cross Si Ahmed. "And it's not good if you're seen begging too often," the caïd had told him.

Belkhodja had understood what was in that *too often*. He had to choose the occasions, preferably when people were leaving the great mosque once a week, without seeming overly poor, to beg without begging, just to receive the discreet alms of some believers who had once known him, nothing more, but those were the conditions for receiving the more substantial help that the caïd gave him—he had to appear in a state of need before the community . . . And so when they saw him, people could be reminded of the sins that Belkhodja had committed. There was alcohol, of course, and drugs, and gambling, and whores, and unreimbursed debts, but that wasn't the worst: the worst was to have come up against Si Ahmed. They didn't know exactly how, but it had to do with that hasty departure of his son, yes, more than a year ago. It was said that through vengeance Belkhodja had denounced the caïd's son to the French police, in the capital, perhaps not denounced, but he had at least committed some guilty indiscretions, or really did denounce him, and wrongly. The caïd's son wasn't harmed, nor was his father, but people weren't sure, and young Raouf had perhaps left voluntarily to discover Europe, and it did him a lot of good, by the way, as did his year in Paris. He has been much less agitated lately. He was even heard saying that he was no longer interested in politics; the country wasn't yet old enough for politics; he wanted to become an observer. That didn't seem to be a true profession, but it was less dangerous than being a Bolshevist or a nationalist.

The caïd kept Belkhodja's head above water, and in exchange Belkhodja agreed to beg, rarely, but well. Sometimes he even had the illusion of being a man like anyone else, upright, affable. He said hello to an old acquaintance, led the conversation, played at being someone who is free, laughed, forgetting that the steel rims of his glasses were held together with black thread, but one thing reminded him of what he truly was: he no longer dared go near his former shop or La Porte du Sud. The little band at the café knew everything.

Out of caution, and also so as not to recall his flight, the young men pretended to have forgotten Raouf's denunciation, but something else weighed on them: the police raid at the café that Laganier had organized, their exit in handcuffs, like criminals, blows by gun butts and knees, and interrogations, and for the ones who didn't have a social status, being beaten with a stick on the bottom of their feet, which led them to believe that Laganier was taking his revenge on them for not being able to put his hands on the caïd's son. He had even interrogated some of the young men himself, including Karim, using a new technique imported from Paris. It didn't leave any marks, blows to the head using a thick commercial phonebook with a soft cover.

"I'm not asking you much," Laganier had said, "I know you're a nationalist, but not rabid. I've got nothing on you. What I would like are two or three precise things on the connections one of your friends has with the Reds, you know who I'm talking about?"

Karim didn't say anything. Then Marfaing put a stop to his deputy's excesses:

"If you keep going at them they're going to stay in the Arab city. Can you keep an eye on them there as well as you do here?"

It would have been difficult for Karim and the others to spit on the ground in front of Laganier, but to do so in front of Belkhodja, or even on Belkhodja himself, would have been a well-deserved pleasure. And so Belkhodja avoided giving them the opportunity. He felt safe only in the old city, where he now had the time to stroll and talk with the people who sometimes forgot to turn their backs on him. He would sometimes stop in front of a storyteller on the square, or in front of an argument between a vegetable merchant and his vendor, the shock of a driver whose cart had lost a wheel, the crowds in front of a brand-new Citroën bus. He watched, listened, escaped for a moment from the despair of the poor. There was also the market where he was perfectly friendly and talked with the merchants while casually putting a hand on a few dates, a peach, a half-slice of watermelon. He examined what he had picked up, as if ready to put it back if it wasn't of the desired quality, then quickly ate it and left saying goodbye. Around noon he went to the harbor, at the hour when the fishermen were finishing up, dropping little red mullets that a beignet vendor, a bit farther away, allowed Belkhodja to dip into his boiling oil.

Around five in the afternoon he went back to his quarter, a square, with a hammam and an oven, the flames of the oven also heating the stones of the hammam. Belkhodja was struck by the good smell of grilled lamb and bread that came out of the oven, remembering the time when, in his house, his table was always full. He also passed in front of kids who laughed and shouted, and threw stones on the roof when they spotted a cat. Belkhodja knew why: the cat is a domestic enemy; it eats rats, but it also takes the meat that a maid has left unattended for two minutes in the courtyard, under a cloth, and the maid would have bruises for two weeks. So when the kids can spot a cat that doesn't belong to any house, a true thief, they go after it. Sometimes they succeed in cornering the cat on a roof, hidden behind a chimney, and they bombard the roof with stones, which always provokes the fury of the people who live below, especially when the roof is covered with tiles. The kids have to work quickly. They have to finish the cat off before a man comes out of the house and gives them all a good slap. The worst is when you throw stones while watching for the man to come out, watching the front door of his house, and the man comes out from behind, around the corner of the street, and becomes a man who walks quickly while picking a kid up by his ear, and the kid moans, cries, asks for his mother. It won't do any good to call for your mother: you have neither father nor mother. Those kids of the street, most often, don't have a true family. They come from the countryside when it has been very dry for two or three years in a row, not really *come*, rather they are deposited, abandoned, and forgotten, and they are called orphans because one mustn't abandon one's child. If you do you are cursed. So you "confer" him, and forget him. To him you are dead. He's an orphan, and a man can then pick him up by his ear without incurring the anger of a known family. And once again Si Azzedine caught one. He had a heavy hand. The kid was shrieking. His ear was bloody, but he was at a point in his life when it wasn't so bad to be picked up by the ear, because at least it was an adult who had caught him, in public.

When it was the teenagers in the area who caught one of the throwers it could go a lot worse, and the kid might find himself in a sort of cellar, with two or three of them, punches raining down. The kid would shout. They would stick a rag in his mouth, more punching, and one of the teenagers would finally say: "That's enough, he's softened."

"Yes," says another, "He's a little softie!"

The teenagers would laugh and calm down, their voices nicer: Don't cry. They take the rag out of the kid's mouth, give him something to drink: It's over, you swear you won't do it again? The kid swears, a hundred times, and when he swears the teenagers laugh, saying that he really should do it again, for the fun of it—that is, for their fun, to come back and see them. And they give him more water, a piece of bread. It's gritty, it must have been lying on the ground. The teenagers continue to laugh, kindly: Did that make you hungry? Eat! One of the teenagers opens a can of sardines: Go on, take one, I'm sure you like sardines in oil, virgin oil. More laughter: You'll see the good it does. They hold out the can. He takes a sardine: Do you like sardines? Is it good? And one of the teenagers says to the others: You see, he took the biggest! Laughter, the kid is doing better. They give him more bread to dip in the sauce. They take back the can: Don't soak up all the oil, we're going to need it. More laughter. They put the rag back in the kid's mouth, and later, if he tells anyone about what happened, he's a goner.

When Belkhodja was a child he had a family. He had thrown stones at cats but had escaped those sorts of reprisals, and now he felt sorry for the hunted beasts. He shook his head, snorted, looked toward the hammam. Stones continued to rain down on the tile roof.

The former merchant felt a presence on his left. He didn't move. A European eau de cologne, he turned his head: Laganier. He said hello. Laganier also said hello with a nice smile while sizing him up. Belkhodja's features were drawn, his eyelids drooping to his cheekbones, torn clothing, dirty shoes, *Does this Arab know he's at the end of the road? No, and he must be told the opposite, and we must hurry to use him before he dies* . . . Laganier congratulated Belkhodja on his appearance. Belkhodja returned his smile. After a few minutes Belkhodja moved a few steps away from Laganier. He didn't want to seem to be with him, but he couldn't turn his back on him, either. Between moving his feet and two or three movements of his head and shoulders to the right, he managed to place six feet between them, a space that Laganier cheerfully filled by taking Belkhodja's left arm while pointing out with his other hand a kid armed with a slingshot: "They're having fun, but they're going to get in trouble, it's not worth it!"

Belkhodja allowed Laganier his hasty conclusion. He knew that, in spite of the risks, it was worth it, it was a true competition, to be the first to knock the cat down, because in this game the first to get a cat in spite of the risks became head of the band for a week. He no longer had to worry about finding food. He didn't even have to shine shoes in the European quarter. Shining is very hard. Not the shining itself, that's quickly learned, at the age of four—shining, two brushes, rag, all of it in a wooden box carried across your body. You shine kneeling down. You brush, without forgetting to spit. The client is standing, his foot on the box, a clacking of the brush against the box to indicate the client should change feet. You brush very quickly because you often do that not far from adult shiners and it was forbidden. That's what's hard, the kicks from the adult shiners that are on avenue Jules-Ferry, and it's also hard because there is always another kid to dispute your corner of the sidewalk. To dispute means taking you by the throat and throwing you to the ground, and squeezing, and you try to get away with punches, or with a stone, and the other quickly squeezes to take away your strength, with men all around you. They're laughing; some have begun to bet. The other kid starts bleeding. He tries to finish you off by giving you a blow on your nose with his head. You start bleeding, too, and an adult finally separates you, calling you children of Satan or sons of whores, and giving you, with each curse, blows that hurt even more than those inflicted between kids. That's why it's good to knock a cat off of a roof. When you do that you become the leader. You give your shoeshine box to a weaker kid. He'll shine instead of you, and in the evening he'll give you the money from the day, all the money, and if he cheats you, you beat him. With food it's the same: you're the leader. The other kids bring you what you ask for, and you can also ask for gifts, even shoes, black, with a buckle, European-style, and the other kids shine them for you, even if they are too big to walk in the street, and that's better anyway because the real owner might recognize them. Laganier was wrong. It really was worth knocking a cat off a roof with a stone, provided you don't take too long.

But this time, all around the building, the kids didn't really seem to be in a hurry. They threw their stones calmly, without worrying about the din the stones were making when they hit the green tiles, and the tiles also fell when a stone broke one and it was detached. Usually that cost the kids dearly, the roof tiles, because you have to repair a tile right away, otherwise the rain can get in, or an evil bird, and you have to put salt on the tail of the bird before getting it out, and the wife tells the husband to replace the tiles, and the husband says he will do it, and he doesn't do it, but every day he thinks of the kids that did that, and when he sees one hanging around, "I told you never to come back to this quarter," he gets one. But this time, the kids were joking about the noise, the tiles, wives and husbands. They were bombarding the roof, shouting, "Thief," at the cat. They were looking for the cat, couldn't see it. Someone, an adult, also cried, "Thief!" and another man began to laugh: "Yes, a thief, I even know what he came to steal!"

The stones were becoming heavier and heavier. It wasn't a cat they were aiming at, of course, it was a man-cat. He was trying to hide on the roof. He had flattened himself on the tiles at the base of the chimney, and there were an increasing number of adults in the street, and they also threw stones, even bigger ones. They didn't need a slingshot. They went around the building, and the man-cat climbed around the chimney to hide. People weren't talking about cats, or thieves anymore, but of a dog, a pig.

Some stones must have hit their target because cries were mixed with the shouts of men. Sometimes the throwing stopped because someone shouted: "You're breaking the tiles of the hammam!" Then it started again, a dozen men in the street now, as many kids, a mixture of stones in slingshots and stones in a man's hand, and there were also women, who came out of the building, running, straw baskets in their hands. They were furious. They yelled at the owner of the hammam: Shame on you, Si Abbade, you let this happen, you're not watching your hammam. Honorable women think they're safe there, and any pig can climb up on the roof and watch them. Shame on that man who is only a pig, and shame on you for allowing a pig to watch us!

A lot of the kids stopped throwing. They gave their stones to the adults. It was a competition among adults now, and Si Azzedine hit the target, like a seasoned thug, he, a respected notary. The women's shouts got louder, and the cries from above, on the roof, like a sort of death rattle, and the man knew what was awaiting him, all those indignant people.

Two guards had managed to climb up on the roof. The stone-throwing stopped. The man must have seen their batons, not pickax handles, but real guard batons, heavier than pickax handles, with a very heavy head, a head with studs on it, and the guards wielded them like jugglers, spun them around, and with the weight of the head of the baton, the speed of the spinning, that's what makes the blows so violent. Laganier responded to the worried look Belkhodja gave him:

"No, you well know that I can't do anything. This type of thing is handled by the boss of the quarter. It's the work of the *moqaddem!*"

Each spin of the baton was accompanied by a "son of a dog," a "pig," or a "you're not a man," and the first baton blow hit a shoulder, a shriek more shattering than the others, and it spun, it fractured—no, not the head, the guards weren't killers, but the back, the legs, an exposed forearm. People heard it cracking.

After a moment the *moqaddem* arrived and the two guards stopped beating. What happened next no one really understood. A frightened guy is not very agile, especially when he begins not to have any more limbs in good condition. Did one of the guards make him roll off the roof like a stone? Did he fall by himself? No one knew. And when he reached the ground he made a funny noise on the hard-packed earth in a cloud of dust, the wind adding more dust, and not much remained of the life of that man.

"It's Driss," someone said, and someone else added:

"The chaouch of the water company," and someone else:

"Yes, poor guy, a bit crazy."

"No, not *a bit*, he was a true loony . . . He never knew what he was doing, maybe he wasn't even watching, if we knew, we would have stopped sooner . . . *Allah irahmu*, may God have mercy on him."

Laganier took Belkhodja by the arm:

"It's horrible, isn't it? A lynching is always horrible! The mob that doesn't control itself under the pretext that it is defending right from wrong . . . and there's worse than that . . ."

Laganier had small eyes, as if they were being eaten by his large eyelids, and he laughed:

"Imagine, for example, if one day the police lets the name of one of their informants slip out, and in addition people learn that the informant didn't denounce just one person . . . that he's been doing it for twenty years, a true second profession, right? . . . It's the type of profession that can still be protected, but if in addition the police say that they no longer give a fuck about the informant, he'll be like . . . a cat on a roof . . ."

Laganier was talking without looking at Belkhodja. He wasn't holding on to his arm any longer. He was speaking softly and slowly: All things considered, one wasn't forced to reach such a conclusion, the police can also be quiet, a file can be lost.

"We understand each other, don't we? But if I help you it can only be between us, we won't talk about it to anyone, will you allow me to hold your arm? Otherwise people will think that we are having a friendly conversation! You know that these little beggars are also extras for the Americans? I'd like to talk to you about that, quickly, it's strange, the interest the Americans have in little beggars, isn't it? Do you know what they're doing in the film? They don't talk about it in the medina? That's strange, too, they should talk about it, even if no one knows anything specific, we're going to talk about it, aren't we? You and I, in confidence . . . And above all, don't try to find protection with our dear caïd, Si Ahmed is even more conniving than I, you know something about that . . . And yet, he doesn't know everything . . . Don't you want to pay him back for everything he's done to you? Yes, very good, act like you're trying to leave me, that I'm holding you by force, people will like you . . . Those little beggars, do we agree? Your coreligionists have a right to be informed . . . Here, I'm going to give you a token of my goodwill. I'm going to put the stupidest of my men on your tracks. The more people see that you're being followed by a snitch, the less you'll seem to be one, and then we'll be able to work together without any difficulty . . . Those Americans, don't you find that they really think they can do anything? I'll show you a photo, you'll see!"

43

THE FACE

At the bar of the Grand Hôtel, there was more news from Hollywood. They joked about it but braced themselves for a storm. This time it involved George Macphail, a director, a "good guy," and an artist, very fastidious. One morning when Macphail was working on his set, the big boss, Lakorsky, came by for a friendly visit. It was rare, it put everyone in a good mood, and what's more, they were shooting a comedy. Lakorsky was delighted with the scenery and the accessories, real, huge spiders, and their webs, in a corner, and a special staff person hired to take care of them. They're for a semi-close-up, Macphail said. Lakorsky was impressed. He also opened up the drawers of a chest: there was real silverware. Are you shooting a dinner? Lakorsky asked, and Macphail replied no, but the scenery had to be as realistic as possible, and then, you know, I showed the contents to the actors; they know that they are acting in front of real silver; that's important.

Lakorsky nodded his approval. They took a break and Macphail even went for a walk in the sun with the big boss, both smoking Havana cigars, a half-hour of promising conversation. Lakorsky asked Macphail what he was working on, another comedy? A drama? What budget would he need? For how long? Macphail wasn't born yesterday. He was careful not to put too much into that, but even so . . . And then the boss said: Good, I must go, come see me whenever you want. Macphail said good-bye and returned to his set, only to find another director in his place. Yes, I'm taking over the film, Lakorsky's orders. No, that's all I know. You should go talk to him, and if you want your spiderwebs they're in the studio entrance. Neil knew Macphail well enough to know that he wouldn't go see Lakorsky for a month, and he wouldn't protest; he was too concerned with keeping his salary for that. That's what the studios were like. The producers wanted to control everything, and they were using the Arbuckle affair and the leagues of virtue to do it. There were other rumors, butchered films, to attract larger audiences.

In the bar, Cavarro's publicist, Samuel Katz, was getting angrier and angrier: *To project a restorative image* — are you kidding me? They couldn't care less about the way we fuck, what's important to them are the films, what we show in them . . . Neil added, two films abandoned since January . . . on peasants . . . two films without sentimentality! And Samuel continued: The Vigilantes want to suck the soul out of movies, and Lakorsky is quite happy for them to light a fire under his ass! Samuel's anger was unstoppable in spite of the efforts that Francis and the others made to calm him down. Samuel doesn't realize, said Francis, he should stop barking all the time at the foot of the wrong tree. In Hollywood he is always spending time with the unions. As long as he does his work well and is with me the producers won't touch him, but if the police get involved that will be another story. He shouldn't talk so much, even if McGhill is no longer here to snitch . . . Samuel opened his mouth and told them the amount Lakorsky paid to hire Hays, the guy responsible for having modesty and morality rule in Hollywood—a hundred thousand dollars! Yes, a hundred thousand . . . The same amount he paid a blackmailer four years ago! Samuel interrupted himself, he was holding his audience, he resumed: Lakorsky had been with some other production bigwigs in a hotel, outside of Boston, for a party, with women. At the time the press had called them "willing women," whores that cost a thousand dollars, the group rate. Some of the women were married, and two months later, a Boston prosecutor, Tufts, said to Lakorsky that the husbands were suing, but he, the prosecutor, he thought it was a simple story of a drinking party, he didn't want to bore himself with that, and if Lakorsky agreed to compensate the plaintiffs and pay their lawyers' fees, he would close the matter without prejudice, for a hundred thousand dollars . . . Obviously, Cavarro added, it was a brilliant move, Lakorsky-the-moral-policeman had been trapped. He was afraid of the publicity, and he paid. And three years later, said Samuel even more bitterly, there was still a trial, in spite of the hundred thousand dollars. No, not because the story had gotten out: to tell that Lakorsky had paid a thousand dollars to screw and a hundred times more than that so no one would talk about it, might just make you laugh. It became interesting when there started to be competition among the Boston prosecutors to get reelected. Such information was a weapon, and during a reelection campaign one uses weapons. The district attorney decided to go after the corrupt prosecutor. People really like it when a prosecutor goes to prison now and then, and it's good for morale, and it's good for crooks. It's like a train accident: people say there won't be another one for some time. Tufts denied everything, but the prosecution showed his bank statements, and he was ultimately dismissed by the Massachusetts supreme court.

The ruling was a gift, said Samuel, in that affair Tufts had "behaved the way a deceitful prosecutor would have acted to stick it to the rich." Yes, he had behaved the way one *would have* . . . And the best was at the end, the court specified that "the question of knowing whether Tufts was guilty in the case in point did not need to be settled." They had cut off Tufts's balls, with a saw that wasn't very clean, but still cut them off—that's what justice is like back home—and Lakorsky still managed to turn everything in his favor: a guy who can pay such a sum just to get laid, that meant he had means, so he was a trustworthy producer! And then he hired Hays to oversee the entire movie industry, for the same amount! That screwer of whores no longer lets anyone get a divorce, let alone remarry, all of that because he's afraid of churches and their Vigilantes. He has cold feet, because he, Mayer, and Schenk are afraid of attacks against Jews, when the Vigilantes should be told that we are the salt of the earth, and make real films, saying *screw* your morality, but those three don't want to: that would give artists power!

Gabrielle and her friends understood Samuel, but not his virulence or the anguish in his voice. They quickly had an explanation: the Americans had just learned that a catastrophe was on the way. The catastrophe was called The Face.

The Face's real name was Arnold Belfrayn, a fat man, with the beard of a lumberjack, a small voice, and food in his beard, a muckraker who worked for the *Los Angeles Herald*, not very good. He saw only what he wanted to see, and wrote with too many adjectives, adverbs, with pleonasms and clichés. He was capable of coming up with things such as "silence and indifference are jetties that prevent entering the port of an expression of authentic morality," and he sulked if a bureau chief cut the sentence. When his bosses realized that he hadn't written anything for two weeks, he was threatened with being fired, but they also said the same thing when they read what he wrote. So he could have been at the end of his rope and end up in obscurity in a corner sorting telegrams, but his guarantee of employment was that he informed his boss about colleagues' moods. He also had a sense of detail, and the panties of a star, with her initials embroidered in pearls, that had been found in the back of a taxi . . .

Why was he called The Face? You just had to look at him, the nose of a drinker, pockmarked cheeks, little slits for eyes, enough to hate Douglas Fairbanks or John Gilbert for a long time. He shot down celebrities, in America people like to see actors climb really high, really fast: it makes you dream, it seems so simple; and they also like to see them fall: that consoles them for having to stay where they are.

In Hollywood, toward the end of April, Belfrayn sensed that his situation was becoming increasingly precarious. He needed a big scoop and he thought of Neil Daintree. He had Daintree in his sights because no one had been able to bring him down, sitting as he was on cloud nine. Usually, for a director, all Belfrayn would have had to say is that he was an *intellectualist*, and three-quarters of the country would be against him; but the problem with Daintree was that he was a war veteran, with rare honors: try to bring down a guy like that in a country where when veterans and their medals go through a train station everyone stands up and applauds them! And Daintree thought he could do anything, such as refusing to take Belfrayn's calls.

Belfrayn had sold his project directly to the big boss of the newspaper:

"If we find any hanky-panky they're hiding over there, it could be bigger than the Arbuckle affair. Over there I'd hear everything. I speak French, I will see everything. That little group is too clean. Hearst has increased sales by twenty percent with that Arbuckle pig, we could do as well with the escapades of Cavarro and Daintree. They were in the San Francisco hotel with Arbuckle, they managed to escape. I'm sure that's made them careless."

When he heard the names Cavarro and Daintree, the big boss smelled a big story. It would cost something, of course. He pointed at Belfrayn:

"Travel, hotel, that's going to cost us a lot of money. If you screw up with this you're finished!" Then he smiled: "Fine, let's do it!"

The smile was because he knew that the cost of Belfrayn's mission wouldn't even be the price of a good meal with the board of directors at Aldo's, with French wine and cognac that were as old as the Declaration of Independence. He also told Belfrayn to find out what the French were doing in that country over there: Look around, they say they're *protecting*, but it seems they're looking for oil.

Belfrayn was succeeding with his plan. The cost of his mission had gotten around and had impressed those who had never had lunch at Aldo's. The colleagues who hated Belfrayn had organized a good-bye party in his honor, and they got stinking drunk into the wee hours before accompanying the lucky guy to his boat, telling him to bring back some real dirt on those kings and queens of the screen. They sang, "For He's a Jolly Good Fellow," emphasizing the "which nobody can deny" . . . my ass! That sack of shit was sailing off for a two-month vacation courtesy of the newspaper!

At the bar of the Grand Hôtel Samuel finally calmed down, but he was really afraid of a catastrophe and even thought about going home before Belfrayn arrived, to avoid having Francis run the slightest risk, a difficult decision to make because it was he who would have to make it—Francis would never force him to do that—and Samuel was also afraid that his departure wouldn't matter, and that Francis might even take advantage of his absence to do something stupid about which Belfrayn would have no difficulty finding out. He started to talk about it to Kathryn and Tess, asking them to keep an eye on his friend just in case he decided to leave.

"You shouldn't," Kathryn told him, "You can't give in to those bastards."

Tess knew Belfrayn. She added:

"I was forced to put him in his place with my knee." And Kathryn: "That wasn't the smartest thing you've ever done."

"It was at your place. He was asking for it, and I know he's a coward."

For Tess, Belfrayn was one of the worst:

"When he's not busy denouncing whites, he tries to screw blacks! And it's not that he likes blacks . . . It's to hate himself more! He reminds me of a joke back home, the guy from the South who goes to a hotel in New York, brought there by two friends. He wants a room for the night and to be woken up at dawn. The hotel manager has only a room with two beds. One of the beds is already occupied:

'That doesn't matter, I'm used to that.'

'But . . . the guest is somewhat peculiar . . .'

'I don't give a damn about that. Do his feet stink, is that it?'

'No, he's . . . a man of color . . .'

The guy's friends laugh, tell him that at that time of night he won't find anything else:

'Take the room, we'll empty another bottle, and you won't think of the negro again!'

The guy agrees."

"I wonder," said Samuel, laughing, "if he would have agreed if they had told him the guy was a queer."

"Being black back home is a curse," said Tess, also laughing, "not a mortal sin!"

"Do you believe in mortal sins?" asked Samuel.

"Only greed is a sin for Tess," said Kathryn, "especially in bosses."

Tess continued: "The guy agrees, ordering the manager to wake him at five in the morning. He proceeds to get dead drunk, and goes to bed without waking up the black, immediately falls asleep. His friends take advantage of his stupor to put shoe polish on his face . . . At dawn the hotel manager shakes him, the guy gets dressed quickly, rushes to the train station, just manages to get his train, starts to relax. The other passengers look at him strangely, he goes to the toilets to wash up, sees himself in the mirror, and says: "Damned hotel manager . . . He woke up the negro!"

"If you tell your joke too often," said Samuel, "a screenwriter will end up stealing it from you!"

"We couldn't care less about The Face," Neil said to Ganthier, "but the guy is a plague." And as in the past before a plague arrived, the Americans decided that they had nothing more urgent to do than take advantage of the good days they had left.

44

GANTHIER'S PARTY

To celebrate Kid's recovery at the healing hands of the veterinarian Ganthier held a dinner at his home.

"I'm sorry, I don't have a dining room," he said.

They dined in the surprising salon-library on his farm. When coffee was served they left the table and went onto the terrace, a circle of armchairs, footstools, and sofas. Some even sat on the arms so they wouldn't enlarge the circle. People chatted with their neighbors. Sometimes two or three, sometimes even the entire group listened. Kid went from one guest to the next, batting his eyes, trying in vain to find someone who wouldn't follow his master's instructions: No treats, his liver is the size of an almond.

Montaubain had come. Ganthier and he had argued a lot before the war, when Ganthier made fun of the "Grand Soir" and the "Red Dawn," and Montaubain of the colonists "incapable of civilizing except with barbed wire," but in the past few years they had begun to talk and to respect each other, Ganthier saying: "Montaubain doesn't have the defect of most teachers, he never acts like he's talking to idiots." At one point Montaubain nodded his head toward Raouf and said to Ganthier, laughing affectionately: "He tries to act like a clever Parisian, but I remember the time when he only pretended to understand." Raouf heard that remark:

"You realized that, and you didn't mention it?"

"Yes, because when one pretends, in order not to be caught out, one has to catch up quickly . . . Your friend David was more open, but he was faster than you only in math."

Everyone started to talk about their school days, and Ganthier asked Gabrielle if she had been a good student. Gabrielle admitted she had won some awards, especially in her last years of *lycée*, which ones? She talked about placing third in sewing, "'You never manage to go beyond third place,' my mother always said to me, 'You could make a little effort!' I tried, everything went well up until hems, but I always messed up with buttonholes and tacking, so it was third place . . . I also won things she talked about less, first place in French composition . . . and Greek translation . . . and history . . . and other things. I came home from the awards ceremonies with my mother, very proud, my arms filled with big books with gilded edges, which smelled great, leather, and my mother told me to go straight up to my room, because your father, you understand, he's already fed up that your brothers don't do anything at *lycée*, but if in addition you start bringing home awards . . ."

Gabrielle was talking a lot more than usual. It was rare, said Ganthier softly, usually she was the one who listened or who was content to make brief remarks to get others to speak. This time they let her speak. She looked at Ganthier, adjusted the ivory barrette she wore at the back of her head with her right hand, and Kathryn was silently amused to see Ganthier's obedient eyes follow the rising of Gabrielle's hand, elbow and breast.

"My two brothers were terrible students, but each had a bicycle that they hadn't even had to ask for. I asked for one, but without success, and if I insisted, I was told that my haircut cost more than the boys'. At the time I had long hair, brown waves, a tendency to frizz, but not too much. At fifteen my mother made me change my hairdresser. The new one let my hair down and said: 'It's full, thick, soft, shiny, a rare shine, and it falls almost to your ankles!' He ran his hand through my hair while congratulating me. I was proud, but at the same time I knew it had nothing to do with me. He turned to my mother: 'Seven hundred francs, Madame, if you allow me to cut it from the nape, seven hundred francs!' My mother refused, that reassured me. The hairdresser was sad, he must have had buyers waiting. My mother said: 'Obviously, that would buy the bicycle you keep asking for . . . ' and after a pause: 'We'll be back!' She didn't want to stay in front of the temptation. I said: 'You can cut it, but for eight hundred francs!' My mother scolded me, she said to the hairdresser: 'We don't barter in our family!' and I answered: 'It's my hair, I'm bartering!' The hairdresser agreed. I got a bicycle, more beautiful than those of my brothers, and a subscription to *L'Illustration*. My father didn't like that publication, he thought it was reactionary. I thought so, too, but it made me dream, and dreams are rarely reactionary."

Ganthier said to Kathryn: "Did you also have to have your hair cut?" Kathryn replied that at fifteen she was already living in Hollywood, an extra with short hair, because long hair was for the great actresses.

Raouf's attention was caught by a gesture between Francis Cavarro and Samuel Katz. They were seated side by side on one of the sofas, and were speaking together softly, very different from how they acted on the set or at the bar of the Grand Hôtel. They were helping each other light cigarettes, one of them cupping with his two hands the hand that held the flame even though there wasn't any wind. A Legion officer was also there.

"We were together with General Lyautey in another life," said Ganthier, "It makes a difference."

At one point the officer recited to Gabrielle what he called an adage of the country: "Love lasts seven seconds, infatuation seven minutes, and misery one's entire life." The men laughed. "I feel sorry for your wives," Gabrielle said. At the beginning of the evening Raouf had been surprised to see that Tess was there, not to help with the dinner, but as a guest, and not at the end of the table. Now he was looking for her, but couldn't find her; then he saw her sitting on a windowsill behind the armchairs, next to Wayne, and he understood what Kathryn had meant when, in Germany, she had spoken of a situation that was difficult to share. He smiled at the couple, he was going to be able to talk about Montparnasse with them. Tess and Wayne responded to his smile, Tess thinking that Raouf was acting almost naturally toward them, almost . . . because she sensed in his kindness a bit of concern for acting correctly, but he must know about that, too, he must sense it, I imagine, the excess kindness, people who take advantage of your presence to show how tolerant and benevolent they are . . . a hypocritical benevolence . . . But in the end everyone wins.

The other Americans seemed completely aware, as they were about Francis and Samuel. Gabrielle started to talk with Kathryn. Raouf didn't hear what they were saying. Gabrielle had sensed Raouf watching them and said to Kathryn, a bit more loudly:

"We should share our little stories with him."

"Absolutely not," Kathryn said, "He doesn't deserve them, he's no longer a cherub, he's a Casanova, who wreaks havoc between Berlin and Paris!"

Kathryn's gaze caressed Raouf. Gabrielle asked:

"How are the young ladies in Paris, Raouf?"

"Like you."

"That's nice, but can you be more specific?"

"I repeat, like you they have lovely lips, but they don't like you to watch their lips when they say interesting things."

Everyone laughed. Cavarro said:

"You're a real son . . . ," he interrupted himself, he refrained from saying *of a bitch*. He learned that some expressions don't travel well from one continent to another.

The night was still young. Conversations were getting softer. There was almost a full moon, a blue moon. Raouf had had a bit to drink, he liked everyone; the terrace undulated when he looked at the stars. Kathryn joined him, asking:

"What are you thinking about?" He looked up at the stars:

"*Tasiru bina hadi llayali ke'annaha*, these nights carry us off like . . . *safa'inu bahrin* . . . like ships on the sea . . . that don't have an anchor . . . *ma lahunna marasi* . . ."

"I know who that is."

"You can understand Arabic now?"

"Neil told me that you were having him translate Al-Ma'arri, and he's struggling!"

Ganthier was now standing on the edge of the veranda and talking with a young American woman, a set photographer. They said it was Neil's new mistress. Gabrielle got up, joined them, and began to talk about photography with the young woman, telling Ganthier to stay, putting a hand on his shoulder and keeping it there.

The cool air was late in arriving, and the stones of the terrace continued to emit the heat they had absorbed during the day. When the wind finally picked up, they realized that it was coming, not from the sea, but from the south. It was even warmer than the ambient air, and in the light of the lamps they could make out bits of red sand. Even by using a fan, they couldn't obtain an illusion of cool. Gabrielle asked while looking into the night:

"The light, over there, what is it?"

"Your friend Rania's farm," Ganthier answered, "She must see us, as well . . ."

"But she can't come over," added Gabrielle . . . "Do you still ride in front of her house to get to your piece of land? You know that in France people would gossip . . ."

Gabrielle wanted to take a car and go get Rania . . . But she would refuse, she said to herself, she would tell me that it would be an absolute scandal, she would thank me and give me a kiss, and would think I'm a disaster.

Ganthier wiped his forehead and neck with a handkerchief and asked the group:

"Who has been to Aboulfaraj's?"

Aboulfaraj was a Syrian, or Iraqi, or Lebanese, no one really knew, who had opened a wonderful night spot in the heart of the old city. They would be able to find a bit of cool air there. Ganthier had never been, but he knew that Raouf had taken Montaubain and he was jealous.

"You want to take us to a place of ill repute?" joked Gabrielle. And Ganthier said, laughing:

"Do you think we're going to ring bells in the dark?"

Everyone piled into three cars, the windows lowered or the top down, seeking a bit of air on their skin. A half hour later they were in the medina, parked on the square of the hammam. They continued on foot, through the sleeping souks, all the stalls closed and locked. From time to time a lantern threw a pale light and revealed shadows that moved around it: bats. Kathryn was startled and seized the opportunity to take Raouf's hand. Sometimes, above their heads, a ceiling of reeds or beams made it seem they were walking down a corridor.

The ceiling could also turn into a vault of stone. The street became narrower, forcing them to walk single file, turning at right angles. It became wider. Ganthier pointed out on the side a superposition of stones that were larger than the others:

"A Roman column!"

"He's happy!" said Raouf. A bark, followed by two or three others: some skinny dogs on a pile of garbage, and cats waiting a few yards away. Gabrielle couldn't manage to get close to Ganthier, thinking he was keeping his distance on purpose. They walked in a street that was cleaner, but with doors that were as decrepit as the others.

"This is the street where Belkacem lives," said Raouf, pointing to a rickety door, "He's a wholesaler, what's inside is worth millions, and there's a real door behind that one."

A shadow seated on a road marker, a beggar?

"An armed beggar, he's one of the guards," said Raouf, squeezing Kathryn's hand and thinking, I'm the one who is guiding Ariane in the labyrinth. It was simple, two hands that took each other, rather retook each other, and suddenly a year was wiped away, and the break, the jealousy, and the fights. We are but a pleasure being prepared, for the end of the night, not this night, wait for tomorrow afternoon, at Gabrielle's, no, the hotel, when we come back from Aboulfaraj's, too bad for the gossip, everyone knows everything now, no, wait, it would be too risky for her, even if she says that she doesn't care, even if she takes advantage to accuse me of being too rational, as usual, this time I will say, *So what?* That's it, respond: *Yes, rational, so what?* And we'll be in love until the next departure, without hurting each other so much this time, we're forewarned.

The deeper they went into the city the cooler it became. They sometimes passed by the smell of garbage.

"When the sun doesn't come through," said Ganthier, "the odors rise up!"

At one point the road descended slightly for about a hundred and fifty feet under a vault. Yes, there were houses above them. It was an impasse closed by a door with an ordinary dirty copper knocker, an odor of gas lamps. They went into a small courtyard, two waiters with spotless clothes, and then a large rectangular room, the walls covered with white and pale green porcelain tiles. In the middle a fountain, surrounded by round tables with straw-bottom chairs, a dozen or so solitary customers, great silence, very cool, nothing nauseating. They could breathe!

"This is your night spot?" Gabrielle asked Raouf, "Your debauchees seem more like great melancholics to me!"

"In the land of sun, melancholia is cultivated like a vice," Raouf replied.

They went into a second room, more comfortable, with whitewashed walls, with a fragment of Roman mosaic in the middle of one of them.

"Orpheus fighting wild animals . . . Long live poetry and its optimism," said Ganthier to Raouf. He got closer, passed a finger along the little tiles, then, in a scholarly tone:

"Your Aboulfaraj must have some arrangement with the inspector of historical monuments . . . original mosaic . . . third century . . . C.E. . . . ."

Raouf didn't react to the *C.E.* He asked:

"Are you talking about the time when Rome granted citizenship to all the inhabitants of the empire?"

Under the mosaic hung two grimacing terra-cotta masks, with grotesque hollows for mouths and eyes. There were no chairs in the room, but banquettes arranged in several circles around low tables. In the middle there was also a marble fountain with water shooting up, a large opening in the roof above the fountain, an upside-down well, that revealed a nice round piece of the starry sky.

The little band from La Porte du Sud were already seated, most of them in silk jebbas. They said hello. The new arrivals went to sit a bit farther away. Gabrielle managed to seat herself next to Ganthier. They were brought glasses and bottles.

"In the past, they would have served us fig or palm alcohol," said Raouf, "but Aboulfaraj understood that today it's better to sell whiskey and even vodka."

On the tables, in small dishes there were fresh almonds in their shells, pistachios, honey cakes. A man came in holding necklaces of orange flowers in one hand and in the other a platter of horns made out of fig leaves. Wayne wanted to buy the necklaces. No, said Kathryn, there's something better! Raouf and Ganthier smiled. She bought several fig leaf horns, passed them around. They opened them. You're going to learn something, said Kathryn, very proud, to Tess, Wayne, Francis, and Samuel. Here they don't buy things ready-made, we have the night ahead! Each horn contained pine needles, a blade of esparto grass, and jasmine buds, thirty-two buds, thirty-two corollas to put on a pine needle. You assembled everything into a bouquet and tied it with a blade of esparto, Kathryn saying:

"When you're done you can breathe in the perfume with your eyes closed."

They heard laughter from around the little band's table.

"It's Karim, one of my friends," Raouf told Francis and Samuel, "He's telling them a story, rather, he's reading it to them, that's one of the ways we 'practice' literature. We call it a 'session.' We get together and read out loud and comment on good authors."

He listened, adding for the whole group:

"It's an old story, it takes place in Baghdad, in your tenth century, our fourth. It's a story of winos, very drunk, who leave their tavern and go to the mosque and sit down in the first row of the faithful, behind the imam . . . During prayers the imam notices them by the smell of alcohol. He denounces them to the gathering of the faithful: 'They have come to soil a sacred place, they should be put to death!' The crowd tears off the drunkards' clothes, cutting their necks. They are chased down the street. The drunks manage to escape; they take refuge in a brothel, *wa qad j'alna addinar imaman* . . . 'the dinar was our imam . . . they led us to a woman with a perfect shape, with an undone belt,' yes," said Raouf, "I should translate the rhymes, it is rhymed and rhythmed prose, the woman covering the escapees with kisses . . ." Karim stopped reading, closed the book, and said, as if challenging him:

"The rest, Raouf!" adding for the benefit of the Americans and the French:

"He knows it all by heart!"

Karim got up and held out his glass, saying:

"To friendship!"

They touched glasses.

"Come over!" said Neil and Kathryn, the Americans and the French enlarged their circle, the two groups now made one.

"The rest, Raouf!"

Raouf started to recite, translating himself, or summing up during the recitation: The woman with the perfect shape is the . . . she's not the owner, what do you call it? Raouf asked Ganthier.

"She's the madam," said Gabrielle, and Ganthier, laughing:

"You know some things!"

Raouf continued:

"The madam serves the escapees wine . . . *khamrun keriqi fi l'udhu* . . . liquor like my saliva . . . for sweetness, and delectation . . . liquor the depositor of the ages . . . only the bouquet remains . . . the bite of the snake . . ." And, in the story, the owner of the brothel ultimately arrives: It's the imam who had wanted to kill the drunks and who begins to drink with them. Everyone applauded.

"They certainly knew how to live, in the fourth century," said Karim, "They nicknamed the author of this book Badi' al-Zaman, the Marvel of Time."

There was some noise at the entrance to the room. A tall, thin man came in, bottles in his hands. The group greeted him with warm shouts of approval.

"I'd like to introduce Aboulfaraj, proprietor and great purveyor!" said Raouf. Behind the man there followed several customers from the first room, with their glasses. The man said hello and began reciting in turn, *ana min koulli ghuba-*

rin, ana min koulli makani . . . Raouf translated: *I am from all the dust, from all places . . . sometimes at the mosque, and sometimes at the . . . bistro . . .* "No, for the rhyme you need another word, a synonym for bistro."

"*Cheap cabaret!*" said Ganthier.

"I'm not the only one who knows things," said Gabrielle. Raouf continued: *And sometimes at the cheap cabaret, thus acts reason that chases it all away!* More applause. Raouf introduced Aboulfaraj to his friends. Aboulfaraj offered a round, saying: I have alcohol, kif, loving women, oblivion, poetry, contraband, intrigue, and pleasure, no pleasure without contraband . . . His right eye was serious, the left was twinkling. They raised their glasses, and they continued to talk louder and louder. They exchanged anecdotes and snippets of novels or poems. Ganthier even recited *Death of the Wolf.* Gabrielle thought it was the first time that a poem by Vigny had had an effect on her, and then dared say to Ganthier:

"Don't die right away, we need you . . ."

She didn't go any further. If she said too much he wouldn't know what to do . . . Tess began to sing, accompanied by Samuel on the harmonica, a blues tune, "Mama Don't Allow No Easy Riders Here."

At one point Aboulfaraj made a large gesture toward the little band and the customers who had come in with him: I'm shirking my duties, I neglected to introduce you to my little social group, my society of crumbs, a world that alcohol brings together but which is torn apart by many schisms. It's the times that dictate that, that offer us many different roles, and we play them while pretending they are imposed on us . . . Aboulfaraj's hand pointed at the people one by one, as if he were playing eeny, meeny, miny, moe: There is the resigned traditionalist and, next to him, the active or Salafist traditionalist, then the radical nationalist, the moderate nationalist, the democratic socialist, the revolutionary socialist, the communist, the falsely accused—we have several examples of that, with one or two real victims (the movement of the hand was accelerating). There is also the Sufi mystic, beloved by the Westerners, the bourgeois radical, the organized plotter, the solitary anarchist, the believer, who says that if one believes it will be better, the unbeliever for whom all evil comes from believing, but the unbeliever appears in all his splendor only when alcohol has flowed well, and it is a rather temporary role. There is also the Pan-Arab, and even a Turkophile Kemalist!

Aboulfaraj spun around, filled a few glasses, continued: One of our favorite expressions is *na'aldine Franca,* cursed is the religion of France! The short form is "cursed is France!" but (a gesture of peace toward Ganthier and the Legion officer), because everything has another side, it also happens that we become partisans of that same France and its colonialism. It is a role that each of us can assume in function of the evil that has been inflicted on us during the day by those that the colonists call our "coreligionists," and in that case the victim says *hchouma 'aleina*, shame on us, and may then call on France, which is then no longer cursed, to free us as quickly as possible from the old customs and traditions that are the refuge of evildoers and shame, but in general France doesn't want to; it prefers that we remain in the state in which we are; it costs less. So after midnight we pour everything into *qalaq*, which you call *spleen*, and some double it with a sort of relative atheism. We distance ourselves from God, so as not to trouble him, but we are not absolute miscreants, we have limits. We don't eat pork, we are content to behave like the animal we don't eat, and we sometimes do worse, because the pig never eats where it excretes!

Aboulfaraj stopped talking. He seemed to be afraid of his own mouth. His oration had made them laugh, but the end of it, as Ganthier later said, had broken the mood. They started drinking again, were able to laugh more or less, recited other poems, told anecdotes. Then the melancholia returned, stronger, and they decided to go home. As they were leaving, Aboulfaraj took Raouf aside. He rocked from side to side while looking at the mosaic of Orpheus and the two grimacing masks:

"I've heard a story about the little beggars that involves the Americans. Come back and see me. It doesn't smell good."

45

THE BLASTER

Belfrayn traveled to Southampton, then on to Le Havre and Paris. He spent three days in Paris, to find out about the state of the country, its politics, the people in the news. He went to the Assemblée nationale and a brothel. The brothel had cost a bit much, but the *French kiss* was included and he met a lot of people there. Then there was the train south, and Marseille, another brothel, with the smell of garlic, he wrote in his notebook. He also thought about what he was going to do, the *authorized* interviews, the questions on the choice of North Africa, their life there, their relations with the natives, the actors' work, not forgetting the problems in the country—no one could refuse to respond to such questions, not even Daintree—when the press knows how to act the whore, there's nothing you can do to resist it.

But for Belfrayn what was essential was what he would be able to do on the side. Over there, in that asshole of the world, they must now be aware of his arrival. They must be busy preparing themselves. That wasn't going to make things easier. Rather, yes, one mustn't be put off by the caution of people, their way of thinking *muckraker* when they smile at you. There was an advantage in being considered a muckraker. It always ended up attracting a talker or two. Not immediately, a talker needs time to get excited, and a place conducive to talking, and the talker will never say that he's talking: the talker exchanges confidences. You have to tell the talker juicy confidences, provoke a competition of confidences, while drinking good alcohol that the talker is delighted not to pay for. And you have to give him time to combine his confidences with the desire to be seen well in the press, and when the talker has begun to talk, you have to watch for the moment when remorse begins to clench his stomach, not to fight against the remorse. Don't attack the talker's good conscience: faced with an obstacle it would begin to develop. Don't contradict it, but make the talker understand that he hasn't given enough information for the listener to be able to hide the source of the information, and he really needs to tell the whole story, doesn't he? Don't blackmail him directly. Rather make use of the infernal machine that he, himself, set into motion. He's not responsible for it, but if he wants to get out of it, he must tell him everything.

But it would still be tricky: they would still just be chatting, and Belfrayn hadn't come all this way to report hearsay. Such things were only of interest because they then led to the taking of photos, or to them being taken. He would have to hire an Arab for that, much less noticeable, teach him how to use a Kodak, to get the *candid* shot, Cavarro in a candid shot, in the company of the true love of his life . . . The charmer of all those ladies watching a sunset, his arm around the waist of his boyfriend, or on an isolated beach, not be content with gossip, get a successful black-and-white victory, and the essential question: What would be best, the glory of the scoop or the money he could get out of Cavarro? Or even Lakorsky? Probably from Lakorsky, he would pay twice as much to avoid the scandal, like Cavarro, but also to have something to hold over Cavarro. And not to stop with Cavarro: that little world must be letting loose over there, rediscovering their old orgy habits, discreetly this time, alongside which what one does in brothels lacked the enthusiasm that *good people* know how to put into dirty games. There is also Daintree's wife, the Bishop woman. They didn't have anything on her. It wasn't possible, an actress who only sleeps with her husband for four years, when the husband always has a debutante on his couch, everyone says so: she has no one else, maybe she likes women, that would be too perfect. Or maybe during that stay in Germany? Improbable . . . Must check it out in any case.

And then that other story, the seed of a rumor. Only one person in Hollywood had talked to him about it, nothing more than that, a true bomb if it were true. Bishop's negress, Belfrayn had a score to settle with that negress. Those movie people thought they could live in a separate world, he was going to teach them what they owed to their country, and what it could cost a white man to play chocolate milk with a maid, and what that could cost the maid, a pretty girl, that one, a real bitch, a real mouth on her, must find something on her, and talk to her about it, that would make her docile . . . Belfrayn closed his eyes, unfastened his trousers, said, "Be careful, my blue velvet, it has to feel good," and then he stopped himself from believing it too much, but in any event, he felt like a blaster choosing his best targets . . . Cash in on his silence about Cavarro, bring down the Bishop woman and Daintree-the-untouchable, and if God exists I'll find something on the maid. Belfrayn was going to blow up at least half that group.

When he arrived in the capital he decided to get his bearings before going to Nahbès. He stayed a few days, enjoyed couscous, tagine, fricassees, and fried fish, and visited two high-quality brothels. He also talked a lot, with the French and Arabs. The French all said the same thing, that everything was going well, and that all would go better if they increased the number of colonists and gendarmes. Some even wanted to bring in other Europeans, Spanish, Italians, other

Christians. As for the Arabs, they were just as good drinkers as Americans. He quickly got along with them. He had met a group of fans of America dressed in Western-style clothes. They asked him about New York and Hollywood, the movies, skyscrapers, how to earn money. They listened to him and tried to repeat *just do it . . . move on . . . land of opportunity* . . . with a dreamy look. They adored stories of America, and to get them from him, they told him a lot about their country, about the court of the sovereign, the quarrels between ministers, between ministers and princes, between the French, between French and Italians, between Italians and Jews. They would launch into wild political imaginings, alluding to what President Wilson said on the rights of people. Belfrayn didn't like Wilson, didn't understand much about him, and quickly changed the subject.

He would drink with his Arab friends in the afternoon, in a café or at one or another's house. The discussions were cynical and cheerful, and the day before he was to leave for Nahbès, he was laughing with them in an apartment, in front of glasses of anisette, when the French police arrived. It was the first time in his life that he was treated like that. He was thrown into a cell at the central police station, sitting on the bare ground, next to a pile of shit buzzing with flies that then came to land on him. He didn't understand.

An attaché from the American consulate came to get him. They took a carriage, went down avenue Gambetta. Belfrayn was able to breathe again. Then he realized that they were going along the lagoon.

"Where are we going?" he asked.

"To the docks!" the attaché replied, "Right now!"

He gestured for him to be quiet and continued:

"Are you here to meet filmmakers or rabble-rousers? Your pals are in big trouble! A great mixture of sons of whores: communists and nationalists! And there were forty pounds of propaganda in the apartment! Can you imagine, the French are going to tell the sovereign that Americans are mixed up in all that! You're going home! Right now! Why? Because you are a double asshole! . . . If that doesn't suit you I'll take you back to the station and there will be two reports on you, mine and the French police's, two, one for each of your assholes! . . . No, listen to me—your boss is going to love this story of contacts with Reds, he's going to open your belly old-school-style, and he'll unroll your intestines down Sunset Boulevard! You were set up? It's a plot? Too bad! If you're a true journalist you don't find yourself in a canoe, without a paddle, in the middle of a river of shit! Go on, be a good boy, go back home now!" The horses were trotting. From time to time the coachman cracked his whip above their heads, toward the back of the coach to prevent kids from grabbing onto it.

The American consulate truly had been horrified. That's what the French police had wanted, as did their director, with whom Marfaing had had a nice telephone conversation a few days earlier: You understand, dear friend, no one needs a troublemaker. This film, this Franco-American project, it's a good way to earn back some credit with them, especially since we owe them billions that Germany doesn't want to pay us. You can see what's at stake, can't you?

Marfaing was happy to do this favor for his American friends and for Gabrielle, who had asked him to do the *impossible* to help them. She had chosen that word on purpose, knowing that he would in turn find an occasion when he might ask the impossible of her, Gabrielle saying to herself that she would never even need to say no: the presence of Thérèse Pagnon alone was enough to contain the ardor of the contrôleur civil.

46

THE BARLEY WIND

In Nahbès, the Americans relaxed when they learned of Belfrayn's hasty departure, but Neil couldn't forgive Lakorsky for that close call. The muckraker couldn't have managed to come over without the blessing of the producer in a direct agreement with the owner of the *Herald*, collusion among the powerful. Lakorsky must have said to himself that if the *Herald* exposed his people that would make them more docile. He had also written to Neil that it would be good if the missionary building that housed the children in the film had a cross on top of the pediment. And at the end of his letter he added that if Neil didn't have a subject to propose for a new "local" film, he should return home with his team.

Neil had refused what he called the "cross gag." The aim of my missionaries, he had replied, is that they welcome human beings, not clients for their parish. Lakorsky let it drop. Neil knew what that meant: in Hollywood a film editor would be instructed to slip into the film an image of a building with a cross on top to please the Vigilantes.

At the bar of the Grand Hôtel, Neil talks about it calmly. It was simple, either Lakorsky agreed to let him approve the final cut, or he would leave and set up shop somewhere else, in France, for example. He was liked in France, that's the advantage of wars, there's friendship among survivors:

"Or I could stay here, I think I have a subject, the story of lovers, someone just told it to me, a brief news item, but not just any story, lovers who die, obviously, otherwise it wouldn't be a true subject for a film."

Neil begins thinking out loud, a fourth whiskey in his hand, in front of his friends, a story with a landscape, a horizon, two lovers, a huge plain, great spaces, huge desires, that's the movies, a landscape of harvests, and two bodies, superb, and it could be called . . . how do you say, Raouf?—*rih achcha'ir . . . the barley wind*—that would be a lovely title, wouldn't it? And beautiful images, a plain covered with barley that undulates, reality and metaphor, two beautiful, young lovers, beauty gives the right, youth gives the audacity, right, Raouf?

Neil looks at Raouf, then glances over at Wayne. Wayne is already sitting apart, in a low chair. They can hardly see him. He is taking notes. Neil will find them the next morning on his desk. It reassures him, he can start talking. Not easy to be lovers in the country, and even less so in this country. Do you think that lovers here can take three steps together? Neil looks at his wife, who remains motionless, and Kathryn tells herself that Neil has set off on a new project. There was *Eugénie Grandet*, tomorrow it will be *The Barley Wind*, and the day after that something else, and today it's our project that he can't complete because he no longer likes his film. It will bring in money, but he doesn't like it anymore, he should have finished it a year ago. He's dragging his feet, and he wants to do in a new film what he can't do in this one, and he pretends to defend his originality by refusing a cross on a building. He's right, but to refuse a cross on a building is not enough to make you an artist. Kathryn is thinking of Wiesner's films . . . that woman in the shadows of a cell, her head against the wall, light from a barred window falling in intervals on her face, it was unbelievable and absorbing, and each time the shadow returned, placing dark gaps on the face. She also remembers the crazy rhythm, and Wiesner's ill temper, a camera operator saying: He works well only when he has first scared the shit out of us . . . Wiesner's models, a giant articulated dragon, with two men inside to move it, make the eyes roll and shoot out flames . . .

And, in front of his friends, Neil pursues his dream of a film. Even when there isn't even a cat on the landscape there are always the eyes of people to see the lovers, so the lovers choose a silo where barley is stored, away from the eyes of others. They go there separately, the barley wind . . .

"I have the title before I have the film. Back home they say that a woman has skin as soft as a grain of barley, so lovers who make love in the softness of barley, the shadow and coolness of the silo, the rustling of the grain under their bodies. No, they aren't assassinated, it's not a typical story. I imagine they end up falling asleep, the scene ends."

Neil lights a cigarette, drinks a large mouthful of whiskey, starts talking again, and the story doesn't stop there, not with a common ending, either, so there aren't any guards who burst in, no denunciation, no jealous ones who take revenge. Death, of course, but all alone, death that comes from itself. No, in fact it is already there, they came to death without knowing it, *mektub!*

Kathryn thinks Neil is making progress, *When he said* mektub *he didn't look at Raouf.* Neil continues:

"And death catches them by surprise, because barley defends itself, not against lovers, of course, but against rodents . . . It ferments . . . a deadly gas, that's the *barley wind.* How do you film what isn't even a wind, how do you film a metaphor? Death that enters with each gasp of pleasure, with gestures that become desperate . . . And what makes it tragic?"

Kathryn thinking: He really has it in for lovers, all this rambling, all this aggression, it might make a good film, basically he's mad at me for taking Raouf away from him, that's why he's doing this . . .

"Death is not enough," says Neil, "Death is a brief news item, that's all! To be tragic the audience must say to themselves that those two could have escaped death, but that they erred, through excessive love, they loved each other too much, that's what cannot be pardoned, but that's still not enough to make it tragic, except in newspapers. I'm not pointing at you, Gabrielle," Neil smiles at Gabrielle, *I wonder what role you might have played with my wife and my dear Raouf, I'm sure that the initiative came from Kathryn, and that you helped her, it didn't come from Raouf, at his age one doesn't betray a friend like that.*

After a pause, Neil says that for a tragedy you need something more—a rat! A dead rat, in the first silo, they saw a rat, "Or a field mouse," says Raouf. "Is the gentleman a specialist of silos or fauna?" asks Ganthier. Neil resumes:

"The lovers didn't try to understand. They were content to go somewhere else, to the second silo. Barley defends itself against rodents, and it is the lovers who suffer from it . . . The rat is important, it is the tragic error. If I just show the lovers' death it's a soap opera. With the rat or the field mouse it's tragic because they made a mistake that they could have avoided! But that's still not enough. I have the story, I have the error, I have the death, Wayne, what am I missing?"

"Fleshing out?"

"Exactly, a true story needs to be fleshed out!"

Neil keeps a thought to himself: I don't have any imagination, I don't know how to invent, I have to find something to use, to rewrite, like Shakespeare did with Plutarch.

Again Neil's voice, full of self-assurance: The context? As usual we'll go get it from the great William, so we'll cross the barley wind with a Shakespearean death of lovers, Romeo and Juliet, obviously, families that don't want that love, competing families, and I already have a nice scene, a camel fight; each family has its contestant, no one has yet to put that in a film. So there's a confrontation between the families, but no suicide, do the opposite of Shakespeare. The families reconcile much earlier than in Shakespeare. They agree on the marriage, that's it—it will seem that we're moving toward a happy ending. I can already hear my colleagues: Daintree uses Shakespeare to make a Hollywood story with a happy ending, he's given in to Lakorsky, the big mouth is a flunkey like everyone else, welcome aboard! I'll revise *Romeo and Juliet,* Neil continues, but with families who agree on the marriage. The two fathers negotiate, they begin to prepare the festivities, they look for the lovers, and they find them in the silo . . . Who's *they?* Maybe another couple of lovers visiting the silo, for the same reasons, but then you can't have shown the death of the first couple, only their sleep, their smiles. We'll leave them right after their pleasure. They are naked, the barley covers them almost entirely, the boy is on his back, the girl against him. You don't know where her hand is, no, just an outline, and if the viewer wants to imagine what the hand is doing, he's free to do so. We leave them with this image, and later the other couple goes into the first silo, again, desire is in the air. They, too, see the rat. They go to the second silo . . . Shriek! They discover Romeo and Juliet, two arched bodies, rigid, with bulging, wide-open eyes, two mouths grotesquely open through asphyxia. Don't hold the shot too long, don't be predictable . . .

Cavarro interrupts: "If you're not predictable you'll never have an audience."

And Samuel: "So what? He will have created a masterpiece!"

"I will have made a German film that no one will want because I'm not German!" says Neil, looking at Kathryn.

Samuel continues: "Balance! Cut some things, leave others . . ." A silence, then Neil:

"I want to end with sorrow."

"In a novel you can," says Gabrielle, "but not in performance. Even in Shakespeare, at the end there are no open wounds. They suture, life goes on . . ."

"I'm going to use the other couple," says Neil, "The girl runs home, the boy will sound the alarm, and I'll finish on the theme of 'life goes on,' with a true sentimental question for the audience: How can you still want to fuck when you've seen the cadavers of two lovers on a pile of grain?"

Around the bar things were heating up. Everyone had an idea for a screenplay for what Neil called a work of art for the general public, Cavarro defending the general public, recalling the quarrel people have with the movies, with all performance, with everything that gathers people outside their homes, everything that makes them an audience, facilities for the audience. One thinks that audiences are unhealthy, that only the individual has value, in his armchair, in his parlor, in front of the fireplace, a book in hand, with ample time. The problem is that they forget that a lot of people don't have a parlor with a fireplace, and not a lot of time! And when Gabrielle interrupted him to ask who was that *they* who forgot people without fireplaces, Cavarro answered:

"Wealthy people, those who have a lot of money and gather in clubs where they forbid others to enter. They proclaim that the movies are a diversion for slaves!"

Raouf was listening, thinking of Cavarro's Rolls . . . but remembering something Kathryn had said: "Francis comes from a place where, when you're five years old and get your first cap, you have to defend it with your fists." Samuel continued what Francis was saying:

"They create the slaves and they criticize those who entertain them."

"That's ingratitude," said Neil, "because the movies prevent slaves from slitting their masters' throats."

"How?" asked Raouf.

"We show people that poverty is the result of the moral sins of an evil person who will be punished," said Samuel, "They just have to be patient, and denounce the sins!"

His face had hardened. He looked at Francis:

"I dream of films that will instruct individuals, instead of just gathering together the herd!"

"So make those films!" Francis cried. Samuel jumped off his stool and disappeared.

"You're rough," Kathryn said to Francis.

"The *herd*," Francis answered, "That's an attack against my audience and the way I act."

Ganthier hadn't said anything, then he said softly:

"There's nothing you can do, movies are the theater, and it's in the theater that people become the herd, livestock, and that stupidity becomes contagious . . ."

He lit a cigarette, then:

"It is there that the *neighbor* reigns, it is there that one *becomes* a neighbor . . ."

He fell silent. That was pure Ganthier, provocateur, doomsayer, sententious . . . Cavarro told him so, cheerfully, with a slap on the shoulder, and before Ganthier could add anything Gabrielle began to laugh:

"*It is there that one becomes a neighbor . . .* He got you, that's not Ganthier, *da wird man Nachbar* . . . that's Nietzsche!" Ganthier started laughing. Gabrielle continued:

"It's in *The Joyful Wisdom,* and what's more our reactionary is a bit of a coward, he forgot a piece of the quote, go ahead, tell them everything, go for it!"

Ganthier didn't say anything. Gabrielle continued:

"He forgot to say what Nietzsche inserted between *become a herd* and *becomes livestock*, he wrote that at a performance the audience *becomes a woman . . .*"

"Thank you for the combination," said Kathryn.

"I censored it on purpose," said Ganthier, "because I don't think that."

"But it makes sense," said Gabrielle.

"I like Nietzsche," said Neil, "He forces you to think against him."

"Germans do that better than we do," said Kathryn. Neil didn't say anything.

47

EQUAL PAY FOR EQUAL WORK

And a week later there was the demonstration. It wasn't supposed to happen. Everything came from those rabble-rousers whom the authorities in Nahbès allowed too much free rein, said some, rather, said others, because they pay as little as possible to people who extract and transport phosphate, and pay even less to those among them who are just natives. That had worked for a long time, however, the French workers comparing their fate to that of the natives and even to that of the Italians, and they were content, one salary for the French, another for the Italians and other Christians (the Spanish weren't happy to be grouped with Italians), and the remainder for the natives, and now the natives were protesting. Things could have still stayed as they were, as long as the French felt happy with their situation, seeing profits grow, but with the economic crisis they were beginning to lose money, and they had the impression that they were getting dangerously close to those whom fate, history, God, or the law of the jungle had placed beneath them. However, even that wouldn't have been enough to move the workers, but they had begun to say to one another that the owners were taking advantage of the lower salaries they were paying the natives to rationalize freezing those of the French, "If you're not happy we'll ask a Mohammed to take your place," and then the others had to get involved, all those guys in Paris who thought the way they do in Moscow and who wanted folks to think like that in Nahbès, and that new slogan, "Equal pay for equal work," can you imagine? When after all the Arabs have fewer needs! And the Italians and Spanish who are getting mixed up in that! In fact, all of this is coming from the Bolshevists, said Pagnon, and their union! And from that left-wing cartel who wants the same laws in Paris to be applied here, added Doly, as if the lesson of two years ago hadn't been enough, and now Herriot and his cartel have raised the lid, the Bolshevists are taking advantage!

Things might not have gone any further if the natives hadn't abandoned their *inch Allah* and their *mektub*, okay, with the crisis they no longer had enough to eat, they said, but there have been crises before, and as long as they have their mint tea in the evening, and are able to break off a piece of sugar to put in the teapot, and a bit of bread, in front of a nice sunset, they didn't have much to complain about, even if the price of a block of sugar, as well as that of wheat, has gone up a bit—it was cyclical, and necessary, they had to be patient; the swipe of a rag and it would improve again; it was a cycle, the law of the market, do you know of any other? Anyway, it used to be much worse . . . But there were also the caps . . . We should have taken precautions when the Arab workers started wearing caps like the French and Italians. It began with the dockworkers, a cap, the ideas that go with it, if you can call them ideas, said Pagnon, and the dock-workers' union indeed was agitating because the new assistant harbormaster didn't want to hear about unions anymore. He's right, said Laganier, no unions in the empire. With the natives there will always be war, it's like Verdun here every morning!

And in the interior of the country, ninety miles from Nahbès, the phosphate workers had also been on strike for a week, and the railroad workers transporting the phosphates to the port; the first time that had happened in the region, that was modernity! The Prépondérants besieged Marfaing, no subversion, no more than in France, even less! The unions decided on a demonstration in Nahbès. The Prépondérants wanted an immediate crackdown, with rifle butts to begin with. But Marfaing knew that the tide was turning in Paris. He wanted to calm things down. A demonstration in itself isn't bad, he said. They will shout, chant, and sing all afternoon, they will tell themselves that they have shown their strength, they will have seen that they don't have very much, and the leaders will be able to say that action will be pursued in forms other than strikes . . . A dem-onstration, when it puts an end to a strike, that's not so bad, I won't prevent it. One must never put one's adversary's back to the wall, said Marfaing, let's have a demonstration, a disciplined march, but on one condition: nothing in the city centers, not in the European city or in the Arab city!

The unofficial discussion with the unions was hard. They spoke of militants sent from Paris, David Chemla, a boy from here, you realize, said the lawyer Doly, those, yes, you know the ones I'm talking about. We've done everything for them. We've welcomed them, educated them, given them French nation-ality, and this is how they thank us? By wanting to destroy everything?

And it was also noted that this Chemla was accompanied by another Moscow-phile native who stayed hidden, a certain Mokhtar. Nothing in the city, repeated Marfaing, otherwise I can't be held responsible. You can march outside the city, all the processions you'd like, but nothing inside the city. During the discussion the city center became the entire city, a prohibition against any demonstration in the city. In the end the union representatives agreed: it was the first time the authorities were authorizing a demonstration, they said (not *authorize*, but *tol-erate*, Marfaing clarified), that's already a victory, we are not the strongest, let's start with showing the strength that they let us show. In any case it will be called a "demonstration in Nahbès." Even *L'Humanité* will talk about it, and we will have proven that we are the only true defenders of the workers of the country, unlike the socialists, those valets of the colonial bourgeoisie!

And so there was a demonstration, on the outskirts of the city, caps, red scarves, banners, the CGT, raised fists, a fanfare in the front, drums and trumpets, several hundred men, many bicycles being pulled along, and behind there were also fife-players, darbukas, tambourines, and children, a disciplined procession in the countryside. Some were amazed at the large number of locusts they were crushing while walking, then they stopped paying attention. There weren't to be any confrontations; a delegation was even to be received later by the general secretary of the *contrôle civil*. That was Marfaing's sadism, to force Laganier, reaction incarnated, to meet with the Reds, and perhaps even have a photo taken with them. Chemla called it a demonstration by the worker class. They went through fields while avoiding crops. They sang, "Arise the damned of the earth!" in the middle of blue cardoons and nettles, *hubbu dhahaya-l-idhtihad!* Raouf and Gabrielle had slipped in among their ranks. This is an ideal spot for my reporting, Gabrielle had said. She was wearing trousers and a khaki shirt, and had looked with amusement at Raouf's dark gray suit, telling him that it was going to get dusty. Raouf looked around him. These people are carrying each other along. I am in the middle of them, but I don't feel carried, because soon I will be in Paris again? When he learns that I was in this march my father is going to let me have it. No, he won't do anything, I am escorting a French journalist, the demonstration is authorized, more or less . . . Do I believe in the "Internationale"? Am I unable to believe in it because of my *class affiliation*, as David tells me? Two years ago, under the sovereign's balcony, it was simpler. We thought that history was being made. This looks more like Mayenburg, a valiant last stand . . .

There was something light-hearted in that "Internationale" with fifes and tambourines, a feeling of a country wedding, assorted people, the level-headed, the entertainers, the crazies. There are probably even foremen, Chemla said: When the little leaders are upset, it rocks the boat for the owners. Raouf had passed that on to Gabrielle. She thought Raouf was lacking animation when he spoke. He was very different from how he had been in Germany, less emotional. Look, said Raouf, pointing off the path, a man who was working a pendulum well: He's doing the same thing that was done a thousand years ago, with the same tool, he's drawing water with goat skins, he's watching us and nothing bothers him . . . Gabrielle thought that Raouf would make a good journalist, he likes great writers and small details, I should talk to him about that one day.

There were also peasants marching, agricultural workers, and even *kham-mes*, Raouf told Gabrielle, explaining that it was the first time he had seen such a thing, the *khammes* rising up. They must really be hurting to demonstrate like that, usually they are the most passive, the most resigned people. Yes, the one-fifth sharecroppers, that's what they're called in French. They work the land for only a fifth of what they produce, while reimbursing a usurer that they will never be able to reimburse. In the countryside they are in the majority. If the *khammes* really calculated they wouldn't farm, and what is a man who makes them work like that worth? asked Raouf. And the one who lends to them at close to one hundred percent interest? And what about the third man, the one who tells the *khammes* every Friday that it is the will from On High, and that all would be better if people renounced corruption, that of the soul, of course? How would the life of a *khammes* be different if there weren't any corruption? And what about another life, that of the day laborer, who picks olives while wondering if there would still be picking to do the next day, or ditches to dig? And all that for half a loaf of bread and three mint leaves? Destroy everything and start again, like the Bolshevists? Raouf knew that basically, for Chemla, one could not pull anything *politically* from the peasants. Only workers could make history, behind their advanced guard of professional revolutionaries. That sounded good, and the triumphant proletariat would then emancipate the *khammes*, said Chemla, adding, "after sending the social traitors to the garbage dump of history!"

Raouf thought his friend was going a bit far. He didn't understand why, for Chemla, the main enemies were now the socialists more than the owners. Socialism here, said Chemla, is the socialism of the little whites. Just when they're about to take the plunge they back down and align themselves with the colonists. They don't set the trap, but they direct the people right into it, and abandon them. They will never recognize nationalities, only Lenin was able . . .

Raouf and David's friends made fun of their discussions: You're becoming heavier and heavier with what you say about the proletariat, almost as heavy as the devout who talk to us of prayers and good intentions. Your defect is that you don't know how to drink. You don't drink enough, never enough to reach the moment of truth!

And on another occasion Ganthier had said to Raouf: The peasant, the *khammes*, he doesn't reason as you do. You pass over the land, whereas he considers himself rooted, in a land that his ancestors owned, and if he is no longer the owner, it is not because other owners ruined him, it is because bad fortune struck him, it's not the same. He wants to go back to the old order, his roots, and if you tell him he's a victim of exploitation, that he must prepare a classless future—the land going to those who work it, bright tomorrows—the *khammes* will ask you how you know about tomorrow, and the peasant owners in the area will call you a diviner and an apostate. You'll end up stoned by the guys you want to liberate. Will you allow me to prepare your eulogy? Things you'd like to see highlighted? "He liked Hallaj, La Rochefoucauld, Ibn Khaldun, Apollinaire, and Marx." You like too many things, that will be your downfall. "He liked progress and morality, not too much religion" . . . No, I wouldn't say that, I would make you a sincere believer . . . No need to be controversial at a graveside.

Being cynical was Ganthier's way of then placing an arm around Raouf's shoulders, to beg pardon. He would never have dared to make that gesture as a sign of pure affection.

48

A COMPLEX OPERATION

Caps, fanfare, slogans, and more or less organized rows, several hundred people, two banners: on one, "Equal Pay for Equal Work!" and on the other, "A Forty-Five-Hour Workweek Now!"

Insanity, said Pagnon at the Cercle des Prépondérants, foreign competition would kill us. Then Pagnon calmed down. It was only a march. They were going to wind around, two, three hours. They like that, winding around, do arabesques in the countryside, in the native style. The oriental soul likes arabesques. And there won't be a forty-five-hour workweek.

Everything could have ended peacefully if there hadn't been the other march. In fact it wasn't a real march, rather a sort of shapeless mass. It wasn't immediately understood what it was, a large and murmuring mass, and it didn't even have to be kept out of the city: that's what had been surprising. A few dozen men had started to move around in the old city and instead of regrouping in the center, they went to the poorest and most populated zone in the outskirts, the place where people lived between boards, under tarps, with walls made of clay and pieces of wavy sheet metal, a place without water or name, and even if a name had been written on a sign, no one in that place would have been able to read it. And those men from the old city had gathered twenty, thirty times more people when they passed through than they had in the beginning, a mass of beggars coming out of their shacks, walking where grass, cardoons, nettles, and stones still had the right to exist, and there were even yellow flowers, on a land that no one cultivated because they knew that houses would come, and the road would also come, or the railroad, or workshops, or it would become a quarter of villas for the rich. Until then they called these empty spaces, the shapeless mass moving over that land, and farther there was the countryside, the real one, with its olive trees or its wheat or esparto grass fields, and even farther there were dunes, not the real desert, rather sand that had come from the sea, but if one took care not to show the sea one could give the impression that it was the desert—that's what the Americans did for their film—the mass advancing through the vacant spaces, then the countryside, and the French officers quickly gave orders to the cavalry to watch that mass, the horses of the Spahis and the gendarmes galloping amid poppies, it seems that makes good harvests, and there were a lot more locusts than usual—it had been almost twenty-five years since they had seen so many locusts, no time to think about that. When the mass saw the riders, it accelerated; there were shouts, invocations to God, sometimes sickles raised high.

At one point those in the disorganized mass saw the marching strikers in the distance. They started to go faster. It was clear they wanted to join them, in the middle of the countryside, and a few snitches were finally able to give some information to the officers. The people in the mass wanted to go to the Americans' film set, in the dunes. It wasn't clear why, but it was troubling. It was surprising that Laganier and his men hadn't known anything about it up to then, and now that mass was turning and running toward the marching workers.

And that was out of the question, Colonel Audibert said, such a mixture would be explosive. Another piece of information arrived. All those beggars wanted to get their children. What children? Those on the film set, the extras that the star, Cavarro, as a noble sheikh, was supposed to have saved from the evil Turkish robbers . . . A rumor in the morning, they hadn't paid attention, but now things were heating up. The people were saying that the Americans were going to convert the children, with the help of the French, and would take them to their Christian land, thousands of people whipped into a frenzy who could finally vent their fury, not furious about their miserable salaries—they didn't have salaries—or against poverty—most accepted poverty as the order of the world—but at the ones stealing their children, that was legitimate fury: the American Christians were going to convert the little shoeshine boys and little maids they had rented from the families where they worked!

At first the Americans had used children from better circumstances, but they behaved too well. Neil Daintree had protested, "It should be a group of orphans, not some kids who have been taught to wipe their noses." He had assigned Wayne the task of finding some, and Wayne had found some, by spending a morning on avenue Jules-Ferry just when the review of the little shoeshine boys was taking place. They were seated side by side on the edge of the sidewalk, their boxes sitting in front of them, looking respectfully at the captain of the French army, who was inspecting them as he would have inspected true soldiers, or only seeming to look at him like that, because some of them must have been saying to themselves: What an idiotic son of a bitch with his switch like a dog's tail that he puts under his arm instead of up his ass, the kids smiling with what the officer called "the atavistic devotion of the young native." Wayne had negotiated with the captain, and the captain had put some twenty kids at his disposal by promising them—no, not promising, I'm not going to make promises to these scum—the captain told them that they would obey Wayne without causing problems and that they could leave the set and return to the city every day after five in the evening—that was when they would have the most customers—and no one would replace them in the meantime, and if one of them decided to desert the set he would immediately have his box and badge taken away. Yes, a captain of the greatest army in the world, a bachelor, was officially in charge of the little shoeshine boys in the European city. As for the little maids, the Americans could take their pick. They were all true actresses. They just had to be prevented from dancing all the time in front of the cameras.

The mass was almost running now, true believers who were going to liberate their children, believers inspired by emotion. In the morning, Belkhodja and a few others had passed around a photo Laganier had provided, smiling children in front of a building, and the few people who had seen the photo had told the others, swearing on the heads of their own children, that it was true, since the cross was on the photo it was true, and everything they had endured suddenly became unendurable. Anything but the children. They could endure blows, confiscated land, forbidden land, obligatory work, taxes, fees, and forced labor when they couldn't pay the taxes and fees, going through the city with chains on their legs, six months breaking stone before finding themselves without land, scavenging in the big piles of garbage outside the city. All of that was *mektub*, but suddenly there was something stronger, and which could not be *mektub*, and which was made much worse by all that they had been able to endure without complaining, and later the officers' report would say that the people had transformed into furies. They had seen hands stick stones into the open stomach of a soldier's body, hundreds and hundreds of men running in the countryside, slowing to regroup, making a bloc, *allahu akbar*, running again to wrench the children out of the hands of the Christians, a rush now through the fields, not winding on a path like the people with caps, but a true wave, no singing, but a permanent hum *allahu akbar*. The officer who was riding at the head of the cavalry had already heard that, more than ten years ago, a bad moment.

And the marching workers saw the others. There was some wavering; that hadn't been expected. Two militants sent out to scout said that they were mainly people from the slums. Another militant spoke of "*Lumpen.*" No one understood. *Lumpenproletariat*, said Mokhtar, it's the proletariat in rags. So not the proletariat, said another voice. They were wary, and the two processions were not far from each other.

We can't let them converge, said Colonel Audibert, his voice emotional. He was going to be able to indulge in the joys of a complex operation to prevent the convergence. It would remain in the annals of the empire. We'll do as Napoleon did; we'll charge in between: the company of Senegalese will get out of the trucks and slip immediately between the two groups, and the gendarmes will cover the CGT, as a screen, and the Spahis will cover the rabble, with some of them facing them. The others will surround them on the wings, with the Legion in reserve! However, Audibert hadn't been to the war in Europe. At fifty-three he was only a colonel, but he wasn't going to let himself be outdone by a mix of fanatics and Moscowphiles; penetrate into the center, a double surrounding from the wings, they'll talk about it for a long time, as far as Saint-Cyr! The colonel got out of his car. The two army photographers were there. He adjusted his uniform. He was happy; he embodied the pure concept of a uniform in the land of Saint Louis. A man in a great uniform, "with a capital 'U,'" as they say, embodies the idea of order, fighting against all that is flabby and anarchic in life; and the uniform on a human body, when it is squeezed to the last inch of the neck by all those fasteners, buttons, and straps, becomes an impeccable sheath, without a single fold that isn't desired; even the back is straight and without a wrinkle. One forgets one's perspiration, one's odors; the body becomes the instrument of values, not that of their loss. We will confront the enemy to the sound of our own heels, and a glorious death is a death in full uniform! The colonel wasn't going to die, but he would have his glory.

What followed was a scene during which nothing could prevent the butt of a rifle from finding a spine or a liver, butts also coming down on a hand protecting a jaw, shoving the hand into the jaw, the violence of the butt canceling out the protection of the phalanxes, breaking the phalanxes and shattering the teeth that fall out in a flow of blood, into the eyes, blinding, and the body on the ground under the stomping of laced boots, arms raised up to protect the head, providing large openings to the stomach or the sides, and sometimes the crunch of a heel on a spine. That one won't be throwing stones anymore, said the soldier who needed a reason for what he was doing. The others were content to blindly knock heads, and at one point two Spahis found themselves alone, pitchforks lunging, bayonets parrying and responding, stabbing, a bayonet stuck in the bone of an enraged combatant. No way to get it out, yes, a method learned over there, in the great school of death on the Somme. Don't try to pull the rifle out, that won't work, the body will come with it. You just have to pull the trigger, bam! And it's freed! Another soldier went too far ahead. He found himself surrounded by the enemy, knives, and could hardly feel the slight burning on his neck. He brought his hand up, avoided the next blow too late, and retaliated for having been struck. One can't pardon a knife in the stomach. He aimed, fired, and saw a body fall. His vision was failing. He was struck by a sickle in his side. The steel blade continued its movement in the arc of a circle, cut through a kidney, came back out. The soldier fell, shrieking, on the body of a demonstrator whose carotid was still pouring blood onto the ground. A Spahi officer ordered the soldiers to open fire. The crowd retreated. The forces of order had brought back order.

There were a half dozen bodies on the ground. Farther away, a young man in a dark gray suit, lying on his back, was no longer breathing. And a French woman, kneeling next to him, was weeping.

In the evening a militia of colonists scoured the countryside, and for the first time there were a lot of Italians and Spanish among them. They opened fire on figures in the fields and even inspected the large farms. "Get out!" Ganthier, in tears, shouted at them. He had just learned of Raouf's death. He was on horseback, standing on the stirrups, forbidding the militia access to his land or that of Rania. He shouted as if he thought his shouts would keep him alive: "You want to act like the French and kill Arabs, but only France has the right to kill Arabs! Do you hear? Only France!"

49

BEASTS FROM HELL

And the next day it was learned that another mass was descending on the city and the surrounding region. It came from the south. Everyone knew it would eventually arrive. It had been more than twenty-five years since they had seen the insects, and these days attention had been so focused on what was going on with humans that they didn't notice the exhausted locusts that were dragging themselves through the streets of the city . . . They had been seen in the countryside, too, but no one really talked about them, as if silence could prevent the unthinkable from happening. They put their trust in time, in destiny, in the Master of the two worlds. It couldn't happen so it wouldn't happen. Then it became hard to ignore, and everything began to move fast.

The French were the ones who ultimately said the word: an invasion. They saw them from their airplanes, military planes that returned after flying very high, and the pilots spoke of a single, huge cloud under their wings, a greenish gray carpet. It covered the horizon, it had crossed the desert, it was above the steppe. Even the pilots who had been in the Great War, their voices trembled: they'll be here tomorrow, or the day after. Ganthier, his face waxen, recalled the Revelation of John, "And there came out of the smoke locusts upon the earth: and unto them was given power, as the scorpions of the earth have power . . ." There were enough of them to destroy anything that resembled a plant within a radius of sixty miles, and many people calmed down. Rather, the anger of the demonstrations was replaced with fear, with the promise of a catastrophe affecting everyone that would be much worse than the misfortune of some. A ton of locusts can in one day eat as much food as twenty thousand people, and some remembered the famines of the past, when one's skin was like folds, drooping like wax on candles. In the city there were now so many insects that it didn't do any good to sweep them up, and they were just the advance guard. People waited for word from the authorities, which didn't come, no orders for mobilization, or of requisition. Yet it was essential to react immediately, but it was as if they wanted to allow panic to overcome the people, make them experience it, and after they had tried to confront it, they would need a strong power, one that coordinates, organizes, decides, one that fights plagues. That's also what a state is for, said Marfaing.

Gabrielle, shattered, tried to continue to work, to write a dispatch on this new catastrophe. She tried to obtain information from Marfaing. Marfaing was no longer at the *contrôle civil*. The rumor spread that he had been recalled to the capital; he might even be going back to France, dismissed from his post. No, he was there, in the countryside, already in the field, making preparations, but he was letting the spring tense up, he was waiting for the right moment, he said. And it was lucky that the coolness of the early evening had numbed the insects. Most of the cloud had landed after more than twelve hours of flying, at the edges of crops, the locusts worn out. They hadn't managed to reach the real vegetation, masses of them on the ground, as far as the eye could see, over dozens and dozens of square miles, insects now busy eating those among them who had been exhausted by the voyage. The idea was to prevent them from taking off in the morning en route to the grain, the barley, the wheat, and everything else—they eat everything, even the esparto, millions and millions of insects seeking all the young shoots, tender, green, of all the plants. At five in the evening Marfaing had launched a pre-alert, and, an hour later, the order for a general mobilization. The people were ready, no need to persuade them, or to round them up. It was a moment when the entire population spontaneously came together, wrote Gabrielle, in tears, everyone wanted to participate and to be seen participating.

And at midnight there were thousands of men in the middle of the countryside, in front of the carpet of herbivores whose weakened rustling still made the hair on their arms stand up, people arranged in groups, obedient, efficient. They had come in military or requisitioned trucks. Some were carrying brooms or shovels, others sheets of metal on which the stars were sometimes reflected. Everyone, said the authorities, is expected to provide the assistance necessary to destroy the locusts, and to comply with the requisition of personnel, matériel, tools, and animals necessary for the destruction of the locusts. Yes, the requisition of animals, it was almost laughable, because of the racket the turkeys and chickens made when they ate the locusts. And out there, in the field, one mustn't forget the pigs, those of the colonists, the enthusiasm of some hundred pigs when they're let loose on a carpet of locusts, each pig capable of consuming twenty pounds all at once . . . And Marfaing liked this battle against the locusts: a plague, orders, techniques, a short and intense struggle, a photographer, and everyone united against those nasty insects, the big, the small, the ex-striker, the colonist, the native, the owner, the *khammes*, the merchant, the dockworker, the Maltese, young and old, the Americans, everyone working in the middle of the night, elbow to elbow, under the authority of the state, of Marfaing and the caïd, a sleepwalking Si Ahmed, whom Marfaing looked after like a nursemaid, forcing him to drink, discreetly taking him by the arm when he sensed he was on the verge of collapse. Si Ahmed's eyes were red. He refused to rest, saying: "Do you know what I see when I don't look at those beasts from hell? I see hell itself! Since the day before yesterday I have been in hell!"

In the fight against the beasts from hell Marfaing became the generalissimo of a righteous battle, and he managed, at the heart of the battle, the differences between the proponents of traditional methods (chickens, turkeys, pigs, blows with shovels, collecting in sacks) and the modernists, who proposed fire, mainly petrol fire, the most spectacular, being careful not to harm the land. So first push the drowsy locusts, using rakes and brooms, toward the canvas barricades or the zinc panels whose only opening was into ditches. The insects fall into them, and are crushed. Two or three locusts flew off, traveling a few yards at eye-level, and people had goose bumps because they said to themselves that the others could do the same, and *the others* meant millions. No, they're too drowsy. There were places where people stomped on them like grapes, singing. Then they poured gasoline, burned them, a great spectacle, tall flames reaching to the stars, and the photographer took advantage of the light to catch Marfaing in his jodhpurs, his colonial shirt and helmet, pointing at the flames. And there was something even more modern than fire, a machine that arrived by train from the capital. It was made of a dozen enormous rollers with twenty circular blades each, arranged in staggered rows, pulled by a tractor. It crushed and shredded the insects. Marfaing wanted everyone to see it, steel against locusts, a twentieth-century battle! On the periphery, there were still some natives who were gathering the insects and putting them in sacks, and they were given salt to eat. Locusts eat everything, and everyone can eat them, they say, or at least the poor can.

Raouf's funeral had taken place the day before. There were a lot of people, including Marfaing; he recounted the official version, a tragedy, a stray bullet while he was trying to protect the French journalist he was accompanying. Laganier pointed out to him that it was a bit contradictory, protection and a stray bullet. Marfaing told him to shut the hell up. The burial went rather quickly, Raouf in three sheets, prayer, formulas, *minha khalaqnakum wa fiha nu'idukum* . . . it is of earth that We created you, We return you to it . . .

The little band of La Porte du Sud was there, led by Karim. Aboulfaraj was there, the Americans, too, all of them, Kathryn between Tess and Wayne, who were holding her up, and Montaubain, who had found Chemla. Chemla expected to be arrested. He was concentrating on his pain, and Montaubain was observing him. Like him, Chemla had his right hand in his pocket. He was probably doing the same thing. In his head Montaubain was singing "L'Internationale," his fist closed, without knowing if Raouf would have wanted that song. Taïeb was there. His father had sent him to get Si Ahmed and bring him to the capital in an ambulance. He had decided to have the caïd stay with him. Taïeb stood next to Rania, who had demanded to be present. At one point he felt sick, and wondered why, then realized it came from his sister's suffering. That surprised him. They were standing apart from everyone else, and since Rania was with her brother, Ganthier was able to approach them.

A few days later, the Americans and their equipment set off from the port of Nahbès on a large cargo ship chartered by the studio. Before leaving, they held a memorial for Raouf at the bar of the Grand Hôtel. Gabrielle and Montaubain had the strength to go. Not Ganthier. Kathryn and Tess were wearing black. Neil spoke about the Arabic lessons Raouf had been giving him:

"We laughed a lot. He used examples from erotic literature to help me retain the rules of grammar . . . But he didn't let me get away with any errors."

People made toasts. Neil concluded with a phrase that everyone approved:

"He was a boy who flattered no one." And Kathryn came out of her silence to say, smiling:

"Not even me."

Gabrielle stayed in Nahbès. She tried to take care of Rania and Ganthier. Both were even more devastated than she. She wrote dispatches while traveling between the two farms. Ganthier worried her, he was somber and determined, he was going to put it all behind him. I am accustomed, he said, in fact no, I'm not, the war makes one sensitive. He was there when they put Si Ahmed in the ambulance. Don't wish anything for me, Si Ahmed had said, *yuhatti-muna raybu ezzamane ka'anana zujaj.* Ganthier bent over to give him a hug. He had recognized a verse that Raouf would recite when he despaired of the world, "The vicissitudes of time shatter us like glass."

The next day Ganthier told Gabrielle that he was going to sell everything and move to the Ardennes, to finish up his days there, adding: "What's worst in all of this, is that I no longer want to love anyone!" Ganthier looked at Gabrielle, but she wasn't focusing. Usually she always had the last word, but here she was at a loss. Ganthier didn't say anything else. Only his old servant woman knew he wasn't sleeping. Gabrielle tried to comfort him. I no longer love anything, he repeated, that is truly hell.

In the capital he had had a long conversation with the superior of the order of White Fathers. The superior had told him:

"We have a center in the mountains where we collect the traditions of this country, the tales, the poems, the songs, the proverbs, the customs . . . You are a good Arabist, that's also our specialty, and you speak Berber. Think it over. You have been a true Christian, we welcome you with open arms, stay with us, as a librarian. Perhaps one day your work will be useful, to another generation, other young people from this country, like him."

Ganthier bequeathed his estate to the White Fathers. He tried to give half to Rania, who refused. She saw him at her house, answering, "I don't care," to her servant, who said that receiving a non-Muslim . . . Her face and hair were uncovered. They spoke for a long time of Raouf. When he was about to leave the servant was still there. Rania didn't dare say what she had planned to say. She simply brushed his cheek lightly with her hand. Ganthier had asked the White Fathers to create scholarships for Franco-Arabic studies, then he had a moment's hesitation: "I really think I'm an atheist." The superior replied: "For the library, that's not a big problem."

Gabrielle ultimately decided to go back to Paris. She paid a final visit to Rania. It was very dark that night. Rania was retreating into herself so that her unhappiness would not overwhelm her. She pointed to the sky:

"Here they say that day and night are only the black and white rings of the same snake."

They were on the veranda, trying not to cry. At one point Gabrielle said:

"Ganthier is entering a monastery . . . It's like he's committing suicide."

"I know," said Rania. Her voice was almost aggressive, and Gabrielle was bold enough to ask:

"Which of the two . . . ?"

Rania answered: "What does it matter now?" And a bit later: "Those who leave, they leave us with the illness of living . . ."

With Si Ahmed gone from Nahbès, Belkhodja no longer had anyone to help him. He was hungry. And the fishmonger, by closing his door with a hard look, made him understand that he shouldn't get too close to the merchandise before it was thrown out.

Back in the United States, Neil and Kathryn divorced. Neil also broke with Lakorsky in spite of the success of *Warrior of the Sands*. He started an independent studio along with a few friends, including Wayne, Samuel, and George Macphail. Six months later, Kathryn joined them. Neil is working on *Eugénie Grandet*.

GLOSSARY

Annamite A native of Annam, former kingdom and French protectorate along the east coast of French Indochina, now part of Vietnam. Ho Chi Minh was also known by the name *Quôc*.

babouches North African leather slippers.

Baedeker *Baedeker Guides* are famous travel guide books published by the Karl Baedeker firm of Germany beginning in the 1830s.

baksheesh A sum of money given as a bribe.

bicot Pejorative term for a North African.

bordj A large, fortified house in North Africa.

caïd (also spelled *qaid* or *kaid*) A provincial governor.

CGT The General Confederation of Labour (French: Confédération générale du travail, *CGT*) is a national trade union center, the first of the five major French confederations of trade unions.

chaouch A North African low-level bureaucrat.

civil list An annual stipend paid to a royal ruler.

contrôleur civil Under the French protectorate, the *contrôleur civil* was responsible for overseeing the French government's interests on the provincial level. He was the one who held true power.

darbuka The "goblet drum" is a single-head membranophone with a goblet-shaped body used mostly in the Middle East, North Africa, South Asia, and eastern Europe.

djellaba A loose, hooded cloak, typically woolen, traditionally worn in Arab countries.

dolichocephalic Having a relatively long head.

douar A camp or village of tents in an Arabic country.

Duc d'Aumale A specific sexual position named after Henri-Eugène-Philippe-Louis d'Orléans, Duc d'Aumale (1822–1897), who is believed to have invented it. The woman is straddling the man, who is lying on his back.

fatma A term used by North African colonists for their female servants. It is the contracted form of the very common name Fatima.

felucca A traditional wooden sailing boat used in protected waters of the Red Sea and eastern Mediterranean, including Malta, and particularly along the Nile in Egypt, Sudan, Iraq, and the Maghreb. Its rig consists of one or two lateen sails.

Guide Bleu A series of French-language travel guides published by Hachette Livre, which started in 1841 as the Guide Joanne. The *Guide Bleu* was addressed to those seeking "discovery in depth."

Hallaj *Mansur al-Hallaj* (c. 858–March 26, 922) (Hijri c. 244 AH–309 AH) was a Persian mystic, revolutionary writer, and teacher of Sufism. He is most famous for his saying

"I am the Truth," which many saw as a claim to divinity, while others interpreted it as an instance of mystical annihilation of the ego which allows God to speak through the individual.

hammam Turkish bath.

houri In Islamic mythology, houris are commonly described as "splendid companions of equal age (well-matched)," "lovely eyed," of "modest gaze," "pure beings" or "companions pure" of paradise, denoting humans and jinn (genies) who enter Jannah (paradise) after being reborn in the hereafter.

Ifriqiya or Ifriqiyah The area during medieval history that comprises what is today Tunisia, Tripolitania (western Libya), and the Constantinois (eastern Algeria), all part of what was previously included in the Africa Province of the Roman Empire.

Intercolonial Union A group of exiles from the French colonies in Vietnam dedicated to the propagation of communism. It published two papers, one in French, *Le Paria*, and one in Vietnamese, the *Soul of Vietnam*, which carried emotional articles denouncing the abuses of colonialism.

jebba A traditional Maghrebi robe made of silk and wool typically worn by men.

Kemalist *Kemalism*, also known as *Atatürkism*, or the *Six Arrows*, is the founding ideology of the Republic of Turkey. Kemalism, as it was implemented by Mustafa Kemal Atatürk, was defined by sweeping political, social, cultural, and religious reforms designed to separate the new Turkish state from its Ottoman predecessor and embrace a westernized way of life, including the establishment of democracy, civil and political equality for women, secularism, state support of the sciences and free education, and the adoption of the modern Turkish alphabet, many of which were first introduced to Turkey during Atatürk's presidency in his reforms.

"La Marseillaise" The national anthem of France. The song was written in 1792 by Claude-Joseph Rouget de Lisle in Strasbourg after France declared war against Austria, and was originally titled "Chant de guerre pour l'Armée du Rhin" (War song for the Rhine army). The French National Convention adopted it as the republic's anthem in 1795. "La Marseillaise" was a revolutionary song, an anthem to freedom, a patriotic call to mobilize all the citizens, and an exhortation to fight against tyranny and foreign invasion. It acquired its nickname after being sung in Paris by volunteers from Marseille marching on the capital. During the European revolutions of 1848, the German people sang "La Marseillaise."

The Muallaqaat ("The Suspended Odes") Long, classical Arabic poems written in the pre-Islamic period.

madrassa An Islamic religious school.

makroud North African pastry. The dough is made mainly of semolina, not flour, which gives the pastry a very specific texture and flavor. Makroud are often filled with dates or almonds.

marabout In the Maghreb, a *marabout* is a recognized local Muslim saint whose tomb can be the object of a popular cult. The *marabout* is often attributed with the ability to grant wishes and even perform miracles. The name is also given, through metonymy, to the tomb itself.

méchoui In the cuisine of Northern Africa, *méchoui* is a whole sheep or a lamb spit-roasted on a barbecue. The word comes from the Arabic word *šawa*, "grilled, roasted." This dish is very popular in North Africa.

Numidia An ancient kingdom of the Numidians in what is now Algeria and a smaller part of Tunisia, in North Africa.

Pola Negri (1897–1987) A Polish stage and film actress who achieved worldwide fame during the silent and golden eras of Hollywood and European film for her tragedienne and femme fatale roles.

quintal A unit of weight equal to 100 kilos, or about 220 pounds.

Walther Rathenau (1867–1922) A German statesman who helped manage the German economy during World War I and who served as foreign minister at the beginning of the Weimar Republic. Rathenau initiated the Treaty of Rapallo, which removed major obstacles to trading with Soviet Russia. Although Russia was already aiding Germany's secret rearmament program, right-wing nationalist groups branded Rathenau a revolutionary when he was in fact a moderate liberal who openly condemned Soviet methods. Anti-Semites also resented his background as a successful Jewish businessman. Two months after signing the treaty, he was assassinated in Berlin by the right-wing terrorist group Organization Consul. The public viewed Rathenau as a democratic martyr until the Nazis banned all commemorations of him.

Les Renseignements généraux The intelligence arm of the French Ministry of the Interior, keeping tabs on political parties, trade unions, lobby groups, and various individuals. The Direction centrale des Renseignements généraux (DCRG), often called Renseignements généraux (RG), was a branch of French intelligence under the Direction générale de la Police nationale (DGPN). Created in 1907 under that name, the primary purpose of the RG was to inform the government about any activity that might threaten the state.

resident general Under the French protectorate, the head of the French administration, which "doubled" the local government at every level, from the sovereign to the caïd. The *resident general* held true power in the country.

Rif The *Rif War*, also called the *Second Moroccan War*, was fought in the early 1920s between the colonial power Spain (later joined by France) and the Berbers of the Rif mountainous region.

Saint-Cyr—Saint-Cyr-l'École Former training school for officers of the French army, the École spéciale militaire de Saint-Cyr (ESM), was relocated to Coëtquidan in 1945.

Scaramouche (1923) A silent costume adventure, by Rex Ingram, based on the novel by Rafael Sabatini.

The Sphinx and the Miramar The names of famous brothels.

Spahis Light cavalry regiments of the French army recruited primarily from the indigenous populations of Algeria, Tunisia, and Morocco. The modern French army retains one regiment of *Spahis* as an armored unit, with personnel now recruited in mainland France.

Tharaud brothers These brothers, Jérôme (1874–1953) and Jean (1877–1952), were first known as travel writers. They were also the authors of numerous "colonial" novels and reminiscences. Both were elected to the French Academy—Jérôme in 1938, Jean in 1946.

thé dansant Tea dance, a summer or autumn afternoon or early evening gathering from 4:00 p.m. to 7:00 p.m., sometimes preceded in the English countryside by a garden party. The function evolved from the concept of afternoon tea.

HÉDI KADDOUR is a professor of French literature at the New York University of France and the author of two novels, *Waltenberg* (Gallimard, 2005, winner of the Goncourt Prize for a first novel), and *Savoir-Vivre* (Gallimard, 2010), published in English as *Little Grey Lies* (Seagull Books, 2013).

TERESA LAVENDER FAGAN is a freelance translator living in Chicago. She has published numerous translations, including Hédi Kaddour's *Little Grey Lies* (Seagull Books, 2013).